About the Authors

Caitlin Crews discovered her first romance novel at the age of twelve and has since conducted a life-long love affair with romance novels, many of which she insists on keeping near her at all times. She currently lives in the Pacific Northwest, with her animator/comic book artist husband and their menagerie of ridiculous animals.

A New York Times bestselling author, **Christine Rimmer** has written over ninety contemporary romances for Mills & Boon. Christine has won the Romantic Times BOOKreviews Reviewers Choice Award and has been nominated six times for the RITA® Award. She lives in Oregon with her family. Visit Christine at http://www.christinerimmer.com

Brenda Harlen is a multi-award winning author for Mills & Boon who has written over twenty-five books for the company.

The Princes

COLLECTION

Deceiving Her Prince

CAITLIN CREWS

CHRISTINE RIMMER

BRENDA HARLEN

MILLS & BOON

First Published in Great Britain 2020
By Mills & Boon, an imprint of HarperCollins*Publishers*
1 London Bridge Street, London, SE1 9GF

DECEIVING HER PRINCE © 2020 Harlequin Books S.A.

The Prince's Nine-Month Scandal © 2017 Caitlin Crews
How to Marry a Princess © 2013 Christine Rimmer
The Prince's Cowgirl Bride © 2008 Brenda Harlen

ISBN: 978-0-263-28137-8

MIX
Paper from
responsible sources
FSC™ C007454

FSC
www.fsc.org

This book is produced from independently certified FSC™ paper to ensure responsible forest management.

For more information visit: www.harpercollins.co.uk/green

Printed and bound in Spain
by CPI, Barcelona

THE PRINCE'S NINE-MONTH SCANDAL

CAITLIN CREWS

CHAPTER ONE

NATALIE MONETTE HAD never done a rash thing in her entire twenty-seven years, something she'd always viewed as a great personal strength. After a childhood spent flitting about with her free-spirited, impetuous mother, never belonging anywhere and without a shred of anything resembling permanence including an address, Natalie had made her entire adulthood—especially her career—a monument to all things *dependable* and *predictable*.

But she'd finally had enough.

Her employer—never an easy man at the best of times—wasn't likely to accept her notice after five long years with anything like grace. Natalie shook her head at the very notion of grace and her cranky billionaire boss. He preferred a bull-in-china-shop approach to most things, especially his executive assistant. And this latest time, as he'd dressed her down for an imagined mistake in front of an entire corporate office in London, a little voice inside her had whispered: *enough*.

Enough already. Or she thought she might die. Internally, anyway.

She had to quit her job. She had to figure out what her life was like when not at the beck and call of a tyrant—because there had to be better things out there. There

had to be. She had to do *something* before she just…
disappeared.

And she was thinking that a rash move—like quitting here and now and who cared if her boss threw a
tantrum?—might just do the trick.

Natalie was washing her hands in the marbled sink
in the fancy women's bathroom that was a part of the
moneyed elegance evident everywhere in the high-class
lounge area at her boss's preferred private airfield outside
London. She was trying to slow her panicked breathing
and get herself back under control. She prided herself
on being unflappable under normal circumstances, but
nothing about the messy things swirling around inside
of her today felt *normal*. She hardly paid any attention
when one of the heavy stall doors behind her opened
and a woman stepped up to the sink beside hers. She had
the vague impression of the sort of marked glamour that
was usually on display in these places she only visited
thanks to her job, but then went back to wondering how
on earth she was going to walk out of this bathroom and
announce that she was done with her job.

She couldn't imagine how her boss would react. Or
she could, that was the trouble. But Natalie knew she had
to do it. *She had to do it.* Now, while there was still this
feverish thing inside her that kept pushing at her. Because if she waited, she knew she wouldn't. She'd settle
back in and it would be another five years in an instant,
and then what would she do?

"I beg your pardon, but you seem to look a great deal
like someone I know."

The woman's voice was cultured. Elegant. And it
made Natalie feel…funny. As if she'd heard it before
when she knew that was impossible. Of course she
hadn't. She never knew anyone in these ultra high-class

places her job took her. Then she looked up and the world seemed to tilt off its axis. She was shocked she didn't crumple to the ground where she stood.

Because the woman standing beside her, staring back at her through the mirror, had her face. *The exact same face.* Her coppery hair was styled differently and she wasn't wearing Natalie's dark-rimmed glasses over her own green eyes, but there was no denying that every other aspect was *exactly the same*. The fine nose. The faintly pointed chin. The same raised eyebrows, the same high forehead.

The other woman was taller, Natalie realized in a rush of something more complicated than simple relief. But then she looked down to see that her impossible, improbable twin was wearing the sort of sky-high stilettos only women who didn't have to walk very often or very far enjoyed, easily making her a few inches taller than Natalie in the far more serviceable wedges she wore that allowed her to keep up with her irascible employer's long, impatient stride.

"Oh." The other woman breathed the syllable out, like a sigh, though her eyes gleamed. "I thought there was an amusing resemblance that we should discuss, but this…"

Natalie had the bizarre experience of watching her own mouth move on another woman's face. Then drop open slightly. It was unnerving. It was like the mirror coming alive right in front of her. It was *impossible*.

It was a great deal more than an "amusing resemblance."

"What is this?" she asked, her voice as shaky as she felt. "How…?"

"I have no idea," the other woman said quietly. "But it's fascinating, isn't it?" She turned to look at Natalie directly, letting her gaze move up and down her body as if measuring her. Cataloging her. Natalie could hardly blame her. If she wasn't so frozen, she'd do the same.

"I'm Valentina."

"Natalie."

Why was her throat so dry? But she knew why. They said everyone on earth had a double, but that was usually a discussion about mannerisms and a vague resemblance. Not *this*. Because Natalie knew beyond the shadow of any possible doubt that there was no way this person standing in front of her, with the same eyes and the same mouth and even the same freckle centered on her left cheekbone wasn't related to her. No possible way. And that was a Pandora's box full of problems, wasn't it? Starting with her own childhood and the mother who had always rather sternly claimed she didn't know who Natalie's father was. She tried to shake all that off—but then Valentina's name penetrated her brain.

She remembered where she was. And the other party that had been expected at the same airfield today. She'd openly scoffed at the notification, because there wasn't much on this earth she found more useless than royalty. Her mother had gotten that ball rolling while Natalie was young. While other girls had dressed up like princesses and dreamed about Prince Charming, Natalie had been taught that both were lies.

There's no such thing as happily-ever-after, her mother had told her. *There's only telling a silly story about painful things to make yourself feel better. No daughter of mine is going to imagine herself anything but a realist, Natalie.*

And so Natalie hadn't. Ever.

Here in this bathroom, face-to-face with an impossibility, Natalie blinked. "Wait. You're that princess."

"I am indeed, for my sins." Valentina's mouth curved in a serene sort of half smile that Natalie would have said she, personally, could never pull off. Except if someone with an absolutely identical face could do it, that meant she could, too, didn't it? That realization was...unnerving. "But I suspect you might be, too."

Natalie couldn't process that. Her eyes were telling her a truth, but her mind couldn't accept it. She played devil's advocate instead. "We can't possibly be related. I'm a glorified secretary who never really had a home. You're a royal princess. Presumably your lineage—and the family home, for that matter, which I'm pretty sure is a giant castle because all princesses have a few of those by virtue of the title alone—dates back to the Roman Conquest."

"Give or take a few centuries." Valentina inclined her head, another supremely elegant and vaguely noble gesture that Natalie would have said could only look silly on her. Yet it didn't look anything like silly on Valentina. "Depending which branch of the family you mean, of course."

"I was under the impression that people with lineages that could lead to thrones and crown jewels tended to keep better track of their members."

"You'd think, wouldn't you?" The princess shifted back on her soaring heels and regarded Natalie more closely. "Conspiracy theorists claim my mother was killed and the death hushed up. Senior palace officials assured me that no, she merely left to preserve her mental health, and is rumored to be in residence in a hospital devoted to such things somewhere. All I know is that I haven't seen her since shortly after I was born. According to my father, she preferred anonymity to the joys of motherhood."

Natalie wanted to run out of this bathroom, lose herself in her work and her boss's demands the way she usually did, and pretend this mad situation had never happened. This encounter felt rash enough for her as it was. No need to blow her life up on top of it. So she had no idea why instead, she opened up her mouth and shared her deepest, secret shame with this woman.

"I've never met my father," she told this total stranger who looked like an upscale mirror image of herself. There was no reason she should feel as if she could trust a random woman she met in a bathroom, no matter whose face she wore. It was absurd to feel as if she'd known this other person all her life when of course she hadn't. And yet she kept talking. "My mother's always told me she has no idea who he was. That Prince Charming was a fantasy sold to impressionable young girls to make them silly, and the reality was that men are simply men and untrustworthy to the core. And she bounces from one affair to the next pretty quickly, so I came to terms with the fact it was possible she really, truly didn't know."

Valentina laughed. It was a low, smoky sound, and Natalie recognized it, because it was hers. A shock of recognition went through her. Though she didn't feel like laughing. At all.

"My father is many things," the princess said, laughter and something more serious beneath it. "Including His Royal Majesty, King Geoffrey of Murin. What he is not now, nor has ever been, I imagine, is forgettable."

Natalie shook her head. "You underestimate my mother's commitment to amnesia. She's made it a life choice instead of a malady. On some level I admire it."

Once again, she had no idea why she was telling this stranger things she hardly dared admit to herself.

"My mother was the noblewoman Frederica de Burgh,

from a very old Murinese family." Valentina watched Natalie closely as she spoke. "Promised to my father at birth, raised by nuns and kept deliberately sheltered, and then widely held to be unequal to the task of becoming queen. Mentally. But that's the story they would tell, isn't it, to explain why she disappeared? What's your mother's name?"

Her hands felt numb, so Natalie shifted her bag from her shoulder to the marble countertop beside her. "She calls herself Erica."

For a moment neither one of them spoke. Neither one of them mentioned that *Erica* sounded very much like a shortened form of *Frederica,* but then, there was no need. Natalie was aware of too many things. The far-off sounds of planes outside the building. The television in the lounge on the other side of the door, cued to a twenty-four-hour news channel. She was vaguely surprised her boss hadn't already texted her fifteen furious times, wondering where she'd gone off to when it was possible he might have need of her.

"I saw everyone's favorite billionaire, Achilles Casilieris, out there in the lounge," Valentina said after a moment, as if reading Natalie's mind. "He looks even more fearsome in person than advertised. You can almost *see* all that brash command and dizzying wealth ooze from his pores, can't you?"

"He's my boss." Natalie ran her tongue over her teeth, that reckless thing inside of her lurching to life all over again. "If he was really oozing anything, anywhere, it would be my job to provide first aid until actual medical personnel could come handle it. At which point he would bite my head off for wasting his precious time by not curing him instantly."

She had worked for Achilles Casilieris—and by extension the shockingly hardy, internationally envied and recession-proof Casilieris Company—for five very long years. That was the first marginally negative thing she'd said about her job, ever. Out loud, anyway. And she felt instantly disloyal, despite the fact she'd been psyching herself up to quit only moments ago. Much as she had when she'd opened her mouth about her mother.

How could a stranger who happened to look like her make Natalie question who *she* was?

But the princess was frowning at the slim leather clutch she'd tossed on the bathroom counter. Natalie heard the buzzing sound that indicated a call as Valentina flipped open the outer flap and slid her smartphone out, then rolled her eyes and shoved it back in.

"My fiancé," she said, meeting Natalie's gaze again, her own more guarded. Or maybe it was something else that made the green in her eyes darker. The phone buzzed a few more times, then stopped. "Or his chief of staff, to be more precise."

"Congratulations," Natalie said, though the expression on Valentina's face did not look as if she was precisely awash in joyous anticipation.

"Thank you, I'm very lucky." Valentina's mouth curved, though there was nothing like a smile in her eyes and her tone was arid. "Everyone says so. Prince Rodolfo is objectively attractive. Not all princes can make that claim, but the tabloids have exulted over his abs since he was a teenager. Just as they have salivated over his impressive dating history, which has involved a selection of models and actresses from at least four continents and did not cease in any noticeable way upon our engagement last fall."

"Your Prince Charming sounds…charming," Natalie murmured. It only confirmed her long-held suspicions about such men.

Valentina raised one shoulder, then dropped it. "His theory is that he remains free until our marriage, and then will be free once again following the necessary birth of his heir. More discreetly, I can only hope. Meanwhile, I am beside myself with joy that I must take my place at his side in two short months. Of course."

Natalie didn't know why she laughed at that, but she did. More out of commiseration than anything else, as if they really were the same person. And how strange that she almost felt as if they were. "It's going to be a terrific couple of months all around, then. Mr. Casilieris is in rare form. He's putting together a particularly dramatic deal and it's not going his way and he…isn't used to that. So that's me working twenty-two-hour days instead of my usual twenty for the foreseeable future, which is even more fun when he's cranky and snarling."

"It can't possibly be worse than having to smile politely while your future husband lectures you about the absurd expectation of fidelity in what is essentially an arranged marriage for hours on end. The absurdity is that *he* might be expected to curb his impulses for a year or so, in case you wondered. The expectations for *me* apparently involve quietly and chastely finding fulfillment in philanthropic works, like his sainted absentee mother who everyone knows manufactured a supposed health crisis so she could live out her days in peaceful seclusion. It's easy to be philanthropically fulfilled while living in isolation in Bavaria."

Natalie smiled. "Try biting your tongue while your famously short-tempered boss rages at you for no reason, for the hundredth time in an hour, because he pays you to stand there and take it without wilting or crying or selling whinging stories about him to the press."

Valentina's smile was a perfect match. "Or the hours

and hours of grim palace-vetted pre-wedding press interviews in the company of a pack of advisors who will censor everything I say and inevitably make me sound like a bit of animated treacle, as out of touch with reality as the average overly sweet dessert."

"Speaking of treats, I also have to deal with the board of directors Mr. Casilieris treats like irritating schoolchildren, his packs of furious ex-lovers each with her own vendetta, all his terrified employees who need to be coached through meetings with him and treated for PTSD after, and every last member of his staff in every one of his households, who like me to be the one to ask him the questions they know will set him off on one of his scorch-the-earth rages."

They'd moved a little bit closer then, leaning toward each other like friends. *Or sisters,* a little voice whispered. It should have concerned Natalie like everything else about this. And like everything else, it did and it didn't. Either way, she didn't step back. She didn't insist upon her personal space. She was almost tempted to imagine her body knew something about this mirror image version of her that her brain was still desperately trying to question.

Natalie thought of the way Mr. Casilieris had bitten her head off earlier, and her realization that if she didn't escape him now she never would. And how this stranger with her face seemed, oddly enough, to understand.

"I was thinking of quitting, to be honest," she whispered. Making it real. "Today."

"I can't quit, I'm afraid," the impossibly glamorous princess said then, her green eyes alight with something a little more frank than plain mischief. "But I have a better idea. Let's switch places. For a month, say. Six weeks at the most. Just for a little break."

"That's crazy," Natalie said.

"Insane," Valentina agreed. "But you might find royal protocol exciting! And I've always wanted to do the things everyone else in the world does. Like go to a real job."

"People can't *switch places*." Natalie was frowning. "And certainly not with a princess."

"You could think about whether or not you really want to quit," Valentina pointed out. "It would be a lovely holiday for you. Where will Achilles Casilieris be in six weeks' time?"

"He's never gone from London for too long," Natalie heard herself say, as if she was considering it.

Valentina smiled. "Then in six weeks we'll meet in London. We'll text in the meantime with all the necessary details about our lives, and on the appointed day we'll just meet up and switch back and no one will ever be the wiser. Doesn't that sound like *fun*?" Her gaze met Natalie's with something like compassion. "And I hope you won't mind my saying this, but you do look as if you could use a little fun."

"It would never work." Natalie realized after she spoke that she still hadn't said no. "No one will ever believe I'm you."

Valentina waved a hand between them. "How would anyone know the difference? I can barely tell myself."

"People will take one look at me and know I'm not you," Natalie insisted, as if that was the key issue here. "You look like a *princess*."

If Valentina noticed the derisive spin she put on that last word out of habit, she appeared to ignore it.

"You too can look like a princess. This princess, anyway. You already do."

"There's a lifetime to back it up. You're elegant. Poised.

You've had years of training, presumably. How to be a diplomat. How to be polite in every possible situation. Which fork to use at dinner, for God's sake."

"Achilles Casilieris is one of the wealthiest men alive. He dines with as many kings as I do. I suspect that as his personal assistant, Natalie, you have, too. And have likely learned how to navigate the cutlery."

"No one will believe it," Natalie whispered, but there was no heat in it.

Because maybe she was the one who couldn't believe it. And maybe, if she was entirely honest, there was a part of her that wanted this. The princess life and everything that went with it. The kind of ease she'd never known—and a castle besides. And only for a little while. Six short weeks. Scarcely more than a daydream.

Surely even Natalie deserved a daydream. Just this once.

Valentina's smile widened as if she could scent capitulation in the air. She tugged off the enormous, eye-gouging ring on her left hand and placed it down on the counter between them. It made an audible *clink* against the marble surface.

"Try it on. I dare you. It's an heirloom from Prince Rodolfo's extensive treasury of such items, dating back to the dawn of time, more or less." She inclined her head in that regal way of hers. "If it doesn't fit we'll never speak of switching places again."

And Natalie felt possessed by a force she didn't understand. She knew better. Of course she did. This was a ridiculous game and it could only make this bizarre situation worse, and she was certainly no Cinderella. She knew that much for sure.

But she slipped the ring onto her finger anyway, and it fit perfectly, gleaming on her finger like every dream she'd ever had as a little girl. Not that she could live a magical life, filled with talismans that shone the way this ring did, because that was the sort of *impracticality* her mother had abhorred. But that she could have a home the way everyone else did. That she could *belong* to a man, to a country, to the sweep of a long history, the way this ring hugged her finger. As if it was meant to be.

The ring had nothing to do with her. She knew that. But it felt like a promise, even so.

And it all seemed to snowball from there. They each kicked off their shoes and stood barefoot on the surprisingly plush carpet. Then Valentina shimmied out of her sleek, deceptively simple sheath dress with the unselfconsciousness of a woman used to being dressed by attendants. She lifted her brows with all the imperiousness of her station, and Natalie found herself retreating into the stall with the dress—since she was not, in fact, used to being tended to by packs of fawning courtiers and therefore all but naked with an audience. She climbed out of her own clothes, handing her pencil skirt, blouse and wrap sweater out to Valentina through the crack she left open in the door. Then she tugged the princess's dress on, expecting it to snag or pull against her obviously peasant body.

But like the ring, the dress fit as if it had been tailored to her body. As if it was hers.

She walked out slowly, blinking when she saw…herself waiting for her. The very same view she'd seen in the mirror this morning when she'd dressed in the room Mr. Casilieris kept for her in the basement of his London town house because her own small flat was too far away to be to-ing and fro-ing at odd hours, according to him, and it was easier to acquiesce than fight. Not that it had kept him from firing away at her. But she shoved that aside because Valentina was laughing at the sight of Natalie in obvious astonishment, as if she was having the same literal out-of-body experience.

Natalie walked back to the counter and climbed into the princess's absurd shoes, very carefully. Her knees protested beneath her as she tried to stand tall in them and she had to reach out to grip the marble counter.

"Put your weight on your heels," Valentina advised. She was already wearing Natalie's wedges, because apparently even their feet were the same, and of course she had no trouble standing in them as if she'd picked them out herself. "Everyone always wants to lean forward and tiptoe in heels like that, and nothing looks worse. Lean back and you own the shoe, not the other way around." She eyed Natalie. "Will your glasses give me a headache, do you suppose?"

Natalie pulled them from her face and handed them over. "They're clear glass. I was getting a little too much attention from some of the men Mr. Casilieris works with, and it annoyed him. I didn't want to lose my job, so I started wearing my hair up and these glasses. It worked like a charm."

"I refuse to believe men are so idiotic."

Natalie grinned as Valentina took the glasses and slid them onto her nose. "The men we're talking about weren't exactly paying me attention because they found me enthralling. It was a diversionary tactic during negotiations and yes, you'd be surprised how many men fail to see a woman who looks smart."

She tugged her hair tie from her ponytail and shook out her hair, then handed the elastic to Valentina. The princess swept her hair back and into the same ponytail Natalie had been sporting only seconds before.

And it was like magic.

Ordinary Natalie Monette, renowned for her fierce work ethic, attention to detail and her total lack of anything resembling a personal life—which was how she'd become the executive assistant to one of the world's most ferocious and feared billionaires straight out of college and now had absolutely no life to call her own—became Her Royal Highness, Princess Valentina of Murin in an instant. And vice versa. Just like that.

"This is crazy," Natalie whispered.

The real Princess Valentina only smiled, looking every inch the smooth, super competent right hand of a man as feared as he was respected. Looking the way Natalie had always *hoped* she looked, if she was honest. Serenely capable. Did this mean…she always had?

More than that, they looked like twins. They had to be twins. There was no possibility that they could be anything but.

Natalie didn't want to think about the number of lies her mother had to have told her if that was true. She didn't want to think about all the implications. She couldn't.

"We have to switch places now," Valentina said softly, though there was a catch in her voice. It was the catch that made Natalie focus on her rather than the mystery that was her mother. "I've always wanted to be…someone else. Someone normal. Just for a little while."

Their gazes caught at that, both the exact same shade of green, just as their hair was that unusual shade of copper many tried to replicate in the salon, yet couldn't. The only difference was that Valentina's was highlighted with streaks of blond that Natalia suspected came from long, lazy days on the decks of yachts or taking in the sunshine from the comfort of her very own island kingdom.

If you're really twins—if you're sisters—it's your is-

land, too, a little voice inside whispered. But Natalie couldn't handle that. Not here. Not now. Not while she was all dressed up in princess clothes.

"Is that what princesses dream of?" Natalie asked. She wanted to smile, but the moment felt too precarious. Ripe and swollen with emotions she couldn't have named, though she understood them as they moved through her. "Because I think most other little girls imagine they're you."

Not her, of course. Never her.

Something shone a little too brightly in Valentina's gaze then, and it made Natalie's chest ache.

But she would never know what her mirror image might have said next, because her name was called in a familiar growl from directly outside the door to the women's room. Natalie didn't think. She was dressed as someone else and she couldn't let anyone see that—so she threw herself back into the stall where she'd changed her clothes as the door was slapped open.

"Exactly what are you doing in here?" growled a voice that Natalie knew better than her own. She'd worked for Achilles Casilieris for five years. She knew him much, much better than she knew herself. She knew, for example, that the particular tone he was using right now meant his usual grouchy mood was being rapidly taken over by his typical impatience. He'd likely had to actually take a moment and look for her, rather than her magically being at his side before he finished his thought. He hated that. And he wasn't shy at all about expressing his feelings. "Can we leave for New York now, do you think, or do you need to fix your makeup for another hour?"

Natalie stood straighter out of habit, only to realize that her boss's typical scowl wasn't directed at her. She was hidden behind the cracked open door of the bathroom stall. Her boss was aiming that famous glare straight at Valentina, and he didn't appear to notice that she wasn't Natalie. That if she was Natalie, that would mean she'd lightened her hair in the past fifteen minutes. But she could tell that all her boss saw was his assistant. Nothing more, nothing less.

"I apologize," Valentina murmured.

"I don't need you to be sorry, I need you on the plane," Achilles retorted, then turned back around to head out.

Natalie's head spun. She had worked for this man, night and day, for *half a decade.* He was Achilles Casilieris, renowned for his keen insight and killer instincts in all things, and Natalie had absolutely no doubt that he had no idea that he hadn't been speaking to her.

Maybe that was why, when Valentina reached over and took Natalie's handbag instead of her own, Natalie didn't push back out of the stall to stop her. She said nothing. She stood where she was. She did absolutely nothing to keep the switch from happening.

"I'll call you," Valentina mouthed into the mirror as she hurried to the door, and the last Natalie saw of Her Royal Highness Valentina of Murin was the suppressed excitement in her bright green eyes as she followed Achilles Casilieris out the door.

Natalie stepped out of the stall again in the sudden silence. She looked at herself in the mirror, smoothed her hair down with palms that shook only the slightest little bit, blinked at the wild sparkle of the absurd ring on her finger as she did it.

And just like that, became a fairy princess—and stepped right into a daydream.

CHAPTER TWO

CROWN PRINCE RODOLFO of the ancient and deeply, deliberately reserved principality of Tissely, tucked away in the Pyrenees between France and Spain and gifted with wealth, peace and dramatic natural borders that had kept things that way for centuries untold, was bored.

This was not his preferred state of existence, though it was not exactly surprising here on the palace grounds of Murin Castle, where he was expected to entertain the royal bride his father had finally succeeded in forcing upon him.

Not that "entertainment" was ever really on offer with the undeniably pretty, yet almost aggressively placid and unexciting Princess Valentina. His future wife. The future mother of his children. His future queen, even. Assuming he didn't lapse into a coma before their upcoming nuptials, that was.

Rodolfo sighed and stretched out his long legs, aware he was far too big to be sitting so casually on a relic of a settee in this stuffily proper reception room that had been set aside for his use on one of his set monthly visits with his fiancée. He still felt a twinge in one thigh from the ill-advised diving trip he'd taken some months back with a group of his friends and rather too many sharks. Rodolfo rubbed at the scarred spot absently, grateful that while his father had inevitably caught wind of the feminine talent who'd graced the private yacht off the coast of Belize, the fact an overenthusiastic shark had grazed the Crown Prince of Tissely en route to a friend's recently caught fish had escaped both the King's spies' and the rabid tabloids' breathless reports.

It was these little moments of unexpected grace, he often thought with varying degrees of irony, that made his otherwise royally pointless life worth living.

"You embarrass yourself more with each passing year," his father had told him, stiff with fury, when Rodolfo had succumbed to the usual demands for a command appearance upon his return to Europe at the end of last summer, the salacious pictures of his "Belize Booze Cruise" still fresh in every tabloid reader's mind. And more to the point, in his father's.

"You possess the power to render me unembarrassing forevermore," Rodolfo had replied easily enough. He'd almost convinced himself his father no longer got beneath his skin. Almost. "Give me something to do, Father. You have an entire kingdom at your disposal. Surely you can find a single task for your only son."

But that was the crux of the matter they never spoke of directly, of course. Rodolfo was not the son his father had wanted as heir. He was not the son his father would have chosen to succeed him, not the son his father had planned for. He was his father's only *remaining* son, and not his father's choice.

He was not Felipe. He could never be Felipe. It was a toss-up as to which one of them hated him more for that.

"There is no place in my kingdom for a sybaritic fool whose life is little more than an extended advertisement for one of those appalling survival programs, complete with the sensationalism of the nearest gutter press," his father had boomed from across his vast, appropriately majestic office in the palace, because it was so much easier to attack Rodolfo than address what simmered beneath it all. Not that Rodolfo helped matters with his increasingly dangerous antics, he was aware. "You stain the principality with every astonishingly bad decision you make."

"It was a boat ride, sir." Rodolfo had kept his voice even because he knew it irritated his father to get no reaction to his litanies and insults. "Not precisely a scandal likely to topple the whole of the kingdom's government, as I think you are aware."

"What I am aware of, as ever, is how precious little you know about governing anything," his father had seethed, in all his state and consequence.

"You could change that with a wave of your hand," Rodolfo had reminded him, as gently as possible. Which was perhaps not all that gently. "Yet you refuse."

And around and around they went.

Rodolfo's father, the taciturn and disapproving sovereign of Tissely, Ferdinand IV, held all the duties of the monarchy in his tight fists and showed no signs of easing his grip anytime soon. Despite the promise he'd made his only remaining son and heir that he'd give him a more than merely ceremonial place in the principality's government following Rodolfo's graduate work at the London School of Economics. That had been ten years back, his father had only grown more bitter and possessive of his throne, and Rodolfo had…adapted.

Life in the principality was sedate, as befitted a nation that had avoided all the wars of the last few centuries by simple dint of being too far removed to take part in them in any real way. Rodolfo's life, by contrast, was…stimulating. Provocative by design. He liked his sport extreme and his sex excessive, and he didn't much care if the slavering hounds of the European press corps printed every moment of each, which they'd been more than happy to do for the past decade. If his father wished him to be more circumspect, to preserve and protect the life of the hereditary heir to Tissely's throne the way he should—the way he'd raced about trying to wrap Felipe in cotton wool, restricting him from everything only to lose him to something as ignoble and silly as an unremarkable cut in his finger and what they'd thought was the flu—he needed only to offer Rodolfo something else with which to fill his time. Such as, perhaps, something to *do* besides continue to exist, thus preserving the bloodline by dint of not dying.

In fairness, of course, Rodolfo had committed himself to pushing the boundaries of his continued existence as much as possible, with his group of similarly devil-may-care friends, to the dismay of most of their families.

"Congratulations," Ferdinand had clipped out one late September morning last fall in yet another part of his vast offices in the Tisselian palace complex. "You will be married next summer."

"I beg your pardon?"

In truth, Rodolfo had not been paying much attention to the usual lecture until that moment. He was no fan of being summoned from whatever corner of the world he happened to be inhabiting and having to race back to present himself before Ferdinand, because his lord and father preferred not to communicate with his only heir by any other means but face-to-face. But of course, Ferdinand had not solicited his opinion. Ferdinand never did.

When he'd focused on his father, sitting there behind the acres and acres of his desk, the old man had actually looked...smug.

That did not bode well.

"You've asked me for a role in the kingdom and here it is. The Crown Prince of Tissely has been unofficially betrothed to the Murin princess since her birth. It is high time you did your duty and ensured the line. This should not come as any great surprise. You are not exactly getting any younger, Rodolfo, as your increasingly more desperate public displays amply illustrate."

Rodolfo had let that deliberate slap roll off his back, because there was no point reacting. It was what his father wanted.

"I met the Murin princess exactly once when I was ten and she was in diapers." Felipe had been fourteen and a man of the world, to Rodolfo's recollection, and the then Crown Prince of Tissely had seemed about as unenthused about his destiny as Rodolfo felt now. "That seems a rather tenuous connection upon which to base a marriage, given I've never seen her since."

"Princess Valentina is renowned the world over for her commitment to her many responsibilities and her role as her father's emissary," his father had replied coolly. "I doubt your paths would have crossed in all these years, as she is not known to frequent the dens of iniquity you prefer."

"Yet you believe this paragon will wish to marry me."

"I am certain she will wish no such thing, but the princess is a dutiful creature who knows what she owes to her country. You claim that you are as well, and that your dearest wish is to serve the crown. Now is your chance to prove it."

And that was how Rodolfo had found himself both hoist by his own petard and more worrying, tied to his very proper, very dutiful, very, very boring bride-to-be with no hope of escape. Ever.

"Princess Valentina, Your Highness," the butler intoned from the doorway, and Rodolfo dutifully climbed to his feet, because his life might have been slipping out of his control by the second, but hell, he still had the manners that had been beaten into him since he was small.

The truth was, he'd imagined that he would do things differently than his father when he'd realized he would have to take Felipe's place as the heir to his kingdom. He'd been certain he would not marry a woman he hardly knew, foisted upon him by duty and immaculate bloodlines, with whom he could hardly carry on a single meaningful conversation. His own mother—no more enamored of King Ferdinand than Rodolfo was— had long since repaired to her preferred residence, her ancestral home in the manicured wilds of Bavaria, and had steadfastly maintained an enduring if vague health crisis that necessitated she remain in seclusion for the past twenty years.

Rodolfo had been so sure, as an angry young man still reeling from his brother's death, that he would do things better when he had his chance.

And instead he was standing attendance on a strange woman who, in the months of their engagement, had appeared to be made entirely of impenetrable glass. She was about that approachable.

But this time, when Valentina walked into the reception room the way she'd done many times before, so they could engage in a perfectly tedious hour of perfectly polite conversation on perfectly pointless topics as if it was the stifling sixteenth century, all to allow the waiting press corps to gush about their visits later as they caught Rodolfo leaving, everything…changed.

Rodolfo couldn't have said how. Much less why.

But he *felt* her entrance. He *felt it* when she paused in the doorway and looked around as if she'd never laid eyes on him or the paneled ceiling or any part of the run-of-the-mill room before. His body tightened. He felt a rush of heat pool in his—

Impossible.

What the hell was happening to him?

Rodolfo felt his gaze narrow as he studied his fiancée. She looked the way she always did, and yet she didn't. She wore one of her efficiently sophisticated and chicly demure ensembles, a deceptively simple sheath dress that showed nothing and yet obliquely drew attention to the sheer feminine perfection of her form. A form he'd seen many times before, always clothed beautifully, and yet had never found himself waxing rhapsodic about before. Yet today he couldn't look away. There was something about the way she stood, as if she was unsteady on those cheeky heels she wore, though that seemed unlikely. Her hair flowed around her shoulders and looked somehow wilder than it usually did, as if the copper of it was redder. Or perhaps brighter.

Or maybe he needed to get his head examined. Maybe he really had gotten a concussion when he'd gone on an impromptu skydiving trip last week, tumbling a little too much on his way down into the remotest peaks of the Swiss Alps.

The princess moistened her lips and then met his gaze, and Rodolfo felt it like her sultry little mouth all over the hardest part of him.

What the hell?

"Hello," she said, and even her voice was…different, somehow. He couldn't put his finger on it. "It's lovely to see you."

"Lovely to see me?" he echoed, astonished. And

something far more earthy, if he was entirely honest with himself. "Are you certain? I was under the impression you would prefer a rousing spot of dental surgery to another one of these meetings. I feel certain you almost admitted as much at our last one."

He didn't know what had come over him. He'd managed to maintain his civility throughout all these months despite his creeping boredom—what had changed today? He braced himself, expecting the perfect princess to collapse into an offended heap on the polished floor, which he'd have a hell of a time explaining to her father, the humorless King Geoffrey of Murin.

But Valentina only smiled and a gleam he'd never seen before kindled in her eyes, which he supposed must always have been that remarkable shade of green. How had he never noticed them before?

"Well, it really depends on the kind of dental surgery, don't you think?" she asked.

Rodolfo couldn't have been more surprised if the quietly officious creature had tossed off her clothes and started dancing on the table—well, there was no need to exaggerate. He'd have summoned the palace doctors if the princess had done anything of the kind. After appreciating the show for a moment or two, of course, because he was a man, not a statue. But the fact she appeared to be teasing him was astounding, nonetheless.

"A root canal, at the very least," he offered.

"With or without anesthesia?"

"If it was with anesthesia you'd sleep right through it," Rodolfo pointed out. "Hardly any suffering at all."

"Everyone knows there's no point doing one's duty unless one can brag forever about the amount of suffering required to survive the task," the princess said, moving farther into the room. She stopped and rested her hand on the high, brocaded back of a chair that had likely cradled the posteriors of kings dating back to the ninth century, and all Rodolfo could think was that he wanted her to keep going. To keep walking toward him. To put herself within reach so he could—

Calm down, he ordered himself. *Now.* So sternly he sounded like his father in his own head.

"You are describing martyrdom," he pointed out.

Valentina shot him a smile. "Is there a difference?"

Rodolfo stood still because he didn't quite know what he might do if he moved. He watched this woman he'd written off months ago as if he'd never seen her before. There was something in the way she walked this afternoon that tugged at him. There was a new roll to her hips, perhaps. Something he'd almost call a swagger, assuming a princess of her spotless background and perfect genes was capable of anything so basic and enticing. Still, he couldn't look away as she rounded the settee he'd abandoned and settled herself in its center with a certain delicacy that was at odds with the way she'd moved through the old, spectacularly royal room. Almost as if she was more uncertain than she looked...but that made as little sense as the rest.

"I was reading about you on the plane back from London today," she told him, surprising him all over again.

"And here I thought we were maintaining the polite fiction that you did not sully your royal eyes with the squalid tabloids."

"Ordinarily I would not, of course," she replied, and then her mouth curved. Rodolfo was captivated. And somewhat horrified at that fact. But still captivated, all the same. "It is beneath me, obviously."

He sketched a bow that would have made his grandfather proud. "Obviously."

"I am a princess, not a desperate shopgirl who wants nothing more than to escape her dreary life, and must imagine herself into fantastical stories and half-truths presented as gospel."

"Quite so."

"But I must ask you a question." And on that she smiled again, that same serene curve of her lips that had about put him to sleep before. That was not the effect it had on him today. By a long shot.

"You can ask me anything, princess," Rodolfo heard himself say.

In a lazy, smoky sort of tone he'd never used in her presence before. Because this was the princess he was going to marry, not one of the enterprising women who flung themselves at him everywhere he went, looking for a taste of Europe's favorite daredevil prince.

There was no denying it. Suddenly, out of nowhere, he wanted his future wife.

Desperately.

As if she could tell—as if she'd somehow become the sort of woman who could read a man's desire and use it against him, when he'd have sworn she was anything but—Valentina's smile deepened.

She tilted her head to one side. "It's about your shocking double standard," she said sweetly. "If you can cat your way through all of Europe, why can't I?"

Something black and wild and wholly unfamiliar surged in him then, making Rodolfo's hands curl into fists and his entire body go tense, taut.

Then he really shocked the hell out of himself.

"Because you can't," he all but snarled, and there was no pretending that wasn't exactly what he was doing. *Snarling.* No matter how unlikely. "Like it or not, princess, you are mine."

CHAPTER THREE

PRINCE RODOLFO WAS not what Natalie was expecting.

No picture—and there were thousands, at a conservative estimate, every week he continued to draw breath—could adequately capture the *size* of Europe's favorite royal adrenaline junkie. That was the first thing that struck her. Sure, she'd seen the detailed telephoto shots of his much-hallowed abs as he emerged from various sparkling Mediterranean waters that had dominated whole summers of international swooning. And there was that famous morning he'd spent on a Barcelona balcony one spring, stretching and taking in the sunlight in boxer briefs and nothing else, but somehow all of those revealing pictures had managed to obscure the sheer *size* of the man. He was well over six feet, with hard, strong shoulders that could block out a day or two. And more than that, there was a leashed, humming sort of *power* in the man that photographs of him concealed entirely.

Or, Natalie thought, *maybe he's the one who does the concealing.*

But she couldn't think about what this man might be hiding beneath the surface. Not when the surface itself was so mesmerizing. She still felt as dazed as she'd been when she'd walked in this room and seen him waiting for her, dwarfing the furniture with all that contained physicality as he stood before the grand old fireplace. He looked like an athlete masquerading as a prince, with thick dark hair that was not quite tamed and the sort of dark chocolate eyes that a woman could lose herself in for a lifetime or three. His lean and rangy hard male beauty was packed into black trousers and a soft-looking button-down shirt that strained to handle his biceps and his gloriously sculpted chest. His hands were large and aristocratic at once, his voice was an authoritative rumble that seemed to murmur deep within her and then sink into a bright flame between her legs, his gaze was shockingly direct—and Natalie was not at all prepared. For any of it. For *him*.

She'd expected this real-life Prince Charming to be as repellent as he'd always been in the stories her mother had told her as a child about men just like him. Dull and vapid. Obsessed with something obscure, like hound breeding. Vain and huffy and bland, all the way through. Not...*this*.

Valentina had said that her fiancé was attractive in an offhanded, uncomplimentary way. She'd failed to mention that he was, in fact, upsettingly—almost incomprehensibly—stunning. The millions of fawning, admiring pictures of Crown Prince Rodolfo did not do him any justice, it turned out, and the truth of him took all the air from the room. From Natalie's lungs, for that matter. Her stomach felt scraped hollow as it plummeted to her feet, and then stayed there. But after a moment in the doorway where she'd seen nothing but him and the world had seemed to smudge a little bit around its luxe, literally palatial edges, Natalie had rallied.

It was hard enough trying to walk in the ridiculous shoes she was wearing—with her weight back on her heels, as ordered—and not goggle in slack-jawed astonishment at the palace all around her. *The actual, real live palace.* Valentina had pointed out that Natalie had likely visited remarkable places before, thanks to her job, and that was certainly true. But it was one thing to be treated as a guest in a place like Murin Castle. Or more precisely, as the employee of a guest, however valued by the guest in question. It was something else entirely to be treated as if it was all...hers.

The staff had curtsied and bowed when Natalie had stepped onto the royal jet. The guards had stood at attention. A person who was clearly her personal aide had catered to her during the quick flight, quickly filling her in on the princess's schedule and plans and then leaving her to her own devices. Natalie had spent years doing the exact same thing, so she'd learned a few things about Valentina in the way her efficient staff operated around her look-alike. That she was well liked by those who worked for her, which made Natalie feel oddly warm inside, as if that was some kind of reflection on her instead of the princess. That Valentina was not overly fussy or precious, given the way the staff served her food and acted while they did it. And that she was addicted to romance novels, if the stacks of books with bright-colored covers laid out for her perusal was any indication.

Then, soon enough, the plane had landed on the tiny little jewel of an island nestled in the Mediterranean Sea. Natalie's impressions were scattered as they flew in. Hills stretched high toward the sun, then sloped into the sea, covered in olive groves, tidy red roofs and the soaring arches of bell towers and churches. Blue water gleamed everywhere she looked, and white sand beaches nestled up tight to colorful fishing villages and picturesque marinas. There were cheerful sails in the graceful bay and a great, iconic castle set high on a hill. A perfect postcard of an island.

A dream. Except Natalie was wide-awake, and this was really, truly happening.

"Prince Rodolfo awaits your pleasure, Your Highness," a man she assumed was some kind of high-level butler had informed her when she'd been escorted into the palace itself, with guards saluting her arrival. She'd been too busy trying to look as if the splendor pressing in on her from all sides was so terribly common that she hardly noticed it to do more than nod, in some approximation of the princess's elegant inclination of her head. Then she'd had to follow the same butler through the palace, trying to walk with ease and confidence in shoes she was certain were not meant to be walked in at all, much less down endless marble halls.

She'd expected Prince Rodolfo to be seedier in person than in his photos. Softer of jaw, meaner of eye. And up himself in every possible way. She had not expected to find herself so stunned at the sight of him that she'd had to reach out and hold on to the furniture to keep her knees from giving out beneath her, for the love of all that was holy.

And then he'd spoken, and Natalie had understood— with a certain, sinking feeling that only made that breathlessness worse—that she was in more than a little hot water. It had never crossed her mind that *she* might find this prince—or any prince—attractive. It had never even occurred to her that she might be affected in any way by a man who carried that sort of title or courted the sort of attention Prince Rodolfo did. Natalie had never liked *flashy*. It was always a deliberate distraction, never anything real. Working for one of the most powerful men in the world had made her more than a little jaded when it came to other male displays of supposed strength. She knew what real might look like, how it was maintained and more, how it was wielded. A petty little princeling who liked to fling himself out of airplanes could only be deeply unappealing in person, she'd imagined.

She'd never imagined...*this*.

It was possible her mouth had run away with her, as some kind of defense mechanism.

And then, far more surprising, Prince Rodolfo wasn't the royal dullard she'd been expecting—all party and no substance. The sculpted mouth of his...*did things* to her as he revealed himself to be something a bit more intriguing than the airhead she'd expected. Especially when that look in his dark eyes took a turn toward the feral.

Stop, she ordered herself sternly. *This is another woman's fiancé, no matter what she might think of him.*

Natalie had to order herself to pay attention to what was happening as the Prince's surprisingly possessive words rang through the large room that teemed with antiques and the sort of dour portraits that usually turned out to have been painted by ancient masters, were always worth unconscionable amounts of money and made everyone in them look shriveled and dour. Or more precisely, she had to focus on their conversation, and not the madness that was going on inside her body.

You are mine didn't sound like the kind of thing the man Valentina had described would say. Ever. It didn't sound at all like the man the tabloids drooled over, or all those ex-lovers moaned about in exclusive interviews, mostly to complain about how quickly each and every one of them was replaced with the next.

In fact, unless she was mistaken, His Royal Highness, Prince Rodolfo, he of so many paramours in so many places that there were many internet graphs and user forums dedicated to tracking them all, looked as surprised by that outburst as she was.

"That hardly seems fair, does it?" she asked mildly, hoping he couldn't tell how thrown she was by him. Hoping it would go away if she ignored it. "I don't see why I have to confine myself to only you when you don't feel compelled to limit yourself. In any way at all, according to my research."

"Is there someone you wish to add to your stable, princess?" Rodolfo asked, in a smooth sort of way that was at complete odds with that hard, near-gold gleam in his dark eyes that set off every alarm in her body. Whether she ignored it or not. "Name the lucky gentleman."

"A lady never shares such things," she demurred. Then smiled the way she always had at the officious secretaries of her boss's rivals, all of whom underestimated her. Once. "Unlike you, Your Highness."

"I cannot help it if the press follows me everywhere I go." She sensed more than heard the growl in his voice. He was still standing where he'd been when she arrived, arranged before the immense fireplace like some kind of royal offering, but if he'd thought it made him look idle and at his ease he'd miscalculated. All she could see when she looked at him was how *big* he was. Big and hard and beautiful from head to toe and, God help her, she couldn't seem to control her reaction to him. "Just as I cannot keep them from writing any fabrication they desire. They prefer a certain narrative, of course. It sells."

"How tragic. I had no idea you were a misunderstood monk."

"I am a man, princess." He didn't quite bare his teeth. There was no reason at all Natalie should feel the cut of them against her skin. "Were you in some doubt?"

Natalie reminded herself that she, personally, had no stake in this. No matter how many stories her mother had told her about men like him and the careless way they lived their lives. No matter that Prince Rodolfo proved that her mother was right every time he swam with sharks or leaped from planes or trekked for a month in remotest Patagonia with no access to the outside world or thought to his country should he never return. And no matter the way her heart was kicking at her and her breath seemed to tangle in her throat. This wasn't about *her* at all.

I'm going to sort out your fiancé as a little wedding gift to you, she'd texted Valentina when she'd recovered from her shell shock and had emerged from the fateful bathroom in London to watch Achilles Casilieris's plane launch itself into the air without her. The beauty of the other princess having taken her bag when she'd left— with Natalie's phone inside it—was that Natalie knew her own number and could reach the woman who was inhabiting her life. You're welcome.

Good luck with that, Valentina had responded. He's unsortable. Deliberately, I imagine.

As far as Natalie was concerned, that was permission to come on in, guns blazing. She had nothing to lose by saying the things Valentina wouldn't. And there was absolutely no reason she should feel that hot, intent look he was giving her low and tight in her belly. No reason at all.

She made a show of looking around the vast room the scrupulously correct butler who had ushered her here had called a *parlor* in ringing tones. She'd had to work hard not to seem cowed, by the butler or the scale of the private wing he'd led her through, all dizzying chandeliers and astoundingly beautiful rooms clogged with priceless antiques and jaw-dropping art.

"I don't see any press here," she said, instead of debating his masculinity. For God's sake.

"Obviously not." Was it her imagination or did Rodolfo sound a little less...civilized? "We are on palace grounds. Your father would have them whipped."

"If you wanted to avoid the press, you could," Natalie pointed out. With all the authority of a person who had spent five years keeping Achilles Casilieris out of the press's meaty claws. "You don't."

Was it possible this mighty, beautiful prince looked... ill at ease? If only for a moment?

"I never promised you that I would declaw myself, Valentina," he said, and it took Natalie a moment to remember why he was calling her Valentina. Because that's who he thought she was, of course. Princess Valentina, who had to marry him in two months. Not mouthy, distressingly common Natalie, who was unlikely to marry anyone since she spent her entire life embroiled in and catering to the needs of a man who likely wouldn't be able to pick her out of a lineup. "I told you I would consider it after the wedding. For a time."

Natalie shrugged, and told herself there was no call for her to feel slapped down by his response. He wasn't going to marry *her*. She certainly didn't need to feel wounded by the way he planned to run his relationship. Critical, certainly. But not *wounded*.

"As will I," she said mildly.

Rodolfo studied her for a long moment, and Natalie forced herself to hold that seething dark glare while he did it. She even smiled and settled back against the delicate little couch, as if she was utterly relaxed. When she was nothing even remotely like it.

"No," he said after a long, long time, his voice dark

and lazy and something else she felt more than heard. "I think not."

Natalie held back the little shiver that threatened her then, because she knew, somehow, that he would see it and leap to the worst possible conclusion.

"You mistake me," she said coolly. "I wasn't asking your permission. I was stating a fact."

"I would suggest that you think very carefully about acting on this little scheme of yours, princess," Rodolfo said in that same dark, stirring tone. "You will not care for my response, I am certain."

Natalie crossed her legs and forced herself to relax even more against the back of her little couch. Well. To look it, anyway. As if she had never been more at her ease, despite the drumming of her pulse.

She waved a hand the way Valentina had done in London, so nonchalantly. "Respond however you wish. You have my blessing."

He laughed, then. The sound was rougher than Natalie would have imagined a royal prince's laugh ought to have been, and silkier than she wanted to admit as it wrapped itself around her. And all of that was a far second to the way amusement danced over his sculpted, elegant face, making him look not only big and surprisingly powerful, but very nearly approachable. Magnetic, even.

Something a whole lot more than magnetic. It lodged itself inside of her, then glowed.

Good lord, Natalie thought in another sort of daze as she gazed back at him. *This is the most dangerous man I've ever met.*

"I take it this is an academic discussion," Rodolfo said when he was finished laughing like that and using up all the light in the world, so cavalierly. "I had no idea you felt so strongly about what I did or didn't do, much less with whom. I had no idea you cared what I did at all. In fact, princess, I wasn't certain you heard a single word I've uttered in your presence in all these months."

He moved from the grand fireplace then, and watching him in motion was not exactly an improvement. Or it was a significant improvement, depending on how she looked at it. He was sleek for such a big man, and moved far too smoothly toward the slightly more substantial chair at a diagonal to where Natalie sat. He tossed himself into the stunningly wrought antique with a carelessness that should have snapped it into kindling, but didn't.

It occurred to her that he was far more aware of himself and his power than he appeared. That he was something of an iceberg, showing only the slightest bit of himself and containing multitudes beneath the surface. She didn't want to believe it. She wanted him to be a vapid, repellant playboy who she could slap into place during her time as a make-believe princess. But there was that assessing gleam in his dark gaze that told her that whatever else this prince was, he wasn't the least bit vapid.

And was rather too genuinely *charming* for her peace of mind, come to that.

He settled in his chair and stretched out his long, muscled legs so that they *almost* brushed hers, then smiled.

Natalie kept her own legs where they were, because shifting away from him would show a weakness she refused to let him see. She refused, as if her life depended on that refusal, and she didn't much care for the hysterical notion that it really, truly did.

"I don't care at all what you do or don't do," she assured him. "But it certainly appears that you can't say the same, for some reason."

"I am not the one who started making proclamations about my sexual intentions. I think you'll find that was you. Here. Today." That curve of his mouth deepened. "Entirely unprovoked."

"My mistake. Because a man who has grown up manipulating the press in no way sends a distinct message when he spends the bulk of his very public engagement 'escorting' other women to various events."

His gaze grew warmer, and that sculpted mouth curved. "I am a popular man."

"What I am suggesting to you is that you are not the only popular person in this arrangement. I'm baffled at your Neanderthal-like response to a simple statement of fact, when you have otherwise been at such pains to present yourself as the very image of modernity in royal affairs."

"We are sitting in an ancient castle on an island with a history that rivals Athens itself, discussing our upcoming marriage, which is the cold-blooded intermingling of two revered family lines for wealth and power, exactly as it might have been were we conducting this conversation in the Parthenon." His dark brows rose. "What part of this did you find particularly modern?"

"The two of us, I thought, before I walked in this room." She smiled brightly and let her foot dangle a bit too close to his leg. As if she didn't care at all that he was encroaching into her personal space. As if the idea of even so innocuous a touch did nothing at all to her central nervous system. As if he were not the sort of man she'd hated all her life, on principle. *And as if he were not promised to another,* she snapped at herself in disgust, but still, she didn't retreat the way she should have. In case she was wondering what kind of person she was.

"Now I suspect the Social Media Prince is significantly more caveman-like than he wants his millions of adoring followers to realize."

"I am the very soul of a Renaissance man, I assure you. I am merely aware of what the public will and will not support and I hate to break it you, princess, but the tabloids are not as forgiving of royal indiscretions as you appear to be."

"You surprise me again, Your Highness. I felt certain that a man in your position could not possibly care what the tabloid hacks did or did not forgive, given how much material you give them to work with. Daily."

"The two of us can sit in this room and bask in our progressive values, I am sure," Rodolfo murmured, and the look in his dark eyes did not strike Natalie as particularly progressive. "But public sentiment, I think you will find, is distressingly traditional. People may enjoy any number of their own extramarital affairs. It doesn't make them tolerant when a supposed fairy-tale princess strays from her charmed life. If anything, it makes the stones they cast heavier and more pointed."

"So, to unpack that, you personally wish to carry on as if we are single and free, but are prevented from following your heart's desire because you suddenly fear public perception?" She eyed him balefully and made no attempt to hide it. "That's a bit hard to believe, coming from the man who told me not twenty minutes ago that he refused to be *declawed*."

"You are not this naive, princess." And the look he gave her then seemed to prickle along her skin, lighting fires Natalie was terribly afraid would never go out. "You know perfectly well that I can do as I like with only minimal repercussions. It is you who cannot. You have built an entire life on your spotless character. What would happen were you to be revealed as nothing more or less than a creature as human as the rest of us?"

CHAPTER FOUR

RODOLFO HAD LONG ceased recognizing himself. And yet he kept talking.

"It will be difficult to maintain the fiction that you are a saint if your lovers are paraded through the tabloids of Europe every week," he pointed out, as if he didn't care one way or the other.

Somehow, he had the sense that the confounding woman who sat close enough to tempt him near to madness knew better. He could see it in the way her green eyes gleamed as she watched him. She was lounging in the settee as if it was a makeshift throne and she was already queen. And now she waved a languid hand, calling attention to her fine bones and the elegant fingers Rodolfo wanted all over his body. Rather desperately.

"It is you who prefer to ignore discretion," she said lightly enough. "I assume you get something out of the spotlight you shine so determinedly into your bedroom. I must congratulate you, as it is not every man who would be able to consistently perform with such an audience, so many years past his prime."

"I beg your pardon. Did you just question my... performance?"

"No need to rile yourself, Your Highness. The entire world has seen more than enough of your prowess.

I'm sure you are marvelously endowed with the—ah—necessary tools."

It took Rodolfo a stunned moment to register that the sensation moving in him then was nothing short of sheer astonishment. Somewhere between temper and laughter and yet neither at once.

"Let me make sure I am following this extraordinary line of thought," he began, trying to keep himself under control somehow—something that he could not recall ever being much of an issue before. Not with Princess Valentina, certainly. Not with any other woman he'd ever met.

"Whether or not it is extraordinary is between you and your revolving selection of aspiring hyphenates, I would think." When he could only stare blankly at her, she carried on almost merrily. "Model slash actress slash waitress slash air hostess, whatever the case may be. You exchange one for another so quickly, it's hard to keep track."

"I feel as if I've toppled off the side of the planet into an alternate reality," Rodolfo said then, after a moment spent attempting to digest what she'd said. What she'd actually dared say directly to his face. "Wherein Princess Valentina of Murin is sitting in my presence issuing veiled insults about my sexual performance and, indeed, my manhood itself."

"In this reality, we do not use the word *manhood* when we mean penis," Princess Valentina said with the same serene smile she'd always worn, back when he'd imagined she was boring. He couldn't understand how he'd misread her so completely. "It's a bit missish, isn't it?"

"What I cannot figure out is what you hope to gain from poking at me, Valentina," he said softly. "I am not given to displays of temper, if that is what you hoped.

Perhaps you forgot that I subject myself to extreme stress often. For fun. It is very, very difficult to get under my skin."

She smiled with entirely too much satisfaction for his comfort. "Says the man who had a rather strong reaction to the idea that what he feels constitutes reasonable behavior for him might also be equally appropriate for his fiancée."

"I assume you already recognize that there is no stopping the train we're on," he continued in the same quiet way, because it was that or give in to the simmering thing that was rumbling around inside of him, making him feel more precarious than he had in a long, long time. "The only way to avoid this marriage is to willfully cause a crisis in two kingdoms, and to what end? To make a point about free will? That is a lovely sentiment, I am sure, but it is not for you or me. We are not free. We belong to our countries and the people we serve. I would expect a woman whose very name is synonymous with her duty to understand that."

"That is a curious statement indeed from the only heir to an ancient throne who spends the bulk of his leisure time courting his own death." She let that land, that curve to her lips but nothing like a smile in her direct green stare. And she wasn't done. "Very much as if he was under the impression he did, in fact, owe nothing to his country at all."

Rodolfo's jaw felt like granite. "I can only assume that you are a jealous little thing, desperate to hide what you really want behind all these halfhearted feints and childish games."

The princess laughed. It was a smoky sound that felt entirely too much like a caress. "Why am I not surprised that so conceited a man would achieve that conclusion so quickly? Alas, I am hiding nothing, Your Highness."

He felt his lips curl in something much too fierce to be polite. "If you want to know whether or not I am marvelously endowed, princess, you need only ask for a demonstration."

She rolled her eyes, and perhaps that was what did it. Rodolfo was not used to being dismissed by beautiful women. Quite the contrary, they trailed around after him, begging for the scraps of his attention. He'd become adept at handling them before he'd left his teens. The ones who pretended to dislike him to get his attention, the ones who propositioned him straight out, the ones who acted as if they were shy, the ones so overcome and starstruck they stammered or wept or could only stare in silence. He'd seen it all.

But he had no way to process what was happening here with this woman he'd dismissed as uninteresting and uninterested within moments of their meeting as adults last fall. He had no idea what to do with a woman who set him on fire from across a room, and then treated him like a somewhat sad and boring joke.

He could handle just about anything, he realized, save indifference.

Rodolfo simply reached over and picked the princess up from the settee, hauling her through the air and setting her across his lap.

It was not a smart move. At best it was a test of that indifference she was flinging around the palace so casually, but it still wasn't smart.

But Rodolfo found he didn't give a damn.

The princess's porcelain cheeks flushed red and hot. She was a soft, slight weight against him, but his entire body exulted in the feel of her. Her scent was something so prosaic it hit him as almost shockingly exotic—soap. That was all. Her hands came up to brace against his chest, her copper hair was a silky shower over his arm and she was breathing hard and fast, making her exactly as much of a liar as he'd imagined she was.

She was many things, his hidden gem of a princess bride, but she was not *indifferent* to him. It felt like a victory.

"Do you think I cannot read women?" he asked her, his face temptingly, deliciously close to hers.

Her gaze was defiant. "There has long been debate about whether or not you can read anything else."

"I know you want me, princess. I can see it. I can feel it. The pulse in your throat, the look in your eyes. The way you tremble against me."

"That is sheer amazement that you think you can manhandle me this way, nothing more."

He moved the arm that wasn't wrapped around her back, sliding his hand to the delectable bit of thigh that was bared beneath the hem of her dress and just held it there. Her skin was a revelation, warm and soft. And her perfect, aristocratic oval of a face was tipped back, his for the taking.

Maybe he was the Neanderthal she'd claimed he was, after all. For the first time in his life, he felt as if he was that and more. A beast in every possible way, inside and out.

"What would happen if I slid my hand up under your skirt?" he asked her, bending even closer, so his mouth was a mere breath from hers.

"I would summon the royal guard and have you cast into the dungeons, the more medieval the better."

He ignored that breathy, insubstantial threat, along with the oddity of the Princess of Murin talking of dungeons in a palace that had never had any in the whole of its storied history. He concentrated on her body instead.

"What would I find, princess? How wet are you? How much of a liar will your body prove you to be?"

"Unlike you," she whispered fiercely, "I don't feel the need to prove myself in a thousand different sexual arenas."

But she didn't pull away. He noted that she didn't even try.

"You don't need to concern yourself with any arena but this one," he said, gruff against her mouth and his palm still full of her soft flesh. "And you need not prove yourself to anyone but me."

Rodolfo had kissed her once before. It had been a bloodless, mechanical photo op on the steps of Murin Castle. They had held hands and beamed insincerely at the crowds, and then he had pressed a chaste, polite sort of closemouthed kiss against her mouth to seal the deal. No muss, no fuss. It hadn't been unpleasant in any way. But there hadn't been anything to it. No fire. No raw, aching need. Rodolfo had experienced more intense handshakes.

That was not the way he kissed her today. Because everything was different, somehow. Himself included.

He didn't bother with any polite, bloodless kiss. Rodolfo took her mouth as if he owned it. As if there was nothing *arranged* about the two of them and never had been. As if he'd spent the night inside her, making her his in every possible way, and couldn't contain himself another moment.

Her taste flooded his senses, making him glad on some distant level that he'd had the accidental foresight to remain seated, because otherwise he thought she might have knocked him off his feet. He opened his mouth over hers, angling his jaw to revel in the slick, hot fit.

She was a marvel. And she was his, whether she liked it or not. No matter what inflammatory thing she said to rile him up or insult him into an international incident that would shame them both, or whatever the hell she was doing. How had he thought otherwise for even a moment?

Rodolfo lost his mind.

And his lovely bride-to-be did not push him off or slap his face. She didn't lie there in icy indifference. Oh, no.

She surged against him, wrapping her arms around his neck to pull him closer, and she kissed him back. Again and again and again.

For a moment there was nothing but that fire that roared between them. Wild. Insane. Unchecked and unmanageable.

And then in the next moment, she was shoving away from him. She twisted to pull herself from his grasp and then clambered off his lap, and he let her. Of course he bloody let her, and no matter the state of him as she went. That it was a new state—one he'd never experienced before, having about as much experience with frustrated desire as he did with governing the country he would one day rule—was something he kept to himself. Mostly because he hardly knew what to make of it.

The princess looked distressed as she threw herself across the room and away from him. She was trembling as she caught herself against the carved edge of the stone fireplace, and then she took a deep, long breath. To settle herself, perhaps, if she felt even a fraction of the things he did. Or perhaps she merely needed to steady herself in those shoes.

"Valentina," he began, but her name seemed to hit

her like a slap. She stiffened, then held up a hand as if to silence him. Yet another new experience.

And he could still taste her in his mouth. His body was still clamoring for her touch. He wanted her, desperately, so he let her quiet him like an errant schoolboy instead of the heir to an ancient throne.

"That must never happen again," she said with soft, intense sincerity, her gaze fixed on the fireplace, where an exultant flower arrangement took the place of the fires that had crackled there in the colder months.

"Come now, princess." He didn't sound like himself. Gruff. Low. "I think you know full well it must. We will make heirs, you and I. It is the primary purpose of our union."

She stood taller, then turned to face him, and he was struck by what looked like *torment* on her face. As if this was hard for her, whatever the hell was happening here, which made no sense. This had always been her destiny. If not with Rodolfo, then with some other Crown-sanctioned suitor. The woman he'd thought he'd known all these months had always seemed, if not precisely thrilled by the prospect, resigned to it. He imagined the change in her would have been fascinating if he wasn't half-blind from *wanting* her so badly.

"No," she said, and he was struck again by how different her voice sounded. But how could that be? He shook that off and concentrated instead on what she'd said.

"You must be aware that there can be no negotiation on this point." He tamped down on the terrible need making his body over into a stranger's, and concentrated instead on reality.

She frowned at him. "What if we can't produce heirs? It's more common than you think."

"And covered at some length in the contracts we

signed," he agreed, trying to rein in his impatience. "But we must try, Valentina. It is part of our agreement." He shook his head when she started to speak. "If you plan to tell me that this is medieval, you are correct. It is. Literally. The same provisions have covered every such marriage between people like us since the dawn of time. You cannot have imagined that a royal wedding at our rank would allow for anything else, can you?"

Something he would have called fierce inhabited her face for a moment, and then was gone.

"You misunderstand me." She ran her hands down the front of her dress as if it needed smoothing, but all Rodolfo could think of was the feel of her in his arms and the soft skin of her thigh against his palm. "I have every intention of doing my duty, Your Highness. But I will only be as faithful to you as you are to me."

He shook his head. "I am not a man who backs down from a challenge, princess. You must know this."

"It's not a challenge." Her gaze was dark when it met his. "It's a fact. As long as you ignore your commitments, I'll do the same. What have I got to lose? I'll always know that our children are mine. Let's hope you can say the same."

And on that note—while he remained frozen in his chair, stunned that she would dare threaten him openly with such a thing—Rodolfo's suddenly fascinating princess pulled herself upright and then swept out of the room.

He let her go.

It was clear to him after today that not only did he need to get to know his fiancée a whole lot better than he had so far, he needed to up his game overall where she was concerned. And when it came to games, Rodolfo had the advantage, he knew.

Because he'd never, ever lost a single game he'd ever played.

His princess was not going to be the first.

It was difficult to make a dramatic exit when Natalie had no idea where she was going.

She was on her third wrong turn—and on the verge of frustrated tears—when she hailed a confused-looking maid who, after a stilted conversation in which Natalie tried not to sound as if she was lost in what should have been her home, led her off into a completely different part of the palace and into what were clearly Valentina's own private rooms. Though "rooms" was an understated way to put it. The series of vast, exquisitely furnished chambers were more like a lavish, sprawling penthouse contained in the palace and sporting among its many rooms a formal dining area, a fully equipped media center and a vast bedroom suite complete with a wide balcony that looked off toward the sea and a series of individual rooms that together formed the princess's wardrobe. The shoe room alone was larger than the flat Natalie kept on the outskirts of London, yet barely used, thanks to her job.

Staff bustled about in the outer areas of the large suite, presumably adhering to the princess's usual schedule, but the bedroom was blessedly empty. It was there that Natalie found a surprisingly comfortable chaise, curled herself up on it with a sigh of something not quite relief and finally gave herself leave to contemplate the sort of person she'd discovered she was today.

It left a bitter taste in her mouth.

She'd always harbored a secret fantasy that should she ever stumble over a Prince Charming type—and not be forced into studied courtesy because she represented her employer—she'd shred him to pieces. Because even if the man in question wasn't the one who'd taught her mother to be so bitter, it was a fair bet that he'd ruined someone else's life. That was what Prince Charmings *did*. Even in the fairy tale, the man had left a trail of mutilated feet and broken families behind him everywhere he went. Natalie had been certain she could slap an overconfident ass like that down without even trying very hard.

And instead, she'd kissed him.

Oh, she tried to pretend otherwise. She tried to muster up a little outrage at the way Rodolfo had put his hands on her and hauled her onto his lap—but what did any of that matter? He hadn't held her there against her will. She could have stood up at any time.

She hadn't. Quite the contrary.

And when his mouth had touched hers, she'd *imploded*.

Not only had Natalie kissed the kind of man she'd always hated on principle, but she'd kissed one promised to another woman. If that wasn't enough, she'd threatened to marry him and then present him with children that weren't his. As punishment? Just to be cruel? She had no idea. She only knew that her mouth had opened and out the threat had come.

The worst part was, she'd seen that stunned, furious look on the Prince's face when she'd issued that threat. Natalie had no doubt that he believed that she would do exactly that. Worse, that *Princess Valentina* was the sort of person who, apparently, thought nothing of that kind of behavior.

"Great," she muttered out loud, to the soft chaise beneath her and the soothing landscapes on the walls. "You've made everything worse."

It was one thing to try to make things better for Valentina, who Natalie imagined was having no fun at all contending with the uncertain temper of Mr. Casilieris. Natalie was used to fixing things. That was what she did with her life—she sorted things out to be easier, smoother, better for others. But Rodolfo hadn't been as easily managed as she'd expected him to be, and the truth was, she'd never quite recovered from that first, shocking sight of him.

There was a possibility, Natalie acknowledged as she remained curled up on a posh chaise in a princess's bedroom like the sort of soft creature she'd never been, that she still hadn't recovered. *And that you never will,* chimed in a voice from deep inside her, but she dismissed it as unnecessary dire.

Her clutch—Valentina's clutch—had been delivered here while she'd been off falling for Prince Charming like a ninny, sitting on an engaged man's lap as if she had no spine or will of her own, and making horrible threats about potential royal heirs in line to a throne. Was that treason in a kingdom like Murin? In Tissely? She didn't even know.

"And maybe you should find out before you cause a war," she snapped at herself.

What she did know was that she didn't recognize herself, all dressed up in another woman's castle as if that life could ever fit her. And she didn't like it.

Natalie pushed up off the chaise and went to sweep up the clutch from where it had been left on the padded bench that claimed the real estate at the foot of the great four-poster bed. She'd examined the contents on the plane, fascinated. Princesses apparently carried very little, unlike personal assistants, who could live out of their shoulder bags for weeks in a pinch. There was no money or identification, likely because neither was necessary when you had access to an entire treasury filled with currency stamped with your own face. Valentina carried only her mobile, a tube of extremely high-end lip gloss and a small compact mirror.

Natalie sat on the bench with Valentina's mobile in her hand and looked around the quietly elegant bedroom, though she hardly saw it. The adrenaline of the initial switch had given way to sheer anxiety once she'd arrived in Murin. She'd expected to be called out at any moment and forced to explain how and why she was impersonating the princess. But no one had blinked, not even Prince Rodolfo.

Maybe she shouldn't be surprised that now that she was finally alone, she felt a little lost. Maybe that was the price anyone could expect to pay when swapping identities with a complete stranger. Especially one who happened to be a royal princess to boot.

It was times like this that Natalie wished she had the sort of relationship with her mother that other people seemed to have with theirs. She'd like nothing more than to call Erica up and ask for some advice, or maybe just so she could feel soothed, somehow, by the fact of her mother's existence. But that had never been the way her mother operated. Erica had liked Natalie best when she was a prop. The pretty little girl she could trot out when it suited her, to tug on a heartstring or to prove that she was maternal when, of course, she wasn't. Not really. Not beyond the telling of the odd fairy tale with a grim ending, which Natalie had learned pretty early on was less for her than for her mother.

No wonder Natalie had lost herself in school. It didn't matter where they moved. It didn't matter what was going on in whatever place Erica was calling home that month. Natalie could always count on her studies. Whether she was behind the class or ahead of it when she showed up as the new kid, who cared? School always gave her a project of one sort or another. She'd viewed getting into college—on a full academic scholarship, of course, because Erica had laughed when Natalie had asked if there would be any parental contributions to her education and then launched into another long story about the evils of rich, selfish men—as her escape. College had been four years of an actual place to call home, at last. Plus classes. Basically nirvana, as far as Natalie had been concerned.

But that kind of overachieving behavior, while perfect for her eventual career as the type A assistant to the most picky and overbearing man alive, had not exactly helped Natalie make any friends. She'd always been the new kid in whatever school she'd ended up in. Then, while she wasn't the new kid at college, she was so used to her usual routine of studying constantly that she hadn't known how to stop it. She and her freshman-year roommate had gotten along well enough and they'd even had lunch a few times over the next few years, all very pleasant, but it hadn't ever bloomed into the sort of friendships Natalie knew other women had. She'd had a boyfriend her junior year, which had been more exciting in theory than in fact. And then she'd started working for Mr. Casilieris after graduation and there hadn't been time for anything but him, ever again.

All of this had been perfectly fine with her yesterday. She'd been proud of her achievements and the fact no one had helped her in equal measure. Well. She'd wanted to quit her job, but surely that was a reasonable response to five years of Achilles Casilieris. And today, sitting on the cushioned bench at the foot of a princess's bed with a medieval castle looming all around her like an accusation, it was clear to Natalie that really, she could have used someone to call.

Anyone except the person she knew she had to call, that was.

But Natalie hadn't dealt with a terrifying man like Achilles Casilieris for years by being a coward, no matter how tempting it was to become one now. She blew out a breath, then dialed her own mobile number. She knew that the flight she should have been on right now, en route to New York City, hadn't landed yet. She even knew that all the calls she'd set up would likely have ended—but she wasn't surprised when Valentina didn't answer. Mr. Casilieris was likely tearing strips out of the princess's hide, because no matter how she'd handled the situation, it wouldn't have been to his satisfaction. She was a bit surprised that Valentina hadn't confessed all and that the Casilieris plane wasn't landing in Murin right now to discharge her—and so Achilles Casilieris could fire Natalie in person for deceiving him.

Really, it hadn't been nice of Natalie to let Valentina take her place. She'd known what the other woman was walking into. God help the poor princess if she failed to provide Mr. Casilieris with what he wanted three seconds before he knew he wanted it. When she'd started, Achilles Casilieris had been famous for cycling through assistants in a matter of hours, sometimes, depending on the foulness of his mood. Everyone was an idiot, as he was all too happy to make clear, especially the people he paid to assist him. Everyone fell short of his impossibly high standards. If he thought Natalie had lost her ability to do her job the way he liked it done, he'd fire her without a second thought. She'd never been in any doubt about that.

Which meant that really, she should have been a little more concerned about the job Valentina was almost certainly botching up right this very minute, somewhere high above the Atlantic Ocean.

But she found she couldn't work up the usual worry over that eventuality. If he fired her, he fired her. It saved her having to quit, didn't it? And when she tried to stress out about losing the position she'd worked so hard to keep all these years, all she could think of instead was the fact he hadn't known Valentina wasn't her in that bathroom. That despite spending more time with Natalie than with his last ten mistresses combined, he'd failed to recognize her. And meanwhile, Rodolfo had looked at *her*. As if he wanted to climb inside of her. As if he could never, ever get enough. And that mouth of his was sculpted and wicked, knowing and hot...

She heard her own voice asking for a message and a phone number on the other end of the line, but she didn't leave a voice mail at the beep. What would she say? Where would she start? Would she jump right into the kissing and claims that she'd sleep her way around Europe in payback for any extramarital adventures Prince Rodolfo might have? She could hardly believe she'd done either of those things, much less think of how best to tell someone else that she had. Particularly when the someone else was the woman who was expected to marry the man in question.

The fact was, she had no idea what Valentina expected from her arranged marriage. A dry tone in a bathroom to a stranger when discussing her fiancé wasn't exactly a peek into the woman's thoughts on what happily-ever-after looked like for her. Maybe she'd been fine with the expected cheating, like half of Europe seemed to be. Maybe she hadn't cared either way. Natalie had no way to tell.

But it didn't matter what Valentina's position on any of this was. It didn't make Natalie any happier with herself that she was hoping, somewhere in there, that Valentina might give her blessing. Or her forgiveness, anyway. And it wasn't as if she could blame the Prince, either. Prince Rodolfo thought she *was* Valentina. His behavior was completely acceptable. He'd had every reason to believe he was with his betrothed.

Natalie was the one who'd let another woman's fiancé kiss her. So thoroughly her breasts still ached and her lips felt vulnerable and she felt a fist of pure need clench tight between her legs at the memory. Natalie was the one who'd kissed him back.

There was no prettying that up. *That* was who she was.

Natalie put the phone aside, then jumped when it beeped at her. She snatched it back up, hoping it was Valentina so she could at least unburden her conscience— another indication that she was not really the good person she'd always imagined herself to be, she was well aware—but it was a reminder from the princess's calendar, telling her she had a dinner with the king in a few hours.

She wanted to curl back up on that chaise and cry for a while. Perhaps a week or so. She wanted to look around for the computer she was sure the princess must have secreted away somewhere and see if she could track her actual life as it occurred across the planet. She wanted to rewind to London and her decision to do this insane thing in the first place and then think better of pulling such a stunt.

But she swallowed hard as she looked down at that reminder on the mobile screen. *The king.*

All those things she didn't want to think about flooded her then.

If Erica had shortened her name... If all that moving around had been less *wanderer's soul* and more *on the run*... If there was really, truly only one reasonable explanation as to how a royal princess and a glorified secretary could pass for each other and it had nothing to do with that tired old saying that *everyone had a twin somewhere*...

If all of those things were true, then the King of Murin—with whom she was about to have a meal—wasn't simply the monarch of this tiny little island kingdom, well-known for his vast personal wealth, many rumors of secret affairs with the world's most glamorous women and the glittering, celebrity-studded life he lived as the head of a tiny, wealthy country renowned for its yacht-friendly harbors and friendly taxes.

He was also very likely her father.

And that was the lure, it turned out, that Natalie couldn't resist.

CHAPTER FIVE

A LITTLE OVER a week later, Natalie thought she might actually be getting the hang of this princess thing. Or settling into her role well enough that she no longer had to mystify the palace staff with odd requests that they lead her to places she should have been able to find on her own.

She'd survived that first dinner with the king, who might or might not have been her father. The truth was, she couldn't tell. If she'd been expecting a mystical, magical sort of reunion, complete with swelling emotions and dazed recognition on both sides, she'd been bitterly disappointed. She'd been led to what was clearly her seat at one end of a long, polished table in what looked like an excruciatingly formal dining room to her but was more likely the king's private, casual eating area given that it was located in his private wing of the palace. She'd stood there for a moment, not knowing what she was supposed to do next. Sit? Wait? Prepare to curtsy?

The doors had been tossed open and a man had strode in with great pomp and circumstance. Even if she hadn't recognized him from the pictures she'd studied online and the portraits littering the castle, Natalie would have known who he was. King Geoffrey of Murin didn't exude the sort of leashed, simmering power Rodolfo did, she couldn't help thinking. He wasn't as magnificently built, for one thing. He was a tall, elegantly slender man who would have looked a bit like an accountant if the suit he wore hadn't so obviously been a bespoke masterpiece and if he hadn't moved with a sort of bone-deep imperiousness that shouted out his identity with each step. It was as if he expected marble floors to form themselves beneath his foot in anticipation that he might place it there. And they did.

"Hello," she'd said when he approached the head of the table, with perhaps a little too much *meaning* in those two syllables. She'd swallowed. Hard.

And the king had paused. Natalie had tensed, her stomach twisting in on itself. *This is it,* she'd thought. *This is the moment you'll not only be exposed as not being Valentina, but recognized as his long-lost daughter—*

"Are you well?" That was it. That was all he'd asked, with a vaguely quizzical look aimed her way.

"Ah, yes." She cleared her throat, though it didn't need clearing. It was her head that had felt dizzy. "Quite well. Thank you. And you?"

"I hope this is not an example of the sort of witty repartee you practice upon Prince Rodolfo," was what Geoffrey had said. He'd nodded at her, which Natalie had taken as her cue to sit, and then he'd settled himself in his own chair. Only then did he lift a royal eyebrow and summon the hovering servants to attend them.

"Not at all," Natalie had managed to reply. And then some demon had taken her over, and she didn't stop there. "A future king looks for many things in a prospective bride, I imagine, from her bloodlines to whether or not she is reasonably photogenic in all the necessary pictures. But certainly not wit. That sort of thing is better saved for the peasants, who require more entertainment to make it through their dreary lives."

"Very droll, I am sure." The king's eyes were the same as hers. The same shape, the same unusual green. And showed the same banked temper she'd felt in her own too many times to count. A kind of panicked flush had rolled over her, making her want to get up and run from the room even as her legs felt too numb to hold her upright. "I trust you know better than to make such an undignified display of inappropriate humor in front of the prince? He may be deep in a regrettable phase with all those stunts he pulls, but I assure you, at the end of the day he is no different from any other man in his position. Whatever issues he may have with his father now, he will sooner or later ascend the throne of Tissely. And when he does, he will not want a comedienne at his side, Valentina. He will require a queen."

Natalie was used to Achilles Casilieris's version of slap downs. They were quicker. Louder. He blazed into a fury and then he was done. This was entirely different. This was less a slap down and more a deliberate *pressing down,* putting Natalie firmly and ruthlessly in her place.

She'd found she didn't much care for the experience. Or the place Valentina was apparently expected to occupy.

"But you have no queen," she'd blurted out. Then instantly regretted it when Geoffrey had gazed at her in amazement over his first course. "Sir."

"I do not appreciate this sort of acting out at my table, Valentina," he'd told her, with a certain quiet yet ringing tone. "You know what is expected of you. You were promised to the Tisselians when I still believed I might have more children, or you would take the throne of

Murin yourself. But we are Murinese and we do not back out of our promises. If you are finding your engagement problematic, I suggest you either find a way to solve it to your satisfaction or come to a place of peace with its realities. Those are your only choices."

"Was that your choice?" she'd asked.

Maybe her voice had sounded different then. Maybe she'd slipped and let a little emotion in. Natalie hadn't known. What she'd been entirely too clear on was that this man should have recognized her. At the very least, he should have known she wasn't the daughter he was used to seeing at his table. And surely the king knew that he'd had twins. He should have had some kind of inkling that it was *possible* he'd run into his other daughter someday.

And yet if King Geoffrey of Murin noticed that his daughter was any different than usual, he kept it to himself. In the same way that if he was racked nightly by guilt because he'd clearly misplaced a twin daughter some twenty-seven years ago, it did not mar his royal visage in any way.

"We must all make choices," he'd said coolly. "And when we are of the Royal House of Murin, each and every one of those choices must benefit the kingdom. You know this full well and always have. I suggest you resign yourself to your fate, and more gracefully."

And it was the only answer he'd given.

He'd shifted the conversation then, taking charge in what Natalie assumed was his usual way. And he'd talked about nothing much, in more than one language, which would have made Natalie terrified that she'd give herself away, but he hadn't seemed to want much in the way of answers. In Italian, French, or English.

Clearly, the princess's role was to sit quietly and listen as the king expounded on whatever topic he liked. And not to ask questions. No wonder she'd wanted a break.

I have a confession to make, Natalie had texted Valentina later that first night. She'd been back in the princess's absurdly comfortable and elegant bedroom, completely unable to sleep as her conscience was keeping her wide awake.

Confession is good for the soul, I'm reliably informed, Valentina had replied after a moment or two. Natalie had tried to imagine where she might be. In the small room in Mr. Casilieris's vast New York penthouse she thought of as hers? Trying to catch up on work in the office suite on the lower floor? *I've never had the pleasure of a life that required a confession. But you can tell me anything.*

Natalie had to order herself to stop thinking about her real life, and to start paying attention to Valentina's life, which she was messing up left and right.

Rodolfo kissed me. There. Three quick words, then the send button, and she was no longer keeping a terrible secret to herself.

That time, the pause had seemed to take years.

That sounds a bit more like a confession Rodolfo ought to be making. Though I suppose he wouldn't know one was necessary, would he?

In the spirit of total honesty, Natalie had typed resolutely, because there was nothing to be gained by lying at that point and besides, she clearly couldn't live with herself if she didn't share all of this with Valentina no matter the consequences, *I kissed him back.*

She'd been sitting up against the headboard then, staring at the phone in her hand with her knees pulled up beneath her chin. She'd expected anger, at the very least. A denunciation or two. And she'd had no idea what that would even look like, coming from a royal princess— would guards burst through the bedroom doors and haul her away? Would Valentina declare her an imposter and have her carried off in chains? Anything seemed possible. Likely, even, given how grievously Natalie had slipped up.

If she'd been a nail-biter, Natalie would have gnawed hers right off. Instead, she tried to make herself breathe.

Someone should, I suppose, Valentina had texted back, after another pause that seemed to last forever and then some. I've certainly never touched him.

Natalie had blinked at that. And had then hated herself, because the thing that wound around inside of her was not shame. It was far warmer and far more dangerous.

I never will again, she'd vowed. And she'd wanted to mean it with every fiber of her being. I swear.

You can do as you like with Rodolfo, Valentina had replied, and Natalie could almost hear the other woman's airy tone through the typed words. You have my blessing. Really. A hundred Eastern European models can't be wrong!

But it wasn't Valentina's blessing that she'd wanted, Natalie realized. Because that was a little too close to outright permission and she'd hardly been able to control herself as it was. What she wanted was outrage. Fury and consequences. Something—*anything*—to keep her from acting like a right tart.

And instead it was a little more than a week later and Rodolfo was outplaying her at the game she was very much afraid she'd put into motion that first day in her new role as the princess. By accident—or at least, without thinking about the consequences—but that hardly mattered now.

Worse, he was doing it masterfully, by not involving her at all. Why risk what might come out of her mouth when he could do an end run around her and go straight to King Geoffrey instead? On some level, Natalie admired the brilliance of the move. It made Rodolfo look like less of a libertine in the king's eyes and far more of the sort of political ally for Murin he would one day become as the King of Tissely.

She needed to stop underestimating her prince. Before she got into the kind of trouble a text couldn't solve.

"Prince Rodolfo thinks the two of you ought to build more of an accessible public profile ahead of the wedding," the king said as they'd sat at their third dinner of the week, as was apparently protocol.

It had taken Natalie a moment to realize Geoffrey was actually waiting for her response. She'd swallowed the bite of tender Murinese lamb she'd put in her mouth and smiled automatically, playing back what he'd said—because she'd gotten in the terrible habit of nodding along without really listening. She preferred to study the King's features and ask herself why, if he was her father, she didn't *feel* it. And he didn't either, clearly. Surely she should *know him* on a deep, cellular level. Or something. Wasn't blood supposed to reveal itself like that? And if it didn't, surely that meant that she and Valentina only happened to resemble each other by chance.

In every detail. Down to resembling Geoffrey, too. So much so that the King himself couldn't tell the difference when they switched.

Natalie knew on a level she didn't care to explore that it was unlikely to be chance. That it couldn't be chance.

"A public profile?" she echoed, because she had to say something, and she had an inkling that flatly refusing to do anything Rodolfo suggested simply because it had come from him wouldn't exactly fly as far as the king was concerned.

"I rather like the idea." King Geoffrey's attention had returned to his own plate. "It is a sad fact that in these modern times, a public figure is judged as much on the image he presents to the world as his contributions to it. More, perhaps."

He didn't order her to do as Rodolfo asked. But then, he didn't have to issue direct orders. And that was how Natalie found herself flying off to Rome to attend a star-studded charity gala the very next day, because Rodolfo had decided it was an excellent opportunity to "boost their profile" in the eyes of the international press corps.

If she ignored the reason she was taking the trip and the man who'd engineered it, Natalie had to admit that it was lovely to have her every need attended to, for a change. All she had to do was wake up the following morning. Everything else was sorted out by a fleet of others. Her wardrobe attendant asked if she had any particular requests and, when Natalie said she didn't, nodded decisively and returned with tidily packed luggage in less than an hour. Which footmen then whisked away. Natalie was swept off to the same private jet as before, where she was fed a lovely lunch of a complicated, savory salad and served sparkling water infused with cucumber. Things she didn't know she craved, deeply, until they were presented to her.

"Your chocolate, Your Highness," the air steward said with a smile after clearing away the salad dishes, presenting her with two rich, dark squares on a gold-embossed plate. "From the finest chocolatiers in all of the kingdom."

"I do like my chocolate," Natalie murmured.

More than that, she liked the princess's style, she thought as she let each rich, almost sweet square dissolve on her tongue, as if it had been crafted precisely to appeal to her.

Which, if she and Valentina were identical twins after all, she supposed it had.

And the pampering continued. The hotel she was delivered to in Rome, located at the top of the Spanish Steps to command the finest view possible over the ancient, vibrant city, had been arranged for and carefully screened by someone else. All she had to do was walk inside and smile as the staff all but kowtowed before her. Once in her sprawling penthouse suite, Natalie was required to do nothing but relax as her attendants bustled around, unpacking her things in one of the lavishly appointed rooms while they got to work on getting the princess ready for the gala in another. A job that required the undivided attention of a team of five stylists, apparently, when Natalie was used to tossing something on in the five minutes between crises and making the best of it.

Her fingernails were painted, her hair washed and cut and styled just so, and even her makeup was deftly applied. When they were done, Natalie was dressed like a fairy-tale princess all ready for her ball.

And her prince, something inside her murmured.

She shoved that away. Hard. There'd been no room for fairy tales in her life, only hard work and dedication. Her mother had told her stories that always ended badly, and Natalie had given up wishing for happier conclusions to such tales a long, long time ago. Even if she and Val-

entina really were sisters, it hardly mattered now. She
was a grown woman. There was no being swept off in
a pumpkin and spending the rest of her life surrounded
by dancing mice. That ship had sailed.

She had no time for fairy tales. Not even if she happened
to be living one.

Natalie concentrated on the fact that she looked like
someone else tonight. Someone she recognized, yet
didn't. Someone far more sophisticated than she'd ever
been, and she'd thought her constant exposure to billionaires
like Mr. Casilieris had given her a bit of polish.

You look like someone beautiful, she thought in a
kind of wonder as she studied herself in the big, round
mirror that graced the wall in her room. *Objectively
beautiful.*

Her hair was swept up into a chignon and secured
with pins that gleamed with quietly elegant jewels. Her
dress was a dove-gray color that seemed to make her
skin glow, cascading from a strapless bodice to a wide,
gorgeous skirt that moved of its own accord when she
walked and made her look very nearly celestial. Her
shoes were high sandals festooned with straps, there
was a clasp of impossible sapphires and diamonds at her
throat that matched the ring she wore on her hand and
her eyes looked fathomless.

Natalie looked like a princess. Not just Princess Valentina,
but the sort of magical, fantasy princess she'd
have told anyone who asked she'd never, ever imagined
when she was a child, because she'd been taught better
than that.

Never ever. Not once.

She nodded and smiled her thanks at her waiting attendants,
but Natalie didn't dare speak. She was afraid
that if she did, that faint catch in her throat would tip over

into something far more embarrassing, and then worse, she'd have to explain it. And Natalie had no idea how to explain the emotions that buffeted her then.

Because the truth was, she didn't know how to be beautiful. She knew how to stick to the shadows and more, how to excel in them. She knew how to disappear in plain sight and use that to her—and her employer's—advantage. Natalie had no idea how to be the center of attention. How to be *seen*. In fact, she'd actively avoided it. Princess Valentina turned heads wherever she went, and Natalie had no idea how she was going to handle it. If she *could* handle it.

But it was more than her shocking appearance, so princessy and pretty. This was the first time in all her life that she hadn't had to be responsible for a thing. Not one thing. Not even her own sugar consumption, apparently. This was the first time in recent memory that she hadn't had to fix things for someone else or exhaust herself while making sure that others could relax and enjoy themselves.

No one had ever taken care of Natalie Monette. Not once. She'd had to become Princess Valentina for that to happen. And while she hadn't exactly expected that impersonating royalty would feel like a delightful vacation from her life, she hadn't anticipated that it would feel a bit more like an earthquake, shaking her apart from within.

It isn't real, a hard voice deep inside of her snapped, sounding a great deal like her chilly mother. *It's temporary and deeply stupid, as you should have known before you tried on that ring.*

Natalie knew that, of course. She flexed her hand at her side and watched the ring Prince Rodolfo had given another woman spill light here and there. None of this was real. Because none of this was hers. It was a short, confusing break from real life, that was all, and there was no use getting all soppy about it. There was only surviving it without blowing up the real princess's life while she was mucking around in it.

But all the bracing lectures in the world couldn't keep that glowing thing inside her chest from expanding as she gazed at the princess in the mirror, until it felt as if it was a part of every breath she took. Until she couldn't tell where the light of it ended and that shaking thing began. And she didn't need little voices inside of her to tell her how dangerous that was. She could feel it deep in her bones, knitting them into new shapes she was very much afraid she would have to break into pieces when she left.

Because whatever else this was, it was temporary. She needed to remember that above all.

"Your Highness." It was the most senior of the aides who traveled with the princess, something Natalie had known at a glance because she recognized the older woman's particular blend of sharp focus and efficient movement. "His Royal Highness Prince Rodolfo has arrived to escort you to the gala."

"Thank you," Natalie murmured, as serenely and princessy as possible.

And this was the trouble with dressing up like a beautiful princess who could be whisked off to a ball at a moment's notice. Natalie started to imagine that was exactly who she was. It was so hard to keep her head, and then she walked into the large, comfortably elegant living room of her hotel suite to find Prince Rodolfo waiting for her, decked out in evening clothes, and everything troubling became that much harder.

He stood at the great glass doors that slid open to one

of the terraces that offered up stunning views of Rome at all times, but particularly now, as the sun inched toward the horizon and the city was bathed in a dancing, liquid gold.

More to the point, so was Rodolfo.

Natalie hadn't seen him since that unfortunate kissing incident. Not in person, anyway. And once again she was struck by the vast, unconquerable distance between pictures of the man on a computer screen and the reality before her. He stood tall and strong with his hands thrust into the pockets of trousers that had clearly been lovingly crafted to his precise, athletic measurements. His attention was on the red-and-gold sunset happening there before him, fanciful and lovely, taking over the Roman sky as if it was trying to court his favor.

He wasn't even looking at her. And still he somehow stole all the air from the room.

Natalie felt herself flush as she stood in the doorway, a long, deep roll of heat that scared her, it was so intense. Her pulse was a wild fluttering, everywhere. Her temples. Her throat. Her chest.

And deep between her legs, like an invitation she had no right to offer. Not this man. Not ever this man. If he was Prince Charming after all, and she was skeptical on that point, it didn't matter. He certainly wasn't hers.

She must have made some noise through that dry, clutching thing in her throat, because he turned to face her. And that wasn't any better. In her head, she'd downgraded the situation. She'd chalked it up to excusable nerves and understandable adrenaline over switching places with Valentina. That was the only explanation that had made any sense to her. She'd been so sure that when she saw Rodolfo again, all that power and compulsion that had sparked the air around him would be gone.

He would just be another wealthy man for her to handle. Just another problem for her to solve.

But she'd been kidding herself.

If anything, tonight he was even worse, all dressed up in an Italian sunset.

Because you know, something inside her whispered. *You know, now.*

How he tasted. The feel of those lean, hard arms around her. The sensation of that marvelous mouth against hers. She had to fight back the shudder that she feared might bring her to her knees right there on the absurdly lush rug, but she had the sneaking suspicion he knew anyway. There was something about the curve of his mouth as he inclined his head.

"Princess," he murmured.

And God help her, but she felt that everywhere. *Everywhere.* As if he'd used his mouth directly against her heated skin.

"I hear you wish to build our public profile, whatever that is," she said, rather more severely than necessary. She made herself move forward, deeper into the room, when what she wanted to do was turn and run. She seated herself in an armchair because it meant he couldn't sit on either side of her, and his fascinating mouth twitched as if he knew exactly why she'd done it. "King Geoffrey—" She couldn't bring herself to say *my father,* not even if Valentina would have and not even if it was true "—was impressed. That is obviously the only reason I am here."

"Obviously." He threw himself onto the couch opposite her with the same reckless disregard for the lifespan of the average piece of furniture that he'd displayed back in Murin. She told herself that was reflective of his character. "Happily, it makes no difference to me if you are here of your own volition or not, so long as you are here."

"What a lovely sentiment. Every bride dreams of such poetry, I am certain. I am certainly aflutter."

"There is no need for sarcasm." But he sounded amused. "All that is required is that we appear in front of the paparazzi and look as if this wedding is our idea because we are a couple in love like any other, not simply a corporate merger with crowns."

Natalie eyed him, wishing the Roman sunset was not taking quite so long, nor quite so many liberties with Rodolfo's already impossible good looks. He was bathed in gold and russet now, and it made him glow, as if he was the sort of dream maidens might have had in this city thousands of years ago in feverish anticipation of their fierce gods descending from on high.

She tried to cast that fanciful nonsense out of her head, but it was impossible. Especially when he was making no particular effort to hide the hungry look in his dark gaze as he trained it on her. She could feel it shiver through her, lighting her on fire. Making it as hard to sit still as it was to breathe.

"I don't think anyone is going to believe that we were swept away by passion," she managed to say. She folded her hands in her lap the way she'd seen Valentina do in the videos she'd watched of the princess these past few nights, so worried was she that someone would be able to see right through her because she forgot to do some or other princessy thing. Though she thought she gripped her own fingers a bit more tightly than the princess had. "Seeing as how our engagement has been markedly free of any hint of it until now."

"But that's the beauty of it." Rodolfo shrugged. "The story could be that we were promised to each other and were prepared to do our duty, only to trip over the fact we were made for each other all along. Or it could be that it was never arranged at all and that we met, kept everything secret, and are now close enough to our wedding that we can let the world see what our hearts have always known."

"You sound like a tabloid."

"Thank you."

Natalie glared at him. "There is no possible way that could be construed as a compliment."

"I've starred in so many tabloid scandals I could write the headlines myself. And that is what we will do, starting tonight. We will rewrite whatever story is out there and make it into a grand romance. The Playboy Prince and His Perfect Princess, etcetera." That half smile of his deepened. "You get the idea, I'm sure."

"Why would we want to do something so silly? You are going to be a king, not a Hollywood star. Surely a restrained, distant competence is more the package you should be presenting to the world." Natalie aimed her coolest smile at him. "Though I grant you, that might well be another difficult reach."

The sun finally dripped below the city as she spoke, leaving strands of soft pink and deep gold in its wake. But it also made it a lot easier to see Prince Rodolfo's dark, measuring expression. And much too easy to feel the way it clattered through her, making her feel…jittery.

It occurred to her that the way he lounged there, so carelessly, was an optical illusion. Because there wasn't a single thing about him that wasn't hard and taut, as if he not only kept all his brooding power on a tight leash— but could explode into action at any moment. That notion was not exactly soothing.

Neither was his smile. "We will spend the rest of the

night in public, princess. Fawned over by the masses. So perhaps you will do me the favor of telling me here, in private, exactly what it is that has made you imagine I deserve a steady stream of insult. One after the next, without end, since I last saw you."

Natalie felt chastened by that, and hated herself for it in the next instant. Because her own feelings didn't matter here. She shouldn't even have feelings where this man was concerned. Valentina might have given her blessing to whatever happened between her betrothed and Natalie, but that was neither here nor there. Natalie knew better than to let a man like this beguile her. She'd been taught to see through this sort of thing at her mother's knee. It appalled her that his brand of patented princely charm was actually *working*.

"Are you not deserving?" she asked quietly. She made herself meet his dark gaze, though something inside her quailed at it. And possibly died a little bit, too. But she didn't look away. "Are you sure?"

"Am I a vicious man?" Rodolfo's voice was no louder than hers, but there was an intensity to it that made that lick of shame inside of her shimmer, then expand. It made the air in the room seem thin. It made Natalie's heart hit at her ribs, hard enough to bruise. "A brute? A monster in some fashion?"

"Only you can answer that question, I think."

"I am unaware of any instance in which I have deliberately hurt another person, but perhaps you, princess, know something I do not about my own life."

It turned out the Prince was as effective with a slap down as her boss. Natalie sat a bit straighter, but she didn't back down. "Everyone knows a little too much about your life, Your Highness. Entirely too much, one might argue."

"Tabloid fantasies are not life. They are a game. You should know that better than anyone, as we sit here discussing a new story we plan to sell ourselves."

"How would I know this, exactly?" She felt her head tilt to one side in a manner she thought was more her than Valentina. She corrected it. "I do not appear in the tabloids. Not with any frequency, and only on the society pages. Never the front-page stories." Natalie knew. She'd checked.

"You are a paragon, indeed." Rodolfo's voice was low and dark and not remotely complimentary. "But a rather judgmental one, I fear."

Natalie clasped her hands tighter together. "That word has always bothered me. There is nothing wrong with rendering judgment. It's even lauded in some circles. How did *judgmental* become an insult?"

"When rendering judgment became a blood sport," Rodolfo replied, with a soft menace that drew blood on its own.

But Natalie couldn't stop to catalog the wounds it left behind, all over her body, or she was afraid she'd simply…collapse.

"It is neither bloody nor sporting to commit yourself to a woman in the eyes of the world and then continue to date others, Your Highness," she said crisply. "It is simply unsavory. Perhaps childish. And certainly dishonorable. I think you'll find that there are very few women on the planet who will judge that behavior favorably."

Rodolfo inclined his head, though she had the sense his jaw was tighter than it had been. "Fair enough. I will say in my defense that you never seemed to care one way or the other what I did, much less with whom, before last week. We talked about it at length and you said nothing. Not one word."

Valentina had said he talked at her, defending himself—hadn't she? Natalie couldn't remember. But she also wasn't here to poke holes in Valentina's story. It didn't matter if it was true. It mattered that she'd felt it, and Natalie could do something to help fix it. Or try, anyway.

"You're right, of course," she said softly, keeping her gaze trained to his. "It's my fault for not foreseeing that your word was not your bond and your vows were meaningless. My deepest apologies. I'll be certain to keep all of that in mind on our wedding day."

He didn't appear to move, and yet suddenly Natalie couldn't, as surely as if he'd reached out and wrapped her in his tight grip. His dark gaze seemed to pin her to her chair, intent and hard.

"I've tasted you," he reminded her, as if she could forget that for an instant. As if she hadn't dreamed about exactly that, night after night, waking up with his taste on her tongue and a deep, restless ache between her legs. "I know you want me, yet you fight me. Is it necessary to you that I become the villain? Does that make it easier?"

Natalie couldn't breathe. Her heart felt as if it might rip its way out of her chest all on its own, and she still couldn't tear her gaze away from his. There was that hunger, yes, but also a kind of *certainty* that made her feel...liquid.

"Because it is not necessary to insult me to get my attention, princess," Rodolfo continued in the same intense way. "You have it. And you need not question my fidelity. I will touch no other but you, if that is what you require. Does this satisfy you? Can we step away from the bloodlust, do you think?"

What that almost offhanded promise did was make

Natalie feel as if she was nothing but a puppet and he was pulling all her strings, all without laying a single finger upon her. And what sent an arrow of shame and delight spiraling through her was that she couldn't tell if she was properly horrified by that notion, or…not.

"Don't be ridiculous," was the best she could manage.

"You only confirm my suspicions," he told her then, and she knew she wasn't imagining the satisfaction that laced his dark tone. "It is not who I might or might not have dated over the past few months that so disturbs you. I do not doubt that is a factor, but it is not the whole picture. Will you tell me what is? Or will I be forced to guess?"

And she knew, somehow, that his guesses would involve his hands on her once more and God help her, she didn't know what might happen if he touched her again. She didn't know what she might do. Or not do.

Who she might betray, or how badly.

She stood then, moving to put the chair between them, aware of the way her magnificent gown swayed and danced as if it had a mind of its own. And of the way Rodolfo watched her do it, that hard-lit amusement in his dark eyes, as if she were acting precisely as he'd expected she would.

As if he was a rather oversize cat toying with his next meal and was in absolutely no doubt as to how this would all end.

Though she didn't really care to imagine him treating her like his dinner. Or, more precisely, she refused to allow herself to imagine it, no matter how her pulse rocketed through her veins.

"My life is about order," she said, and she realized as she spoke that she wasn't playing her prescribed role. That the words were pouring out of a part of her she hadn't even known was there inside of her. "I have duties, responsibilities, and I handle them all. I *like* to handle them. I like knowing that I'm equal to any task that's put in front of me, and then proving it. Especially when no one thinks I can."

"And you are duly celebrated for your sense of duty throughout the great houses of Europe." Rodolfo inclined his head. "I salute you."

"I can't tell if you're mocking me or not, but I don't require celebration," she threw back at him. "It's not about that. It's about the accomplishment. It's about putting an order to things no matter how messy they get."

"Valentina…"

Natalie was glad he said that name. It reminded her who she was—and who she wasn't. It allowed her to focus through all the clamor and spin inside of her.

"But your life is chaos," she said, low and fierce. "As far as I can tell, it always has been. I think you must like it that way, as you have been careening from one death wish to another since your brother—"

"Careful."

He looked different then, furious and something like thrown, but she only lifted her chin and told herself to ignore it. Because the pain of an international playboy had nothing to do with her. Prince Charming was the villain in all the stories her mother had told her, never the hero. And the brother he'd lost when he was fifteen was a means to psychoanalyze this man, not humanize him. She told herself that again and again. And then she forged on.

"He died, Rodolfo. You lived." He hissed in a breath as if she'd struck him, but Natalie didn't stop. "And yet your entire adult life appears to be a calculated attempt to change that. You and I have absolutely nothing in common."

Rodolfo stood. The glittering emotion she'd seen grip him a moment ago was in his dark gaze, ferocious and focused, but he was otherwise wiped clean. She would have been impressed if she'd been able to breathe.

"My brother's death was an unfortunate tragedy." But he sounded something like hollow. As if he was reciting a speech he'd learned by rote a long time ago. His gaze remained irate and focused on her. "I never intended to fill his shoes and, in fact, make no attempt to do so. I like extreme sports, that is all. It isn't a death wish. I am neither suicidal nor reckless."

He might as well have been issuing his own press release.

"If you die while leaping out of helicopters to get to the freshest ski slope in the world, the way you famously do week after week in winter, you will not only break your neck and likely die, you will leave your country in chaos," Natalie said quietly. His gaze intensified, but she didn't look away. "It all comes back to chaos, Your Highness. And that's not me."

She expected him to rage at her. To argue. She expected that dark thing in him to take him over, and she braced herself for it. If she was honest, she was waiting for him to reach out and his put his hands on her again the way he had the last time. She was waiting for his kiss as surely as if he'd cast a spell and that was her only hope of breaking it—

It was astonishing, really, how much of a fool she was when it counted.

But Rodolfo's hard, beguiling mouth only curved as if there wasn't a world of seething darkness in his eyes, and somehow that sent heat spiraling all the way through her.

"Maybe it should be, princess," he said softly, so softly, as if he was seducing her where he stood. As if he was the spell and there was no breaking it, not when he was looking at her like that, as if no one else existed in all the world. "Maybe a little chaos is exactly what you need."

CHAPTER SIX

THE CHARITY GALA took place in a refurbished ancient villa, blazing with light and understated wealth and dripping with all manner of international celebrities like another layer of decoration. Icons from the epic films of Bollywood mingled with lauded stars of the stages of the West End and rubbed shoulders with a wide selection of Europe's magnificently blooded aristocrats, all doing what they did best. They graced the red carpet as if they found nothing more delightful, smiling into cameras and posing for photographs while giving lip service to the serious charity cause du jour.

Rodolfo escorted his mouthy, surprising princess down the gauntlet of the baying paparazzi, smiling broadly as the press went mad at the sight of them, just as he'd suspected they would.

"I told you," he murmured, leaning down to put his mouth near her ear. As much to sell the story of their great romance as to take pleasure in the way she shivered, then stiffened as if she was trying to hide it from him. Who could have imagined that his distant betrothed was so exquisitely sensitive? He couldn't wait to find out where else she was this tender. This sweet. "They want nothing more than to imagine us wildly and madly in love."

"A pity my imagination is not quite so vivid," she replied testily, though she did it through a smile that perhaps only he could tell was not entirely serene.

But the grin on Rodolfo's face as they made their way slowly through the wall of flashing cameras and shouting reporters wasn't feigned in the least.

"You didn't mention which charity this gala benefits," the princess said crisply as they followed the well-heeled crowd inside the villa, past dramatic tapestries billowing in the slight breeze and a grand pageant of colored lights in the many fountains along the way.

"Something critically important, I am sure," he replied, and his grin only deepened when she slid a reproving look at him. "Surely they are all important, princess. In the long run, does it matter which one this is?"

"Not to you, clearly," she murmured, nodding regally at yet another photographer. "I am sure your carelessness—excuse me, I mean thoughtfulness—is much appreciated by all the charities around who benefit from your random approach."

Rodolfo resolved to take her out in public every night, to every charity event he could find in Europe, whether he'd heard of its cause or not. Not only because she was stunning and he liked looking at her, though that helped. The blazing lights caught the red in her hair and made it shimmer. The gray dress she wore hugged her figure before falling in soft waves to the floor. She was a vision, and better than all of that, out here in the glare of too many spotlights she could not keep chairs between them to ward him off. He liked the heat of her arm through his. He liked her body beside his, lithe and slender as if she'd been crafted to fit him. He liked the faint scent of her, a touch of something French and something sweet besides, and below it, the simplicity of that soap she used.

There wasn't much he didn't like about this woman, if he was honest, not even her intriguing puritan streak. Or her habit of poking at him the way no one else had ever dared, not even his disapproving father, who preferred to express his endless disappointment with far less sharpness and mockery. No one else ever threw Felipe in his face and if they'd ever tried to do such a remarkably stupid thing, it certainly wouldn't have been to psychoanalyze him. Much less find him wanting.

He took care of that all on his own, no doubt. And the fact that his own father found his second son so much more lacking than his first was common knowledge and obvious to all. No need to underscore it.

Rodolfo supposed it was telling that as little as he cared to have that conversation, he hadn't minded that Valentina had tried. Or he didn't mind too much. He didn't know where his deferential, disappearing princess had gone, the one who had hidden in plain sight when there'd been no one in the room but the two of them, but he liked this one much better.

The hardest part of his body agreed. Enthusiastically. And it didn't much care that they were out in public.

But there was another gauntlet to run inside the villa. One Rodolfo should perhaps have anticipated.

"I take it that you did not make proclamations about your sudden onset of fidelity to your many admirers," Valentina said dryly after they were stopped for the fifth time in as many steps by yet another woman who barely glanced at the princess and then all but melted all over Rodolfo. Right there in front of her.

For the first time in his entire adult life, Rodolfo found he was faintly embarrassed by his own prowess with the fairer sex.

"It is not the sort of thing one typically announces,"

he pointed out, while attempting to cling to his dignity, despite the number of slinky women circling him with that same avid look in their eyes. "It has the whiff of desperation about it, does it not?

"Of course, generally speaking, becoming engaged *is* the announcement." What was wrong with him, that he found her tartness so appealing? Especially when not a bit of it showed on her lovely, serene face? How had he spent all these months failing to notice how appealing she was? He'd puzzled it over for days and still couldn't understand it. "I can see the confusion in your case, given your exploits these last months."

"Yet here I am," he pointed out, slanting a look down at her, amused despite himself. "At your side. Exuding fidelity."

"That is not precisely what you exude," she said under her breath, because naturally she couldn't let any opportunity pass to dig at him, and then they were swept into the receiving line.

It felt like a great many hours later when they finally made it into the actual gala itself. A band played on a raised dais while glittering people outshone the blazing chandeliers above them. Europe's finest and fanciest stood in these rooms, and he'd estimate that almost all of them had their eyes fixed on the spectacle of Prince Rodolfo and Princess Valentina actually out and about together for once—without a single one of their royal relatives in sight as the obvious puppeteers of what had been hailed everywhere as an entirely cold-blooded marriage of royal convenience.

But their presence here had already done exactly what Rodolfo had hoped it would. He could see it in the faces of the people around them. He'd felt it on the red carpet outside, surrounded by paparazzi nearly incandescent with joy over the pictures they'd be able to sell of the two of them. He could already read the accompanying headlines.

Do the Daredevil Prince and the Dutiful Princess Actually Like *Each Other After All?*

He could feel the entire grand ballroom of the villa seem to swell with the force of all that speculation and avid interest.

And Rodolfo made a command decision. They could do another round of the social niceties that would cement the story he wanted to sell even further, assuming he wasn't deluged by more of the sort of women who were happy to ignore his fiancée as she stood beside him. Or he could do what he really wanted to do, which was get his hands on Valentina right here in public, where she would have no choice but to allow it.

This was what he was reduced to. On some level, he felt the requisite shame. Or some small shadow of it, if he was honest.

Because it still wasn't much of a contest.

"Let's dance, shall we?" he asked, but he was already moving toward the dance floor in the vast, sparkling ballroom that seemed to swirl around him as he spoke. His proper, perfect princess would have to yank her arm out of his grip with some force, creating a scene, if she wanted to stop him.

He was sure he could see steam come off her as she realized that for herself, then didn't do it. Mutinously, if that defiant angle of her pointed chin was any clue.

"I don't dance," she informed him coolly as he stopped and turned to face her. He dropped her arm but stood a little too close to her, so the swishing skirt of her long dress brushed against his legs. It made her have to tip her head back to meet his gaze. And he was well aware it created the look of an intimacy between them. It suggested all kinds of closeness, just as he wanted it to do.

As much to tantalize the crowd as to tempt her.

"Are you certain?" he asked idly.

"Of course I'm certain."

Other guests waltzed around them, pretending not to stare as they stood still in the center of the dance floor as if they were having an intense discussion. Possibly an argument. Inviting gossip and rumor with every moment they failed to move. But Rodolfo forgot about all the eyes trained on them in the next breath. He gazed down at his princess, watching as the strangest expression moved over her face. Had she been anyone else, he would have called it panic.

"Then I fear I must remind you that you have been dancing since almost before you could walk," he replied, trying to keep his voice mild and a little bit lazy, as if that could hide the intensity of his need to touch her. As if every moment he did not was killing him. He felt as if it was.

He reached over and took her hands in his, almost losing his cool when he felt that simple touch everywhere—from his fingers to his feet and deep in his aching sex—far more potent than whole weekends he could hardly recall with women he wouldn't remember if they walked up and introduced themselves right now. What the hell was she doing to him? But he ordered himself to pull it together.

"There is that iconic portrait of you dancing with your father at some or other royal affair. It was the darling of the fawning press for years. You are standing on his shoes while the King of Murin dances for the both of you." Rodolfo made himself smile, as if the odd intensity that gripped him was nothing but a passing thing. The work of a moment, here and then gone in the swirl of the stately dance all around them. "I believe you were six."

"Six," she repeated. He thought she said it oddly, but then she seemed to recollect herself. He saw her blink, then focus on him again. "You misunderstand me. I meant that I don't dance with *you*. By which I mean, I won't."

"It pains me to tell you that, sadly, you are wrong yet again." He smiled at her, then indulged himself—and infuriated her—by reaching out to tug on one of the artful pieces of hair that had been left free of the complicated chignon she wore tonight. He tucked it behind her ear, marveling that so small a touch should echo inside of him the way it did then, sensation chasing sensation, as if all these months of not quite seeing her in front of him had been an exercise in restraint instead of an oddity he couldn't explain to his satisfaction. And this was his reward. "You will dance with me at our wedding, in front of the entire world. And no doubt at a great many affairs of state thereafter. It is unavoidable, I am afraid."

She started to frown, then caught herself. He saw the way she fought it back, and he still couldn't understand why it delighted him on a deep, visceral level. His glass princess, turned flesh and blood and brought to life right there before him. He could see the way her lips trembled, very slightly, and he knew somehow that it was the same mad fire that blazed in him, brighter by the moment.

It made him want nothing more than to taste her here and now, the crowd and royal protocol be damned.

"You should know that I make it a policy to step on the feet of all the men I dance with, as homage to that iconic photograph." Her smile was razor sharp and her eyes had gone cool again, but he could still see that soft little tremor that made her mouth too soft. Too vulnerable.

He could still see the truth she clearly wanted to hide, and no matter that he couldn't name it. "Prepare yourself."

"All you need to do is follow my lead, princess," Rodolfo said then, low and perhaps a bit too dark, and he didn't entirely mean the words to take on an added resonance as he said them. But he smiled when she pulled in a sharp little breath, as if she was imagining all the places he could lead her, just as he was. In vivid detail. "It will be easy and natural. There will be no trodding upon feet. Simply surrender—" and his voice dipped a bit at that, getting rough in direct correlation to that dark, needy thing in her gaze "—and I will take care of you. I promise."

Rodolfo wasn't talking about dancing—or he wasn't only talking about a very public waltz—but that would do. He studied Princess Valentina as she stood there before him, taut and very nearly quivering with the same dark need that made him want to behave like a caveman instead of a prince. He wanted to throw her over his shoulder and carry her off into the night. He wanted to throw her down on the floor where they stood and get his mouth on every part of her, as if he could taste what it was that had changed in her, cracking her open to let the fascinating creature inside come out and making her irresistible seemingly overnight.

He settled for extending his hand, very formally and in full view of half of Europe, even throwing in a polite bow that, as someone more or less equal in rank to her, could only be construed as a magnanimous, even romantic gesture. Then he stood still in the center of the dance floor and waited for her to take it.

Her green eyes looked a little bit too wide and still far too dark with all the same simmering need and deep hunger he knew burned bright in him. She looked more beautiful than he'd ever seen her before, but then, he was closer than he'd ever been. He couldn't count those hot, desperate moments in the palace reception room where he'd tasted her with all the finesse of an untried adolescent, because he'd been too out of control—and out of his mind—to enjoy it.

This was different. This—tonight—he had every intention of savoring.

But he wasn't sure he would ever savor anything more than when she lifted that chin of hers, faintly pointed and filled with a defiance her vulnerable mouth contradicted, and placed her hand in his.

Rodolfo felt that everywhere, as potent as if she'd knelt down before him and declared him victor of this dark and delicious little war of theirs.

He pulled her a step closer with his right hand, then slid his left around to firmly clasp the back she'd left bared in the lovely dress she wore that poured over her slender figure like rain, and he heard her hiss in a breath. He could feel the heat of her like a furnace beneath his palm. He wanted to bend close and get his mouth on her more than he could remember wanting anything.

But he refrained. Somehow, he held himself in check, when he was a man who usually did the exact opposite. For fun.

"Put your hand on my shoulder," he told her, and he didn't sound urbane or witty or anything like lazy. Not anymore. "Have you truly forgotten how to perform a simple waltz, princess? I am delighted to discover how deeply I affect you."

He felt the hard breath she took, as if she was bracing herself. And he realized with a little shock that he had no idea what she would do. It was as likely that she'd yank herself out of his arms and storm away as it was that she'd melt into him. He had no idea—and he couldn't deny he felt that like a long, slow lick against the hardest part of him.

She was as unpredictable as one of his many adventures. He had the odd thought that he could spend a lifetime trying to unravel her mysteries, one after the next, and who knew if he'd ever manage it? It astonished him that he wanted to try. That for the first time since their engagement last fall, he wanted their wedding day to hurry up and arrive. And better than that, their wedding night. And all the nights thereafter, all those adventures lined up and waiting for him, packed into her lush form and those fathomless green eyes.

He could hardly wait.

And it felt as if ten years had passed when, with her wary gaze trained on him as if he couldn't be trusted not to harm her somehow, Valentina put her hand where it belonged.

"Thank you, princess." He curled his fingers around hers a little tighter than necessary for the sheer pleasure of it and smiled when the hand she'd finally placed on his shoulder dug into him, as if in reaction. "You made that into quite a little bit of theater. When stories emerge tomorrow about the great row we had in the middle of a dance floor, you will have no one to blame but yourself."

"I never do," she replied coolly, but that wariness receded from her green gaze. Her chin tipped up higher and Rodolfo counted it as a win. "It's called taking responsibility for myself, which is another way of acknowledging that I'm an adult. You should try it sometime."

"Impossible," he said, gripping her hand tighter in his and smiling for all those watching eyes. And because her defiance made him want to smile, which was far more dangerous. And exciting. "I am far too busy leaping out of planes in a vain attempt to cheat death. Or court death. Which is it again? I can't recall which accusation you leveled at me, much less when."

And before she could enlighten him, he started to move.

She was stiff in his arms, which he assumed was another form of protest. Rodolfo ignored it, sweeping her around the room and leading her through the steps she appeared to be pretending not to know, just as he'd promised he would.

"You cannot trip me up, princess," he told her when she relaxed just slightly in his hold and gave herself over to his lead. "I was raised to believe a man can only call himself a man when he knows how to dance well, shoot with unerring accuracy and argue his position without either raising his voice or reducing himself to wild, unjustified attacks on his opponent."

"Well," she said, and she sounded breathless, which he felt in every part of his body like an ache, "you obviously took that last part to heart."

"I am also an excellent shot, thank you for asking."

"Funny, the tabloids failed to report that. Unless you're speaking in innuendo? In which case, I must apologize, but I don't speak twelve-year-old boy."

He let out a laugh that had the heads nearest them turning, because no one was ever so giddy when on display like this, especially not him. Rodolfo was infamous because he called attention to himself in other ways, but never like this. Never in situations like these, all stuffy protocol and too many spectators. Never with anything that might be confused for *joy*.

"You must be feeling better if you're this snappish, princess."

"I wasn't feeling bad. Unless you count the usual dismay anyone might feel at being bullied onto a dance floor in the company of a rather alarming man who dances very much like he flings himself off the sides of mountains."

"With a fierce and provocative elegance? The envy of all who witness it?"

"With astonishing recklessness and a total lack of regard for anyone around you. Much in the same vein as your entire life, Your Highness, if the reports are true." She lifted one shoulder, then let it drop in as sophisticated and dismissive a shrug as he'd ever seen. "Or even just a little bit true, for that matter."

"And if you imagine that was bullying, princess, you have led a very charmed life, indeed. Even for a member of a royal house dating back to, oh, the start of recorded history or thereabouts, surrounded by wealth and ease at every turn."

"What do you want, Rodolfo?" she asked then, and that near-playful note he was sure he'd heard in her voice was gone. Her expression was grave. As if she was yet another stranger, this one different than before. "I don't believe that this marriage is anything you would have chosen, if given the opportunity. I can't imagine why you're suddenly pretending otherwise and proclaiming your commitment to fidelity in random hotel suites. What I do understand is that we're both prepared to do our duty and have been from the start. And I support that, but there's nothing wrong with maintaining a civil, respectful distance while we go about it."

"I would have agreed with you in every respect," he said, and he should have been worried about that fervent intensity in his tone. He could feel the flames of it licking through him, changing him, making him something other than the man he'd thought he was all this time.

Something that should have set off alarms in every part of him, yet didn't. "But that was before you walked into your father's reception rooms and rather than blending into the furniture the way you usually did, opted to attack me instead."

"Of course." And Rodolfo had the strangest sensation that she was studying him as if he was a museum exhibit, not her fiancé. Hardly even a man—which should have chastened him. Instead, it made him harder. "I should have realized that to a man like you, with an outsize ego far more vast and unconquerable than any of the mountain peaks you've summited in your desperate quest for meaning, any questioning of any kind is perceived as an attack."

"You are missing the point, I think," Rodolfo said, making no attempt to hide either the laughter in his voice or the hunger in his gaze, not put off by her character assassinations at all. Quite the opposite. "Attack me all you like. It doesn't shame me in the least. Surely you must be aware that *shame* is not the primary response I have to you, princess. It is not even close."

She didn't ask him what he felt instead, but he saw a betraying, bright flush move over her face. And he knew she was perfectly aware of the things that moved in him, sensation and need, hunger and that edgy passion—and more, that she felt it, too.

Perhaps that was why, when they danced past a set of huge, floor-to-ceiling glass doors that led out to a wide terrace for the third time, he led her out into the night instead of deeper into the ballroom.

"Where are we going?" she asked.

Rodolfo thought it was meant to be a demand—a rebuke, even—but her cheeks were too red. Her eyes were too bright. And most telling, she made no attempt to tug her hand from his, much less lecture him any further about chaos and order and who was on which side of that divide.

"Nothing could be less chaotic than a walk on a terrace in full view of so many people," he pointed out, not bothering to look behind him at the party they'd left in full swing. He had no doubt they were all staring after him, the way they always did, and with more intensity than ever because he was with Valentina. "Unless you'd like it to be?"

"Certainly not. Some people admire the mountain from afar, Your Highness. They are perfectly happy doing so, and feel no need whatsoever to throw themselves off it or climb up it or attempt to ski down the back of it."

"Ah, but some people do not live, princess. They merely exist."

"Risking death is not living. It's nihilistic. And in your case, abominably selfish."

"Perhaps." He held her hand tighter in his. "But I would not underestimate the power of a little bout of selfishness, if I were you. Indulge yourself, princess. Just for an evening. What's the worst that could happen?"

"I shudder to think," she retorted, but there was no heat in it.

Rodolfo pretended not to hear the catch in her throat. But he smiled. He liberated two glasses of something exquisite from a passing servant with a tray, he pulled his fascinating princess closer to his side and then he led her deeper into the dark.

CHAPTER SEVEN

MAYBE IT WAS the music. Maybe it was the whirl of so many gleaming, glorious people.

Natalie had the suspicion that really, it was Rodolfo.

But no matter what it was, no matter why—she forgot.

That she wasn't really a princess, or if she was, she was the discarded kind. The lost and never-meant-to-be-found sort that had only been located by accident in a bathroom outside London.

She forgot that the dress wasn't hers, the ball inside the pretty old building wasn't a magical spectacle put on just for her and, most of all, that the man at her side— gripping her hand as he led her into temptation—wasn't ever going to be hers, no matter what.

He'd danced with her. It was as simple and as complicated as that.

Natalie had never thought of herself as beautiful before she'd seen herself in that mirror tonight, but it was more than that. She couldn't remember the last time anyone had treated her like a *woman*. Much less a desirable one. Not a pawn in whatever game the man in question might have been playing with her employer, which had only ever led to her wearing her hair in severe ponytails and then donning those clear glasses to keep the attention off her. Not an assistant. Not the person responsible for every little detail of every little thing and therefore the first one to be upbraided when something went wrong.

Rodolfo looked at her as if she was no more and no less than a beautiful woman. He didn't see a list of all the things she could *do* when he gazed at her. He saw only her. A princessed-out, formally made-up version of her, sure. And she couldn't really gloss over the fact he called her by the wrong name because he had every reason to believe she was someone else. Even so, she was the woman he couldn't seem to stop touching, who made his eyes light up with all that too-bright need and hunger.

And it was that, Natalie found, she couldn't resist.

She'd never done a spontaneous thing in her life before she'd switched places with Valentina in that bathroom. Left to her own devices, she thought it was likely she'd never have given her notice at all, no matter how worked up she'd been. And now it seemed she couldn't stop with the spontaneity. Yet somehow Rodolfo's grip on her hand, so strong and sure, made her not mind very much at all. She let this prince, who was far more charming than she wanted to admit to herself, tug her along with him, deeper into the shadows, until they were more in the dark than the light.

He turned to face her then, and he looked something like stern in the darkness. He set the two glasses of sparkling wine down on the nearby balustrade, then straightened again. Slowly. Deliberately, even. Natalie's heart thudded hard against her ribs, but it wasn't from fear. He pulled her hand that he'd been holding high against his chest and held it there, and Natalie couldn't have said why she felt as caught. As gripped tight. Only that she was—and more concerning, had no desire to try to escape it.

If anything, she leaned closer into him, into the shelter of his big body.

"Where did you come from?" he asked, his voice a mere scrape against the night. "What the hell are you doing to me?"

Natalie opened her mouth to answer him. But whatever that dark, driving force had been inside her, urging her to poke back at him and do her best to slap down the only real Prince Charming she'd ever met in the flesh, it was gone. Had she imagined herself some kind of avenging angel here? Flying into another woman's royal fairy tale of a life to do what needed doing, the way she did with everything else? Fighting her mother's battles all these years later and with a completely different man than the one Erica had never explicitly named?

It didn't matter, because that had been before he'd taken her in his arms and guided her around a dance floor, making her feel as if she could dance forever when she'd never danced a waltz before in her life. She had a vague idea of what it entailed, but only because she'd had to locate the best ballroom dancing instructor in London when Achilles Casilieris had abruptly decided he needed a little more polish one year. She'd watched enough of those classes—before Mr. Casilieris had reduced the poor man to tears—to understand the basic principle of a waltz.

But Rodolfo had made her feel as if they were flying.

He looked down at her now, out here in the seductive dark, and it made her tremble deep inside. It made her forget who she was and what she was doing. Her head cleared of everything save him. Rodolfo. The daredevil prince who made her feel as if she was the one catapulting herself out of airplanes every time his dark, hungry gaze caught hers. And held.

He took her bare shoulders in his hands, drawing her closer to him. Making her shiver, deep and long. On some distant level she thought she should push away from him. Remind them both of her boundaries, maybe. But she couldn't seem to remember what those were. Instead she tilted her head back while she drifted closer to his big, rangy body. And then she made everything worse by sliding her hands over the steel wall of his chest, carefully packaged in that gorgeous suit that made him look almost edible. To push him away, she told herself piously.

But she didn't push at him. She didn't even try.

His dark eyes gleamed with a gold she could feel low in her belly, like a fiery caress. "The way you look at me is dangerous, princess."

"I thought you courted danger," she heard herself whisper.

"I do," he murmured. "Believe me, I do."

And then he bent his head and kissed her.

This time, the first brush of his mouth against hers was light. Easy. Electricity sparked and sizzled, and then he did it again, and it wasn't enough. Natalie pressed herself toward him, trying to get more of him. Trying to crawl inside him and throw herself into the storm that roared through her. She went up on her toes to close the remaining distance between them, and her reward was the way he smiled, that dangerous curve of his mouth against hers.

It seemed to wash over her like heat then pool in a blaze of fire, high between her legs. Natalie couldn't keep herself from letting out a moan, needy and insistent.

And obvious. So terribly, blatantly obvious it might as well have been a scream in the dark. She felt Rodolfo turn to stone beneath her palms.

Then he angled his head, took the kiss deeper and wilder and everything went mad.

Rodolfo simply…took her over. He kissed her like he was already a great king and she but one more subject to his rule. His inimitable will. He kissed her as if there had never been any doubt that she was his, in every possible way. His mouth was demanding and hot, intense and carnal, and her whole body thrilled to it. Her hands were fists, gripping his jacket as if she couldn't bear to let go of him, and he only took the kiss deeper, wilder.

She arched against him as he plundered her mouth, taking and taking and taking even more as he bent her over his arm, as if he could never get enough—

Then he stopped, abruptly, muttering a curse against her lips. It seemed to pain him to release her, but he did it, stepping back and maneuvering so he stood between Natalie and what it took her far too long to realize was another group of guests making use of the wide terrace some distance away.

But she couldn't bring herself to care about them. She raised a hand to her lips, aware that her fingers trembled. And far more aware that he was watching her too closely as she did it.

"Why do you look at me as if it is two hundred years ago and I have just stolen your virtue?" he asked softly, his dark eyes searching hers. "Or led you to your ruin with a mere kiss?"

Natalie didn't know what look she wore on her face, but she felt…altered. There was no pretending otherwise. Rodolfo was looking at her the way any man might gaze at the woman he was marrying in less than two months, after kissing her very nearly senseless on the terrace of a romantic Roman villa.

But that was the trouble. No matter what fairy tale

she'd been spinning out in her head, Natalie wasn't that woman.

She was ruined, all right. All the way through.

"I'm not looking at you like that." Her voice hardly sounded like hers. She took a step away from him, coming up against the stone railing. She glanced down at the two glasses of sparkling wine that sat there and considered tossing them back, one after the next, because that might dull the sharp thing that felt a little too much like pain, poking inside of her. Only the fact that it might dull her a little *too* much kept her from it. Things were already bad enough. "I'm not looking at you like anything, I'm sure."

Rodolfo watched her, his eyes too dark to read. "You are looking at me as if you have never been kissed before. Much as that might pander to my ego, which I believe we've agreed is egregiously large already, we both know that isn't true." His mouth curved. "And tell the truth, Valentina. It was not so bad, was it?"

That name slammed into her like a sucker punch. Natalie could hardly breathe through it. She had to grit her teeth to keep from falling over where she stood. How did she keep forgetting?

Because you want to forget, a caustic voice inside her supplied at once.

"I'm not who you think I am," she blurted out then, and surely she wasn't the only one who could hear how ragged she sounded. How distraught.

But Rodolfo only laughed. "You are exactly who I think you are."

"I assure you, I am not. At all."

"It is an odd moment for a philosophical turn, princess," he drawled, and there was something harder about him then. Something more dangerous. Natalie could feel it dance over her skin. "Are any of us who others think we are? Take me, for example. I am certain that every single person at this gala tonight would line up to tell you exactly who I am, and they would be wrong. I am not the tabloid stories they craft about me, pimped out to the highest bidder. My wildest dream is not surviving an adventure or planning a new one, it's taking my rightful place in my father's kingdom. That's all." His admission, stark and raw, hung between them like smoke. She had the strangest notion that he hadn't meant to say anything like that. But in the next instant he looked fierce. Almost forbidding. "We are none of us the roles we play, I am sure."

"Are you claiming you have a secret inner life devoted to your sense of duty? That you are merely misunderstood?" she asked, incredulous.

"Do you take everything at face value, princess?" She told herself she was imagining that almost hurt look on his face. And it was gone when he angled his head toward her. "You cannot really believe you are the only one with an internal life."

"That's not what I meant."

But, of course, she couldn't tell him what she meant. She couldn't explain that she hadn't been feeling the least bit philosophical. Or that she wasn't actually Princess Valentina at all. She certainly couldn't tell this man that she was Natalie Monette—a completely different person.

Though it occurred to her for the first time that even if she came clean right here and now, the likelihood was that he wouldn't believe her. Because who could believe something so fantastical? Would she have believed it herself if it wasn't happening to her right now—if she wasn't standing in the middle of another woman's life?

And messing it up beyond recognition, that same interior voice sniped at her. *Believe that, if nothing else.*

"Do you plan to tell me what, then, you meant?" Rodolfo asked, dark and low and maybe with a hint of asperity. Maybe with more than just a hint. "Or would you prefer it if I guessed?"

The truth hit Natalie then, with enough force that she felt it shake all the way through her. There was only one reason that she wanted to tell him the truth, and it wasn't because she'd suddenly come over all honest and upstanding. She'd switched places with another person—lying about who she was came with the territory. It allowed her to sit there at those excruciatingly proper dinners and try to read into King Geoffrey's facial expressions and his every word without him knowing it, still trying to figure out if she really thought he was her father. And what it would mean to her if he was. Something that would never happen if she'd identified herself. If he'd been on the defensive when he met her.

She didn't want to tell Rodolfo the truth because she had a burning desire for him to know who she was. Or she did want that, of course, but it wasn't first and foremost.

It made her stomach twist to admit it, but it was true: what she wanted was him. This. She wanted what was happening between them to be real and then, when it was, she wanted to keep him.

He is another woman's fiancé, she threw at herself in some kind of despair.

Natalie thought she'd never hated herself more than she did at that moment, because she simply couldn't seem to govern herself accordingly.

"I need to leave," she told him, and she didn't care if she sounded rude. Harsh and abrupt. She needed to remove herself from him—from all that temptation he wore entirely too easily, like another bespoke suit—before she made this all worse. Much, much worse. In ways she could imagine all too vividly. "Now."

"Princess, please. Do not run off into the night. I will only have to chase you." He moved toward her and Natalie didn't have the will to step away. To ward him off. To do what she should. And she compounded it by doing absolutely nothing when he fit his hand to her cheek and held it there. His dark eyes gleamed. "Tell me."

He was so big it made her heart hurt. The dark Roman night did nothing to obscure how beautiful he was, and she could taste him now. A kind of rich, addicting honey on her tongue. She thought that alone might make her shatter into pieces. This breath, or the next. She thought it might be the end of her.

"I need to go," she whispered, aware that her hands were in useless, desperate fists at her sides.

She wanted to punch him, she told herself, but Natalie knew that was a lie. The sad truth here was she was looking for any excuse to put her hands on him again. And she knew exactly what kind of person that made her.

And even so, she found herself leaning into that palm at her cheek.

"I never wanted what our parents had," Rodolfo told her then, his voice low and commanding, somehow, against the mild night air. "A dance in front of the cameras and nothing but duty and gritted teeth in private. I promised myself that I would marry for the right reasons. But then it seemed that what I would get instead was a cold shoulder and a polite smile. I told myself it was more than some people in my position could claim. I thought I had made my peace with it."

Natalie found she couldn't speak. As if there was a hand around her throat, gripping her much too tight.

Rodolfo didn't move any closer, though it was as if he shut out the rest of the world. There was nothing but that near-smile on his face, that hint of light in his gaze. There was nothing but the two of them and the lie of who she was tonight, but the longer he looked at her like that, the harder it was to remember that he wasn't really hers. That he could never be hers. That none of the things he was saying to her were truly for her at all.

"Rodolfo…" she managed to say. Confession or capitulation, she couldn't tell.

"I like my name in your mouth, princess," he told her, sending heat dancing all over her, until it pooled low and hot in her belly. "And I like this. There is no reason at all we cannot take some pleasure in our solemn duty to our countries. Think of all the dreadfully tedious affairs we will enjoy a great deal more when there is this to brighten up the monotony."

His head lowered to hers again, and she wanted nothing more than to lose herself in him. In the pleasure he spoke of. In his devastating kiss, all over again.

But somehow, Natalie managed to recollect herself in the instant before his lips touched hers. She yanked herself out of his grip and stepped away from him, the night feeling cool around her now that she wasn't so close to the heat that seemed to come off him in waves.

"I'm sorry." She couldn't seem to help herself. But she kept her gaze trained on the ground, because looking at him was fraught with peril. Natalie was terribly afraid it would end only one way. "I shouldn't have…" She trailed off, helplessly. "I need to go back to my hotel."

"And do what?" he asked, and something in his voice made her stand straighter. Some kind of foreboding, perhaps. When she looked up at him, Rodolfo's gaze had gone dark again, his mouth stern and hard. "Switch personalities yet again?"

Valentina jerked as if he'd slapped her, and if he'd been a little more in control of himself, Rodolfo might have felt guilty about that.

Maybe he already did, if he was entirely honest, but he couldn't do anything about it. He couldn't reach out and put his hands on her the way he wanted to do. He couldn't do a goddamned thing when she refused to tell him what was going on.

The princess looked genuinely distraught at the thought of kissing him again. At the thought that this marriage they'd been ordered into for the good of their kingdoms could be anything but a necessary, dutiful undertaking to be suffered through for the rest of their lives.

Rodolfo didn't understand any of this. Didn't she realize that this crazy chemistry that had blazed to life out of nowhere was a blessing? The saving grace of what was otherwise nothing more than a royal chore dressed up as a photo opportunity?

Clearly she did not, because she was staring at him with something he couldn't quite read making her green eyes dark. Her lovely cheeks looked pale. She looked shaken—though that made no sense.

"What do you mean by that?" she demanded, though her voice sounded as thrown as the rest of her looked. "I have the one personality, that's all. This might come as a shock to you, I realize, but many women actually have *layers*. Many humans, in fact."

Rodolfo wanted to be soothing. He did. He prided himself on never giving in to his temper. On maintaining his cool under any and all extreme circumstances. There was no reason he couldn't calm this maddening woman, whether he understood what was going on here or not.

"Are you unwell?" he asked instead. And not particularly nicely.

"I am feeling more unwell by the moment," she threw back at him, stiff and cool. "As I told you, I need to leave."

He reached over and hooked a hand around her elbow when she made as if to turn, holding her there where she stood. Keeping her with him. And the caveman in him didn't care whether she liked it or not.

"Let go of me," she snapped at him. But she didn't pull her elbow from his grasp.

Rodolfo smiled. It was a lazy, edgy sort of smile, and he watched the color rush back into her face.

"No."

She stiffened, but she still didn't pull away. "What do you mean, *no*?"

"I mean that I have no intention of releasing you until you tell me why you blow so hot and cold, princess. And I do not much care if it takes all night. It is almost as if you are two women—"

Her green eyes flashed. "That or I find you largely unappealing."

"Until, of course, you do not find me unappealing in the least. Then you melt all over me."

Her cheeks pinkened further. "I find it as confusing as you do. Best not to encourage it, I think."

He savored the feel of her silky skin beneath his palm. "Ah, but you see, I am not confused in the least."

"If you do not let go of me, right now, I will scream," she told him.

He only smiled at her. "Go ahead. You have my blessing." He waited, and cocked an eyebrow when she only glared at him. "I thought you were about to scream down the villa, were you not? Or was that another metaphor?"

She took what looked like a shaky breath, but she didn't say anything. And she still didn't pull her elbow away. Rodolfo moved a little closer, so he could bend and get his face near hers.

"Tell me what game this is," he murmured, close to her ear. She jumped, and he expected her to pull free of him, but she didn't. She settled where she stood. He could feel her breathe. He could feel the way her pulse pounded through her. He could smell her excitement in the heated space between them, and he could feel the tension in her, too. "I am more than adept at games, I promise you. Just tell me what we're playing."

"This is no game." But her voice sounded a little broken. Just a little, but it was enough.

"When I met you, there was none of this fire," he reminded her, as impossible as that was to imagine now. "We sat through that extraordinarily painful meal—"

She tipped her head back so she could look him dead in the eye. "I loved every moment of it."

"You did not. You sat like a statue and smiled with the deepest insincerity. And then afterward, I thought you might have nodded off during my proposal."

"I was riveted." She waved the hand that wasn't trapped between them. "Your Royal Highness is all that is charming and so on. It was the high point of my life, etcetera, etcetera."

"You thanked me in your usual efficient manner, yes. But riveted?" He slid his hand down her forearm, abandoning his grip on her elbow so he could take her hand in his. Then he played with the great stone she wore on her finger that had once belonged to his grandmother and a host of Tisselian queens before her. He tugged it this way, then that. "You were anything but that, princess. You used to look through me when I spoke to you, as if I was a ghost. I could not tell if I was or you were. I imagined that I would beget my heirs on a phantom."

Something moved through her then, some electrical current that made that vulnerable mouth of hers tremble again, and she tugged her hand from his as if she'd suddenly been scalded. And yet Rodolfo felt as if he might have been, too.

"I'm not sure what the appropriate response is when a man one has agreed to marry actually sits there and explains his commitment to ongoing infidelity, as if his daily exploits in the papers were not enough of a clue. Perhaps you should count yourself lucky that all I did was look through you."

"Imagine my surprise that you noticed what I did, when you barely appeared to notice me."

"Is that what you need, Rodolfo?" she demanded, and this time, when she stepped back and completely away from him, he let her go. It seemed to startle her, and she pulled in a sharp breath as if to steady herself. "To be noticed? It may shock you to learn that the entire world already knows that, after having witnessed all your attention-seeking theatrics and escapades. That is not actually an announcement you need to make."

Rodolfo didn't exactly thrill to the way she said that, veering a bit too close to the sorts of things his father was known to hurl at him. But he admired the spirit in her while she said it. He ordered himself to concentrate on that.

"And now you are once again *this* Valentina," he replied, his voice low. "The one who dares say things to my face others would be afraid to whisper behind my back. Bold. Alluring. Who are you and what have you done with my dutiful ghost?"

She all but flinched at that and then she let out a breath that sounded a little too much like a sob. But before he could question that, she clearly swallowed it down. She lifted her chin and glared at him with nothing but sheer challenge in her eyes, and he thought he must have imagined the vulnerability in that sound she'd made. The utter loneliness.

"This Valentina will disappear soon enough, never fear," she assured him, a strange note in her voice. "We can practice that right now. I'm leaving."

But Rodolfo had no intention of letting her go. This time when she turned on her heel and walked away from him, he followed.

CHAPTER EIGHT

RODOLFO CAUGHT UP to her quickly with his long, easily athletic stride, and then refused to leave her side. He stayed too close and put his hand at the small of her back, guiding her through the splendid, sparkling crowd whether she wanted his aid or not. Natalie told herself she most emphatically did not, but just as she hadn't pulled away from him out on the terrace despite her threats that she might scream, she didn't yank herself out of his grasp now, either. She assured herself she was only thinking about what would be best for the real princess, that she was only avoiding the barest hint of scandal—but the truth was like a brand sunk deep in her belly.

She wanted him to touch her. She liked it when he did.

You are a terrible person, she told herself severely.

Natalie wanted to hate him for that, too. She told herself that of course she did, but that slick heat between her legs and the flush that she couldn't quite seem to cool let her know exactly how much of a liar she was. With every step and each shifting bit of pressure his hand exerted against her back.

He summoned their driver with a quick call, and then walked with her all the way back down the red carpet, smiling with his usual careless charm at all the paparazzi who shrieked out his name. Very much as if he enjoyed all those flashing lights and impertinent questions.

It was Natalie who wanted to curl up into a ball and hide somewhere. Natalie who wasn't used to this kind of attention—not directed at her, anyway. She'd fended off the press for Mr. Casilieris as part of her job, but she'd never been its focus before, and she discovered she really, truly didn't like it. It felt like salt on her skin. Stinging and gritty. But she didn't have the luxury of fading off into the background to catch her breath in the shadows, because she wasn't Natalie right now. She was Princess Valentina, who'd grown up with this sort of noisy spectacle everywhere she went. Who'd danced on her doting father's shoes when she was small and had cut her teeth on spotlights of all shapes and sizes and hell, for all she knew, enjoyed every moment of it the way Rodolfo seemed to.

She was Princess Valentina tonight, and a princess should have managed to smile more easily. Natalie tried her best, but by the time Rodolfo handed her into the gleaming black SUV that waited for them at the end of the press gauntlet, she thought her teeth might crack from the effort of holding her perhaps not so serene smile in place.

"I don't need your help," she told him, but it was too late. His hand was on her arm again as she clambered inside and then he was climbing in after her, forcing her to throw herself across the passenger seat or risk having him…all over her.

She hated that she had to remind herself—sternly— why that would be a bad idea.

"Would you prefer it if I had drop-kicked you into the vehicle?" he asked, still smiling as he settled himself beside her.

There was a gleam in his dark gaze that let her know he was fully aware of the way she was clinging to the far door as if it might save her. From him. As ever, he appeared not to notice the confines or restrictions of whatever he happened to be sitting on. In this case, he sprawled out in the backseat of the SUV, taking up more than his fair share of the available room and pretty much all of the oxygen. Daring her to actually come out and comment on it, Natalie was fairly sure, rather than simply twitching her skirts away from his legs in what she hoped was obvious outrage.

"I think you are well aware that neither I nor anyone else would prefer to be drop-kicked. And also that there exists yet another option, if one without any attendant theatrics. You could let me get in the car as I have managed to do all on my own for twenty-seven years and keep your hands to yourself while I did it."

He turned slightly in his seat and studied her for a moment, as the lights of Rome gleamed behind him, streaking by in the sweet, easy dark as they drove.

"Spoken like someone who has not spent the better part of her life being helped in and out of motorcades to the roars of a besotted crowd," Rodolfo said, his dark brows high as his dark eyes took her measure. "Except you have."

Natalie could have kicked herself for making such a silly mistake, and all because she'd hoped to score a few points in their endless little battle of words. She thought she really would have given herself a pinch, at the very least, if he hadn't been watching her so closely. She sniffed instead, to cover her reaction.

"You've gone over all literal, haven't you? Back on the terrace it was all metaphor and now you're parsing what I say for any hint of exaggeration? What's next?

Will you declare war on parts of speech? Set loose the Royal Tisselian Army on any grammar you dislike?"

"I am looking for hints, Valentina, but it is not figurative language that I find mysterious. It is a woman who has already changed before my eyes, more than once, into someone else."

Natalie turned her head so she could hold that stern, probing gaze of his. Steady and long. As if she really was Valentina and had nothing at all to hide.

"No one has changed before your eyes, Your Highness. I think you might have to face the fact that you are not very observant. Unless and until someone pricks at your vanity. I might as well have been a piece of furniture to you, until I mentioned I planned to let others sit on me." She let out a merry little laugh that was meant to be a slap, and hit its mark. She saw the flare of it in his gaze. "You certainly couldn't have *that*."

"Think for a moment, please." Rodolfo's voice was too dark to be truly impatient. Too rich to sound entirely frustrated. And still, Natalie braced herself. "What is the headline if I am found to be cavorting outside the bounds of holy matrimony?"

"A long, weary sigh of boredom from all sides, I'd imagine." She aimed a cool smile his way. "With a great many exclamation points."

"I am expected to fail. I have long since come to accept it is my one true legacy." Yet that dark undercurrent in his low voice and the way he lounged there, all that ruthless power simmering beneath his seeming unconcern, told Natalie that Rodolfo wasn't resigned to any such thing. "You, on the other hand? It wouldn't be *my* feelings of betrayal you would have to worry about, however unearned you might think they were. It would be the entire world that thought less of you, forever after. Is that really what you want? After you have gone to such lengths to create your spotless reputation?"

Natalie laughed again, but there was nothing funny. There was only a kind of heaviness pressing in upon her, making her feel as if she might break apart if she didn't get away from this man before something really terrible happened. Something she couldn't explain away as a latent Cinderella fantasy, lurking around inside of her without her knowledge or permission, that had put a ball and a prince together and then thrown her headfirst into an unfortunate kiss.

"What does it matter?" she asked him, aware that her voice was ragged, giving too much away—but she couldn't seem to stop herself. "There's no way out of this, so we might as well do as we like no matter what the headlines say or do not. It will make no difference. We will marry. You will have your heirs. Our kingdoms will be linked forever. Who cares about the details when that's the only part that truly matters in the long run?"

"An argument I might have made myself a month ago," Rodolfo murmured. "But we are not the people we were a month ago, princess. You must know that."

From a distance he would likely have looked relaxed. At his ease, with his legs thrust out and his collar loosened. But Natalie was closer, and she could see that glittering, dangerous thing in his gaze. She could feel it inside her, like a lethal touch of his too-talented hands, stoking fires she should have put out a long time ago.

"What I know," she managed to say over her rocketing pulse and that quickening, clenching in her core, "is that it is not I who am apparently unwell."

But Rodolfo only smiled.

Which didn't help at all.

The rest of the drive across the city was filled with

a brooding sort of silence that in many ways was worse than anything he might have said. Because the silence grew inside of her, and Natalie filled it with…images. Unhelpful images, one after the next. What might have happened if they hadn't been interrupted on that terrace, for example. Or if they'd walked a little farther into the shadows, maybe even rounding the corner so no one could see them. Would Rodolfo's hands have found their way beneath her dress again? Would they have traveled higher than her thigh—toward the place that burned the hottest for him even now?

"Thank you for the escort but I can see myself—" Natalie began when they arrived at her hotel, but Rodolfo only stared back at her in a sort of arrogant amazement that reminded her that he would one day rule an entire kingdom, no matter what the tabloids said about him now.

She restrained the little shiver that snaked down her spine, because it had nothing to do with apprehension, and let him usher her out of the car and into the hushed hotel lobby, done in sumptuous reds and deep golds and bursting with dramatic flowers arranged in stately vases. Well. It wasn't so much that she *let* him as that there was no way to stop him without causing a scene in front of all the guests in the lobby who were pretending not to gawk at them as they arrived—especially because really, yet again, Natalie didn't much *want* to stop him. Until she'd met Rodolfo, she'd never known that she was weak straight through to her core. Now she couldn't seem to remember that everywhere but here, she was known for being tough. Strong. Unflappable.

That Natalie seemed like a distant memory.

Rodolfo nodded at her security detail as he escorted her to the private, keyed elevator that led only to the

penthouse suite, and then followed her into it. The door
swished shut almost silently, and then it was only the
two of them in a small and shiny enclosed space. Natalie braced herself, standing there just slightly behind
him, with a view of his broad, high, solidly muscled
back and beyond that, the gold-trimmed elevator car. She
could feel the heat of him, and all that leashed danger,
coming off him like flames. He surrounded her without
even looking at her. He seemed to loop around her and
pull tight, crushing her in his powerful grip, without
so much as laying a finger upon her. She couldn't hear
herself think over the thunder of her heart, the clatter
of her pulse—

But nothing happened. They were delivered directly
into the grand living room of the hotel's penthouse. Rodolfo stepped off and moved into the room, shrugging
out of his jacket as he went. Natalie followed after him
because she had no choice—or so she assured herself.
It was that or go back downstairs to the hotel lobby,
where she would have to explain herself to her security,
the hotel staff, the other guests still sitting around with
mobile phones at the ready to record her life at will.

The elevator doors slid shut behind her, and that was
it. The choice was made. And it left her notably all alone
in her suite's living room with the Prince she very desperately wanted to find the antithesis of charming.

There was no Roman sunset to distract her now. There
was only Rodolfo, far too beautiful and much too dangerous for anyone's good. She watched the way he moved
through the living room with a kind of liquid athleticism.
The light from the soft lamps scattered here and there
made the sprawling space feel close. Intimate.

And it made him look like some kind of god all over

again. Not limned in red or gold, but draped in shadows and need.

Her throat was dry. Her lungs ached as if she'd been off running for untold miles. Her fingers trembled, and she realized she was as jittery as if she'd pulled one of her all-nighters before a big meeting and had rivers of coffee running through her veins in place of blood. It made her stomach clench tight to think that it wasn't caffeine that was messing with her tonight. It was this man before her who she should never have touched, much less kissed.

What was she going to do now?

The sad truth was, Natalie couldn't trust herself to make the right decision, or she wouldn't still be standing where she was, would she? She would have gone straight on back to her bedchamber and locked the door. She would have summoned her staff, who she knew had to be nearby, just waiting for the opportunity to serve her and usher Rodolfo out. She would have done *something* other than what she did.

Which was wait. Breathlessly. As if she really was a princess caught up in some or other enchantment. As if she could no more move a muscle than she could wave a magic wand and turn herself back into Natalie.

Rodolfo shrugged out of his jacket and tossed it over the back of one of the fussy chairs, and then he took his time turning to face her again. When he did, his dark eyes burned into her, the focused, searing hunger in them enough to send her back a step. In a wild panic or a kind of dizzy desire, she couldn't have said.

Both, something whispered inside of her. And not with any trace of fear. Not with anything the least bit like fear.

"Rodolfo," she managed to say then, in as measured

a tone as she could manage, because she thought she should have been far more afraid of all those things she could feel in the air between them than she was. Either way, this was all too much. It was all temptation and need, and she could hardly think through the chaos inside of her. "This has all gotten much too fraught and strange. Why don't I have some coffee made? We can sit and talk."

"I am afraid, *princesita*, that it is much too late for talk."

He moved then. His long stride ate up the floor and he was before her in an instant. Or perhaps it was that she didn't want to move out of his reach. She couldn't seem to make herself run. She couldn't seem to do anything at all. All she did was stand right where she was and watch him come for her, that simmering light in his dark eyes and that stern set to his mouth that made everything inside her quiver.

Maybe there was no use pretending this wasn't what she'd wanted all along. Since the very first moment she'd crossed the threshold of that reception room at the palace and discovered he was so much more than his pictures. She'd wanted to eviscerate him and instead she'd ended up on his lap with his tongue in her mouth. Had that really been by chance?

Something dark and guilty kicked inside of her at that, and she opened her mouth to protest—to do *something,* to say *anything* that might stop this—but he was upon her. And he didn't stop. Her breath left her in a rush, because he kept coming. She backed up when she thought he might collide into her, but there was nowhere to go. The doors to the elevator were at her back, closed up tight, and Rodolfo was there. *Right there.* He crowded into her. He laid a palm against the smooth metal on either side of her head and then he leaned in, trapping her between the doors of the elevator and his big, hard body.

And there was nothing but him, then. He was so much bigger than her that he became the whole world. She could see nothing past the wall of his chest. There was no sky but his sculpted, beautiful face. And if there was a sun in the heated little sliver of space that was all he'd left between their bodies, Natalie had no doubt it would be as hot as that look in his eyes.

"I think," she began, because she had to try.

"That is the trouble. You think too much."

And then he simply bent his head and took her mouth with his.

Just like that, Natalie was lost. The delirious taste of him exploded through her, chasing fire with more fire until all she did was burn. His kiss was masterful. Slick and hot and greedy. He left absolutely no doubt as to who was in control as he took her over and sampled her, again and again, as if he'd done it a thousand times before tonight alone. As if he planned to keep doing it forever, starting now. Here.

There was no rush. No desperation or hurry. Just that endless, erotic tasting as if he could go on and on and on.

And Natalie forgot, all over again, who she was and what she was meant to be doing here.

Because she could feel him everywhere. In her fingers, her toes. In the tips of her ears and like a breeze of sensation pouring down her spine. She pushed up on her feet, high on her toes, trying to get as close to him as she could. His arms stayed braced against the elevator doors like immovable barriers, leaving her to angle herself closer. She did it without thought, grabbing hold of his soft shirt in both fists and letting the fire that burned through her blaze out of control.

Sensation stormed through her, making and remaking her as it swept along. Telling her stark truths about herself she didn't want to know. She felt flushed and wild from her lips to the tight, hard tips of her breasts, all the way to that ravenous heat between her legs.

She would have climbed him if she could. She couldn't seem to get close enough.

And then Rodolfo slowed down. His kiss turned lazy. Deep, drugging—but he made no attempt to move any closer. He kept his hands on the wall.

After several agonies of this same stalling tactic, Natalie tore her lips from his, jittery and desperate.

"Please…" she whispered.

His mouth chased hers, tipped up in the corners as he sampled her, easy and slow. Teasing her, she understood then. As if this was some kind of game, and one he could play all night long. As if she was the only one being burned to a crisp where she stood. Over and over again.

"Please, what?" he asked against her mouth, an undercurrent of laughter making her hot and furious and decidedly needy all at once. "I think you can do better than that."

"Please…" she tried again, and then lost her train of thought when his mouth found the line of her jaw.

Natalie shivered as he dropped lower, trailing fire down the side of her neck and somehow finding his way to every sensitive spot she hadn't known she had. And then he used his tongue and his teeth to taunt her with each and every one of them.

"You will have to beg," he murmured against her flushed, overwarm skin, and she could feel the rumble of his voice deep inside of her, low in her belly where all that heat seemed to bloom into a desperate softness that made her knees feel weak. "So that later, there can be no confusion, much as you may wish there to be. Beg me, *princesita.*"

Natalie told herself that she would do no such thing. Of course not. Her mother had raised a strong, tough, independent woman who did not *beg,* and especially not from a man like this. Prince Charming at his most dangerous.

But she was writhing against him. She was unsteady and wild and out of her mind, and all she wanted was his hands on her. All she wanted was *more.* And she didn't care what that made her. How could she? She hardly knew who the hell she was.

"Please, Rodolfo," she whispered, because it was the only way she could get her voice to work, that betraying little rasp. "Please, touch me."

His teeth grazed her bare shoulder, sending a wild heat dancing and spinning through her, until it shuddered into the scalding heat at her core and made everything worse.

Or better.

"I am already touching you."

"With your hands." And her voice was little more than a moan then, which ought to have embarrassed her. But she was far beyond that. "Please."

She thought he laughed then, and she felt that, too, like another caress. It wound through her, stoking the flames and making her burn brighter, hotter. So hot she worried she might simply...explode.

And then Rodolfo dropped his arms from the wall, leaning closer to her as he did. He took her jaw in his hand and guided her mouth to his. The kiss changed, deepened, losing any semblance of laziness or control. Natalie welcomed the crush of his chest against her, the contrast between all his heat and the cool metal at her back. She wound her arms around his neck and held on to all that corded strength as he claimed her mouth over and over, as if he was as starved for her as she was for him.

She hardly dared admit how very much she wanted that to be true.

With his other hand, he reached down and began pulling up the long skirt of her dress. He took his time, plundering her mouth as he drew the hem higher and higher. She felt the faintest draft against her calf. Her knee. Then her thigh, and then his hand was on her flesh again, the way it had been that day in the palace.

Except this time, he didn't leave it one place.

He continued to kiss her, again and again, as he smoothed his way up her thigh, urging her legs apart. And Natalie felt torn in two. Ripped straight down the center by the intensity of the hunger that poured through her, then. A tumult of need and hunger and the wild flame within her that Rodolfo kept burning at a fever pitch.

When his seeking fingers reached the edge of the satiny panties she wore, he lifted his head just slightly, taking his mouth away from her. It felt like a blow. Like a loss almost too extreme to survive.

It hurts to breathe, Natalie thought dimly, still lost in the mad commotion happening everywhere in her body. Still wanting him—needing him—almost more than she could bear.

"I will make it stop," Rodolfo said, and she realized with a start that she'd spoken out loud. His mouth crooked slightly in one corner. "Eventually."

And then he dipped his fingers beneath the elastic of her panties and found the heat of her.

Natalie gasped as he stroked his way through her

folds, bold and sure, directly into her softness. His other hand was at her neck, his thumb moving against her skin there the way his clever fingers played with her sex below. He traced his way around the center of her need, watching her face as she clutched at his broad wrist— but only to maintain that connection with him, not to stop him. Never that. Not now.

And then, without warning, he twisted his wrist and drove two fingers into her, that hard curve of his mouth deepening when she moaned.

"Like that, princess," he murmured approvingly. "Sing for me just like that."

And Natalie lost track of what he was doing, and how. He dropped his head to her neck again, teasing his way down to toy with the top of her bodice. He dragged his free hand over her nipples, poking hard against the fabric of the dress, and it was like lightning storming straight down the center of her body to where she was already little more than a flame. And he was stoking that fire with every thrust of his long, blunt fingers deep into her, as if he knew. As if he knew everything. Her pounding heart, that slick, impossible pleasure crashing over her, and that delicious tightening that was making her breath come too fast and too loud.

She lost herself in the slide, the heat. His wicked, talented hands and what they were doing to her. Her hips lifted of their own accord, meeting each stroke, and then the storm took her over. She let her head fall back against the elevator doors. She let herself go, delivering herself completely into his hands, as if there was nothing but this slick, insistent rhythm. As if there was nothing but the sensation he was building in her, higher and higher.

As if there was nothing left in all the world but him.

And then Rodolfo did something new, twisting his wrist and thrusting in a little bit deeper, and everything seemed to shudder to a dangerous halt. Then he did it again, and threw her straight over the edge into bliss.

Sheer, exultant bliss.

Natalie tumbled there, lost to herself and consumed by all that wondrous fire, for what seemed like a very long time.

When the world stopped spinning he was shifting her, lifting her up and into his arms. She had the vague thought that she should protest as he held her high against his chest so her head fell to his wide shoulder when she couldn't hold it up, but his gaze was dark and hungry—still so very hungry—and she couldn't seem to find her tongue to speak.

Rodolfo carried her to the long couch that stretched out before the great wall of windows with all of Rome winking and sparkling there on the other side, like some kind of dream. He laid her down carefully, as if she were infinitely precious to him, and it caught at her. It made the leftover fire still roaring inside of her bleed into…something else. Something that ached more than it should.

And that was the trouble, wasn't it?

Natalie wanted this to be real. She wanted all of this to be real. She wanted to stay Valentina forever, so it wouldn't matter what she did here because *she* would live the consequences of it. She could marry Rodolfo herself. She could—

You could lose yourself in him, a voice that sounded too much like her mother's, harsh and cold, snapped at her. It felt like a face full of cold water. *And then you could be one more thing he throws away when he gets bored. This is a man who has toys, not relationships.*

How can you be so foolish as to imagine otherwise—no matter how good he is with his hands?

"I should have done this a long time ago," he was saying, in a contemplative sort of way that suggested he was talking to himself more than her. But his gaze was so hot, so hungry. It made her shiver, deep inside, kindling the same fire she would have sworn was already burned out. "I think it would have made for a far better proposal of marriage, don't you?"

"Rodolfo…" she began, but he was coming down over her on the couch. He held himself up on his arms and gazed down at her as he settled himself between her legs, fitting his body to hers in a way that made them both breathe a little bit harder. Audibly. And there was no pretending that wasn't real. It made her foolish. "You may imagine you know who I am, but you don't. You really don't."

"Quiet, *princesita*," he said in a low sort of growl that made everything inside her, still reeling from what he'd done with his hands alone, bloom into a new, even more demanding sort of heat. He shifted so he could take her face between his hands, and that was better. Worse. Almost too intense. "I am going to taste you again. Then I will tell you who are, though I already know. You should know it, too." He let his chest press against her, and dipped his chin so his mouth was less than a gasp away. Less than a breath. *"Mine."*

And then he set his mouth to hers and the flames devoured her.

Again.

This time, Natalie didn't need to be told to beg for him. There was no space between them, only heat and the intense pressure of the hardest part of him, flush against her scalding heat. There was no finesse, no strategy, no teasing. Only need.

And that hunger that rolled between them like so much summer thunder.

She didn't know who undressed whom and she didn't—couldn't—care. She only knew that his mouth was a torment and a gift, both at the same time. His hands were like fire. He pulled down her bodice and feasted on the nipples he'd played with before, until Natalie was nothing but a writhing mess beneath him. Begging. Pleading. Somehow his shirt was open, and she was finally able to touch all those hard muscles she'd only imagined until now. And he was so much better than the pictures she'd seen. Hot and extraordinarily male and perfect and *here,* right here, stretched out on top of her. It was her turn to use her mouth on him, tasting the heat and salt of him until his breath was as heavy as hers, and everything was part of the same shattering, impossible magic.

At some point she wondered if it was possible to survive this much pleasure. If anyone could live through it. If she would recognize herself when this was done— but that was swept away when he took her mouth again.

She loved his weight, crushing her down into the cushions. She loved it even more when he pulled her skirts out of the way and found her panties again. This time, he didn't bother sneaking beneath them. This time he simply tugged, hard and sure, until they tore away in his hand.

And somehow that was so erotic it seemed to light her up inside. She could hardly breathe.

Rodolfo reached down and tore at his trousers, and when he shifted back into place Natalie felt him, broad and hard, nudging against her entrance. His gaze trav-

eled over her body from the place they were joined to
the skirt of the dress rucked up and twisted around her
hips. Then higher, to where her breasts were plumped
up above the dress's bodice, her nipples still tight and
swollen from his mouth. Only then did his gaze touch
her face.

Suddenly, the world was nothing but that shuddering
beat of her heart, so hard she thought he must surely feel
it, and that stark, serious expression he wore. He dropped
down to an elbow, bringing himself closer to her.

This was happening. This was real.

He was the kind of prince she'd never dared admit
she dreamed about, so big and so beautiful it hurt to be
this close to him. It hurt in a way dreams never did. It
ached, low and deep, and everywhere else.

"Are you ready, princess?" he asked, and his voice
was another caress, rough and wild.

Natalie wanted to say something arch. Witty. Something to cut through the intensity and make her feel in
control again. Anything at all that might help make this
less than it was. Anything that might contain or mini-
mize all those howling, impossible things that flooded
through her then.

But she couldn't seem to open her mouth. She couldn't
seem to find a single word that might help her.

Her body knew what to do without her guidance or
input. As if she'd been made for this, for him. She lifted
her hips and pushed herself against him, impaling herself on his hardness, one slow and shuddering inch. Then
another. He muttered something in what she thought was
the Spanish he sometimes used, but Natalie was caught
in his dark gaze, still fast on her face.

"What are you doing to me?" he murmured. He'd
asked it before.

Like then, he didn't wait for an answer. He didn't give her any warning. He wrapped an arm around her hips, then hauled them high against him. And in the next instant, slammed himself in deep.

"Oh, my God," Natalie whispered as he filled her, and everything in her shuddered again and again, nudging her so close to the edge once more that she caught her breath in anticipation.

"'Your Highness' will do," Rodolfo told her, a thread of amusement beneath the stark need in his voice.

And then he began to move.

It was a slick, devastating magic. Rodolfo built the flames in her into a wildfire, then fanned the blaze ever higher. He dropped his mouth to hers, then shifted to pull a nipple into the heat of his mouth.

Natalie wrapped herself around him, and gave herself over to each glorious thrust. She dug her fingers into his back, she let her head fall back and then she let herself go. As if the woman she'd been when she'd walked into this room, or into this life, no longer existed.

There was only Rodolfo. There was only this.

Perfect, she thought, again and again, so it became a chant inside her head. *This is perfect.*

She might even have chanted it aloud.

He dropped down closer, wrapping his arms around her as his rhythm went wilder and more erratic. He tucked his face in her neck and kept his mouth there as he pounded into her, over and over, until he hurled her straight back off that cliff.

And he followed her only moments later, releasing himself into her with a roar that echoed through the room and deep inside of Natalie, too, tearing her apart in a completely different way as reality slammed back into her, harsh and cruel.

Because she'd never felt closer to a man in all her life, and Rodolfo had called out to her as if he felt the same. She was as certain as she'd ever been of anything that he felt exactly the same as she did.

But, of course, he thought she was someone else.

And he'd used the wrong name.

CHAPTER NINE

RODOLFO HAD BARELY shifted his weight from Valentina before she was rolling out from beneath him, pulling the voluminous skirt of her dress with her as she climbed to her feet. He found he couldn't help but smile. She was so unsteady on her feet that she had to reach out and grab hold of the nearby chair to keep from sagging to the ground.

He was male enough to find that markedly satisfying.

"You are even beautiful turned away from me," he told her without meaning to speak. It was not, generally, his practice to traffic in flattery. Mostly because it was never required. But it was the simple truth as far as Valentina was concerned. Not empty flattery at all.

She shivered slightly, as if in reaction to his words, but that was all. She didn't glance back at him. She was pulling her dress back into place, shaking back her hair that had long since tumbled from its once sleek chignon. And all Rodolfo wanted to do was pull her back down to him. He wanted to indulge himself and take a whole lot more time with her. He wanted to strip her completely and make sure he learned every last inch of her sweet body by heart.

He was more than a little delighted at the prospect of a long life together to do exactly that.

Rodolfo zipped himself up and rolled to a sitting position, aware that he felt lighter than he had in a long time. Years.

Since Felipe died.

Because the truth was, he'd never wanted his brother's responsibilities. He'd wanted his brother. Funny, irreverent, remarkably warm Felipe had been Rodolfo's favorite person for the whole of his life, and then he'd died. So suddenly. So needlessly. He'd locked himself in his rooms to sleep through what he'd assumed was a flu, and he'd been gone within the week. There was a part of Rodolfo that would never accept that. That never had. That would grieve his older brother forever.

But Rodolfo was the Crown Prince of Tissely now no matter how he grieved his brother, and that meant he should have had all of the attendant responsibilities whether he liked it or not. His father had felt otherwise. And every year the king failed to let Rodolfo take Felipe's place in his court and his government was like a slap in the face all over again, of course. It was a very public, very deliberate rebuke.

More than that, it confirmed what Rodolfo had always known to be true. He could not fill Felipe's shoes. He could not come anywhere close and that would never change. There was no hope.

Until now, he'd assumed that was simply how it would be. His father would die at some point, having allowed Rodolfo no chance at all to figure out his role as king. Rodolfo would have to do it on the fly, which was a terrific way to plunge a country straight into chaos. It was one of the reasons he'd dedicated himself to the sort of sports that required a man figure out how to remain calm no matter what was coming at him. Sharks. The earth, many thousands of feet below, at great speed. Assorted impossible mountain peaks that had killed many men before him. He figured it was all good practice for the little gift his father planned to leave him, since he suspected the old man was doing his level best to ensure that all his dire predictions about the kind of king Rodolfo would be would come true within days of his own death.

This engagement was a test, nothing more. Rodolfo had no doubt that his father expected him to fail, somehow, at an arranged marriage that literally required nothing of him save that he show up. And perhaps he'd played into that, by continuing to see other women and doing nothing to keep that discreet.

But everything was different now. Valentina was his. And their marriage would be the kind of real union Rodolfo had always craved. Without even meaning to, Rodolfo had beaten his father at the old man's own cynical little game.

And it was more than that. Rodolfo had to believe that if he could make the very dutiful princess his the way he had tonight, if he could take a bloodless royal arrangement and make it a wildfire of a marriage, he could do anything. Even convince his dour father to see him as more than just an unwelcome replacement for his beloved lost son.

For the first time in a long, long while, Rodolfo felt very nearly *hopeful*.

"Princess," he began, reaching out to wrap a hand around her hip and tug her toward him, because she was still showing him her back and he wanted her lovely face, "you must—"

"Stop calling me that!" she burst out, sounding raw. And something like wild.

She twisted out of his grasp. And he was so surprised by her outburst that he let her go.

Valentina didn't stop moving until she'd cleared the vast glass table set before the couch, and then she stood there on the other side, her chest heaving as if she'd run an uphill mile to get there.

His princess did not look anything like *hopeful*. If anything, she looked… Wounded. Destroyed. Rodolfo couldn't make any sense out of it. Her green eyes were dark and that sweet, soft mouth of hers trembled as if the hurt inside her was on the verge of pouring out even as she stood there before him.

"I can't believe I let this happen…" she whispered, and her eyes looked full. Almost blank with an anguish Rodolfo couldn't begin to understand.

Rodolfo wanted to stand, to go to her, to offer her what comfort he could—but something stopped him. How many times would she do this back and forth in one way or another? How many ways would she find to pull the rug out from under him—and as he thought that, it was not lost on Rodolfo that unlike every other woman he'd ever known, he cared a little too deeply about what this one was about. All this melodrama and for what? There was no stopping their wedding or the long, public, political marriage that would follow. It was like a train bearing down on them and it always had been.

From the moment Felipe had died and Rodolfo had been sat down and told that in addition to losing his best friend he now had a different life to live than the one he'd imagined he would, there had been no deviating from the path set before them. Princess Valentina had already been his—entirely his—before he'd laid a single finger on her. What had happened here only confirmed what had always been true, not that there had been any doubt. Not for him, anyway.

The only surprise was how much he wanted her.

Again, now, despite the fact he'd only just had her. She made him…thirsty in a way he'd never experienced before in his life.

But it wouldn't have mattered if she'd stayed the same pale, distant ghost he'd met at their engagement celebration. The end result—their marriage and all the politics involved—would have been the same.

He didn't like to see her upset. He didn't like it at all. It made his jaw clench tight and every muscle in his body go much too taut. But Rodolfo remained where he was.

"If you mean what happened right here—" and he nodded at the pillow beside him as if could play back the last hour in vivid color "—then I feel I must tell you that it was always going to happen. It was only a question of when. Before the wedding or after it. Or did you imagine heirs to royal kingdoms were delivered by stork?"

But it was as if she couldn't hear him. "Why didn't you let me leave the gala alone?"

He shrugged, settling back against the pillows as if he was entirely at his ease, though he was not. Not at all. "I assume that was a rhetorical question, as that was never going to happen. You can blame the unfortunate optics if you must. But there was no possibility that my fiancée was ever going to sneak out of a very public event on her own, leaving me behind. How does that suit our narrative?"

"I don't care about your narrative."

"*Our* narrative, Valentina, and you should. You will. It is a weapon against us or a tool we employ. The choice is ours."

She was frowning now, and it was aimed at him, yet Rodolfo had the distinct impression she was talking to herself. "You should never, ever have come up here tonight."

He considered her for a moment. "This was not a mistake, *princesita*. This was a beginning."

She lifted her hands to her face and Rodolfo saw that they were shaking. Again, he wanted to go to her and again, he didn't. It was something about the stiff way she was standing there, or what had looked like genuine torment on her face before she'd covered it from his view. It gripped him, somehow, and kept him right where he was.

As if, he realized in the next moment, he was waiting for the other shoe to drop. The way he had been ever since he'd discovered at too young an age that anything and anyone could be taken from him with no notice whatsoever.

But that was ridiculous. There was no "other shoe" here. This was an arranged marriage set up by their fathers when Valentina was a baby. One crown prince of Tissely and one princess of Murin, and the kingdoms would remain forever united. Two small countries who, together, could become a force to be reckoned with in these confusing modern times. The contracts had been signed for months. They were locked into this wedding no matter what, with no possibility of escape.

Rodolfo knew. He'd read every line of every document that had required his signature. And still, he didn't much like that thing that moved him, dark and grim, as he watched her. It felt far too much like foreboding.

His perfect princess, who had just given herself to him with such sweet, encompassing heat that he could still feel the burn of it all over him and through him as if he might feel it always, dropped her hands from her face. Her gaze caught his and held. Her eyes were still too dark, and filled with what looked like misery.

Sheer, unmistakable misery. It made his chest feel tight.

"I should never have let any of this happen," she said, and her voice was different. Matter-of-fact, if hollow. She swallowed, still keeping her eyes trained on his. "This is my fault. I accept that."

"Wonderful," Rodolfo murmured, aware his voice sounded much too edgy. "I do so enjoy being blameless. It is such a novelty."

She clenched her hands together in front of her, twisting her fingers together into a tangle. There was something about the gesture that bothered him, though he couldn't have said what. Perhaps it was merely that it seemed the very antithesis of the sort of thing a woman trained since birth to be effortlessly graceful would do. No matter the provocation.

"I am not Princess Valentina."

He watched her say that. Or rather, he saw her lips move and he heard the words that came out of her mouth, but they made no sense.

Her mouth, soft and scared, pressed into a line. "My name is Natalie."

"Natalie," he repeated, tonelessly.

"I ran into the princess in, ah—" She cleared her throat. "In London. We were surprised, as you might imagine, to see…" She waved her hand in that way of hers, as if what she was saying was reasonable. Or even possible. Instead of out-and-out gibberish. "And it seemed like a bit of a lark, I suppose. I got to pretend to be a princess for a bit. What could be more fun? No one was ever meant to know, of course."

"I beg your pardon." He still couldn't move. He thought perhaps he'd gone entirely numb, but he knew, somehow, that the paralytic lack of feeling was better than what lurked on the other side. Much better. "But where, precisely, is the real princess in this ludicrous scenario?"

"Geographically, do you mean? She's back in London. Or possibly Spain, depending."

"All tucked up in whatever your life is, presumably." He nodded as if that idiocy made sense. "What did you say your name was, again?"

She looked ill at ease. As well she should. "Natalie."

"And if your profession is not that of the well-known daughter of a widely renowned and ancient royal family, despite your rather remarkable likeness to Princess Valentina, dare I ask what is it that you do? Does it involve a stage, perhaps, the better to hone these acting skills?"

"I'm a personal assistant. To a very important businessman."

"A jumped-up secretary for a man in trade. Of course." He was getting less numb by the second, and that was no good for anyone—though Rodolfo found he didn't particularly care. He hadn't lost his temper in a long while, but these were extenuating circumstances, surely. She should have been grateful he wasn't breaking things. He shook his head, and even let out a laugh, though nothing was funny. "I must hand it to you. Stage or no stage, this has been quite an act."

She blinked. "Somehow, that doesn't sound like a compliment."

"It was really quite ingenious. All you had to do was walk in the room that day and actually treat me like another living, breathing human instead of a cardboard cutout. After all those months. You must have been thrilled that I fell into your trap so easily."

The words felt sour in his own mouth. But Valentina only gazed back at him with confusion written all over her, as if she didn't understand what he was talking about. He was amazed that he'd fallen for her performance. Why hadn't it occurred to him that her public persona, so saintly and retiring, was as much a constriction as his daredevil reputation? As easily turned off as on. And yet it had never crossed his mind that she was anything but the woman she'd always seemed to be, hailed in all the papers as a paragon of royal virtue. A breath of fresh air, they called her. The perfect princess in every respect.

He should have known that all of it was a lie. A carefully crafted, meticulously built lie.

"The trap?" She was shaking her head, looking lost and something like forlorn, and Rodolfo hated that even when he knew she was trying to play him, he still wanted to comfort her. Get his hands on her and hold her close. It made his temper lick at him, dark and dangerous. "What trap?"

"All of this so you could come back around tonight and drop this absurd story on me. Did you really think I would credit such an outlandish tale? You *happen* to resemble one of the wealthiest and most famous women in the world, yet no one remarked on this at any point during your other life. Until, by chance, you stumbled upon each other. How convenient. And that day in the palace, when you came back from London—am I meant to believe that you had never met me before?"

She pressed her lips together as if aware that they trembled. "I hadn't."

"What complete and utter rubbish." He stood then, smoothing his shirt down as he rose to make sure he kept his damned twitchy hands to himself, but there wasn't much he could do about the fury in his voice. "I am not entirely certain which part offends me more. That you would go to the trouble to concoct such a childish, ridiculous story in the first place, or that you imagined for one second that I would believe it."

"You said yourself that I was switching personalities. That I was two women. This is why. I think—I mean, the only possible explanation is that Valentina and I are twins." There was an odd emphasis on that last word, as if she'd never said it out loud before. She squared her shoulders. "Twin sisters."

Rodolfo fought to keep himself under control, despite the ugly things that crawled through him then, each worse than the last. The truth was, he should have known better than to be hopeful. About anything. He should have known better than to allow himself to think that anything in his life might work out. He could jump out of a thousand planes and land safely. There had never been so much as a hiccup on any of his adventures, unless he counted the odd shark bite or scar. But when it came to his actual life as a prince of Tissely? The things he was bound by blood and his birthright to do whether he wanted to or not? It was nothing but disaster, every time.

He should have known this would be, too.

"Twin sisters," he echoed when he trusted himself to speak in both English and a marginally reasonable tone. "But I think you must mean *secret* twin sisters, to give it the proper soap opera flourish. And how do you imagine such a thing could happen? Do you suppose the king happily looked the other way while Queen Frederica swanned off with a stolen baby?"

"No one talks about where she went. Much less who she went with."

"You are talking about matters of state, not idle gossip." His hands were in fists, and he forced them to open, then shoved them in his pockets. "The queen's mental state was precarious. Everyone knows this. She would hardly have been allowed to retreat so completely from public life with a perfectly healthy child who also happened to be one of the king's direct heirs."

Valentina frowned. "Precarious? What do you mean?"

"Do not play these games with me," he gritted out, aware that his heart was kicking at him. Temper or that same, frustrated hunger, he couldn't tell. "You know as well as I do that she was not assassinated, no matter how many breathless accounts are published in the dark and dingy corners of the internet by every conspiracy theorist who can type. That means, for your story to make any kind of sense, a king with no other heirs in line for his throne would have to release one of the two he did have into the care of a woman who was incapable of fulfilling a single one of her duties as his queen. Or at the very least, somehow fail to hunt the world over for the child once this same woman stole her."

"I didn't really think about that part," she said tightly. "I was more focused on the fact I was in a palace and the man with the crown was acting as if he was my father. Which it turns out, he probably is."

"Enough." He belted it out at her, with enough force that her head jerked back a little. "The only thing this astonishing conversation is doing is making me question your sanity. You must know that." He let out a small laugh at that, though it scraped at him. "Perhaps that is your endgame. A mental breakdown or two, like mother, like daughter. If you cannot get out of the marriage before the wedding, best to start working on how to exit it afterward, I suppose."

Her face was pale. "That's not what this is. I'm trying to be honest with you."

He moved toward her then, feeling his lips thin as he watched her fight to stand her ground when she so clearly wanted to put more furniture between them—if not whole rooms.

"Have I earned this, Valentina?" he demanded, all that numbness inside him burning away with the force of his rage. His sense of betrayal—which he didn't care to examine too closely. It was enough that she'd led him to hope, then kicked it out of his reach. It was more than enough. "That you should go to these lengths to be free of me?"

He stopped when he was directly in front of her, and he hated the fact that even now, all he wanted to do was pull her into his arms and kiss her until the only thing between them was that heat. Her eyes were glassy and she looked pale with distress, and he fell for it. Even knowing what she was willing to do and say, his first instinct was to believe her. What did that say about his judgment?

Maybe his father had been right about him all along.

That rang in him like a terrible bell.

"Here is the sad truth, princess," he told her, standing above her so she was forced to tilt her head back to keep her eyes on him. And his body didn't know that everything had changed, of course. It was far more straightforward. It wanted her, no matter what stories she told. "There is no escape. There is no sneaking away into some fantasy life where you will live out your days without the weight of a country or two squarely on your shoulders. There is no switching places with a convenient twin and hiding from who you are. And I am terribly afraid that part of what you must suffer is our marriage. You are stuck with me. Forever."

"Rodolfo." And her voice was scratchy, as if she had too many sobs in her throat. As if she was fighting to hold them back. "I know it all sounds insane, but you have to listen to me—"

"No," he said with quiet ferocity. "I do not."

"Rodolfo—"

And now even his name in her mouth felt like an insult. Another damned lie. He couldn't bear it.

He silenced her the only way he knew how. He reached out and hooked a hand around her neck, dragging her to him. And then he claimed her mouth with his.

Rodolfo poured all of the dark things swirling around inside of him into the way he angled his jaw to make everything bright hot and slick. Into the way he took her. Tasted her. As if she was the woman he'd imagined she was, so proper and bright. As if he could still taste that fantasy version of her now despite the games she was trying to play. He gave her his grief over Felipe, his father's endless shame and fury that the wrong son had died—all of it. If she'd taken away his hope, he could give her the rest of it. He kissed her again and again, as much a penance for him as any kind of punishment for her.

And when he was done, because it was that or he would take her again right there on the hotel floor and he wasn't certain either one of them would survive that, he set her away from him.

It should have mattered to him that she was breathing too hard. That her green eyes were wide and there were tears marking her cheeks. It should have meant something.

Somewhere, down below the tumult of that black fury that roared in him, inconsolable and much too wounded, it did. But he ignored it.

"I only wanted you to know who I am," she whispered.

And that was it, then. That was too much. He took her shoulders in his hands and dragged her before him, up on her toes and directly in his face.

"I am Rodolfo of Tissely," he growled at her. "The accidental, throwaway prince. I was called *the spare* when I was born, always expected to live in my brother's shadow and never, ever expected to take Felipe's place. Then the spare became the heir—but only in name. Because I have always been the bad seed. I have always been unworthy."

"That's not true."

He ignored her, his fingers gripping her and keeping her there before him. "Nothing I touch has ever lasted. No one I love has ever loved me back, or if they did, it was only as long as there were two sons instead of the one. Or they disappeared into the wilds of Bavaria, pretending to be ill. Or they died of bloody sepsis in the middle of a castle filled with royal doctors and every possible medication under the sun."

She whispered his name as if she loved him, and that hurt him worse than all the rest. Because more than all the rest, he wanted that to be true—and he knew exactly how much of a fool that made him.

"What is one more princess who must clearly hate the very idea of me, the same as all the rest?" And what did it matter that he'd imagined that she might be the saving of him, of the crown he'd never wanted and the future he wasn't prepared for? "None of this matters. You should have saved your energy. This will all end as it was planned. The only difference is that now, I know exactly how deceitful you are. I know the depths of the games you will play. And I promise you this, princess. You will not fool me again."

"You don't understand," she said, more tears falling from her darkened green eyes as she spoke and wetting her pale cheeks. "I wanted this to be real, Rodolfo. I lost myself in that."

He told himself to let go of her. To take his hand off her shoulders and step away. But he didn't do it. If anything, he held her tighter. Closer.

As if he'd wanted it to be real, too. As if some part of him still did.

"You have to believe me," she whispered. "I never meant it to go that far."

"It was only sex," he told her, his voice a thing of granite. He remembered what she'd called herself as she'd spun out her fantastical little tale. "But no need to worry, *Natalie*." She flinched, and he was bastard enough to like that. Because he wanted her to hurt, too—and no matter that he hated himself for that thought. Hating himself didn't change a thing. It never had. "I will be certain to make you scream while we make the requisite heirs. I am nothing if not dependable in that area, if nowhere else. Feel free to ask around for references."

He let her go then, not particularly happy with how hard it was to do, and headed for the elevator. He needed to clear his head. He needed to wash all of this away. He needed to find a very dark hole and fall into it for a while, until the self-loathing receded enough that he could function again. Assuming it ever would.

"It doesn't have to be this way," she said from behind him.

But Rodolfo turned to face her only when he'd stepped into the elevator. She stood where he'd left her, her hands tangled in front of her again and something broken in her gaze.

Eventually, she would have as little power over him as she'd had when they'd met. Eventually, he would not want to go to her when she looked at him like that, as if she was small and wounded and only he could heal her.

Eventually. All he had to do was survive long enough to get there, like anything else.

"It can only be this way," he told her then, and he hardly recognized his own voice. He sounded like a broken man—but of course, that wasn't entirely true. He had never been whole to begin with. "The sooner you resign yourself to it, the better. I am very much afraid this is who we are."

Natalie didn't move for a long, long time after Rodolfo left. If she could have turned into a pillar of stone, she would have. It would have felt better, she was sure.

The elevator doors shut and she heard the car move, taking Rodolfo away, but she still stood right where he'd left her as if her feet were nailed to the floor. Her cheeks were wet and her dress caught at her since she'd pulled it back into place in such a panicked hurry, and her fingers ached from where she'd threaded them together and held them still. Her breathing had gone funny because her throat was so tight.

And for a long while, it seemed that the only thing she could do about any of those things was stay completely still. As if the slightest movement would make it all worse—though it was hard to imagine how.

Eventually, her fingers began to cramp, and she unclasped them, then shook them out. After that it was easier to move the rest of her. She walked on stiff, protesting legs down the long penthouse hallway into her bedroom, where she stood for a moment in the shambles of her evening, blind to the luxury all around her. But that could only last so long. She went to kick off her shoes and realized she'd lost them somewhere, but she didn't want to go back out to the living room and look. She was sure Rodolfo's contempt was still clinging to every gleaming surface out there and she couldn't bring herself to face it.

She padded across the grandly appointed space to the adjoining bathroom suite and stepped in to find the bath itself was filled and waiting for her, steam rising off the top of the huge, curved, freestanding tub like an invitation. That simple kindness made her eyes fill all over again. She wiped the blurriness away, but it didn't help, and the tears were flowing freely again by the time she got herself out of her dress and threw it over a chair in the bedroom. She didn't cry. She almost never cried. But tonight she couldn't seem to stop.

Natalie returned to the bathroom to pull all the pins out of her hair. She piled the mess of it on her head and knotted it into place, ignoring all the places she felt stiff or sore. Then she walked across the marble floor and climbed into the tub at last, sinking into the warm, soothing embrace of the bath's hot water and the salts that some kind member of the staff had thought to add.

She closed her eyes and let herself drift—but then there was no more hiding from the events of the night. The dance. That kiss out on the terrace of the villa. And then what had happened right here in this hotel. His mouth against her skin. His wickedly clever hands. The bold, deep surge of his possession and how she'd fallen to pieces so easily. The smile on Rodolfo's face when he'd turned her around to face him afterward, and how quickly it had toppled from view. And that shuttered, haunted look she'd put in his eyes later, that had been there when he'd left.

As if that was all that remained of what had swelled and shimmered between them tonight. As if that was all it had ever been.

Whatever else came of these stolen days here in Valentina's life, whatever happened, Natalie knew she would never forgive herself for that. For believing in a fairy tale when she knew better and hurting Rodolfo—to say nothing of herself—in the process.

She sat in the tub until her skin was shriveled and the water had cooled. She played the night all the way through, again and again, one vivid image after the next. And when she sat up and pulled the plug to let the water swirl down the drain, she felt clean, yes. But her body didn't feel like hers. She could still feel Rodolfo's touch all over, as if he'd branded her with his passion as surely as he'd condemned her with his disbelief.

Too bad, she told herself, sounding brisk and hard like her mother would have. *This is what you get for doing what you knew full well you shouldn't have.*

Natalie climbed out of the tub then and wrapped herself in towels so light and airy they could have been clouds, but she hardly noticed. She stood in the still-fogged-up bathroom and brushed out her hair, letting the copper strands fall all around her like a curtain and then braiding the heavy mess of it to one side, so she could toss it over one shoulder and forget it.

When she walked back into the bedroom, her dress was gone from the chair where she'd thrown it and in its place was the sort of silky thing Valentina apparently liked to sleep in. Natalie had always preferred a simple T-shirt, but over the past couple of weeks she'd grown to like the sensuous feel of the fine silk against her bare skin.

Tonight, however, it felt like a rebuke.

Her body didn't want silk, it wanted Rodolfo.

She would have given anything she had to go back in time and keep herself from making that confession. To accept that of course he would call her by the wrong name and find a way to make her peace with it. Her mind spun out into one searing fantasy after another about how the night would have gone if only she'd kept her mouth shut.

But that was the trouble, wasn't it? She'd waited too long to tell him the truth, if she was going to. And she never should have allowed him to touch her while he thought she was Valentina. Not back in the palace. Certainly not tonight. She should have kept her distance from him entirely.

Because no matter what her traitorous heart insisted, even now, he wasn't hers. He could never be hers. The ring on her finger belonged to another woman and so did he. It didn't matter that Valentina had given her blessing, whatever that meant in the form of a breezy text. Natalie had never wanted to be the sort of woman who took another woman's man, no matter the circumstances. She'd spent her whole childhood watching her mother flit from one lover to the next, knowing full well that many of the men Erica juggled had been married already. Natalie always vowed that she was not going to be one of those women who pretended they didn't know when a man was already committed elsewhere. In this case, she'd known going in and she'd still ended up here.

How many more ways was she going to betray herself?

How many more lives was she going to ruin besides her own?

Natalie looked around the achingly gorgeous room, aware of every last detail that made it the perfect room for a princess, from the soaring canopy over her high, proud bed to the deep Persian rugs at her feet. The epic sweep of the drapery at each window and the stunning view of Rome on the other side of the glass. The artistry in every carved leg of each of the chairs placed *just so* at different points around the chamber. She looked down at her own body, still warm and pink from her bath and barely covered in a flowy, bright blue silk that cascaded lazily from two spaghetti straps at her shoulders. Her manicure and pedicure were perfect. Her skin was as soft as a baby's after access to Valentina's moisturizing routine with products crafted especially for her. Her hair had never looked so shiny or healthy, even braided over one shoulder. And she was wearing nothing but silk and a ring fit for a queen. Literally.

But she didn't belong here with these things that would never belong to her. She might fit into this borrowed life in the most physical sense, but none of it suited her. *None of it was hers.*

"I am Natalie Monette," she told herself fiercely, her own voice sounding loud and brash in the quiet of the room. Not cool and cultured, like a princess. "My fingernails are never painted red. My toes are usually a disaster. I live on pots of coffee and fistfuls of ibuprofen, not two squares of decadent chocolate a day and healthy little salads."

She moved over to the high bed, where Valentina's laptop and mobile phone waited for her on a polished bedside table, plugged in and charged up, because not even that was her responsibility here.

It was time to go home. It was time to wake up from this dream and take back what was hers—her career— before she lost that, too.

It was time to get back to the shadows, where she belonged.

She picked up the mobile and punched in her own number, telling herself this would all fade away fast when she was back in her own clothes and her own life. When she had too much to do for Mr. Casilieris to waste her time brooding over a prince she'd never see again. Soon this little stretch of time would be like every other fairy tale she'd ever been told as a girl, a faded old story she might recall every now and then, but no part of anything that really mattered to her.

And so what if her heart seemed to twist at that, making her whole chest ache?

It was still time—past time—to go back where she belonged.

"I am Natalie Monette," she whispered to herself as the phone on the other end rang and rang. "I am not a princess. I was never a princess and I never will be."

But it didn't matter what she told herself, because Valentina didn't answer.

Not that night.

And not for weeks.

CHAPTER TEN

RODOLFO WAS CONFLICTED.

He hadn't seen Valentina since that night in Rome. He'd had his staff contact her to announce that he thought they'd carried out their objectives beautifully and there would be no more need for their excursions into the world of the paparazzi. And that was before he'd seen their pictures in all the papers.

The one most prominently featured showed the two of them on the dance floor, in the middle of what looked like a very romantic waltz. Rodolfo was gazing down at her as if he had never seen a woman before in all his life. That was infuriating enough, given what had come afterward. It made his chest feel too tight. But it was the look on the princess's face that had rocked Rodolfo.

Because the picture showed her staring up at the man who held her in his arms in open adoration. As if she was falling in love right then and there as they danced. As if it had already happened.

And it had all been a lie. A game.

The first you've ever lost, a vicious voice inside of him whispered.

Today he stood in the grand foyer outside his father's offices in the palace in Tissely, but his attention was across Europe in Murin, where the maddening, still-more-fascinating-than-she-should-have-been woman who was meant to become his wife was going about her business as if she had not revealed herself to be decidedly unhinged.

She'd kept a low profile these last few weeks. As had Rodolfo.

But his fury hadn't abated one bit.

Secret twins. The very idea was absurd—even if she hadn't been the daughter of one of the most famous and closely watched men in the world. There was press crawling all over Murin Castle day and night and likely always had been, especially when the former queen had been pregnant with the heir to the country's throne.

"Ridiculous," he muttered under his breath.

But his trouble was, he didn't want to be bitter. He wanted to believe her, no matter how unreasonable she was. That was what had been driving him crazy these past weeks. He'd told himself he was going to throw himself right back into his old habits, but he hadn't. Instead he'd spent entirely too much time mired in his old, familiar self-pity and all it had done was make him miss her.

He had no earthly idea what to do about that.

The doors opened behind him and he was led in with the usual unnecessary ceremony to find his father standing behind his desk. Already frowning, which Rodolfo knew from experience didn't bode well for the bracing father/son chat they were about to have.

Ferdinand nodded at the chair before his desk and Rodolfo took it, for once not flinging himself down like a lanky adolescent. Not because doing so always irritated his father. But because he felt like a different man these days, scraped raw and hollow and made new in a variety of uncomfortable and largely unpleasant ways he could blame directly on his princess, and he didn't have it in him to needle his lord and king whenever possible.

His father's frown deepened as he beheld his son before him, because, of course, he always had it in him to poke at his son. It was an expression Rodolfo knew well. He had no idea why it was harder to keep his expression impassive today.

"I hope you have it in you to acquit yourself with something more like grace at your wedding," Ferdinand said darkly, as if Rodolfo had been rousted out of a den of iniquity only moments before and still reeked of excess. He'd tried. In the sense that he'd planned to go out and drown himself in all the things that had always entertained him before. But he'd never made it out. He couldn't call it fidelity to his lying, manipulative princess when the truth was, he'd lost interest in sin—could he? "The entire world will be watching."

"The entire world has been watching for some time," Rodolfo replied, keeping his tone easy. Even polite. Because there was no need to inform his father that he had no intention of marrying a woman who had tried to play him so thoroughly. How could he? But he told himself Ferdinand could find out when he didn't appear at the ceremony, like everyone else. "Has that not been the major point of contention all these years?"

His father ignored him. "It is one thing to wave at a press call. Your wedding to the Murin princess will be one of the most-watched ceremonies in modern Europe. Your behavior must, at last, be that of a prince of Tissely. Do you think you can manage this, Rodolfo?"

He glared at him as if he expected an answer. And something inside of Rodolfo simply…cracked.

It was so loud that first he thought it was the chair beneath him, but his father didn't react. And it took Rodolfo a moment to understand that it wasn't his chair. It was him.

He died, Rodolfo, his princess had said in Rome, before she'd revealed herself. *You lived.*

And he'd tried so hard to reverse that, hadn't he? He'd told himself all these years that the risks he took were what made him feel alive, but that had been a lie. What he'd been doing was punishing himself. Pushing himself because he hadn't cared what happened to him. Risking himself because he'd been without hope.

Until now.

"I am not merely *a* prince of Tissely," he said with a great calm that seemed to flood him then, the way it always did before he dropped from great heights with only a parachute or threw himself off the sides of bridges and ravines attached to only a bouncy rope. Except this time he knew the calm was not a precursor to adrenaline, but to the truth. At last. "I am the only prince of Tissely."

"I know very well who you are," his father huffed at him.

"Do you, sir? Because you have seemed to be laboring under some misconceptions as to my identity this last decade or two."

"I am your father and your king," his father thundered.

But Rodolfo was done being put into his place. He was done accepting that his place was somehow lower and shameful, for that matter.

All he'd done was live. Imperfectly and often foolishly, but he'd lived a life. He might have been lying to himself. He might have been hopeless. But he'd survived all of that.

The only thing he was guilty of was of not being Felipe.

"I am your son," Rodolfo replied, his voice like steel.

"I am your only remaining son and your only heir. It doesn't matter how desperately you cling to your throne. It doesn't matter how thoroughly you convince yourself that I am worthless and undeserving. Even if it were true, it wouldn't matter. Nothing you do will ever bring Felipe back."

His father looked stiff enough to break in half. And old, Rodolfo thought. How had he missed that his father had grown old? "How dare you!"

He was tired of this mausoleum his father had built around Felipe's memory. He was tired of the games they played, two bitter, broken men who had never recovered from the same long-ago loss and instead, still took it out on each other.

Rodolfo was done with the game. He didn't want to live like this any longer.

He wanted to feel the way he did when he was with Valentina. Maybe it had all been a lie, but he'd been *alive.* Not putting on a show. Not destined to disappoint simply by showing up.

And there was something he should have said a decade or two ago.

"I am all you have, old man." He stood then, taking his time and never shifting his gaze from his father's, so perhaps they could both take note of the fact that he towered over the old man. "Whether you like it or do not, I am still here. Only one of your sons died all those years ago. And only you can decide if you will waste the rest of your life acting as if you lost them both."

His father was not a demonstrative man. Ferdinand stood like a stone for so long that Rodolfo thought he might stand like that forever. So committed to the mausoleum he'd built that he became a part of it in fact.

But Rodolfo wanted no part of it. Not anymore. He

was done with lies. With games. With paying over and over for sins that were not his.

He inclined his head, then turned for the door. He was reaching for the knob to let himself out—to leave this place and get on with his life—when he heard a faint noise from behind him.

"It is only that I miss him," came his father's voice, low and strained. It was another man's sob.

Rodolfo didn't turn around. It would embarrass them both.

"I know, Papa," he said, using a name he hadn't thought, much less spoken aloud, since he was little more than a baby himself. But it was the only one that seemed appropriate. "I do, too."

The first week after that shattering trip to Rome, Natalie tried Valentina so many times she was slightly afraid it would have bordered on harassment—had she not been calling her own mobile number. And it didn't matter anyway, because the princess never answered, leaving Natalie to sit around parsing the differences between a ringing phone that was never picked up and a call that went straight to voice mail like an adolescent girl worrying over a boy's pallid attentions.

And in the meantime, she still had to live Valentina's life.

That meant endless rounds of charity engagements. It meant approximately nine million teas with the ladies of this or that charity and long, sad walks through hospitals filled with ill children. It was being expected to "say a few words" at the drop of a hat, and always in a way that would support the crown while offending no one. It meant dinners with King Geoffrey, night after night, that she gradually realized were his version of preparing Valentina for the role she would be expected to fill once she married and was the next Queen of Tissely. It also meant assisting in the planning of the impending royal wedding, which loomed larger with every day that passed.

Every call you don't answer is another questionable decision I'm making for YOUR wedding, she texted Valentina after a particularly long afternoon of menu selecting. *I hope you enjoy the taste of tongue and tripe. Both will feature prominently.*

But the princess didn't respond.

Which meant Natalie had no choice but to carry on playing Valentina. She supposed she could fly to London and see if she was there, but the constant stream of photographs screeching about her *fairy-tale love affair* in the papers made her think that turning up at Achilles Casilieris's property this close to Valentina's wedding would make everything worse. It would cause too much commotion.

It would make certain that when they finally did switch, Natalie wouldn't be able to seamlessly slip back into her old life.

Meanwhile, everything was as Rodolfo had predicted. The public loved them, and the papers dutifully recycled the same pictures from Rome again and again. Sometimes there were separate shots of them going about their business in their separate countries, and Natalie was more than a little embarrassed by the fact she pored over the pictures of Rodolfo like any obsessed tabloid reader. One day the papers were filled with stories about how daredevil, playboy Rodolfo encouraged Valentina to access her playful side, bringing something real and rare to her stitched-up, dutiful life. The next day the same papers were crowing about the way the proper princess had brought noted love cheat Rodolfo to heel, presumably with the sheer force of her *goodness*. It didn't matter what story the papers told; the people ate it up. They loved it.

Natalie, meanwhile, was miserable. And alone.

Everything was in ruins all around her—it was just too bad her body didn't know it.

Because it wanted him. So badly it kept her up at night. And made her hoard her vivid, searing memories of Rome and play them out again and again in her head. In her daydreams. And all night long, when she couldn't sleep and when she dreamed.

She was terribly afraid that it was all she would ever have of him.

The longer she didn't hear from Rodolfo or see him outside of the tabloids, the more Natalie was terrified that she'd destroyed Valentina's marriage. Her future. Her destiny. That come the wedding day, there would be no groom at the altar. Only a princess bride and the wreck Natalie had made of her life.

Because she was a twin that shouldn't exist. A twin that couldn't exist, if Rodolfo had been right in Rome.

Do you suppose the king happily looked the other way while Queen Frederica swanned off with a stolen baby? he'd asked, and God help her, but she could still see the contempt on his face. It still ricocheted inside of her, scarring wherever it touched.

And it was still a very good question.

One afternoon she locked herself in Valentina's bedroom, pulled out her mobile and punched in her mother's number from memory.

Natalie and her mother weren't close. They never had been, and while Natalie had periodically wondered what it might be like to have the mother/daughter bond so many people seemed to enjoy, she'd secretly believed she was better off without it. Still, she and Erica were civil. Cordial, even. They might not get together for holidays or go off on trips together or talk on the phone every Sunday, but every now and then, when they were in the same city and they were both free, they had dinner. Natalie wasn't sure if that would make pushing Erica for answers harder or easier.

"Mother," she said matter-of-factly after the perfunctory greetings—all with an undercurrent of some surprise because they'd only just seen each other a few months back in Barcelona and Natalie wasn't calling from her usual telephone number—were done. "I have to ask you a very serious question."

"Must you always be so intense, Natalie?" her mother asked with a sigh that only made her sound chillier, despite the fact she'd said she was in the Caribbean. "It's certainly not your most attractive trait."

"I want the truth," Natalie forged on, not letting her mother's complaint distract her. Since it was hardly anything new. "Not some vague story about the evils of some or other Prince Charming." Her mother didn't say anything to that, which was unusual. So unusual that it made a little trickle of unease trail down Natalie's back... but what did she have to fear? She already knew the answer. She'd just been pretending, all this time, that she didn't. "Is your real name Frederica de Burgh, Mother? And were you by chance ever married to King Geoffrey of Murin?"

She was sitting on the chaise in the princess's spacious bedroom with the laptop open in front of her, looking at pictures of a wan, very unsmiling woman, pale with copper hair and green eyes, who had once been the Queen of Murin. Relatively few pictures existed of the notorious queen, but it really only took one. The woman Natalie knew as Erica Monette was always tanned. She had dark black hair in a pixie cut, brown eyes and was almost never without her chilly smile. But how hard could it be, for a woman who didn't want to be found or connected to her old self, to cut and dye her hair, get some sun and pop in color contacts?

"Why would you ask such a thing?" her mother asked.

Which was neither an answer nor an immediate refutation of her theory, Natalie noted. Though she thought her mother sounded a little…winded.

She cleared her throat. "I am sitting in the royal palace in Murin right now."

"Well," Erica said after a moment bled out into several. She cleared her throat, and Natalie thought that was more telling than anything else, given that her mother didn't usually do emotions. "I suppose there's no use in telling you not to go turning over rocks like that. It can only lead to more trouble than it's worth."

"Explain this to me," Natalie whispered, because it was that or shout, and she wasn't sure she wanted to give in to that urge. She wasn't sure she'd stop. "Explain *my life* to me. How could you possibly have taken off and gone on to live a regular life with one of the King's children?"

"I told him you died," her mother said matter-of-factly. So matter-of-factly, it cut Natalie in half. She couldn't even gasp. She could only hold the phone to her ear and sit there, no longer the same person she'd been before this phone call. Her mother took that as a cue to keep going, once again sounding as unruffled as she always did. "My favorite maid took you and hid you until I could leave Murin. I told your father one of the twins was stillborn and he believed it. Why wouldn't he? And of course, we'd hid the fact that I was expecting twins from the press, because Geoffrey's mother was still alive then and she thought it was unseemly. It made sense to hide that there'd been a loss, too. Geoffrey never liked to show a weakness. Even if it was mine."

A thousand questions tracked through Natalie's head then. And with each one, a different emotion, each one buffeting her like its own separate hurricane. But she couldn't indulge in a storm. Not now. Not when she had a charity event to attend in a few short hours and a speech to give about its importance. Not when she had to play the princess and try her best to keep what was left of Valentina's life from imploding.

Instead, she asked the only question she could.

"Why?"

Erica sighed. And it occurred to Natalie that it wasn't just that she wasn't close to her mother, but that she had no idea who her mother was. And likely never would. "I wanted something that was mine. And you were, for a time, I suppose. But then you grew up."

Natalie rubbed a trembling hand over her face.

"Didn't it occur to you that I would find out?" she managed to ask.

"I didn't see how," Erica said after a moment. "You were such a bookish, serious child. So intense and studious. It wasn't as if you paid any attention to distant European celebrities. And of course, it never occurred to me that there was any possibility you'd run into any member of the Murinese royal family."

"And yet I did," Natalie pushed out through the constriction in her throat. "In a bathroom in London. You can imagine my surprise. Or perhaps you can't."

"Oh, Natalie." And she thought for a moment that her mother would apologize. That she would try, however inadequately, to make up for what she'd done. But this was Erica. "Always so intense."

There wasn't much to say after that. Or there was, of course—but Natalie was too stunned and Erica was too, well, *Erica* to get into it.

After the call was over, Natalie sat curled up in that chaise and stared off into space for a long time. She tried to put all the pieces together, but what she kept coming back to was that her mother was never going to change. She was never going to be the person Natalie wanted her to be, whether Natalie was a princess or a secretary. None of that mattered, because it was Erica who had trouble figuring out how to be a mother.

And in the meantime, Natalie really, truly was a princess, after all. Valentina's twin with every right to be in this castle. It was finally confirmed.

And Rodolfo still isn't yours, a small voice inside her whispered. *He never will be, even if he stops hating you tomorrow. Even if he shows up for his wedding, it won't be to marry you.*

She let out a long, hard breath. And then she sat up.

It took a swipe of her finger to bring up the string of texts Valentina still hadn't answered.

It turns out we really are sisters, she typed. Maybe you already suspected as much, but I was in denial. So I asked our mother directly. I'll tell you that story if and when I see you again.

She sent that and paused, lifting a hand to rub at the faint, stubborn headache that wouldn't go away no matter how much water she drank or how much sleep she got, which never felt at all like enough.

I don't know when that will be, because you've fallen off the face of the planet and believe me, I know how hard it is to locate Achilles Casilieris when he doesn't wish to be found. But if you don't show up soon, I'm going to marry your husband and I didn't sign up to pretend to be you for the rest of my life. I agreed to six weeks and it's nearly been that.

She waited for long moments, willing the other woman to text back. To give her some clue about…anything. To remind her that she wasn't alone in this madness despite how often and how deeply she felt she was.

If you're not careful, you'll be Natalie Monette forever. Nobody wants that.

But there was nothing.

So Natalie did the only thing she could do. She got to her feet, ignored her headache and that dragging exhaustion that had been tugging at her for over a week now, and went out to play Valentina.

Again.

CHAPTER ELEVEN

A FEW SHORT hours before the wedding, Rodolfo strode through the castle looking for his princess bride, because the things he wanted to say to her needed to be said in person.

He'd followed one servant and bribed another, and that was how he finally found his way to the princess's private rooms. He nodded briskly to the attendants who gaped at him when he entered, and then he strode deeper into her suite as if he knew where he was headed. He passed an empty media center and an office, a dining area and a cheerful salon, and then pushed his way through yet another door to find himself in her bedroom at last.

To find Valentina herself sitting on the end of the grand four-poster bed that dominated the space as if she'd been waiting for him.

She was not dressed in her wedding clothes. In fact, she was wearing the very antithesis of wedding clothes: a pair of very skinny jeans, ballet flats and a slouchy sort of T-shirt. There was an apricot-colored scarf wrapped around her neck several times, her hair was piled haphazardly on the top of her head and she'd anchored the great copper mess of it with a pair of oversize sunglasses. He stopped as the door shut behind him and could do nothing but stare at her.

This was the sort of outfit a woman wore to wander down to a café for a few hours. It was not, by any possible definition, an appropriate bridal ensemble for a woman who was due to make her way down the aisle of a cathedral to take part in a royal wedding.

"You appear to be somewhat underdressed for the wedding," he pointed out, aware he sounded more than a little gruff. Deadly, even. "Excuse me. I mean *our* wedding."

There was something deeply infuriating about the bland way she sat there and did nothing at all but stare back at him. As if she was deliberately slipping back into that old way she'd acted around him. As if he'd managed to push her too far away from him for her to ever come back and this was the only way she could think to show it.

But Rodolfo was finished feeling sorry for himself. He was finished living down to expectations, including his own. He was no ghost, in his life or anyone else's. After their conversation in Tissely, Ferdinand had appointed Rodolfo to his cabinet. He'd called it a wedding gift, but Rodolfo knew what it was: a new beginning. If he could manage it with his father after all these years and all the pain they'd doled out to each other, this had to be easier.

He'd convinced himself that it had to be.

"I am sorry, princess," he said, because that was where it needed to start, and it didn't seem to matter that he couldn't recall the last time he'd said those words. It was Valentina, so they flowed. Because he meant them with every part of himself. "You must know that above all else."

She straightened on the bed, though her gaze flicked away from his as she did. It seemed to take her a long time to look back at him.

"I beg your pardon?"

"I am sorry," he said again. There was too much in

his head, then. Felipe. His father. Even his mother, who had refused to interrupt her solitude for a wedding, and no matter that it was the only wedding a child of hers would ever have. She'd been immovable. He took another step toward Valentina, then stopped, opening up his hands at his sides. "I spent so long angrily not being my brother that I think I forgot how to be me. Until you. You challenged me. You stood up to me. You made me want to be a better man."

He heard what he assumed were her wedding attendants in the next room, but Valentina only regarded him, her green eyes almost supernaturally calm. So calm he wondered if perhaps she'd taken something to settle her nerves. But he forgot that when she smiled, serene and easy, and settled back on the bed.

"Go on," she murmured, with a regal little nod.

"In my head, you were perfect," he told her, drifting another step or so in her direction. "I thought that if I could win you, I could fix my life. I could make my father treat me with respect. I could clean up my reputation. I could make myself the Prince I always wanted to be, but couldn't, because I wasn't my brother and never could be." He shook his head. "And then at the first hint that you weren't exactly who I wanted you to be, I lost it. If you weren't perfect, then how could you save me?"

That was what it was, he understood. It had taken him too long to recognize it. Why else would he have been so furious with her? So deeply, personally wounded? He was an adult man who risked death for amusement. Who was he to judge the games other people played? Normally, he wouldn't. But then, he'd spent his whole life pretending to be normal. Pretending he wasn't looking for someone to save him. Fix him. Grant him peace.

No wonder he'd been destroyed by the idea that the

only person who'd ever seemed the least bit capable of doing that had been deliberately deceiving him.

"I don't need you to save me," he told her now. "I believe you already have. I want you to marry me."

Again, the sounds of her staff while again, she only watched him with no apparent reaction. He told himself he'd earned her distrust. He made himself keep going.

"I want to love you and enjoy you and taste you, everywhere. I do not want a grim march through our contractual responsibilities for the benefit of a fickle press. I want no *heir and spare,* I want to have babies. I want to find out what our life is like when neither one of us is pretending anything. We can do that, princess, can we not?"

She only gazed back at him, a faint smile flirting with the edge of her lips. Then she sat up, folding her hands very nicely, very neatly in her lap.

"I'm moved by all of this, of course," she said in a voice that made it sound as if she wasn't the least bit moved. It rubbed at him, making all the raw places inside him…ache. But he told himself to stand up straight and take it like a man. He'd earned it. Which wasn't to say he wouldn't fight for her, of course. No matter what she said. Even if she was who he had to fight. "But you think I'm a raving madwoman, do you not?"

And that was the crux of it. There was what he knew was possible, and there was Valentina. And if this was what Rodolfo had to do to have her, he was willing to do it. Because he didn't want their marriage to be like his parents'. The fake smiles and churning fury beneath it. The bitterness that had filled the spaces between them. The sharp silences and the barbed comments.

He didn't want any of that, so brittle and empty. He wanted to live.

After all this time being barely alive when he hadn't

felt he deserved to be, when everyone thought he should have died in Felipe's place and he'd agreed, Rodolfo wanted to *live*.

"I do not know how to trust anyone," he told her now, holding her gaze with his, "but I want to trust you. I want to be the man you see when you look at me. If that means you want me to believe that there are two of you, I will accept that." His voice was quiet, but he meant every word. "I will try."

Still, she didn't say anything, and he had to fight back the temper that kicked in him.

"Am I too late, Valentina? Is this—" He cut himself off and studied her clothes again. He stood before her in a morning coat and she was in jeans. "Are you planning to run out on this wedding? Now? The guests have already started arriving. You will have to pass them on your way out. Is that what you planned?"

"I was planning to run out on the wedding, yes," she replied, and smiled as she said it, which made no sense. Surely she could not be so *flippant* about something that would throw both of their kingdoms into disarray—and rip his heart out in the process. Surely he'd only imagined she'd said such a thing. But Valentina nodded across the room. "But the good news is that *she* looks like she's planning to stay."

And on some level he knew before he turned. But it still stole his breath.

His princess was standing in the door to what must have been her dressing room, clad in a long white dress. There was a veil pinned to a shining tiara on her head that flowed to the ground behind her. She was so lovely it made his throat tight, and *her* green eyes were dark with emotion and shone with tears. He looked back to check, to make sure he wasn't losing his own mind, but the spitting image of her was still sitting on the end of the bed, still dressed in the wrong clothes.

He'd known something was off about her the moment he'd walked in. *His* princess lit him up. She gazed at him and he wanted to fly off into the blue Mediterranean sky outside the windows. More, he believed he could.

She was looking at him that way now, and his heart soared.

He thought he could lose himself in those eyes of hers. "How long have you been standing there?"

"Since you walked in the door," she whispered.

"Natalie," he said, his voice rough, because she'd heard everything. Because he really had been talking to the right princess after all. "You told me you were Natalie."

She smiled at him, a tearful, gorgeous smile that changed the world around. "I am," she whispered. "But I would have been Valentina for you, if that was what you wanted. I tried."

Valentina was talking, but Rodolfo was no longer listening. He moved to *his princess* and took her hands in his, and there it was. Fire and need. That sense of homecoming. *Life.*

He didn't hesitate. He went down on his knees before her.

"Marry me, Natalie," he said. Or begged, really. Her hands trembled in his. "Marry me because you want to, not because our fathers decided a prince from Tissely should marry a princess from Murin almost thirty years ago. Marry me because, when you were not pretending to be Valentina and I was not being an ass, I suspect we were halfway to falling in love."

She pulled a hand from his and slid it down to stroke over his cheek, holding him. Blessing him. Making him whole.

"I suspect it's a lot more than halfway," she whispered. "When you said *mine,* you meant it." Natalie shook her head, and the cascading veil moved with her, making her look almost ethereal. But the hand at his jaw was all too real. "No one ever meant it, Rodolfo. My mother told me I grew up, you see. And everything else was a job I did, not anything real. Not anything true. Not you."

"I want to live," he told her with all the solemnity of the most sacred vow. "I want to live with you, Natalie."

"I love you," she whispered, and then she bent down or he surged up, and his mouth was on hers again. At last.

She tasted like love. Like freedom. Like falling end over end through an endless blue sky only with this woman, Rodolfo didn't care if there was a parachute. He didn't care if he touched ground. He wanted to carry on falling forever, just like this.

Only when there was the delicate sound of a throat being cleared did he remember that Valentina was still in the room.

He pulled back from Natalie, taking great satisfaction in her flushed cheeks and that hectic gleam in her green eyes. Later, he thought, he would lay her out on a wide, soft bed and learn every single inch of her delectable body. He would let her do the same when he was sated. He estimated that would take only a few years.

Outside, the church bells began to ring.

"I believe that is our cue," he said, holding fast to her hand.

Natalie's breath deserted her in a rush, and Rodolfo braced himself.

"I want to marry you," she said fiercely. "You have no idea how much. I wanted it from the moment I met you, whether I could admit it to myself or not." She shook her head. "But I can't. Not like this."

"Like what?" He lifted her fingers to his mouth. "What can be terrible enough to prevent us from marrying? I haven't felt alive in two decades, princess. Now that I do, I do not want to waste a single moment of the time I have left. Especially if I get to share that time with you."

"Rodolfo, listen to me." She took his hand between hers, frowning up at him. "Your whole life was plotted out for you since the moment you were born. Even when your brother was alive. My mother might have made some questionable choices, but because she did, I got something you didn't. I lived exactly how I wanted to live. I found out what made me happy and I did it. That's what you should do. *Truly live.* I would hate myself if I stood between you and the life you deserve."

"You love me," he reminded her, and he slid his hand around to hold the nape of her neck, smiling when she shivered. "You want to marry me. How can it be that even in this, you are defiant and impossible?"

"Oh, she's more than that," Valentina chimed in from the bed, and then smiled when they both turned to stare at her. A little too widely, Rodolfo thought. "She's pregnant."

His head whipped back to Natalie and he saw the truth in his princess's eyes, wide and green. He let go of her, letting his gaze move over what little of her body he could see in that flowing, beautiful dress, even though he knew it was ridiculous. He could count—and he knew exactly when he'd been with her on that couch in Rome. To the minute.

He'd longed for her every minute since.

But mostly, he felt a deep, supremely male and wildly possessive triumph course through him like a brand-new kind of fire.

"Bad luck, *princesita,*" he murmured, and he didn't

try very hard to keep his feelings out of his voice. "That means you're stuck with me, after all."

"That's the point," she argued. "I don't want to be stuck. I don't want *you* to be stuck!"

He smiled at her, because if she'd thought she was his before, she had no idea what was coming. He'd waited his whole life to love another this much, and now she was more than that. Now she was a family. "But I do."

And then, to make absolutely sure there would be no talking her way out of this or plotting something new and even more insane than the secret twin sister who was watching all of this from her spot on the bed, he wrenched open the door behind him and called for King Geoffrey himself.

"Make him hurry," he told the flabbergasted attendants as they raced to do his bidding. "Tell him I'm seeing double."

In the end, it all happened so fast.

King Geoffrey strode in, already frowning, only to stop dead when he saw Natalie and Valentina sitting next to each other on the chaise. Waiting for him.

Natalie braced herself as Valentina stood and launched into an explanation. She rose to her feet, too, shooting a nervous look over at Rodolfo where he lounged against one of the bed's four posters, because she expected the king to rage. To wave it all away the way Erica had. To say or do something horrible—

But instead, the King of Murin made a small, choked sound.

And then he was upon them, pulling both Natalie and Valentina into a long, hard, endless hug.

"I thought you were dead," he whispered into Natalie's neck. "She told me you were dead."

And for a long while, there was nothing but the church bells outside and the three of them, not letting go.

"I forget myself," Geoffrey said at last, wiping at his face as he stepped back from their little knot. Natalie made as if to move away, but Valentina gripped her hand and held her fast. "There is a wedding."

"My wedding," Rodolfo agreed from the end of the bed.

The king took his time looking at the man who would be his son-in-law one way or another. Natalie caught her breath.

"You were promised this marriage the moment you became the Crown Prince, of course, as your brother was before you."

"Yes." Rodolfo inclined his head. "I am to marry a princess of Murin. But it does not specify which one."

Valentina blinked. "It doesn't?"

The king smiled. "Indeed it does not."

"But everyone expects Valentina," Natalie heard herself say. Everyone turned to stare at her and she felt her cheeks heat up. "They do. It's printed in the programs."

"The programs," Rodolfo repeated as if he couldn't believe she'd said that out loud, and his dark gaze glittered as it met hers, promising a very specific kind of retribution.

She couldn't wait.

"It is of no matter," King Geoffrey said, sounding every inch the monarch he was. He straightened his exquisite formal coat with a jerk. "This is the Sovereign Kingdom of Murin and last I checked, I am its king. If I wish to marry off a daughter only recently risen from the dead, then that is exactly what I shall do." He started for the door. "Come, Valentina. There is work to be done."

"What work?" Valentina frowned at his retreating

back. But Natalie noticed she followed after him anyway. Instantly and obediently, like the proper princess she was.

"If I have two daughters, only one of them can marry into the royal house of Tissely," King Geoffrey said. "Which means you must take a different role altogether. Murin will need a queen of its own, you know."

Valentina shot Natalie a harried sort of smile over her shoulder and then followed the King out, letting the door fall shut behind her.

Leaving Natalie alone with Rodolfo at last.

It was as if all the emotions and revelations of the day spun around in the center of the room, exploding into the sudden quiet. Or maybe that was Natalie's head— especially when Rodolfo pushed himself off the bedpost and started for her, his dark gaze intent.

And extraordinarily lethal.

A wise woman would have run, Natalie was certain. But her knees were in collusion with her galloping pulse. She sank down on the chaise and watched instead, her heart pounding, as Rodolfo stalked toward her.

"Valentina arrived in the middle of the night," she told him as he came toward her, all that easy masculine grace on display in the morning coat he wore entirely too well, every inch of him a prince. And something far more dangerous than merely charming. "I never had a sister growing up, but I think I quite like the idea."

"If she appears in the dead of night in my bedchamber, princess, it will not end well." Rodolfo's hard mouth curved. "It will involve the royal guard."

He stopped when he was at the chaise and squatted down before her, running his hands up her thighs to find and gently cup her belly through the wedding gown she wore. He didn't say a word, he just held his palm there, the warmth of him penetrating the layers she wore and sinking deep into her skin. Heating her up the way he always did.

"Would you have told me?" he asked, and though he wasn't looking at her as he said it, she didn't confuse it for an idle question.

"Of course," she whispered.

"Yet you told me to go off and be free, like some dreadfully self-indulgent Kerouac novel."

"There was a secret, nine-month limit on your freedom," Natalie said, and her voice wavered a bit when he raised his head. "I was trying to be noble."

His gaze was dark and direct and filled with light.

"Marry me," he said.

She whispered his name like a prayer. "There are considerations."

"Name them."

Rodolfo inclined his head in that way she found almost too royal to be believed, and yet deeply alluring. It was easy to imagine him sitting on an actual throne somewhere, a crown on his head and a scepter in his hand. A little shiver raced down her spine at the image.

"I didn't mean to get pregnant," she told him, very seriously. "I'm not trying to trap you."

"The hormones must be affecting your brain." He shook his head, too much gold in his gaze. "You are already trapped. This is an arranged marriage."

"I wasn't even sick. Everyone knows the first sign of pregnancy is getting sick, but I didn't. I had headaches. I was tired. It was Valentina who suggested I might be pregnant. So I counted up the days and she got a test somewhere, and…"

She blew out a breath.

"And," he agreed. He smiled. "Does that truly require consideration? Because to me it sounds like something of a bonus, to marry the father of your child. But I am alarmingly traditional in some ways, it turns out."

Natalie scoffed at the famous daredevil prince who had so openly made a mockery of the very institutions he came from, saying such things. "What are you traditional about?"

His dark eyes gleamed. "You."

Her heart stuttered at that, but she pushed on. "And we've only had sex the one time. It could be a fluke. Do you want to base your whole life on a fluke?"

His gaze was intent on hers, with that hint of gold threaded through it, and his hands were warm even through layers and layers of fabric.

"Yes," he said. "I do."

It felt like a kiss, like fire and need, but Natalie kept going.

"You barely know me. And the little while you have known me, you thought I was someone else. Then when I told you I wasn't who you thought I was, you were sure I was either trying to con you, or crazy."

"All true." His mouth curved. "We can have a nice, long marriage and spend the rest of our days sorting it out."

"Why are you in such a rush to get married?" she demanded, sounding cross even to her own ears, and he laughed.

It was that rich, marvelous sound. Far better than Valentina's gold-plated chocolate. Far sweeter, far more complex and infinitely more satisfying.

Rodolfo stood then, rising with an unconscious display of that athletic grace of his that never failed to make her head spin.

"We are dressed for it, after all," he said. "It seems a pity to waste that dress."

She gazed up at him, caught by how beautiful he was. How intense. And how focused on her. It was hard to think of a single reason she wouldn't love him wildly and fiercely until the day she died. Whether with him or not.

Better to be with him.

Better, for once in her life, to stay where she belonged. Where after all this time, she finally *belonged*.

"Natalie." And her name—her real name at last—was like a gift on his tongue. "The bells are ringing. The cathedral is full. Your father has given his blessing and your secret twin sister, against all odds, has returned and given us her approval, too, in her fashion. But more important than all of that, you are pregnant with my child. And I have no intention of letting either one of you out of my sight ever again."

She pulled in a breath, then let it out slowly, as if she'd already decided. As if she'd already stayed.

"I risked death," Rodolfo said then, something tender in his gaze. "For fun, princess. Imagine what I can do now I have decided to live."

"Anything at all," she replied, tears of joy in her voice. Her eyes. Maybe her heart, as well. "I think you're the only one who doesn't believe in you, Rodolfo."

"I may or may not," he said quietly. "That could change with the tides. But it only matters to me if you do."

And she didn't know what she might have done then, because he held out his hand. The way he had on that dance floor in Rome.

Daring her. Challenging her.

She was the least spontaneous person in all the world, but Rodolfo made it all feel as if it was inevitable. As if she had been put on this earth for no other purpose but to love him and be loved by him in turn.

Starting right this minute, if she let it.

"Come." His voice was low. His gaze was clear. "Marry me. Be my love. All the rest will sort itself out, *princesita*, while we make love and babies with equal vigor, and rule my country well. It always does." And his smile then was brighter than the Mediterranean sun. "I love you, Natalie. Come with me. I promise you, whatever else happens, you will never regret it."

"I will hold you to that," she said, her heart in her voice.

And then she slipped her hand into Rodolfo's and let him lead her out into the glorious dance of the rest of their lives.

* * * * *

HOW TO MARRY
A PRINCESS

CHRISTINE RIMMER

For MSR,
always.

Chapter One

On the first Wednesday in September, temptation came looking for Alice Bravo-Calabretti.

And she'd been doing so well, too. For more than two weeks, she'd kept her promise to herself. She'd maintained a low profile and carried herself with dignity. She'd accepted no dares and avoided situations where she might be tempted to go too far.

It hadn't been all that difficult. She'd spent her days with her beloved horses and her nights at home. Temptation, it seemed, presented no problem when she made sure there was none.

And then came that fateful Wednesday.

It happened in the stables well before dawn. Alice was tacking up one of the mares, Yasmine, for an early-morning ride. She'd just placed the saddle well forward on the mare's sleek back when she heard a rustling sound in the deserted stable behind her.

Yasmine twitched her tail and whickered softly, her distinctive iridescent coat shimmering even in the dim light provided by the single caged bulb suspended over the stall. A glance into the shadows and Alice registered the source of the unexpected noise.

Over near the arched door that led into the courtyard, a stable hand was pushing a broom. He was no one she recognized, which she found somewhat odd. The palace stables were a second home to her. Alice knew every groom by name. He must be new.

Gilbert, the head groom, came in from the dark yard. He said something to the man with the broom. The man laughed low. Gilbert chuckled, too. Apparently the head groom liked the new man.

With a shrug, Alice gave the beautiful mare a comforting pat and finished tacking up. She was leading Yazzy out of the stall when she saw that Gilbert had gone. The stable hand remained. He'd set his broom aside and lounged against the wall by the door to the courtyard.

As she approached, the man straightened from the wall and gave her a slow nod. "Your Highness." His voice was deep and rather stirring, his attitude both ironic and confident. She recognized his accent instantly: American.

Alice had nothing against Americans. Her father was one after all. And yet...

As a rule, the grooms were Montedoran by birth— and diffident by nature. This fellow was simply not the sort Gilbert usually hired.

The groom raised his golden head. Blue eyes met hers. She saw mischief in those eyes and her heart beat faster.

Temptation. Oh, yes.

Down, girl. Get a grip.

So what if the new groom was hot? So what if just a glance from him had her thinking of how boring her life had become lately, had her imagining all kinds of inappropriate activities she might indulge in with him?

Nothing inappropriate is happening here, she reminded herself staunchly.

And then, in an attempt to appear stern and formidable, she drew her shoulders back and gave the man a slow once-over. He wore a disreputable sweatshirt with the sleeves ripped off, old jeans and older Western boots.

Hot. Definitely. Tall and fit, with a scruff of bronze beard on his lean cheeks. She wondered briefly why Gilbert hadn't required him to dress in the brown trousers, collared shirt and paddock boots worn by the rest of the stable staff.

He stepped forward and her thoughts flew off in all directions. "Such a beautiful girl," he said in a tender tone—to the mare. Alice stared, bemused, as he stroked Yazzy's long, sleek face.

Like most of her ancient hotblood breed, Yasmine was a fiercely loyal, sensitive animal. She gave her trust and affection to very few. But the bold and handsome American worked a certain magic on the golden mare. Yazzy nuzzled him and nickered fondly as he petted her.

Alice permitted his attentions to the horse. If Yazzy didn't mind, neither did she. And watching him with the mare, she began to understand why Gilbert had hired him. He had a way with horses. Plus, judging by his tattered clothing, the fellow probably needed the work. The kindhearted head groom must have taken pity on him.

Finally, the new man stepped back. "Have a nice ride, ma'am." The words were perfectly mundane, the tone pleasant and deferential. *Ma'am* was the proper form of address.

The look in his eyes, though?

Anything but proper. Far from deferential.

"Thank you. I shall." She led the mare out into the gray light of coming dawn.

* * *

The new groom had disappeared when Alice returned from her morning ride. That didn't surprise her. The grooms were often needed outside the stables.

Her country, the principality of Montedoro, was a tiny slice of paradise overlooking the Mediterranean on the Côte d'Azur. The French border lay less than two kilometers from the stables and her family owned a chain of paddocks and pastures in the nearby French countryside. A stable hand might be required to exercise the horses in some far pasture or help with cleanup or fence repair at one of the paddocks.

And honestly, what did it matter to her where the handsome American had gone off to? He was nothing to her. She resisted the urge to ask Gilbert about him and reminded herself that becoming overly curious about one of the grooms was exactly the sort of self-indulgence she couldn't permit herself anymore.

Not after the Glasgow episode.

Her face flamed just thinking about it.

And she *needed* to think about it. She needed to keep her humiliation firmly in mind in order to never allow herself to indulge in such unacceptable behavior again.

Like most of her escapades, it had begun so innocently.

On a whim, she'd decided to visit Blair Castle for the International Horse Trials and Country Fair. She'd flown to Perth the week before the trials thinking she would spend a few days touring Scotland.

She'd never made it to Blair Castle. She'd met up with some friends in Perth and driven with them down to Glasgow. Such fun, a little pub hopping. They'd found this one lovely, rowdy pub and it was karaoke night.

Alice had enjoyed a pint or two more than she should have. Her bodyguard, huge, sweet old Altus, had caught her eye more than once and given her *the look*—the one meant to warn her that she was going too far, the one that rarely did any good.

As usual, she'd ignored *the look*. Repeatedly. And then, somehow, there she was up on the stage singing that Katy Perry song, "I Kissed a Girl." At the time, it had seemed like harmless fun. She'd thrown herself into her performance and acted out the lyrics.

Pictures of her soul-kissing that cute Glaswegian barmaid with her skirt hiked up and her top halfway off had been all over the scandal sheets. The paparazzi had had a field day. Her mother, the sovereign princess, had not been amused.

And after that, Alice had sworn to herself that she would do better from now on—which definitely meant steering clear of brash, scruffy American stable hands who made her pulse race.

The next morning, Thursday, the new groom appeared again. He was there, busy with his broom, when she entered the stables at five. The sight of him, in the same disreputable jeans and torn sweatshirt as the day before, caused a thoroughly annoying flutter in her solar plexus, as well as a definite feeling of breathlessness.

To cover her absurd excitement over seeing him again, she said, "Excuse me," in a snooty abovestairs-at-Downton-Abbey tone that she instantly regretted, a tone that had her wondering if she might be trying *too* hard to behave. "I didn't catch your name."

He stopped sweeping. "Noah. Ma'am."

"Ah. Well. Noah…" She was suddenly as tongue-tied

as a preteen shaking hands with Justin Bieber. Ridiculous. Completely ridiculous. "Would you saddle Kajar for me, please?" She gave a vague wave of her hand toward the stall where the gray gelding waited. As a rule, she personally tacked up any horse she rode. It helped her read the horse's mood and condition and built on the bond she established with each of the animals in her care.

But once she'd opened her mouth, she'd had to come up with a logical excuse for talking to him.

And she was curious. Would he work the same magic, establish the same instant comfortable rapport with Kajar as he had with Yazzy?

The groom—Noah—set aside his broom and went to work. Kajar stood patiently under his firm, calm hands. Noah praised the horse as he worked, calling him fine and handsome and good. The gelding gave no trouble through the process. On the contrary. Twice Kajar turned his long, graceful neck to whicker at Noah as though in approval and affection.

Once the job was done, the groom led the horse from the stall and passed Alice the reins. His long fingers whispered across her gloved palm and were gone. For a moment she caught the scent of his clean, healthy skin. He wore a light aftershave. It smelled of citrus, of sun and cedar trees.

She should have said, "Thank you," and led the horse out to ride. But he drew her so strongly. She found herself instigating an actual conversation. "You're not Montedoran."

"How did you guess?" Softly. With humor and a nice touch of irony.

"You're American."

"That's right." He looked at her steadily, those eyes

of his so blue they seemed almost otherworldly. "I grew up in California, in Los Angeles. In Silver Lake and East L.A." He was watching her in that way he had: with total concentration. A wry smile stretched the corners of his mouth. "You have no idea where Silver Lake is, or East L.A., do you? Ma'am." He was teasing her.

She felt a prickle of annoyance, which only increased her interest in him. "I have a basic understanding, yes. I've been to Southern California. I have a second cousin there. He and his family live in Bel Air."

"Bel Air is a long way from East L.A."

She leaned into Kajar, cupping her hand to his far cheek, resting her head against his long, fine neck. The gelding didn't object, only made a soft snuffling sound. "A long distance, you mean?"

One strong shoulder lifted in a shrug. "It's not so far in miles. However, Bel Air has some of the priciest real estate in the world—kind of like here in Montedoro. East L.A.? Not so much."

She didn't want to talk about real estate. Or class differences. And she needed to be on her way. She went as far as to stop leaning on the horse—but then, what do you know? She opened her mouth and another question popped out. "Do your parents still live there?"

"No. My father was killed working construction when I was twelve. My mother died of the flu when I was twenty-one."

Sympathy for him moved within her, twining with the excitement she felt at his nearness. Kajar tossed his head. She turned to the gelding, reaching up to stroke his elegant face, settling him. And then she said to Noah, "That is too sad."

"It is what it is."

She faced the groom fully again. "It must have been horrible for you."

"I learned to depend on myself."

"Do you have brothers and sisters?"

"A younger sister. Lucy is twenty-three."

She wanted to ask *his* age—but somehow that seemed such an intimate question. There were fine lines at the corners of his eyes. He had to be at least thirty. "What brings you to Montedoro?"

He seemed faintly amused. "You're full of questions, Your Highness."

She answered honestly. "It's true. I'm being very nosy." *And it's time for me to go.* But she didn't go. She kept right on being as nosy as before. "How long have you been here, in my country?"

"Not long at all."

"Do you plan to stay on?"

"That depends…."

"On?"

He didn't answer, only held her gaze.

She felt the loveliest, most effervescent sensation. Like champagne sliding, cool and fizzy, down her throat. "You love horses."

"Yes, I do. And you're wondering how a guy from East L.A. learned to handle horses…."

Tell him that you really do have to go. "I have been wondering exactly that."

"When I was eighteen, I went to work for a man who owned a horse ranch in the Santa Monica Mountains. He taught me a lot. And I learned fast. He kept warm bloods. Hanoverians and Morgans, mostly."

"Excellent breeds." She nodded in approval. "Strong, steady and handsome. Not nearly so testy and sensitive as an Akhal-Teke." All her horses were Tekes. Akhal-Tekes were called the "heavenly horses," the oldest breed on earth. Originating in the rugged deserts of Turkmenistan and northern Iran, the Teke was swift and temperamental and very tough. Both Genghis Khan and Alexander the Great chose Akhal-Tekes to carry them into battle.

"There is nothing like an Akhal-Teke," he said. "I hope to own one someday."

"An admirable goal."

He chuckled and the sound seemed to slide like a sweet caress across her skin. "Aren't you going to tell me that I'll never be able to afford one?"

"That would be rude. And besides, you seem a very determined sort of person. I would imagine that if you want something strongly enough, you'll find a way to have it." He said nothing, only regarded her steadily through those beautiful eyes. She was struck with the sense that there was much more going on here than she understood. "What is it?" she asked finally, when the silence had stretched thin.

"I *am* determined."

She found herself staring at his mouth. The shape of it—the slight bow of his top lip, the fullness below—was so intriguing. She wondered what it might feel like, that mouth of his touching hers. It would be so very easy to step in close, go on tiptoe and claim a kiss....

Stop. No. Wrong. Exactly the sort of foolish, bold, unprincess-like behavior she was supposed to be avoiding at all costs.

"I..." She was still staring at his lips.

"Yeah?" He moved an inch closer.

She clutched the reins tighter. "...really must be on my way."

He instantly stepped back and she wished that he hadn't—which was not only contrary but completely unacceptable. "Ride safe, ma'am."

She nodded, pressing her lips together to keep them from trembling. Then she clucked her tongue at Kajar and turned for the wide-open stable door.

Once again he was gone when she returned from her ride. That day, she worked with a couple of the yearlings and put one of the show jumpers through his paces. Later she went home to shower and change.

In the afternoon, she met with the planning committee for next year's Grand Champions Tour. Montedoro would host the sixth leg of the tour down at the harbor show grounds in June. Through the endless meeting, she tried very hard not to think of blue eyes, not to remember the deep, stirring sound of a certain voice.

That night, alone in her bed, she dreamed she went riding with Noah. She was on Yasmine and he rode the bay stallion Orion. They stopped in a meadow of wildflowers and talked, though when she woke she couldn't remember a thing they had said.

It was a very tame dream. Not once did they touch, and there was none of the heated tension she had felt when she'd actually been near him. In the dream they laughed together. They were like longtime companions who knew each other well.

She woke Friday morning as usual, long before dawn, feeling edgy and dissatisfied, her mind on the American.

Why? She hardly knew this man. She *didn't* know him. She'd seen him twice and shared one brief conversation with him. He should not have affected her so profoundly.

Then again, there was probably nothing profound about it. He was hot and mysterious, untamed and somehow slightly dangerous. He called to her wild side. She found him madly attractive.

Plus, well, maybe she'd been keeping too much to herself. She wanted to avoid getting wild in the streets, but that didn't mean she couldn't have a life. She'd been sticking *too* close to home. This obsession with Noah was clear proof that she needed to get out more.

And she would get out, starting that very evening with a gala party at the palace, a celebration of her sister Rhiannon's recent marriage to Commandant Marcus Desmarais. It would be lovely. She would enjoy herself. She would dance all night.

She rose and dressed and went to the stables, expecting to see Noah again, unsure whether she *wanted* to see him—or wished that he wouldn't be there.

He wasn't there.

And her uncertainty vanished. She *did* want to see him, to hear his voice again, to find out if her response to him was as strong as it had seemed yesterday. As she tacked up the black mare Prizma, she was alert every moment for the telltale sound of someone entering the stables behind her. But no one came.

She went for her ride, returning to find that he still wasn't there. She almost asked Gilbert about him.

But she felt too foolish and confused—which wasn't like her at all. She was a confident person, always had been. She spoke her mind and had few fears. Yes, she was making a definite effort not to get into situations that might attract the attention of the tabloids and embarrass her family. But that didn't mean she was all tied up in emotional knots. She liked to live expansively, to take chances, to have fun.

She was no shy little virgin afraid to ask a few questions about a man who interested her.

The problem was…

Wait a minute. There *was* no problem. She'd met a man and found him attractive. She might or might not see him again. If she ever did get something going with him, well, it *could* be a bit awkward. She was a princess of Montedoro and he was a penniless American from a place called East Los Angeles.

They didn't exactly have a whole lot in common.

Except that they did. She *was* half American after all. And they both loved horses. And she had so enjoyed talking with him. Plus, he was very easy on the eyes.…

She'd made way too much of this and she was stopping that right now. He was only a man she found intriguing. She might see him again.

And she might not. The world would go on turning however things worked out.

At six o'clock, Alice returned to her villa on a steep street in the ward of Monagalla, not far from the palace. Her housekeeper, Michelle Thierry, met her at the front door.

"I thought you'd never get back," the housekeeper chided. "Have you forgotten your sister's party?"

"Of course not. Relax. There's plenty of time."

"You're to be there at eight, you said," Michelle accused.

"Oh, come on. It's definitely doable."

Michelle wrinkled her nose. "What *have* you stepped in?"

"I work all day with horses. Take a guess."

The housekeeper waved her hands. "Don't just stand there. Get out of those boots and come inside. We'll have to hurry. There's so much to do...."

"You are way too bossy."

Michelle granted her a smug smile. "But you couldn't get along without me."

It was only the truth.

In her late forties, Michelle was a wonder. She not only took excellent care of the villa but also cooked beautiful meals and played lady's maid with skill and flair. Michelle loved her work and had impeccable taste. Alice knew she was lucky to have her.

Laughing, she perched on the step and took off her boots, which the housekeeper instantly whisked from her hands.

"The bath," Michelle commanded, waving a soiled boot. "Immediately."

Alice had her bath, did her hair and makeup, put on the red silk-taffeta Oscar de la Renta that Michelle had chosen for her and then sat impatiently, fully dressed except for her shoes, while Michelle repaired her manicure and pedicure and clucked over her for not taking proper care of her hands.

The car was waiting outside when she left the villa at ten of eight. The drive up to Cap Royale, the bluff overlooking the Mediterranean on which the Prince's Palace sprawled in all its white stone glory, should have taken only a few minutes. But the streets were packed with limousines on their way to the party. Alice could have walked it faster—and at one time, she would have simply told the driver to pull over and let her out. But no. The goal was to be more dignified, less of a wild child. She stayed in her limo like everyone else. The car finally reached the palace at 8:28 p.m. Hardly late at all, the way Alice saw it. But her mother would think otherwise. Her Sovereign Highness Adrienne expected the members of her family to arrive promptly at important events.

The guests in their gala finery were still streaming in the red-carpeted main entrance. Alice had the driver take her around to a side door where two stern-faced palace guards waited to let in intimate friends and members of the princely family. She gave her light wrap and bag to a servant.

Then she took a series of marble hallways to another exit—the one that led out to the colonnade above the palace gardens. Alice paused at the top of the white stone stairs leading down to the garden.

Below, a giant white silk tent had been erected. Golden light glowed from within the tent, where dinner for three hundred would be served. The palace, the tent, the gardens, the whole of Montedoro—everything seemed ablaze with golden light.

"There you are." Her sister Rhiannon, five months pregnant and glowing with happiness, clutched the frothy tiered skirts of her strapless ivory gown and sailed up the stairs to Alice's side, her growing baby bump leading the way.

Alice adored all four of her sisters, but she and Rhia shared a special bond. They were best friends. "Sorry I'm a little late. The streets are awash in limousines."

The sisters shared a quick hug and kissed the air by each other's cheeks. Rhia whispered, "I'm just glad you're here. I've missed you...." Flashes went off. There were always photographers lurking around, way too many of them at an event like this.

Alice hooked her arm through Rhia's. They turned as

one to face the cameras. "Smile," Alice advised softly, trying not to move her lips. "Show no weakness."

Rhia braced her free hand proudly on the bulge of her tummy and smiled for the cameras. She had a lot to be happy about. For almost a decade she'd struggled to deny her love for Marcus Desmarais. Now, at last, she and her lifetime love were together in the most complete way. Rhia and Marcus had married in a small private ceremony three weeks ago. They'd flown off for a honeymoon in the Caribbean on the same day Alice had made that fateful trip to Scotland.

The party tonight was in lieu of the usual big wedding. The world needed to see how the Bravo-Calabretti family welcomed the new husband of one of their own.

Rhia's groom had been orphaned soon after his birth. He'd started with nothing—and become a fine man, one who'd gone far in spite of his humble beginnings. The party wasn't just for show. The Bravo-Calabrettis did welcome him.

Alice loved that about her family. They judged a man—or a woman—by his or her behavior and accomplishments. Not by an accident of birth or a string of inherited titles. If Alice were to choose a man with nothing, her family would support her in her choice.

Not that she was anywhere close to choosing anyone. Certainly not a bold blue-eyed American she'd only just met and would likely not see again.

She banished the stable hand from her mind—yet again—as Rhia grabbed her hand and pulled her down the curving staircase. They wove their way through the crowd toward the wide-open entrance to the big white tent. Alice spotted her brother Damien, the youngest of the four Bravo-Calabretti princes, entering the tent, his dark head thrown back as he laughed at something the tall golden-haired man beside him had said....

"Allie?" Rhia turned back to her with a puzzled frown.

Alice realized she'd stopped in midstep at the base of the stairs and was staring with her mouth hanging open. Her brother and the other man disappeared inside the tent. She'd only caught the briefest glimpse of the other man from the back. And then from the side, for that split second when he'd turned his head. "It can't be..."

"Allie?" her sister asked again.

"I could have sworn..."

"Are you all right?" A worried frown creased the space between Rhia's smooth brows.

Alice blinked and shook her head. Lovely. Not only was she obsessing over a near stranger, she was also hallucinating that she saw the same man, perfectly turned out in white tie and tails, chatting up her brother. "Did you see that tall blond man with Dami? They just went inside the tent."

"Dami? I didn't notice."

"You didn't notice Dami, or the man with him?"

"Either. Allie, really. Are you all right?"

"I'm beginning to wonder about that," she muttered.

"You're mumbling. Say again?"

Alice would have loved to drag her favorite sister off somewhere private, where she could tell her all about the scruffy, sexy, unforgettable stable hand—whom she could have sworn she'd just seen wearing a perfectly cut designer tailcoat and evening trousers and sharing a joke with their brother. She wanted a comforting hug and some solid, down-to-earth advice. But now was not the time. She tugged on Rhia's hand. "It doesn't matter. Come on. Let's go in. Marcus will be wondering where you've gone."

The family table was a long one, set up on a dais at the far end of the tent. All their brothers and sisters were there. The married ones had come with their spouses. Even dear Belle, who lived in America now with her horse-rancher husband, Preston McCade, had come all the way from Montana to celebrate with Rhia and Marcus. Only the little nieces and nephews were missing tonight. This was a grown-up party after all.

Rhia whispered, "We never have time to talk anymore."

"I know. I miss you, too."

"Come to our villa at seven Sunday night. We'll have dinner, catch up. Just the two of us."

"What about Marcus?"

"He's dining at the palace with Alex. Something about the CCU." Alexander, Damien's twin, was third-born of their brothers. Alex had created the elite fighting force the Covert Command Unit, in which Marcus served.

"I'll be there," Alice promised.

With a last hug, Rhia left her to join her groom in her seat of honor at the center of the table.

Alice went to greet her parents. Her mother, looking amazing as always in beaded black Chanel, gave her a kiss and a fond, "Hello, my darling," and didn't say a word about her tardiness. Her mother was like that. HSH Adrienne had high expectations, but she'd never been one to nag.

In the past, Alice had crashed a motorcycle in the marketplace, run off with a sheikh for a week in Marrakech, been photographed for *Vanity Fair* wearing only a cleverly draped silk scarf and been arrested in Beijing for participating in a protest march. Among other things.

Until Glasgow, her mother had never done more than gently remind her that she was a princess of Montedoro and expected to behave like one. But after Glasgow, for the first time, Alice had been summoned to her mother's office. HSH Adrienne had asked her to shut the door and then coolly informed her that she'd finally gone too far.

"Alice," her mother had said much too sadly, too gently, "it's one thing to be spirited and adventurous. It's another to be an embarrassment to yourself and our family. In future I am counting on you to exercise better judgment and to avoid situations that will lead to revealing, provocative pictures of you splashed across the front pages of the *Sun* and the *Daily Star*."

It had been awful. Just thinking about it made her feel a little sick to her stomach.

And sad, too. A bit wilted and grim.

Shake it off, she commanded herself. *Let it go.*

Alice looked for her place card and found it between her older sister Belle's husband, Preston McCade, and her younger sister Genevra. Genny wore shimmering teal-blue satin and was giggling over something with another sister, the youngest, Rory, who was seated on Genny's other side.

Damien sat at the opposite end of the table. No sign of the man who looked like Noah. Alice considered hustling down there and asking Dami…what?

Who was that man with the dark blond hair, the one you came in with?

And what if he stared at her blankly and demanded, *Allie, darling, what man?*

She waffled just long enough that she missed her

chance. Her mother rose and greeted the guests. A hush fell over the tent. Then her father stood, as well. He picked up his champagne glass to propose the first toast.

Allie reached for her glass, raised it high and drank on cue. Then she took her seat. She greeted her sisters and Preston, whom she liked a lot. He was charming and a little shy, with a great sense of humor. He bred and trained quarter horses, so they had plenty to talk about.

There were more toasts. Alice paced herself, taking very small sips of champagne, practicing being low-key and composed for all she was worth. By the time the appetizer was served, she felt glad she hadn't asked Dami about the broad-shouldered stranger with the dark gold hair and perfectly cut evening clothes.

It was nothing. It didn't matter. She would have a fine evening celebrating her dearest sister's hard-earned happiness. And no one else would know that she'd imagined she saw someone who wasn't really there. She accepted a second glass of champagne from a passing servant and picked up a spear of prosciutto-wrapped asparagus—and then almost dropped the hors d'oeuvre in her lap when she glanced over and saw Noah.

He wore the same perfect evening attire she'd glimpsed earlier. And he sat between a stunning blonde and a gorgeous redhead several tables away, staring right at her.

Chapter Two

Noah was watching Alice when she spotted him. Her mouth dropped open. Her face went dead white.

About then it occurred to him that maybe he'd carried his innocent deception a little too far.

She pressed her lips together and looked away, turning to her younger sister on her right side, forcing a smile. He waited for her to glance his way again.

Didn't happen.

Jennifer, the redhead seated on his left, put her hand on his thigh and asked him how he was enjoying his visit to Montedoro. He gently eased her hand away and said he was having a great time.

She hit him with a melting, eager look and said, "I'm so pleased to have met you, Noah, and I hope we can spend some time together during your stay. I would just love to show you the *real* Montedoro."

Andrea, the blonde on his other side, cut in, saving him the necessity of giving Jennifer an answer. "I love all of Prince Dami's friends," Andrea said. "Dami and I were once, well, very close. But then he met Vesuvia." A model and sometime actress, Vesuvia was often called simply V. "Dami is exclusive with V now," Andrea added. None of what she'd said was news to Noah. Or to anyone else, for that matter. "They're all over the tabloids, Dami and V," Andrea whispered breathlessly. She was mistress of the obvious in a big, big way.

"Or at least, the prince is *mostly* exclusive with V," Jennifer put in with a wicked little giggle. She fluttered her eyelashes at him. "I mean, they *are* always fighting and I notice that V's not here tonight...."

The meal wore on. Jennifer and Andrea kept up a steady stream of teasing chatter. Noah sipped champagne and hoped that Alice might grant him a second look.

If she did, he failed to catch it.

Had he blown it with her, misjudged her completely? It was starting to look that way.

But no. It couldn't be.

She'd assumed he was an itinerant stable hand and all he'd done was play along. He'd thought she would find the whole thing funny.

It hadn't even occurred to him that she might be upset about it. How could he have gotten it so wrong? He'd done his research on her after all. She was bold and curious and ready for anything, the darling of the scandal sheets. He'd never imagined she would freak out when she finally saw him as he really was.

So what did he do now?

He wouldn't give up, that was for damn sure. Not now that he'd met her, talked to her, seen her smile, looked in those eyes of hers that could be blue or gray or green, depending on the light and her shifting mood. Not now that he'd discovered she was *exactly* the woman he'd been looking for—and more.

Somehow he would have to make amends.

The meal finally ended. Princess Adrienne rose and congratulated the newlyweds again. She wished them a lifetime of married bliss. Then she invited the guests to enjoy the moonlit garden and to dance the night away in the palace ballroom upstairs.

Jennifer whispered an invitation in his ear. He turned to express his regrets.

When he glanced toward the dais again, Alice was gone.

Alice slipped out of the tent through the servants' entrance behind the dais.

She'd recovered from her initial shock at the sight of Noah sitting between those two beautiful women, looking as though he belonged there. At least by the end of dinner, she'd become reasonably certain she wasn't hallucinating. He was not a bizarre figment of her overactive imagination. The man who looked exactly like Noah the stable hand really did exist.

That meant she wasn't losing her mind after all—a fact she found wonderfully reassuring.

But *was* he actually the same man she'd first met sweeping the stable floor before dawn on Wednesday morning? Was this some kind of bizarre practical joke he was playing on her? And if so, did that make him a palace groom posing as a guest at the palace? Or a jet-setter friend of her brother's who enjoyed masquerading as the help?

She considered tracking down Dami and quizzing him about that friend of his who looked exactly like the poverty-stricken groom she'd met Wednesday.

But no. Not tonight. Damien might be able to enlighten her, but then he would have questions of his own. She just wasn't up for answering Dami's questions. And it didn't matter anyway. She knew what to do: forget it. Forget *him*.

It was all too weird. It made no sense and she wasn't going to think about it.

She would enjoy the rest of the evening and move on.

A familiar voice behind her said, "Allie, I haven't seen you in ages."

She turned to smile at a longtime friend. "Robert. How have you been?"

"I can't complain." Robert Bentafaille was compact and muscular, with an open face and kind green eyes. The Bentafailles owned orange groves. Lots of them. He and Alice were the same age and had gone through primary and secondary school together. "You look beautiful, as always."

"And you always say that."

"I hear the orchestra." He cast a glance back at the palace, at the lights blazing in the upstairs ballroom. Music drifted down to them. He offered his hand.

She took it and they turned together to go inside.

Alice danced two dances with Robert.

Then another longtime friend, Clark deRoncleff, tapped Robert on the shoulder. She turned into Clark's open arms and danced some more.

After that she left the floor, accepted a glass of sparkling water from a passing servant and visited with Rhia and Marcus for a bit. Rhia was sharing her plans for the nursery when Alice spotted Dami across the dance floor. He was talking to the man who almost certainly was Noah. She stared for a moment too long.

The man who had to be Noah seemed to sense her gaze on him. He turned. Their eyes met. His were every bit as blue as she remembered.

She had no doubt now. It had to be him. Quickly, she

turned away and gave her full attention to Rhia and her groom.

Noah didn't matter to her. She hardly knew him. She refused to care what he was doing there at her sister's wedding party or what he might be up to.

Marcus asked Rhia to dance. They went off together, holding hands, looking so happy it made Alice feel downright misty-eyed and more than a little bit envious.

Her eldest brother, Maximilian, came toward her. The heir to their mother's throne, Max was handsome and magnetic—like all of her brothers. He used to be a happy man. But three years ago his wife, Sophia, had died in a waterskiing accident. Max had loved Sophia since they were children. Now he was like a ghost of himself. He went through all the motions of living. But some essential element was missing. Sophia had given him two children, providing him with the customary heir and a spare to the throne. He didn't have to marry again—and he probably never would.

"We hardly see you lately," Max chided. "You haven't been to Sunday breakfast in weeks." It was a family tradition: Sunday breakfast in the sovereign's private apartments at the palace. She and her siblings were grown now, but they all tried to show up for the Sunday-morning meal whenever they were in Montedoro.

"I've been busy with my horses."

"Of course you have." Max leaned closer. "You did nothing wrong. Don't ever let them crush your spirit."

She knew whom he meant by *them:* the paparazzi and the tabloid journos. "Oh, Max…"

"You are confident and curious. You like to get out and mix it up. It's who you are. We all love you as you are and we know it was only in fun."

"I'm not so sure about Mother."

"She's on your side and she never judges. You know that."

"What I know is that I've finally managed to embarrass her." It wasn't so much that she'd French-kissed a girl. It was the pictures. They came off so tacky, like something out of *Girls Gone Wild.*

"I think you're wrong. Mother is not embarrassed. And she loves you unconditionally."

Alice didn't have the heart to argue about it, to insist that their mother *was* embarrassed; she'd said so. Instead, she leaned close to him and whispered, "Thank you."

He smiled his sad smile. "Dance?" Though Max would never marry again, women were constantly trying to snare him. They all wanted to console the widower prince who would someday rule Montedoro. So he tried to steer clear of them. At balls, he danced with his mother and his sisters and then retired early.

"I would love to dance with you." She pulled him out onto the floor and they danced through the rest of that number and the next one.

Before they parted, he asked her directly to come to the family breakfast that Sunday. "Please. Say you'll be here. We miss you."

She gave in and promised she would come, and then she walked with him to where their youngest sister, Rory, chatted with Lani Vasquez. Small, dark-haired and curvy, Lani was an American, an aspiring author of historical novels set in Montedoro. She'd come from America with Sydney O'Shea when Sydney had married Rule, the second-born of Alice's brothers.

Alice had assumed Max would dance next with Rory.

But he took Lani's hand instead. The music started up again and Max led the pretty American onto the floor.

Rory said, "Well, well."

"My, my," Alice murmured in agreement. For a moment the two sisters watched in amazement as their tragically widowed eldest brother danced with someone who wasn't his sister.

Then a girlfriend of Rory's appeared out of the crowd. She grabbed Rory's hand and towed her toward the open doors to the balcony. Alice considered following them. It was a lovely night. She could lean on the stone railing and gaze out over the harbor, admire the lights of the casino and the luxury shops and hotels that surrounded it.

"Alice. Dance with me."

The deep, thrilling voice came from directly behind her and affected her just as it had when they were alone in the stables. It seemed to slip beneath her skin, to shiver its way along the bumps of her spine, to create a warm pool of longing down in the deepest core of her.

She didn't turn. Instead, she stared blindly toward the open doors to the balcony. She wasn't even going to acknowledge him. She would start walking and she wouldn't look back.

If he dared to come after her, she would cut him dead.

But really, what would that prove? That she was afraid to deal with him? That she didn't have the stones to stand her ground and face him, to find out from his own mouth what kind of game he was playing with her? That Max had been right and the tacky tabloid reporters, the shameless paparazzi, really had done it? They'd broken her spirit, made her into someone unwilling to face a challenge head-on.

Oh, no. No way.

She whirled on him and glared into his too-blue eyes. "It *is* you."

He nodded. He held out his hand. "Let me explain. Give me that chance."

She kept her arm at her side. "I don't trust you."

"I know." He didn't lower his hand. The man had nerves of steel.

And she couldn't bear it, to let him stand there with his hand offered and untaken. She laid her fingers into his palm. Heat radiated up her arm just from that first contact. Her breath caught and tangled in her chest.

How absurd. Breathe.

With slow care, she sucked in a breath and then let it out as he turned and led her onto the floor. She went into his arms. They danced.

He had the good sense to hold her lightly. For a few endless minutes, neither of them spoke, which was just as well as far as Alice was concerned. She longed to wave her arms about and shriek accusations at him. Unfortunately, shrieking and waving her arms would attract attention, and that would no doubt land her on the front pages of the tabloids again.

She caught a hint of his aftershave. Evergreen and citrus, the same as before. It was all too disorienting. She'd thought he was one person and now here he was, someone else altogether. She felt shy. Tongue-tied. Young.

And at a definite disadvantage. She needed to take back the upper hand here. She had questions for him. And he'd better have good answers.

The next song began, a fast one. Couples separated and danced facing each other, moving to the beat but not touching. Noah didn't let her go, just picked up the rhythm a bit and danced them out of the way of the others.

"You're angry," he said at last.

"What happened to your two girlfriends?"

"What girlfriends?"

"That sexy redhead and the stunning blonde."

"They're not my girlfriends." He kept his voice low, but he did pull her fractionally closer. She allowed that in order to hear him over the music. "They were seated on either side of me at dinner, that's all."

"They seemed very friendly." She spoke quietly, too. She didn't want anyone overhearing, broadcasting their conversation, starting new rumors about her.

He held her even closer and whispered much too tenderly, "Is that somehow my fault?"

She fumed in silence, refusing to answer. Finally, she demanded, "Who are you, really?"

"I'm who I said I was."

"Noah."

"Yes."

"Do you have a last name?"

"Cordell." He turned her swiftly and gracefully to the music, guiding her effortlessly, keeping them to the outer edges of the floor.

"*Are* you a stable hand?"

"No. And I didn't say I was. You assumed that."

"And you never bothered to enlighten me. Do you live in Los Angeles?"

"No. Not for years. I have an estate in Carpinteria, not far from Santa Barbara. I live there most of the time. I also have a flat I keep in London. And a Paris apartment."

"So you should have no trouble affording that Akhal-Teke you said you want."

"No trouble at all. But it's a specific horse I'm after."

She should have known. "Let me guess. One of mine?"

"Orion."

She drew in a sharp breath. In that foolish dream of hers, he'd been riding Orion. "I'm not selling you Orion." That was a bit petty, and she knew it. Not to mention a bad business move. Alice bred her horses for sale—to buyers who would love them and bond with them and treat them well, buyers who appreciated the beauty and rarity of the breed. Her pool of buyers was a small one, as she also demanded a high price for her Tekes. She might be angry with Noah, but he knew horses and loved them. She'd be smarter not to reject him out of hand—as a potential buyer, anyway. "I don't wish to discuss my horses with you right now."

"You brought it up." The next song was a slower one. He effortlessly adjusted to the change in tempo, all the while gazing down at her, watching her mouth. As if he planned to kiss her—a bold move he had better not try.

She accused, "I brought it up as an example of the way that you lied to me. Not with words, maybe. But by implication. By action. The first time I saw you, you were sweeping the stable floor. Gilbert seemed to know you. What else was I to assume but that he'd hired you?"

"Gilbert was joking with me. He saw me sweeping and asked me if I needed a job. Your brother Damien had introduced us the day before. Dami knows I love horses and wanted me to have a chance to ride while I was here. And I had told him I was hoping to buy one of your stallions. He said I would have to talk to you about that."

"You're great friends, then, you and my brother?"

"Yes. I consider Damien a friend."

She thought again of the blonde and the redhead at

dinner. He'd seemed to take their fawning attentions as his due. "You're a player. Like Dami."

"I'm single. I enjoy a good life and I like the company of beautiful women."

"You're a player."

"I am not playing you, Alice." He held her gaze. Steadily. Somehow the very steadiness of his regard excited her.

She did not wish to be excited. "You've been playing me from the moment you picked up that broom and pretended to be someone you're not."

"Everything I told you was true. Everything. Yes, I've got all I'll ever need now, but I started out in L.A. with nothing. My parents were both dead by the time I was twenty-one. I have one sister, Lucy."

"And you went to work on a ranch when you were eighteen?"

"No. I visited that ranch. Often. My boss took a liking to me. He flipped houses in Los Angeles for a living and he hired me as a day laborer to start. I learned the business from the ground up, beginning on his low-end properties in East L.A."

"You're saying you learned fast?" She wasn't surprised.

"Before the crash, I was buying and selling in all the major markets. I got out ahead of the collapse with a nice nest egg. Now I manage my investments and I do what I want with the rest of my time. Oh, and that second cousin you mentioned, the one who lives in Bel Air?"

"Jonas."

He nodded. "I know him. Jonas Bravo and I have done business on a couple of occasions. He's a good man." He pulled her a little closer again. She allowed that, though she knew that she probably shouldn't. They danced without talking for a minute or two.

Finally, she muttered grudgingly, "You should have told me all of this at the first."

"I can see that now." He sounded so...sincere. As though he truly regretted misleading her.

She tried not to soften. "Why didn't you, then?"

"Alice, I..." The words trailed off.

"At a loss? I don't believe it. Just tell me. Why weren't you honest with me from the first?"

"I don't know, exactly. Because it was fun. Exciting. To tease you."

She started to smile and caught herself. "That's not a satisfactory answer."

"Look. I came early to ride and I saw you there, saddling that beautiful mare. It was still dark out and there was no one else around. I didn't want to scare you. I picked up the broom and started sweeping, because what's more nonthreatening than some guy sweeping the floor? And then... I don't know. You thought I was a groom and you talked to me anyway. I liked that. I got into it, that's all. In a way, the Noah you met in the stables really is me. Just...another possible me. The one who didn't make a fortune in real estate. I thought it would be something we would laugh over later."

The dance ended. For a moment they swayed together at the edge of the floor. She should have pulled away.

She stayed right where she was.

He was getting to her. She was liking him again. Believing the things he told her....

Yet another song started.

He pulled her even closer and whispered, his breath warm across her skin, "I screwed up, okay?" He whirled her around. They danced in a circle along the outer rim of the floor.

"You knew who I was from the first. Before we met. Right?"

He pulled back enough to give her a look. Patient. Ironic. "Please. I'm friends with your brother. He's told me about you—and your sisters and brothers. Also, I want one of your stallions and I know you're quite a horse trader, not only brutal when striking a bargain but particular about whom you'll sell to. I've made it my business to learn everything I can about you."

Which meant he would have seen the Glasgow pictures.

Well, so what? She'd done what she'd done. She'd gone over the top and she'd suffered for it. She was tired of being ashamed. "You know all about me? That sounds vaguely stalkerish."

He shrugged, his muscular shoulder lifting and then settling under her hand. "You could look at it that way, I suppose. Or you could admit that it's just good sense to find out what you can about the people you'll be dealing with."

"So of course you won't mind if I track you down online the next chance I get."

"I would expect nothing less." And he smiled, rueful. And somehow hopeful, too. He was way too charming when he smiled. "And when you find out I've told the truth, do I get another chance with you?"

All at once she was too sharply aware of his hand holding hers, his warm fingers and firm palm at her back, his big body brushing hers. Little arrows of sensation seemed to zip around beneath her skin. "A chance with me? I thought we were talking about your buying Orion."

He eased her closer. His breath touched her hair and his body burned into hers. Her skin felt electrified. And he whispered, "You know we're talking about more than the horse. Who's lying now? Ma'am?"

She liked it too much, dancing so close to him. She liked *him* too much. "Please don't hold me so tightly."

He instantly obeyed, loosening his hold so he embraced her easily, lightly, again. "Better?"

She nodded, thinking that this particular Noah, self-assured and sophisticated in evening dress, was every bit as brash and manly as the one she'd assumed was a groom. And smooth, too. She hadn't planned to forgive him for pretending to be a penniless stable hand—but somehow she already had.

And not only had she forgiven him, she was actually considering letting him have Orion after all. Because she did like him and she'd seen him with her horses. Orion would thrive in Noah's care.

He pulled her closer again. She allowed that. It felt good and she wasn't really afraid of him. She was afraid of *herself*, of her too-powerful response to him. And then there was her basic problem: it had always been so easy for her to get carried away. She would have to watch herself.

Then again, her goal tonight had been to get out and have a little fun.

So all right. It shouldn't be too difficult to do both—to have a little fun and yet not get carried away.

They danced the rest of that dance without talking. When it ended, they swayed together until the next dance began and then danced some more.

"Walk in the garden with me," he said when that song was over.

"Yes. I would like that."

He took her hand and led her from the dance floor.

It was going pretty well, Noah thought as he walked with her down the stone stairway that led to the big tent and the palace gardens beyond. She seemed to have gotten past her fury with him for pretending to be someone he wasn't. But he sensed a certain residual wariness in her. Which was fine. Few things worth winning came easily.

"Something to drink?" he asked.

"I would like that."

So they stopped in the tent, where waiters offered wine and cocktails and soft drinks, too. They both took flutes of champagne and went out the back exit behind the dais into the moonlit garden strung with party lights.

She said, "You implied when we talked in the stables that you were staying in Montedoro indefinitely...."

"Not anymore. It turns out there are a couple of meetings I have to get back for. I'll be leaving Thursday."

"Is your sister visiting with you?"

"No, she's at home in California."

"I assume Dami has you staying here at the palace?"

He shook his head. "Lots of guests at the palace this weekend. I went ahead and took a suite at the Belle Époque." The five-star hotel was across from Casino d'Ambre.

Another couple came toward them. They nodded in greeting as they passed. When it was just the two of them again, Alice said, "I love the Belle Époque. We used to go for afternoon tea there now and then when I was a girl, my sisters and I. We would get our favorite table—on the mezzanine of the winter garden, with that amazing dome of stained glass and steel overhead. I would stuff myself with tea cakes, and the governess, Miss Severly, would have to reprimand me."

"Governess? I thought your brother said you all went to Montedoran schools."

"We did. But after we grew out of our nanny, Gerta, we also had Miss Severly. She tutored us between school terms and tried to drum good manners into us."

"Were you scared of your governess?"

"Not in the least. Once reprimanded, I only grew more determined. At tea I would wait until Miss Severly looked the other way and then try to stuff down as many cakes as I could before she glanced at me again."

"Did you make yourself sick?"

She slanted him a glance. "How did you know?"

He thought of all the tabloid stories he'd read about her. Of course she'd been a girl who gobbled cakes when the governess wasn't looking. "Just a guess."

They came out on a point overlooking the sea. An iron bench waited beneath a twisted cypress tree and an iron railing marked the cliff's edge. Alice went to the railing. She sipped her champagne and stared out over the water at the distant three-quarter moon.

As he watched her, he had the oddest feeling of unreality. It was like a dream, really, being there with her. She was a vision in lustrous red, her bare shoulders so smooth, her arms beautifully shaped, muscular in a way that was uniquely feminine.

Eventually, she turned to him. Her eyes were very dark at that moment. Full of shadows and secrets. "I've never been as well behaved as I should be. It's a problem for me. I'm too eager for excitement and adventure. But I'm working on that."

He moved to stand beside her, and leaned back against the railing. "There's nothing wrong with a little adventure now and then."

She laughed, turning toward him, holding her champagne glass up so he could tap his against it. "I agree. But as you said, *now and then*. For me it's like the tea cakes. I just *have* to eat them all." She sighed. And then she drained the glass. "So I'm trying to slow down a little, to think before I jump, to be less...excitable."

"It's a shame to curb all that natural enthusiasm." He wanted to touch her—to smooth her shining hair or run the back of a finger along the sleek curve of her neck. But he held himself in check. He didn't want to spook her.

"Everybody has to grow up sometime." She leaned in closer. Her perfume came to him: like lilies and leather and a hint of the ocean. He could stand there and smell her all night. But she was on the move again. In a rustle of red skirts, she went to the bench and sat down. "Tell me about your sister." She bent to set her empty glass beneath the bench.

"She's much younger than I am. We're twelve years apart. She's been homeschooled for most of her life. She's sensitive and artistic. She could always draw, from when she was very little, and she carries a sketch pad around with her all the time. And she loves to sew. She's better with a thread and needle than any tailor I've ever used. She makes all her own clothes. And now she's suddenly decided that she wants to study fashion design in New York City."

Alice patted the space next to her. "And you don't want her to do what she wants?"

He went to her. She swept her skirt out of the way and he sat beside her. "Lucy was homeschooled because she was sick a lot. She almost died more than once. She had asthma and a problem with a heart valve."

"Had?" She took his empty champagne flute and put it under the bench with hers. "You mean she's better now?"

"The asthma's in remission. And after several surgeries that didn't do much good, two years ago she finally had the one that actually worked."

"So she's well? She can lead a normal life."

"She has to be careful."

Alice was studying him again, and much too closely. "You're overprotective."

"I'm not." He sounded defensive and he knew it.

"But Lucy thinks so...."

He grumbled, "You're too damn smart." He could almost regret not choosing a stupid princess. But then all he had to do was look at her, smell her perfume, hear her laugh, watch her with her horses—and he knew that no silly, malleable princess would do for him. Alice was the one. No doubt about it.

"I certainly am smart," she said. "So you'd better be honest with me from now on. Tell me lies and I'll find you out."

"I *have* been honest." Mostly.

She shook her head. "Do I have to remind you of your alter ego, the stable hand—again?"

"Please. No." He held up both hands palms out in surrender.

"Oh, my." She pretended to fan herself. "You're begging. I think I like that."

He set her straight. "It was a simple request."

"No, no, no." She laughed. She had a great laugh, full-out and all in. "You were definitely begging." Smiling smugly, showing off the dimples that made her almost as cute as she was beautiful, she asked, "You said Lucy is twenty-three, right?"

He kept catching himself watching her mouth. It was plump and pretty and very tempting. But he wasn't going to kiss her, not tonight. He'd just barely salvaged the situation with her and he couldn't afford to push his luck by moving too fast. "Why are we talking about Lucy, anyway?"

"Because she's important to you." She said it simply. Openly.

And all at once he wanted to be...better somehow. It was bewildering. She stirred him, more than he'd ever intended to be stirred. He started talking, started saying *real* things. "When our mom died, we had nothing. Lucy was nine and sick all the time. I was twenty-one, just starting out, working days for that guy with the horse ranch I told you about, taking business classes at night. Our mom died and Child Protective Services showed up the next day to take Lucy away."

"I am sorry...." She said it softly, the three simple words laden with sadness. For him.

He wanted some big things from her. Sympathy wasn't one of them. "Don't be. It was a good thing."

"A good thing that you lost your sister?"

"I didn't lose her. She went to an excellent foster mom, a great lady named Hannah Russo who made me welcome whenever I came to visit."

"Well, that's good."

"It was, yeah. And that they wouldn't let me take care of my sister was a definite wake-up call. I knew I had to get my ass in gear or I would never get custody of her. She was so damn frail. She could have died. I was afraid she *would* die. It was seriously motivating. I was determined, above all, to get her back with me where I could take care of her."

Her eyes were so soft. He could see the moon in them. "How long did it take you?"

"I got custody of her three years after our mom died, when Lucy was twelve. I've taken care of her since then. She's my family. Sometimes she doesn't see it, but I only want what's best for her."

"I know you do." She leaned in close again. He smelled lilies and sea foam. "I like you, Noah." She said his name on a breath. And then she leaned closer still. "You're macho and tough. Kind of. But not. You confuse me. I shouldn't like that. But I do. I like *you* far too much, I think."

He whispered, "Good." His senses spun. She affected him so strongly. Too strongly, really. More strongly than any woman had in a long, long time—maybe ever. Above all, he had to remember not to push too fast. Not to kiss her. Yet.

Her red skirts rustled as she leaned that little bit closer. Her breath brushed his cheek, so warm, so sweet.

What now? Should he back off? Did it count as moving too fast if *she* was the one doing the moving?

She whispered, "I promised myself I wouldn't kiss you...."

"All right." It wasn't all right. Not really. And she was too close, making it way too hard to remember that he wasn't going to kiss her. Not now. Not tonight....

"But, Noah. I really *want* to kiss you."

He held very still, every molecule in his body alert. Hungry. He wanted to go for it, to grab her and haul her into his aching arms. He wanted that way too much for his own peace of mind. "Remember," he said on a bare husk of sound, "you have a plan."

"What plan?" Her gaze kept straying to his mouth.

"You promised yourself you would think before you jump." Did he mean to be helpful? Maybe. But somehow it came out as a challenge.

And, as everything he'd read about her had made crystal clear, Her Highness Alice never could resist a challenge. "To hell with my plan."

"Tomorrow you'll feel differently."

"Tomorrow can take care of itself." She swayed that fraction closer. "Right now I only want to kiss you." She lifted those plump, sweet lips to him.

He made himself wait. He managed, just barely, to hold himself in check until her mouth touched his.

Then, with a low groan, he reached out and wrapped his arms good and tight around her.

Chapter Three

Alice knew very well that she shouldn't be kissing him.

Kissing him, after all, was exactly what she'd said she wouldn't do.

But the scent of him was all around her—like his big strong arms that held her so very tightly. His chest was broad and hard and wonderful beneath the snow-white evening shirt.

And his kiss? Deep and demanding at first, thrilling her. His hot breath burned her mouth; his tongue delved in.

But then a moment later he dialed it down, going gentle, easier. He tempted her all the more forcefully by using tenderness, by taking it slow. His big hands roamed her back, making her shiver with delight. And his lips... Oh, my, the man certainly did know how to kiss. She could go on like this forever, sitting under the moon with the soft sigh of the sea far below them, all wrapped up in Noah's arms.

Then again, anyone might come up on them out here in the open like this. The paparazzi were everywhere. She'd learned that the hard way, over and over again.

If someone got a shot of her now, plastered all over a virtual stranger, soul-kissing him deeper than she had that redheaded barmaid during the karaoke escapade...

With a low moan, she put her hands to his hard chest and pushed him away. He made no move to stop her.

Breathless, still yearning, she faced forward again. Sagging against the iron back of the bench, she stared out beyond the railing at the moonlit sea.

Noah said nothing. She was grateful for that.

Back on the path behind them, a woman laughed. It was more of a giggle, really. A man spoke as though in reply, his voice low and intimate, the words unclear. More feminine laughter, and then the man said something else, the sound of his voice retreating as he spoke. Whoever they were, they had turned and gone back toward the palace.

There was silence. Only the breeze off the sea and the distant cry of a gull.

Alice smoothed her hair and straightened the bodice of her strapless gown. "Sometimes I really disappoint myself."

"Is it possible you're trying too hard to be good?" he asked in that lovely sexy rumble that had stirred her from the first.

She shot him a scoffing glance. "More likely, I'm not trying hard enough."

He caught her hand. Before she could pull away, he pressed his wonderful lips to the back of it. His mouth was so warm, so deliciously soft compared to the rest of him. "You're amazing. Just as you are. Why mess with a great thing?" His words were pure temptation. She wanted only to sigh and sway against him again, to kiss him some more, to give him a chance to flatter her endlessly. She wanted to let him kiss her and touch her until she forgot all the promises she'd made to herself about learning a little discipline, about keeping her actions under control.

Instead, she said, "I would like my hand back, please." He released her. She rose and brushed out her taffeta skirt. "Good night. Please don't follow me." She turned for the trail, glancing back only once before she ducked between the hedges.

He hadn't moved. He sat facing the sea, staring out at the moon.

Alice collected her bag and wrap from the attendant at the side entrance and called for her driver.

Twenty minutes after she'd left Noah staring out to sea, the driver was holding the limo door for her. She slipped into the plush embrace of the black leather seat.

At home she had another bath. A long one, to relax.

But she didn't relax. She lay there amid the lily-scented bubbles and tried not to feel like a complete jerk.

Noah had really stepped up. He'd made an honest, forthright apology for misleading her at the stables. And then he'd gone about being a perfect gentleman. He'd also been open and honest with her about his life, his past. About the tensions between him and his little sister.

He had not put a move on her. She'd made sure that he wouldn't, by going on and on about how from now on she planned to look before she leaped.

After which she had grabbed him and kissed him for all she was worth.

Seriously, now. She was hopeless. She needed a keeper, someone to follow her around and make sure she behaved herself. Twenty-five years old and she couldn't stop acting like an impulsive, greedy child.

Her bath grew cold. She only grew more tense, more annoyed with herself.

Finally, she got out and dried off and put on a robe. It was after two in the morning. Time for bed.

But she couldn't sleep. She kept thinking how Noah had said he had no problem with her looking him up on the internet.

Finally, she threw back the covers, grabbed her laptop and snooped around for a while.

She learned that everything he'd told her that night—and in the stables, for that matter—was the truth. He was quite a guy, really, to have come from a run-down rented bungalow in the roughest part of Los Angeles without a penny to his name and built a real-estate empire before he was thirty. When he was twenty-eight, he'd been one of *Forbes'* thirty top entrepreneurs under thirty. Two years ago he'd been a *People* magazine pick for one of America's ten most eligible bachelors. His Santa Barbara–area estate had been profiled in *House & Garden.*

There were several pages of images. Some of them showed him with Lucy, who had a sweet, friendly smile and looked very young. But most of them were of him with a gorgeous woman at his side—a lot of *different* gorgeous women. He'd never been linked to any one woman for any length of time.

The endless series of beautiful girlfriends reminded her of all the reasons she wouldn't be getting involved with him. The last thing she needed was to fall for a rich player who would trade her in for a newer model at the first opportunity.

It was after four when she finally fell asleep. She woke at noon, ate a quick breakfast, put on her riding clothes and went to the stables.

Noah wasn't there. Excellent. With a little luck, she would get through the last five days of his Montedoran visit without running into him again.

Sunday morning, Alice kept her promise to Max and went to breakfast at the palace. Everyone seemed happy to see her.

Her mother made a special effort to ask her how the plans were coming along for next year's Grand Champions Tour. Alice gave her a quick report and her mother said how pleased they all were with her work. She'd sold two mares, a stallion and a gelding in the past month. The money helped support her breeding program, but a good chunk of it went to important causes. Her mother praised her contribution to the lives of all Montedorans.

Alice basked in the approval. She knew what it meant. Her mother was getting past her disappointment over her antics in Glasgow.

At the table, she ended up next to Damien. He threw an arm across her shoulders and pressed a kiss to her cheek. "Allie. You're looking splendid, as always."

"Flatterer."

Dami shrugged and got to work on his eggs Benedict. He looked a little tired, she thought. But then, he often did. He was quite the globe-trotter. Most people thought he was all about beautiful women and the good life—and he was. But he also held a degree in mechanical engineering and design. He was a talented artist, too. And beyond all that, he loved putting together a profitable business deal almost as much as their second-born brother, Rule. And then there were the charities he worked hard to support.

No wonder he looked as though he needed a long nap.

She was tempted to ply him with questions about Noah. But what was the point? She'd already decided that she and Noah weren't going to be happening, so it didn't matter what Dami might have to tell her about him.

Dami sipped espresso. When he set down the demitasse, he turned to her again and said softly, "I heard you danced more than one dance with Noah Cordell last Friday. After which you went walking in the garden with him...."

Well, all right, then. Apparently, she was going to hear about Noah after all, whether she wanted to or not. "I met him in the stables. He was there Wednesday and Thursday mornings, early. He said you had introduced him to Gilbert."

"That's right."

"We...chatted."

"And danced," he repeated, annoyingly patient. "And walked in the garden."

"Yes, Dami. We did."

"You like him." It wasn't a question. His expression was unreadable.

She answered truthfully. "I do. He's intelligent, fun and a good dancer, as well."

"He's worse with women than I am."

"But you're not so bad—lately. I mean, what about Vesuvia?"

"What about her?" He gave her one of those looks. "We've been on-again, off-again. Now we're permanently off."

"I'm sorry to hear that."

"Don't be. It's for the best."

"But you've settled down a lot. We've all noticed."

He dismissed her argument with a wave. "I'm not a

good bet when it comes to relationships. Neither is Noah. It's always a new woman with him. Take my advice. Stay away from him."

That got her back up. "You ought to know better than to tell me what to do, Dami."

"It's for your own good, I promise you."

She laughed. "You're just making it worse. And you know that. You know how I am. Tell me *not* to do a thing and I just *have* to do it. Or are you *trying* to get me interested in Noah?"

"I'm not that clever."

"Oh, please. We both know you're brilliant."

"Sometimes, my darling, I actually do mean exactly what I say. Please stay away from Noah Cordell."

She really wanted to remind him that he had no right to tell her whom she could or couldn't see. But she let it go. "He wants to buy Orion."

"Do you want to sell him Orion?"

"I told him I wouldn't, but actually, I'm still thinking it over."

"I'll be honest."

"Why, thank you."

"I've been to his California estate. It's a horse farm and a fine one. And he's as good with horses as you are."

Alice had seen how good Noah was with horses. Still, her pride couldn't let that stand. "No one's as good with horses as I am."

"Plus, you're so enchantingly shy and modest."

"Shyness and modesty are overrated."

He turned back to his meal. They ate in silence for a minute or two. Then he said, "Noah's got more money than we do. He would pay whatever price you set for one of your Tekes. And he treats his animals handsomely."

"Then you do think I should sell him the stallion?"

"Yes—but then, I know you, Allie. You're going to do exactly what you want to do."

"I certainly am."

"Just don't let him charm you. Keep your guard up, or you'll get hurt."

Keep your guard up, or you'll get hurt....

Dami had only warned her of what she already knew. And she *would* heed his warning. For once, she wouldn't be contrary for contrary's sake. She would take her brother's advice and steer clear of Noah Cordell. Should she happen to meet up with him again, she would treat him with courtesy.

Courtesy and nothing more.

Her resolve got its first test at the stables that afternoon. Noah appeared as she was consulting with the equine dentist who checked the teeth of all her horses twice yearly. She glanced up and there he was out in the courtyard, the September sun gilding his hair, looking way too tall and fit and yummy for her peace of mind. Just the sight of him caused a curl of heat down low in her abdomen.

But no problem. She could handle this.

Alice asked the dentist to excuse her for a moment.

When Noah entered the stable, she was waiting for him, her smile cool and composed. "Noah. I hardly recognized you."

Gone were the old jeans and battered Western boots. Today he was beautifully turned out in the English style: black breeches, black polo shirt and a fine pair of black field boots. He regarded her distantly. "I was hoping to ride." A flick of a glance at the rows of stalls. "How about

Gadim?" The six-year-old black gelding had energy to spare and could be fractious.

But she knew Noah could handle him. "Excellent choice. Shall I call a groom to tack him up?"

"I can manage, thanks." His tone gave her nothing. Because she'd come on so distant and cool? Or because he'd already lost interest in her?

She couldn't tell.

And she wished that she didn't care.

"Good, then," she said too brightly. "Have a pleasant ride."

She returned to her consultation with the dentist, who had a list of the horses needing teeth pulled or filed.

Noah was off on Gadim when she finished with the dentist. She considered lingering until he came back. She wanted to ask him how he'd enjoyed his ride, to let him know that she might be convinced to sell him Orion.

But that would only be courting trouble.

She liked him too much. She could let down her guard with him so very easily. Not that he even cared at this point. He'd seemed so bored and uninterested earlier.

Which shouldn't matter in the least to her.

But it did.

No. Not a good idea to hang around in the hope of seeing him again.

She left the stables for a far paddock, where she spent the remainder of the afternoon working on leading and tying with a couple of recently weaned foals.

"Don't listen to Dami," Rhia said that evening as they shared dessert on the terrace of her villa overlooking the harbor.

Alice had told her sister everything by then. "But what if Dami's right?"

"That the man's a player? Oh, please. As though Dami has any room to talk."

"Well, but I just don't need to get myself into any more trouble. I really don't."

Rhia enjoyed a slow bite of her chocolate soufflé. "How are you going to get into trouble? You said he's filthy rich."

"Whether or not I get myself in trouble has nothing to do with how much money a man has."

"I *mean* you can rest assured that he's no fortune hunter. You're both single. You both love horses. You enjoy being with him. And you happen to be extremely attracted to him. You should give him a chance." She savored yet another bite. "Mmm." She licked chocolate from her upper lip. "Lately, if it's chocolate, I can't get enough."

"The baby must love chocolate," Alice suggested with a smile.

"That must be it—and what was it you once advised me? 'Rhia, be bold,' you said."

"Oh, please. That was about Marcus."

"So?"

"Marcus loves you. He's *always* loved you."

Rhia frowned. "I wasn't at all sure about that at the time."

"Still, my situation is entirely different."

"Why?"

"Because *we're* so different, you and I. You've always been nothing short of exemplary. Well behaved and *good*. You needed to be told to get out there and go after the only man you've ever loved. I don't require any such encouragement."

"On the contrary, it seems very clear to me that you do."

"One, Noah Cordell is not my lifelong love. I truly hardly know the man. And two, if anything, *I* need to be told *not* to be bold."

Her sister reached across the table and touched her cheek. "You like him. He likes you. You haven't been this worked up over a man in forever."

"I am not worked up."

Rhia clucked her tongue and then began scraping the last of the soufflé out of her ramekin. "I don't know what I'm going to do with you."

"Support me. Sympathize with me."

"As though that's going to help you." Rhia shook her head and licked her spoon.

"Even if I took your advice instead of Dami's, I'm afraid it's too late."

"Too late for what?"

"I'm afraid he's not interested in me anymore. Today in the stables, he acted as though he didn't even *care* what I thought of him."

"Was this before or after you treated him like a stranger?"

"I didn't treat him like a stranger."

"Yes, you did. You *said* that you did."

"I was perfectly civil."

"Civil. Precisely. Are you going to eat your soufflé?" Alice pushed it across the table.

Rhia dug right in, sighing. "Oh, my, yes. *So* good. And you do see what's happening here, don't you?"

"What?"

"You are not being you." Rhia paused to sigh over another big bite of chocolate. "And you're making yourself miserable."

"Not being me? Of course I'm being me. Who else would I be?"

"Allow me to explain...."

"Please."

Rhia pointed with her spoon. "You went a little over the top in Glasgow."

"A *little?*"

"That is what I said. You went over the top, and since then, you've decided you need to be *so* well behaved and subdued. It's just not like you at all. You are a brave, bold person, a person who jumps right into anything that interests her, who lives by her instincts. But you're trying to be someone else, someone careful and controlled, someone who plans ahead, who reasons everything out with agonizing care. And as your favorite sister who loves you more than you'll ever know, it's my responsibility to inform you that being someone you're not isn't working for you."

Alice thought a lot about the things Rhia had said to her. She could see the sense in Rhia's advice, she truly could.

But the thing was that she liked Noah *too* much. She hardly knew him, yet she couldn't stop thinking about him.

It scared her. It really did. She'd never been so powerfully attracted to any man before. What if she did fall in love with him?

And then he dumped her for someone else?

Even a brave, bold woman who lived by her instincts should have the sense not to volunteer for that kind of pain.

She didn't see him on Monday. But then Tuesday she went down to the Triangle d'Or, the area of exclusive shops near the casino, to pick up a Balenciaga handbag she'd ordered. She saw him sitting at a little outdoor café sipping an espresso. He was alone and she was so very tempted to stop and chat with him a little.

But she didn't. Uh-uh. She walked on by, quickly, before he could spot her and wave at her. Or worse, ignore her.

He was leaving on Thursday, he'd said. She only had to get through the next day without doing anything stupid. He would go home to his estate in California, to his frail and artistic little sister. And in time she would forget him.

All day Wednesday she kept thinking that tomorrow he would be gone. He never came to the stables that day—or if he did, she missed seeing him. She went home at a little after six.

Tomorrow he'll be gone....

She wanted to cry.

It was too much. She couldn't stand it anymore, that he would return to America and she might never see him again.

She did the very thing she knew she shouldn't do. She picked up the phone and called the Belle Époque. She asked for his room and they put her right through.

He answered the phone on the second ring. "Yes?"

"It's Alice. Are you still leaving tomorrow?" Her voice came out husky and confident. She sounded like the bold woman Rhia insisted she actually was.

"Alice. I'm surprised." *He* sounded anything but bored. But he didn't sound exactly happy, either.

"You're angry with me."

"Come on. I got the message when you ran away Friday night—and the other day in the stables when I came to ride. I got it loud and clear."

Her heart sank. "I'm sorry. I... Maybe I shouldn't have called."

A silence. And then, with real feeling, "Don't say that. I'm glad that you called."

"You are?"

"Yeah."

She let out a sigh of pure relief. "So, then, are you leaving?"

"Yes. Tomorrow."

"And tonight?" Her throat clutched. She coughed to clear it. "Are you busy tonight?"

Another silence. For a moment she thought he'd hung up. But then he asked, "What game are you playing now, Alice?"

"It's not a game. I promise you."

"Frankly, it feels like a game, a game I'll never win."

She tried for lightness. "Look at it this way—at least I'm not boring and predictable."

More dead air. And then at last he said, "I'm available. For you."

Well, all right. He definitely sounded like a man who wanted to see her again. Suddenly, she was floating on air. "I want to wear a long dress and diamonds. I want to play baccarat and eat at La Chanson." La Chanson de la Mer was right on the water in the Triangle d'Or and arguably the best restaurant on the Riviera.

"I'll arrange everything. Whatever you want."

Her stomach had gone all fluttery. Her heart was racing. Her cheeks felt too warm. Sweet Lord, she was out of control.

And it was fabulous. "Be in front of the casino, by the fountain," she commanded. "Eight o'clock."

"I'll be there."

Noah was waiting right where she'd told him to be, dressed for evening, feeling way too damned anxious to see her again, when her limo pulled up a few feet away.

The driver got out, hustled around and opened her door. She emerged in a strapless gold dress that clung to every sweet curve and had a slit up the skirt to above the knee. Her hair was pinned up loosely, bits of it escaping to curl at her nape.

And she was on her own, as he'd hoped. No bodyguard. Damien had told him that the princely family only used bodyguards outside the principality. Good. He might actually get a chance to be alone with her.

She saw him. A gorgeous, hopeful, glowing smile curved her lips. They stood there like a couple of lovesick teenagers, just looking at each other, as the driver got back behind the wheel and the long black car slid away.

They both started moving at the same time. Three steps and he was with her, in front of her, looking down into those amazing blue-green eyes.

Again, they just stared at each other. He said, "God. You're so beautiful."

And she said, "You came. I was a little worried you wouldn't."

"Are you kidding? Turn down a chance to spend an evening with you? Couldn't do it." Over her shoulder, he saw a man with a camera. "Someone's taking our picture."

"Behave with dignity," she said. "And ignore them. I'll do my very best to follow your lead. Because, as we both know, dignity was never my strong suit."

"You are more than dignified enough," he argued.

She gave him her full-out, beautiful laugh. "Not true, but thanks for trying."

He wanted to kiss her, but not while some idiot was snapping pictures of them. "Dinner first?"

"Perfect." She reached for his arm.

They turned for the restaurant. It was just a short walk across the plaza.

He'd gotten them a table on the patio, which jutted out over the water. The food was excellent and the waitstaff were always there when you needed them, but otherwise invisible. The sky slowly darkened and the moon over the water glowed brighter as the night came on. The sea glittered, reflecting the lights of the Triangle d'Or and those shining from the windows and gardens of the red-roofed villas that crowded the nearby hillsides.

They talked of nothing important during the meal, which was fine with him. He was content right then just to be with her, to listen to her laughter and watch those sweet dimples appear in her cheeks when she smiled.

After they ate, they strolled back across the plaza to the casino. They played craps and roulette and baccarat. People stopped to watch them, to whisper about them. A few took pictures. Noah had foreseen this and called ahead to speak with the manager so that the casino staff was on top of the situation. They made sure none of the gawkers got too close.

Alice won steadily and so did he. Around eleven he

challenged her to play blackjack, two-handed, in one of the exclusive back rooms.

She looked at him with suspicion. But in the end, as he could have predicted, she refused to walk away from a challenge. "Am I going to regret this?"

He simply offered his arm. When she wrapped her hand around it, he led her into the card room in the back, where the table he'd reserved was waiting for them, cordoned off with golden ropes in its own quiet little corner. She eyed the deck of cards and the equally divided stacks of chips as he pulled back her chair for her.

"I thought we would play for something more interesting than money." He pushed in her chair and went around to sit opposite her.

She cast a glance around the big room. Almost every other table was in use. Leaning closer, lowering her voice so only he heard her, she said, "I am not taking off my clothes in a room full of strangers."

He laughed. "Clearly, I should have ordered a private room."

She tried to play it stern but didn't quite succeed. Her dimples gave her away. "Let's just not go there."

"Fair enough." He shuffled the cards.

She watched him, narrow eyed. "All right, then. If not for money, then what?"

He looked up into her eyes. "Orion."

She stared at him for a count of three before she spoke. "Surely you're joking."

He shook his head. "If I win, you agree to sell him to me."

She looked at him sideways, her diamond earrings glittering, scattering the light from the chandeliers above.

"At my price, then. You're only winning the right to buy him."

"That's right."

"Think twice, Noah. It's an astronomical price."

"Name it."

She did.

He looked at her patiently—and counteroffered.

She laughed, glanced away—and then countered his counter.

"Agreed." He slapped the deck in front of her.

Alice cut the cards. "But what if *I* win?"

He took the deck again. "Name your prize."

"Hmm." She grinned slowly. "I know. I want you to donate twenty thousand American dollars to St. Stephens Children's Home. My brother-in-law Marcus was raised there."

He gave her a wry smile. "So either way, I pay."

She dimpled. "Exactly."

He pretended to think it over. Then, "At least it's a worthy cause. Done."

They began to play.

She was an excellent gambler, bold and focused. And fearless, as well. She kept track of the cards seemingly without effort, laughing and chatting so charmingly as she played.

He was down to a very short stack at one point. But he battled his way back, winning. Losing. And then winning again.

It was almost two in the morning when he claimed her last chip from her.

She leaned back in her chair and laughed. "All right, Noah. You win. You may buy Orion for the price we agreed on."

He got the real picture then. "You were going to sell him to me anyway."

Her smile was downright smug. "Yes, I was—and enough of all this." She held out both hands, as though to indicate the whole of the world-famous casino complex. "Let's go somewhere else."

An attendant showed them to a private office where Noah settled up and they collected what they'd won earlier in the evening. The attendant appeared again with Alice's gold wrap and tiny jeweled handbag. A few minutes later they emerged into the glittering Montedoran night.

"What now?" he asked, even though it was a risk; it gave her an out if she suddenly decided she should call it a night. He was betting she wouldn't. She seemed to be having a great time. And he already knew how much she enjoyed calling the shots.

"Somewhere private." She glanced across the plaza where two men with cameras were snapping away. "Somewhere we can talk and not be disturbed."

Noah chuckled, pleased with himself that he'd read her mood correctly. "As though there's anywhere in Montedoro they won't follow us."

She took hold of his arm again and leaned close. He breathed in her scent. Exciting. So sweet. She said, "I have a plan."

"Uh-oh."

She laughed. "That's exactly what my sister Rhia always says when I come up with a fabulous idea." She faked a puzzled frown. "Why is that, do you think?"

He played it safe. "Not a clue."

"Ha!" And then she leaned even closer. "I am having altogether too much fun."

Her words pleased him no end. "There's no such thing as too much fun."

"Yes, there is. But it's all right. It's your last night in Montedoro after all. And we may never see each other again."

Wrong. "I just bought a horse from you, remember?"

"Of course I remember. And you shall have Orion. But you know what I meant."

He decided to let that remark go, but if she thought this was the last evening they would spend together, she didn't know who she was dealing with. "Tell me your plan."

"You're sure? A moment ago you seemed reluctant to hear it."

"I'm sure."

"Well, all right, then." She whispered her scheme in his ear.

Chapter Four

"It just might work," he said, admiring the way the bright lights brought out hints of auburn and gold in her hair.

"Of course it will work."

"All right, then. I'm game." They turned together for his hotel, neither looking back to see if they were being followed. Why bother to look? Of course they were being followed. The paparazzi were relentless. As they entered the lobby, he got out his cell and called his driver.

He led her straight through to the elevators. They got on and rode up to his floor—after which they changed elevators and went back down to the mezzanine level.

They took the service stairway to the first floor again and slipped out the side door, where the car he'd called for was waiting, the engine running. The driver, Talbot, held the door for her. Noah jumped in on the other side.

"Where to?" Talbot asked once they were safely hidden from prying eyes behind tinted windows. Alice rattled off a quick series of directions. The driver nodded and pulled the car away from the curb.

Noah raised the panel between the front and rear seats.

Alice glanced at him and grinned. "Alone at last."

He wrapped his arm around her and drew her closer. "If I kiss you, will you run away again?"

She gazed at him steadily, eyes shining. Then she shook her head. "Not while the car is moving."

He bent closer and brushed his lips across the velvet flesh of her temple. "Remind me to tell Talbot never to stop...."

"It's a tempting idea, being here with you forever...." She tipped her face up to him.

He brushed his mouth across hers, giving her a moment to accept him. When her lips parted slightly on a small tender sigh, he deepened the contact.

She let him in. He tasted the wet, secret surfaces behind her lips, ran his tongue along the smooth, even edges of her pretty white teeth.

Another sigh from her, deeper than the one before.

And he tightened his arm around her, bringing her closer so he could taste her more deeply still.

When she brought her hand up between them and pushed lightly against his chest, he lifted his mouth from hers just enough to grumble, "What now, Alice?"

Her eyes had the night in them. "Dami told me to stay away from you. He says you're a heartbreaker." Bad words scrolled through his mind, but he held them in. She added, "My sister Rhia told me not to listen to Dami."

"I like your sister already." He kissed her again, quickly, a little more ruthlessly than he probably should have. "And I'll talk to your brother."

Her fingers strayed upward. She stroked the nape of his neck. He wished she'd go on doing that for a century or two. "Please don't talk to Dami about me. It's none of his business. He doesn't get to decide who I see or don't see."

Noah had pretty much expected Damien to warn Alice off him. He'd considered explaining his real goal to Dami up front when he'd told Dami he wanted Orion—but he'd decided against it.

Damien wouldn't have believed him anyway. And Alice might be convinced to let him off the hook for a lot of things. But even before their first meeting, he'd known enough about her to figure out that she would never forgive him for telling her brother his real intentions before he revealed them to her.

And come on. He'd never planned to tell her *or* her brother everything. He'd assumed the whole truth wouldn't fly with either of them. The idea had been to meet her, pursue her and win her. To sweep her off her pretty feet.

But now that he'd come to know her a little, he was having second thoughts about the original plan. She was honest. Forthright. And after the near disaster of his playing along when she mistook him for a stable hand, he'd learned his lesson: she expected him to be honest, too.

Which brought him to that other thing, the thing he hadn't been prepared for. The way she made him want to give her everything, to be more than he'd ever been.

It was getting beyond his pride now, way past his idea of who he was and what he'd earned in his life. It was getting downright personal.

She *mattered* to him now, as a person. He didn't really understand it or want to think on it too deeply. It was what it was.

And it meant that he would knock himself out to give her whatever she needed, whatever she wanted from him. Up to and including the unvarnished truth.

So, then. He hadn't decided yet. Should he go there— go all the way, lay the naked truth right out on the table for her?

It was dangerous, a bold move.

Too bold?

Could be. And probably not tonight, anyway. It seemed much too soon....

She laid her soft hand against the side of his face. "Earth to Noah. Are you in there?"

"Forget about Damien." He said it too fiercely, and he knew it. "Kiss me again."

She laughed—and then she kissed him. And then she settled against him with her head on his shoulder and asked, "How did you meet my brother?"

He breathed in the scent of her hair. "I thought we were going to forget about Damien."

She tipped her head up and grinned at him. "You wish—and seriously. How did you meet him?"

"At a party in New York a little over two years ago. We both knew the host. I struck up a conversation with him. We found we had a lot in common."

"Fast cars, beautiful women..."

He shrugged. "I like your brother. We get along—as a rule, anyway."

The car pulled to a stop.

"We're here." She straightened from his embrace. With reluctance, he let her go and lowered the panel between the seats.

"Will you be getting out, sir?" Talbot asked.

"Yes, thanks." The driver jumped out to open the door for Alice. Noah emerged on his side. The car sat on a point near the edge of a sheer cliff with the sea spread out beyond. He could hear the waves on the rocks below. He caught her eye over the roof of the car. "It's beautiful here."

She grinned as though she'd created the setting herself. "I thought you might like it. There's a path down to a fine little slice of beach. A private beach. Is there a blanket or two in the boot?"

There were two. Talbot got them from the trunk. He handed them to Noah and then got back in behind the wheel to wait until they were ready to go.

She'd left her wrap and bag in the car, but her gold sandals had high, delicate heels. Noah eyed them doubtfully. "Are you sure you can make it down a steep trail in those?"

"Good point." She slipped off the flimsy shoes, opened the car door again, and tossed them inside. "Let's go."

Going barefoot didn't seem like a good idea to him. "Alice. Be realistic. You'll cut up your feet."

She waved a hand. "The trail is narrow and steep, yes, but not rocky. I'll be fine." She gathered her gold skirts and took the lead.

The woman amazed him. She led the way without once stumbling, without a single complaint. Halfway down they came out on a little wooden landing with a rail. They stood at the rail together, the breeze off the sea cool and sweet, the dark sky starless, the moon sunk almost to the edge of the horizon now, sending out a trail of shifting light across the water toward the shore.

She said, "We all, my brothers and sisters and me, used to come here together, with my mother and father, when we were children. The observation point above, where we left the car, belongs to my family. The only way down is this trail. The high rocks jut out on either side of the beach, so intruders can't trek in along the shoreline. We've always kept it private. Just for our family, a place to be like other families out for a day by the sea."

"Beautiful," he said. He was looking at her.

She waved a hand, the diamond cuff she wore catching light even in the darkness, sparkling. "But of course, now and then, the paparazzi fly over and get pictures from the air." She sounded a little sad about that. But then she sent him a conspiratorial glance. "Come on." And she turned to take the wooden stairs that led the rest of the way down.

The beach was sandy. He took off his shoes and socks and rolled his trouser legs. They spread one of the blankets midway between the cliffs and the water and sat there together. The breeze seemed chilly now that they were sitting still, so he wrapped the other blanket around her bare shoulders. He put his arm around her and she settled against him as she had in the car, as though she belonged there. For a while they stared out at the moon trail on the water.

Eventually, she broke the companionable silence. "I think I like you too much."

He pressed his lips to her hair. "Don't stop."

She chuckled. "Liking you—or talking?"

"Either."

She laughed again. And then complained, "You're much too attractive."

"I'll try to be uglier."

"But that's not all. You're also funny and irreverent and a little bit dangerous. And a heartbreaker, too, just like Dami said. I really need to remember that and not go making a fool of myself over you."

He put a finger under her chin and lifted her face to him. "I have no intention of breaking your heart. Ever."

She wrinkled her fine nose at him. "I didn't say you would *intend* to do it. Men like you don't go out to hurt women on purpose. They simply get bored and move on and leave a trail of shattered hearts behind them."

He was starting to get a little defensive. "From what I've heard, you've broken a heart or two yourself in the past."

She groaned. "I should have known you would say that. After all, I have no secrets. My whole life is available, with pictures, *lots* of pictures, in the pages of the *National Enquirer* and the *Daily Star*." And then all at once she was shoving away from him, throwing off the blanket and leaping to her feet.

"Alice. Don't…"

"I'm going wading." She gathered up her gold skirts and ran to the water's edge.

He got up and followed her, taking his time about it. Better to give her a moment or two to calm down.

When he reached her, she was just standing there, the foamy waves lapping her slender feet, holding her skirts out of the way. For a moment they stared out at the water together toward the sinking moon on the far horizon.

Then she confessed, "All right, that was a little bit bitchy. Not to mention over the top. Sorry."

He said nothing, only reached out a hand, caught a loose curl of her hair and tucked it behind her ear. He really liked touching her—and he liked even more that she let him. "I was only saying that we're more or less evenly matched."

"But I don't want to be shattered. I don't want to shatter *you*. I want…" Words seemed to fail her.

He ran a finger down the side of her neck. Living silk, her skin. He drank in her slight shiver at his touch. "You want what?"

She gazed out over the water again. "I want to rip off my dress and dive in. Right here. Right now."

A bolt of heat hit him where it counted. Gruffly, he suggested, "Fine with me. I'll join you."

She let her head drop back and stared up at the dark sky. "I can't."

"There's no one here but the two of us."

She lowered her head and turned to him then. "Oh, Noah. That's the thing. I can never be sure, never be too careful. If someone just happened to be lurking back on the trail with a camera and got a shot of me cavorting naked in the waves with you… Oh, God. My mother would never forgive me." She smiled then, but it was a sad smile. "If the paparazzi caught me in the buff now, I don't think I would forgive *myself,* if you want the truth."

"You're being way too hard on yourself. You know that, right?"

"Maybe. I suppose. It didn't used to bother me much. I used to simply ignore it all. I did what I wanted and if the journos had nothing better to do than to take pictures of me and write silly stories about me, so what? But now, well, I feel differently. I'm sick to death of being the wild one, the ready-for-anything, out-of-control Princess Alice."

He had a good idea of what had pushed her over the line. "The pictures from that pub in Glasgow?"

She winced. "You saw them."

"Yeah."

"My mother was pretty upset over them."

He blew out a slow breath. "I thought they were hot."

"More like a hot mess."

"*Hot* still being the operative word."

She turned fully toward him and studied his face, a

deep look, one that made him slightly uncomfortable. And then she said, "I think I really should go home now."

Uh-uh. Not yet. Not this time.

He reached out. He couldn't stop himself. He wrapped his fingers around the back of her neck and pulled her into him. "Kiss me."

"Oh, Noah…"

"Shh." He took her mouth. She made a reluctant sound low in her throat—but then she softened and kissed him back. When he lifted his head, he said, "I've got to get you away from here."

She gazed up at him, eyes shining, lips slightly swollen from the kiss. "Away from where?"

"Away from Montedoro."

She frowned. "That's not going to happen. Tonight is our last night and—"

He stopped her with a gentle finger on her soft lips. "I don't want this to be our last night. And I don't believe that you do, either."

Her slim shoulders drooped. "Noah. Be realistic."

"But I am. Completely. And my point is, it's a fishbowl here—beautiful, glamorous, but still. A fishbowl. Whatever we do together here, there will be pictures and stories in the tabloid press." Plus, it was way too easy for her to escape him here on her own turf. He needed to get her onto his territory for a change. He went for it. "Come back to California with me tomorrow. Come and stay with me for a while."

She pressed her lips together. "Oh, Noah. I really don't think that would be a good idea."

He wasn't giving up. Ever. "Why not? You'll love it there. And I want to show you my world. I want you to meet Lucy."

"Noah, really. I can't just run off with you. Didn't I just explain all this? I'm trying to be more…discreet. Trying to behave myself for a change. Trying to stop throwing myself blindly into crazy situations."

"It's not crazy. The Santa Barbara area is a beautiful place, almost as beautiful as Montedoro. And my stables are world-class. You can ride every day."

"Oh, Noah…" She pulled away from him then. He wanted to grab her and hold her to him, but he knew better. She spun on her heel and raced back up the beach to the blanket again.

He forced himself to stay behind, turning back to the water, staring out at the horizon for a while, giving them both a few minutes to settle down.

When he felt that he could deal calmly and reasonably, he turned to her once more. She sat on the blanket, the other blanket wrapped around her, her knees drawn up, staring at him with equal parts misery and defiance.

He stuck his hands into his pockets and went to her, stopping at the edge of the blanket, not sure what to do or say next.

She tipped her face up to him and demanded, "What are you after, Noah, really? What in the world do you want from me? Because if I'm just another of your conquests, no thank you. I'm not looking for a meaningless hookup right now."

He knew then that he had to go for it, to tell her everything. What else could he do? A clever lie would never satisfy her. "You're not 'just another' anything. You never could be."

"Please don't flatter me."

"I'm not. Will you listen? Will you let me explain?"

He waited for her nod before he said, "I've done damn well for myself."

"Yes, you have. But what does that have to do with—"

"Just go with me here. Let me play this out."

She hugged her drawn-up knees a little tighter. "All right. I'm listening."

"I've done well for myself and I'm proud. Too proud, I suppose. But that's how it is."

She guided a few windblown strands of hair away from that mouth he couldn't stop wanting to kiss. "Yes, well, I get that."

"A few years ago I decided it was about time I got married and founded my dynasty."

"Ah. Of course. Your dynasty." She made a wry little face.

He forged on. "To found a dynasty, there has to be... the right wife. Someone young and strong, someone from a large family, for a higher likelihood of fertility."

She made a scoffing sound. "I don't believe you just said that."

"Believe it. It's true—and here's where my pride comes in. I decided I wanted a princess. A real one."

Her mouth dropped open. "Oh. You are so bad. Incorrigible, really."

He didn't disagree with her. "How do you think I've got as far as I have in life? Not through good behavior and political correctness. I decide what I want and I go after it."

"You know this makes you look reprehensible, right?"

He only gazed down at her, unflinching. "Do you want the truth from me or not?"

She fiddled with the blanket a little and then hitched up her chin. "Yes. I do. Go on."

He continued, "So I started looking. I wanted a special kind of princess, a princess who was different from the rest. No one inbred. Someone beautiful and exciting. If I'm going to be with a woman for the rest of my life, she will damn well *not* be boring—and my kids won't be stupid or dull."

She made a small snorting sound. "Or, God forbid, unattractive."

He asked very softly, "Are you getting the picture here, Alice?"

Her mocking look fled. She swallowed. Hard. "You… chose me?"

"Yes, I did. The first picture I saw of you, I knew you were the one. I read about you—everything I could find. All the tacky tabloid stories. The articles in *Dressage Today* and *Practical Horseman.* It really worked for me that you loved horses. I wanted to meet you, to find out if the chemistry might be right—because in the end, I would have to *want* you. And *you* would have to want *me.* So I found a way to approach you by using my connections to meet your brother first. As it turned out, I liked Damien. We got along. I invited him to visit me in California. And after we'd known each other awhile, he suggested I come to Montedoro. Of course, I took him up on that."

"It was part of your plan."

"That's right. Damien invited me and I came to Montedoro and I found a way to meet you—in the palace stables, where you're most at home. I set out to get your attention. And I found out that my original instinct was solid. Every minute I've spent with you has only made me more certain that my choice is the right one."

"Wait a minute."

"What?"

"Are you going to try to tell me that you're in love with me?"

"Would you believe me if I did?"

She studied him for a moment, her head tipped to the side. "So, then. It's just chemistry. Chemistry and your plan."

"That's why I want you to come to Santa Barbara. We need more time together. I want you to give that to me—to *us*."

"Be realistic, Noah. There isn't any *us*."

He scowled at her. "There will be. And you're thinking too much."

"Right. Because I'm not a stupid princess, remember? You wanted one with a brain."

"Damn it, Alice." He dropped to his knees on the blanket before her. She gasped, but at least she didn't scuttle backward to get away from him. "I'm only telling you that you don't have to worry. You're not just some hookup. I will never dump you. I want you to marry me. I want children with you. And I won't change my mind. You're the one that I want, Alice. I want you for my wife."

Alice wasn't really sure what to say to him at that point.

Strangely, she still liked him after his extraordinary confession. She liked him and wanted him even more than before. Which probably said something really awful about her character. She didn't especially mind that he'd picked her out as a horse trader chooses a broodmare, for her good bloodlines, her sterling temperament, her fine health and conformation—and her excellent pedigree.

What she did care about was the truth, that he'd told

her honestly exactly what he was after—and that she believed him.

Should she have been at least a little appalled?

Probably. But she simply wasn't.

Surprised, yes. She'd known that he wanted her—pretty hard to miss that—but it had never occurred to her he might be seeing her as a wife. As a rule, she wasn't the type of woman a man would set out to marry in advance of even knowing her. Her reputation preceded her and most men looked for someone a bit more sedate when it came time to choose a lifelong companion.

"Alice. My God. Will you please say *something?*"

She hugged the blanket around her more tightly. "Well, I'm not sure what to say. Except that I do appreciate your telling me the truth."

"I didn't know what else to do," he grumbled. "There's something way too straightforward about you. I get it, that you want honesty. And I'm willing to give you whatever you want."

"Well. Thanks. I think."

He braced his hands on his thighs and gritted his strong white teeth. "Please come to California with me."

"Oh, I don't think so...."

He swore low, then turned and sat down beside her. Drawing up his knees, he let them drop halfway open and wrapped his big arms around them. He stared at his lean bare feet. "Why the hell not?"

"Because when I get married, it's going to be to a man I love and trust and know I can count on."

"I didn't ask you to marry me. Yet. I just told you what I'm after. Now we need the time for you to *learn* to trust and count on me."

She turned her head and pinned him with an unwavering look. "You keep leaving out love."

He made a low growling sound. "You make me be honest, and then you want me to come on with hearts and flowers."

"No, I don't want you to come on with hearts and flowers. I truly don't. I want you to be exactly who and what you are. I like you. A lot. Too much. I find you smoking hot. If I wasn't trying to be a better person, I would be rolling around naked on this blanket with you right now."

He shut his eyes and hung his golden head. "Great. Tell me in detail what you're *not* going to do with me."

"Stop it." She leaned toward him.

His head shot up and he wrapped his hand around her neck and pulled her close. "Alice…" His eyes burned into hers.

She whispered, "Please don't…."

With slow care, he released her.

They sat for a minute or two without speaking.

And then she tried again. "For me, right now, running off to Santa Barbara with you tomorrow seems like just another crazy harebrained stunt. I would need a little time to think this over."

He slid her a glance. "So you're not saying no."

"Not yes, either," she warned.

"But you'll think about it."

She nodded. "And you should do some thinking, too—about how you're hoping I'm going to learn to trust and count on you."

He scowled at her. "You're getting at something. Will you just say it, whatever it is?"

"Fine. If we can't talk about love, we can at least talk

about monogamy. Because that's a condition for me. If you ever want me to marry you, your days as a lady-killer are done."

He said very slowly, the words dragging themselves reluctantly out of him, "I haven't been with anyone for months. And I can't believe I'm admitting it to you."

"Good. It's a start." She stood. "I want to go now."

He didn't argue that time. Apparently he agreed that they'd said all they were going to say for one night. He got up, shook out the blanket and tucked it under his arm. She turned and led the way up to the car.

The ride to her villa took only a few minutes. They were very quiet minutes. To Alice it seemed she could cut the silence with a dull knife.

When they pulled up at the curb, she turned to say good-night to him, to thank him for a wonderful evening. Because it *had* been wonderful, even the rockiest parts. Wonderful and true and difficult. And real.

He only reached for her and covered her mouth with his. She swayed against him, sighing, and he wrapped her up tight in his powerful arms.

It was a great kiss, one of the best. So good she almost said yes, she would go with him after all. Anywhere he wanted. To the ends of the earth.

If he would only kiss her like that again.

But instead, she took a card from her jeweled minaudière and pressed it into his hand. "Home and cell. Call me."

Gruffly, he commanded, "Come and stay with me soon."

She leaned close, pressed her cheek to his and whispered, "Noah. Good night." The driver pulled her door open.

She grabbed her shoes and her wrap and jumped out before she could weaken. Then she stood there on the walk, barefoot in her gold dress, and watched his car drive away.

Chapter Five

Noah slept on the plane, but only fitfully. His car and driver were waiting for him at the Santa Barbara Airport when his flight touched down. He'd have one night in his own bed and then in the morning he'd board another plane to San Francisco for meetings with a media firm seeking investors for a TV-streaming start-up.

At the estate, Lucy came running out to greet him. She grabbed him and hugged him and said how she'd missed him. It did him good to see her smile. She seemed to have boundless energy lately. He was pleased at how well she was doing.

They were barely in the front door before she started in on him about college in Manhattan.

He took her by her thin shoulders and held her still. "Lucy."

She looked up at him through those big sweet brown eyes of hers, all innocence. "What?"

"You need to call that school and tell them you won't be attending in the spring."

Her lips thinned to a hard line. "Of course I won't call them. I'm going, one way or another, no matter what."

"Later," he coaxed. "In a year or two, after we're certain you can handle it."

"I *can* handle it. And I'm taking the spring semester. *This* spring semester. You just see if I don't."

Noah tried not to let out a long, weary sigh. She was so completely out there on this—nothing short of obsessed over it. She couldn't go if he didn't write the checks. And he had no intention of allowing her to put her health at risk. "We've been through this. It's too soon."

"No, it's not." She shrugged off his grip. "It's been two years since my last surgery. I am fine. I am *well*. And you know it. It's *not* too soon."

He wanted a stiff drink and dinner and a little peace and quiet before he had to leave again in the morning. He wanted Alice, a lot. But he wasn't going to have her for a while yet, and he understood that. "Please, Lucy. We'll talk more later, all right?"

"But—"

He caught her shoulders again and kissed her forehead. "Later." He said it gently.

She shrugged him off again. "Later to you really means never."

There was no point in arguing anymore over it. Shaking his head, he turned for the stairs.

"I suppose you saw the stories in the *Sun* and the *Daily Mirror*." Alice sipped her sparkling water and poked at her pasta salad.

It was Saturday, two days since Noah had gone back to America. Rhia had come to Alice's for lunch. The sisters sat in the sunlit breakfast room that looked out on Alice's small patio and garden.

Rhia slathered butter on a croissant. "As tabloid stories go, I thought they were lovely."

"Tabloid stories are never lovely."

"In this case, I beg to differ. The pictures were so romantic. Noah looked so handsome and you looked fabulous. Two gorgeous people out enjoying an evening together at Casino d'Ambre. Totally harmless. Nothing the least tacky. Good press for Montedoro and the casino. And you both seemed to be having such a good time together. I don't see what you're so glum about."

She was glum because she missed him. A lot. It didn't make sense, she kept reminding herself, to miss a man she hardly knew. No matter how smoking hot he happened to be. "I sold him Orion. He arranged to have the veterinarian at the stables yesterday for the prepurchase exam and he's already sent the money." He'd wired the whole amount after the exam, before he got the papers to sign. So very, very Noah.

Rhia swallowed more pasta. "You've changed your mind about parting with the stallion, then, and want to back out of the sale?"

Alice scowled. "Of course not. I'm a horse breeder. I can't keep them all."

"Then what *is* the matter?"

"Everything. Nothing. Did you see the flowers in the big Murano glass vase in the foyer?"

"I did. The vase is fabulous. And the lilies... Your favorite."

"Noah sent them—both the flowers and the vase. He also sent a ridiculously expensive hammered-gold necklace studded with rubies."

"You know, I get the distinct impression that he fancies you." Rhia ate more pasta and chuckled to herself.

"What is so funny?"

"Grumpy, grumpy." Rhia was still chuckling.

"He wants me to come and visit him in California."

"Will you?"

"I haven't decided. He also wants to marry me."

Rhia blinked and swallowed the big bite of croissant she'd just shoved into her mouth. Since she hadn't chewed, she choked a little and had to wash it down with sparkling water. "Well," she said when she could talk again. "That was fast."

"You don't know the half of it."

Rhia set down her glass and sat back in her chair. "I'm listening."

"Oh, Rhia…"

"Just tell me. You'll feel better."

So Alice told her sister about taking Noah to the family beach, about his startling confession that he wanted to marry a princess—Alice, specifically. "Is that insane or what?"

Rhia shrugged. "He's very bold. Just like you. And you've admitted there *is* real attraction between you."

"But don't you think it's wildly arrogant and more than a little strange to decide to marry a princess out of thin air like that?"

"I'm not going to judge him. Please don't ask me to. What I think is that you really like him and lately you're not trusting your own instincts, so you think you *shouldn't* like him."

"Oh, Rhia. I don't know what to do…."

Her sister gave her a tender, understanding smile. "I think you do. You just haven't admitted it to yourself yet."

Noah arrived home again from the Bay Area on Saturday afternoon.

Lucy did not run out to greet him. Still sulking over

that damn school she wouldn't be going to, no doubt. Fine. Let her sulk. Eventually, she would see reason and accept that she needed more time at home, where he and Hannah, her former foster mom, who managed the estate now, could take care of her. Maybe at dinner that night, if she wasn't too hostile, he could suggest a few online classes. He needed to get her to slow down a little. There was too much stress and responsibility involved in going to college full-time and living on her own. She needed to ease into all that by degrees.

He thought about Alice. On the plane, he'd read the tabloid stories of their night together at Casino d'Ambre. Just looking at the pictures of her in that amazing gold dress made him want to hop another flight back to Montedoro, where he could kiss her and touch her and take off all her clothes.

She should have come home with him. But she hadn't. He had to be patient; he knew it. He was playing the long game with her. And the prize was a lifetime, the two of them, together.

Unfortunately, being patient about Alice wasn't easy. It made him edgy, made him want to pick a fight with someone like he used to do when he was young and stupid—pick a fight and kick some serious ass.

A ride might lift his spirits a little, get his mind off Alice in that gold dress. He put on old jeans and boots and a knit shirt and went out to the stables, where he greeted the staff and chose the Thoroughbred gelding Solitairio to ride.

He took a series of trails that wound over his thirty-acre estate and on and off neighboring properties. His neighbors owned horses, too. They shared an agreement, giving each other riding access.

An hour after he left the stables, he was feeling better about everything. The meetings with the streaming start-up had gone well. Lucy would see the light eventually and agree to take things more slowly. And in time Alice would be his wife.

Sunday, Alice went to breakfast at the palace with the family. She was a little nervous that her mother might not approve of all the press from her night out with Noah.

But Adrienne only greeted Alice with a hug—and congratulated her on getting such a fine price for Orion. Alice was just breathing a sigh of relief when Damien took the chair next to her at the breakfast table.

He leaned close. "So you sold Noah the horse he wanted."

"I did." Alice sipped her coffee.

"Well." Dami spread his napkin on his knee. "Good enough. And now he's gone back to California where he belongs." She promised herself she was not going to become annoyed with her brother, that he only wanted the best for her. Dami added, "And you won't be seeing him again."

That did it. She turned a blinding smile his way. "Actually, he invited me to come and visit him in California."

Her brother didn't miss a beat. "And, of course, you told him no."

"I told him I would think about it. And that is exactly what I'm doing."

Dami gave her a look. His expression remained absolutely calm. But his eyes shot sparks. "Are you *trying* to get hurt?"

She longed to blurt out the rest of it—that Noah wanted to marry her and she just might be considering that, too. But telling Dami was not the same as confiding in Rhia. Rhia didn't judge. Dami had decided he knew what was best for her. "There's no good way to answer that question, and you know it."

Dami only sat there, still wearing *that* look.

She laid it out for him clear as glass. "Mind your own business. Please."

"But, Allie, it *is* my business." He kept his voice carefully low, just between the two of them. "*I* invited him here."

"What is the matter with you?" She spoke very quietly, too. But she wrapped her whisper in a core of steel. "You'd think I was some wide-eyed little baby, unable to take care of myself. You're way out of line about this. You've already told me what you think I need to know. Now you can back off and stay out of it. Please."

"I think I should talk to him. I should have spoken to him earlier."

"Dami. Hear me. Don't you dare."

Something in the way she said that must have finally gotten through to him. Because he shook his head and muttered, "Don't say I didn't warn you...."

"Stay out of it. Are we clear?"

"Fine. We're clear." He was the one who looked away.

The next day, Alice received another vase—Chinese that time, decorated with cherry blossoms and filled with pink lilies, green anthuriums, plumeria the color of rainbow sherbet and flowering purple artichokes. That night he called her.

"I miss you," he said, his voice low and gruff and way too intimate. "When are you coming to see me?"

She felt an enormous smile bloom and couldn't have

stopped it if she'd wanted to. "The flowers are so beautiful."

"Which ones?"

"All of them—the lilies especially. Both vases, too. And that necklace. You shouldn't have sent that necklace."

"Come and visit me. You can wear it for me."

"Thank you. Now stop sending me things."

"I like sending you things. It's fun. How's my stallion?"

"Beautiful. And a gentleman. I hate to part with him."

"You won't have to if you marry me."

"A telephone proposal. How very romantic."

"It wasn't a proposal. Just a statement of fact. You'll know when I'm proposing, I promise you that. I want you to send Orion on Friday—can you do that?"

"Of course. If you have all the arrangements made?"

"I will. He'll fly into JFK, be picked up in a quarantine van and taken to a beautiful little farm in Maryland for testing." The required quarantine for transporting a stallion from Montedoro to the U.S.A. was thirty days, during which time Orion would be tested for contagious equine metritis. "I'll pay a visit to the farm the day after he arrives to see that he's managed the trip well. And I'll arrange to have him put on a hot walker daily for exercise." During quarantine a stallion couldn't be allowed out to pasture or to be ridden. A mechanical hot walker was a machine designed to cool a horse down after exercise. In this case, the machine would give the quarantined stallion the exercise he needed while in isolation.

She said, "By the end of next month, you will have him."

"Come and visit. You can be here when he arrives at his new home."

"That would be a long visit. I do have a life, you know."

He said nothing for a moment. The silence was warm, full of promise. Companionable. "I don't want to take anything away from you. I only want to give you more. We could live here *and* there in Montedoro. I know your work with your horses means everything to you. You wouldn't have to give that up. However you prefer it, that's how it will be."

"Suddenly we're talking about marriage again—but this isn't a proposal, right?"

"Absolutely not. I told you. When I propose, you won't have to ask if that's what I'm doing."

The next night, Tuesday, he called again. She asked about Lucy.

"She's doing well. Feeling great. And still after me to let her move to New York."

"*Let* her? She's twenty-three, you said."

"So? I told you. She hasn't been well for most of her life."

"But, Noah, she's well now, isn't she?"

"She can't be too careful." His voice had turned flat. Uncompromising.

Alice let the subject go. She'd never met Lucy, didn't really understand the situation. She had no right to nag him in any case. They hardly knew each other. She only *felt* as though she knew him. She needed to remember that.

Wednesday, she sent him a text letting him know she'd taken Orion out during her predawn ride.

Hving 2nd thgts abt selling him. He is 2 fabu.

He zipped one right back.

4get it. He's mine.

Hold the tude.

Come 2 C me.

U R 2 relentless.

Rite away wd b gud.

R U NTS?

They went back and forth like that for at least twenty minutes. She stood on the cobblestones outside the stable door, the sun warm on her back, thumbs flying over her phone. It was so much fun.

And yes, she was starting to think that a visit to California might be a lovely idea.

After that day, they texted regularly. He called every night and sent flowers again on Friday, the day Orion boarded a plane in a special stall-like crate for his flight to America.

Noah flew to Maryland to check on his new stallion and then flew from there to Los Angeles for another series of meetings that would go on over the weekend. They kept up an ongoing conversation in text messages, and he called her each night, which rather impressed her. He always called around eight, a perfect time for her since she was sticking close to home and usually at the villa for the evening by then. With the nine-hour time difference, though, it was eleven in the morning in California when he called. Somehow he always managed to call her anyway.

It pleased her, the way he made a point to take the time to get in touch with her consistently. It pleased her a lot. Maybe too much, she kept telling herself.

On Saturday she was expected at a gala charity auction in Cannes. A driver and her favorite bodyguard, Altus, showed up at seven to take her there. It was nice enough as those things went. She bid on several items and visited with people she'd known all her life and had her picture taken with people whose names she couldn't recall. At the end, she wrote a large check for the decorative mirror and antique side table she'd won.

On the drive home, she felt a little down somehow. For some reason, that made her want to talk to Noah. She got out her phone to text him—and it buzzed in her hand.

A text *from* him.

Still @ auction?

That down feeling? Evaporated.

It's over. Cn U tk?

WCU 1 hr.

She was back at her villa when the phone rang. They talked for two hours. She explained how she'd somehow ended up with a mirror and a side table she didn't even want and he told her all about the movie people he'd met with to discuss a film project he was considering investing in. They laughed together and she felt...understood somehow. Connected. And she couldn't help remembering that dream she'd had right after they'd first met, the dream where they rode through a meadow of wild-flowers and talked and laughed together like longtime companions.

Monday, she found pictures of him on the internet. And yes, it was becoming a habit with her, to look him up online. In the pictures, he was having lunch at the Beverly Hills Hotel with a famous movie producer and a couple of actors she recognized. She teased him about it when they talked that night.

He said, "You're checking up on me." He didn't sound the least bothered by the idea. "How am I doing?"

"So far, so good. Not a single scandal since you left Montedoro. No hot gossip about your newest girlfriend."

"You told me I had to be monogamous, remember?"

She half groaned, half laughed. "If you're only sleeping alone because I told you to, you're missing the point."

"Spoken like a woman. Not only does a guy have to do it your way, he has to *like* doing it your way."

"So you're feeling deprived, are you?"

"Only of your company."

She groaned again. "You *are* good. Too, too good."

"Exactly what I keep trying to tell you."

Tuesday, her mother invited her to lunch at the palace in the sovereign's apartment, just the two of them. Alice wondered what she'd done now. But it was lovely anyway to get a little one-on-one time with her mother in the elegant sitting room where Alice and her siblings used to play when they were children.

They chatted about Alice's plans for the stables and her breeding-and-training program, about how happy Rhia and Marcus were. They laughed over how big Alice's nieces and nephews were getting. Her mother had six grandchildren now, seven once Rhia's baby was born. It was hard to believe that Adrienne Bravo-Calabretti was a grandmother so many times over. She remained slim and ageless, her olive skin seeming to glow from within.

"We missed you at Sunday breakfast," Adrienne said a little too casually when they were sharing a dessert of white-chocolate raspberry-truffle cheesecake.

"I had that thing in Cannes Saturday night." And then there'd been that long, lovely chat with Noah. It had been after three when they'd said good-night. "I didn't make it to the stables for my early ride, either. I was…feeling lazy, I guess."

"Dami got me alone and asked for a word with me," her mother said softly. "He's worried about you."

Alice lost her appetite. She set her half-finished cake down on the coffee table. "I'm going to make a real effort not to roll my eyes right now."

Her mother's smile was patient. "Dami loves you. As do I." Alice kept her mouth shut. She couldn't help hoping that this wasn't about Noah after all. Her mother went on, "Your brother is concerned about your relationship with a friend of his."

So much for her hopes. "Oh, really?" Seriously annoyed and unwilling to make a lot of effort to hide it, she laid on the sarcasm. "Which friend is that?"

"The man from California who bought your stallion Orion. Noah Cordell?"

Alice wanted to grab the small cloisonné vase on the coffee table beside their lunch tray and hurl it at the damask-covered wall. "This isn't like you, Mother."

Adrienne had the grace to look chagrined. "You're right. Your father and I have always tried to stay out of the way, to let our children lead their own lives. But your brother was insistent that I speak with you."

"And since Glasgow, you don't trust me."

Adrienne set down her dessert fork. "That's not so."

"I hope not."

"Please, darling. Don't be upset with me."

Alice let out a low sound of real frustration. "I'm not upset with *you*. Not really. But I think I want to strangle Dami. All of a sudden he's worried for my...what? My virtue? It's laughable—besides being more than a little too late."

"Forgive him. He loves you. And I think he's finally growing up. He's changing, starting to think about his life and his future in a serious way, yet not quite sure how to go about making a change."

"Great. Fabulous. Good for him. But what does that have to do with me?"

"He doesn't want you getting hurt by a man who's just like he used to be, a man you met through him."

"He *told* me he would mind his own business. Instead, he came crying to you. And he has no right to bad-mouth Noah. Noah's never done anything Dami hasn't done. Plus, he and Noah are supposed to be friends."

Her mother raised a hand. "It was nothing that bad, I promise you, only that Noah Cordell is a heartbreaker. Dami just doesn't want you to get hurt."

Alice really did want to break something. "I might have to kill him. With my bare hands."

Her mother reached across and clasped her arm, a soothing touch. "My advice? Let it go. On reflection, I honestly do think that this is more about the changes in your brother than anything else." Adrienne tipped her head to the side, considering. "And I think you do like this man, Noah. I think you like him very much."

Alice had nothing to hide. Why not just admit it? She sat a little straighter. "I do like him. I'm beginning to... care for him. He's tough and competitive and way too smart. He calls me every evening. I can talk with him for hours. He's come a long way in his life and he's very proud and more than a little controlling. But he's also tender and funny and generous, too."

Adrienne's expression had softened. "I see that Dami isn't the only one of my children who is changing, growing more thoughtful, more mature, more capable of truly loving— And how about this? I will speak with your brother again on this subject. I will remind him that your life is your own and I have faith in your judgment."

Her mother's words touched her. "Thank you. Noah's invited me to come and visit him in California."

"Will you go?"

"Yes, Mother. I believe that I will."

Chapter Six

That night when Noah called, Alice told him she would like to come for a visit.

He instantly tried to take over. "Come tomorrow. I'll send a plane for you. I'll handle everything."

She was prepared for that. "Thank you. But no. I'll make my own arrangements. I'll need a little more time."

He made a growling sound. "How long is a *little* more time?"

"A couple of days."

"Thursday, then. You're coming Thursday."

"Friday, actually."

"That's three days. You said two."

"It's so nice that you're eager to see me."

"So, then, you'll come Thursday."

Rather than allow him to keep pushing her when she'd already made it clear she would arrive on Friday, she let a moment of silence speak for her.

"Alice. Alice, are you still there?"

"Right here," she answered sweetly.

"I've been patient."

She couldn't suppress a chuckle. "Oh, you have not."

"Yes, I have. I've waited for you to be ready to come to me. Don't you dare change your mind on me now."

"I'm not changing my mind, Noah."

"How long can you stay?"

"A week?"

"Not long enough," he grumbled. "You should stay for a month, at least. Longer. Forever."

"Let's leave it open-ended, why don't we? We'll see how it goes. I'll have to return by the middle of next month for Montedoro's annual Autumn Faire."

"A fair? That sounds like something you could skip this year."

"I never skip the Autumn Faire. There will be a street bazaar and a parade. I'll wear traditional dress and ride one of my horses."

"Sounds thrilling." His tone implied otherwise.

She held her ground. "I have to return for it. I've already agreed to participate."

He relented. "All right, then—and I have a meeting in San Francisco on Friday," he admitted at last. "No way to reschedule it."

"It's not a problem. I can come later, when you're at home."

"But if you came Thursday, you could fly with me up to the Bay Area. We could—"

"Noah."

"What?"

"Just tell me when you'll be back."

"Never mind," he grumbled. "Come Friday. Lucy and Hannah will be here to welcome you. And I'll be home Saturday."

"Wonderful. I'll see you then."

She took Altus and Michelle with her—Altus because her mother insisted that they all use bodyguards when traveling outside the principality. And Michelle because the housekeeper was an excellent companion who never got flustered by long lines or inconveniences and could pack weeks' worth of gear and clothing in a small number of bags.

With the time difference, they were able to leave Nice Friday morning and arrive at Santa Barbara Airport that afternoon. Altus transferred their bags to the car they had waiting and off they went.

It was a short ride along El Camino Real, less than half an hour from the airport to the gates of Noah's property in Carpinteria. The black iron gates parted as the car approached and they rolled along a curving driveway, past vineyards and orange trees and an olive grove, up the gentle slope of a sunlit hill to the white stucco villa with two wings branching off to either side of the carved-limestone entrance.

Even prettier than the pictures Alice had seen of it online, the house was a beautifully simple Italian-style villa, complete with wrought-iron balconies and a red-tile roof. Four wide arches to the left of the entrance framed a front-garden patio centered around a koi pond and land-scaped with tropical flowers and miniature palms.

The coffered mahogany door swung open as Altus stopped the car. A slim pixie-haired young woman in skinny jeans, pink Chuck Taylor high-tops and a pink-striped peplum T-shirt bounded out, followed at a more sedate pace by a taller, older woman with thick black hair parted in the middle and pinned up in back.

The girl had to be Lucy, and she looked so eager and happy to have visitors that Alice pushed open her door and called out, "Hello."

"Alice!" The girl blushed. "Er, I mean, Your Highness?"

"Just Alice. Please." She got out of the car and shut the door. "And you must be Lucy...."

"It's so good that you're here." Lucy ran up and embraced her. Laughing, Alice returned the hug. And then Lucy was grabbing her hand and pulling her toward the older woman. "And this is Hannah. Once she was my foster mom, and now she lives with us. She takes care of us—of Noah and me...."

The older woman nodded. "Welcome, Your Highness."

"Thank you, Hannah. Noah's told me about you, about how much he appreciates all you've done for him and Lucy—and call me Alice, won't you?"

"Alice, then," said Hannah with a warm smile. "Let's get you settled. Come this way...."

An hour later, Alice was comfortably installed in a large west-facing bedroom suite that overlooked the estate's equestrian fields and tree-lined riding trails. She could see El Camino Real and the endless blue Pacific beyond that. Michelle and Altus each had smaller rooms above Alice's, on the third floor.

Hannah had provided an afternoon snack of cheese, fresh fruit and iced tea. Alice and Lucy sat on the small balcony off of Alice's room, enjoying the view and the afternoon sun.

Lucy chattered away. "I'm *so* glad you're here. Noah told me all about you, and of course I had heard of you before. Who hasn't heard of your family? It's such a totally romantic story, isn't it? Your mother, the last of her line, visiting Hollywood and falling in love with an actor. I adore the pictures of their wedding, that fabulous dress she wore, all that Brussels lace, the gazillion seed pearls,

the yards and yards of netting and taffeta and tulle...."
Lucy sighed and pressed a hand to her chest. "Oh, my racing heart. Like something out of a fairy tale." She plucked a strawberry from the cheese tray and popped it into her mouth. "And they still love each other, don't they, your mother and your father?"

"They do, yes. Very much."

"Wonderful. Perfect. Heaven on earth. My mom and dad were deeply in love, too. But then he died before I was born. And we lost our mom when I was nine—did Noah tell you?"

"Yes, he—"

"Ugh! Noah!" Lucy pretended to strangle herself, complete with the bulging eyes and flapping tongue. And then she laughed. And then she groaned. "Honestly, I love Noah more than anything, but sometimes I wonder if he's *ever* going to let me get out on my own. I used to be sick a lot—he told you that, didn't he? Did he also bother to tell you I'm *well* now? Hello! I am. And that I got accepted to the Fashion Institute of Technology in New York for the spring semester? I did! FIT New York. It's the best fashion and design school in the country. They *loved* my portfolio, and my entry essay was brilliant, if I do say so myself. But I swear, Noah's so careful and so sure I can't handle it. I'm afraid that he won't let me go." She pulled a fat grape off the bunch, ate it—and kept right on talking. "Noah says you're twenty-five. Just two years older than me. But you seem so mature, so sophisticated."

Alice smiled at that. "You're making me feel ancient, you know."

Lucy blinked—and then laughed some more. "Oh, you're just kidding. I can see that."

Alice wasn't kidding, not really. There was something childlike about Lucy. She came across as much younger than twenty-three. But she didn't seem the least bit ill. On the contrary, she bubbled with energy and glowed with good health. "I'm sure Noah only wants the best for you. But on the other hand, every woman needs to get out and mix it up a little, to make her own way in the world."

"Oh, Alice. That is *exactly* what I keep trying to tell him. I mean, he's done *everything* for me, to make sure I had a chance when I was sick all the time, to get me the best doctors, the most advanced surgeries, the care I needed so I finally got well. I owe him everything, and like I said before, I love him so much. But I *am* well now. And one way or another, I have to make him see that I've got a great chance here. And I'm not passing it up just because he won't quit thinking of me as his sickly baby sister. Do you want to see my portfolio? I'm really ridiculously proud of it."

"I would love to see it."

So Lucy jumped up and ran to get it. She was back, breathless and pink cheeked, in no time. She shoved the cheese tray aside, plunked the zippered case down on the balcony table and started flipping through her designs.

"They're fabulous," said Alice. Because they were. They were very much like Lucy. Fun, lighthearted and brimming with energy. She favored bright colors and she freely mixed flowing fabrics with leather and lace. She had skirts made of netting in neon-bright colors combined with slinky silky tops worn under studded structured jackets. And then there were simpler pieces, too. Everyday pieces. Perfect little dresses, tops that would make a pair of jeans into something special.

Lucy chattered on. "I always loved to draw, you know?

And it was something I could do in bed when I wasn't well enough to go anywhere. I used to make up stories to myself of where I would go and what I would do—*and what I would wear*—when I finally got well. So I started drawing the clothes I saw in my fantasies, the clothes I saw myself wearing. I got Hannah to buy me a sewing machine and I taught myself to sew. I started making those clothes I dreamed of."

"Seriously. These are wonderful. You ought to be on one of those fashion-design shows."

Lucy put her hands over her ears and let out a silent squeal of delight. "Oh, you had better believe it, Alice. One of these days I will, just you watch and see." She flopped back into her chair—and then she sat straight up again. "Oh! I heard all about your beautiful horses, your Akhal-Tekes. I'll bet you want to get out to the stables, huh? Meet the guys and the horses. Ride."

"I would love to ride, but maybe I should wait for Noah." Noah. Just saying his name brought a hot little stab of eagerness to see him again. "He might want to show me around himself."

Lucy beamed. "You are so gone. You know that, right? But it's okay. So is he."

A shiver of pure happiness cascaded through her. "You think?"

"Are you kidding me? He was beyond pissed off that he wouldn't be here when you came. He wanted everything to be perfect for you. And he kept nagging poor Hannah about how it all had to be just so, giving her endless new items for the menus, insisting over and over that there had to be Casablanca lilies in your room, as though Hannah doesn't always remember what he asks for the first time."

Alice glanced through the wide-open French doors at the big vase on the inlaid table in the sitting area. "The lilies are so beautiful, and I do love the fragrance of them."

"Yeah. But he was impossible. Hannah finally had to talk back to him. She hardly ever does that, but when she does, believe me, he listens. She told him to back off her case and not get his boxers in a twist."

"No…"

"Yeah. It was so funny I had to clap my hand over my mouth to keep from laughing out loud—because I'm barely speaking to him lately and if he saw me laughing he would start thinking I was giving in and accepting that I'm not going to New York after all." Lucy lowered her voice then and spoke with steely determination. "But I *am* going. You watch me. One way or another. I'm going no matter what."

A few minutes later Hannah bustled in and shooed Lucy out so that Alice could rest after her long flight. "Dinner at seven-thirty," she told Alice. "It will only be you and Lucy, in the loggia off the family room downstairs. Now, you lie down for a little, why don't you? Put your feet up."

Alice stretched out on the bed, just for a minute or two.…

When she woke up, the sun beyond the balcony was half a red-gold ball sinking into the ocean, the sky a hot swirl of orange and purple. The bedside clock said it was quarter of seven. She had a quick shower. When she got out, Michelle was in the bedroom laying out a white dress with a square neckline and a pair of high-heeled red sandals for her.

Alice put on the dress and sandals and went downstairs to the family room off the ultramodern kitchen. The doors were open to the loggia and a table was set for two. Alice sat alone for a few minutes, sipping the iced concoction Hannah had served her, enjoying the fire in the outdoor fireplace that pushed back the slight evening chill, admiring the infinity pool just visible from where she sat and appreciating the expanse of the equestrian fields below.

Eventually, Lucy bounced out to join her, wearing the cutest striped top in mustard and yellow with a pair of cropped black silk pants and high wedge sandals.

"Adorable," said Alice.

Lucy fluttered her lashes and pulled back her chair. "I do my best. You're not so bad yourself." She giggled. "This is nice, isn't it? Just us girls."

"Yes, it is. Very."

"Oh, I knew I would like you. I adore Dami, and I always had a feeling I would get along great with all you Bravo-Calabrettis."

"I didn't realize you knew Dami."

Lucy shrugged. "He's come to stay here several times when he was visiting California. He's always funny and so charming. Right away he insisted that he would just be Dami, not His Highness or anything—the same way you did. I love to talk to him. I could talk to him forever. He takes time, you know, to pay attention to me, even if I am just Noah's little sister."

"You are a lot more than just Noah's sister," Alice chided. "And you're right. Dami *can* be a sweetheart." She'd been so annoyed with him lately she'd lost sight of his good qualities, his lightheartedness and generosity of spirit. She made a mental note to remember the good things about her bossy big brother.

Hannah brought the food and Lucy chattered on. After the meal, Lucy led Alice to the media room, where they shared a bowl of popcorn and laughed over a comedy about four sorority sisters lost in the jungle. It was still pretty early when the movie ended, but Alice couldn't stop yawning. Jet lag had taken its toll. She went upstairs, climbed into bed and was asleep five minutes after switching off the light.

Hours later she woke.

For a moment she didn't know where she was. And then it came to her: Noah's house. The clock by the bed said it was ten after two in the morning. She stared up into the darkness and wondered what had awakened her.

Then she heard a light tap on the door.

And she knew: Noah. She threw back the covers and switched on the lamp as she reached for her robe. Tying the belt as she went, she raced to the door and yanked it wide.

She caught him in the act of raising his hand to knock again. "Noah…" He looked so fine he stole her breath. How could he be even hotter than she had remembered?

"Okay. It's true," he said in that wonderful gruff tone that always made her pulse race. "I caught a midnight flight because I couldn't wait to see you." His gaze ran over her, hot and slow, from the top of her head to the tips of her toes. "You look amazing."

"All squinty eyed and half-asleep, you mean?"

"Exactly."

She scraped her hair out of her eyes and resisted the

urge to launch herself at him. "How long have you been standing out here?"

He braced an arm on the door frame and leaned in close. "About ten minutes, knocking intermittently. I was trying to wake you up without freaking you out."

"Ah. Very...thoughtful."

"You're staring," he whispered, and stared right back.

"Oh, I know. I can't seem to stop. It's just so good to see you." The urge to jump on him and kiss him sense-less kept getting stronger.

With slow, deliberate care, he lifted a hand and guided a wild curl of hair off her temple and behind her ear. The light touch struck hot sparks on her skin. "I don't know what's happening to me," he said in a wondering tone. "Standing outside a woman's bedroom door at two in the morning, patiently knocking at measured intervals... It's not really my style."

She yearned to touch him, yet she felt strangely shy. And that had her casting madly about for something at least reasonably intelligent to say. "How did your busi-ness meeting go?"

"It was a success." Those blue, blue eyes tempted her down to drowning. And oh, she wanted to go there with him, to sink beneath the waves of shared desire, to lose herself in the heat and hardness of his body. He whis-pered, "I invested."

"In?"

"A new company. They stream television shows. It's an interesting start-up—though I have to admit, today I could not have cared less. I had a hell of a time concen-trating in the meetings. I kept thinking that you were on your way and then, in the afternoon, that you must be here. I kept wishing *I* was here. I couldn't get back fast enough." He said the last softly, a little bit desperately. "And why am I telling you all this? It's nothing you really need to know."

"Of course I need to know that you're thinking of me, that you want to be with me," she told him sternly. "It's important that I know."

He chuckled then. "Ah. That's it. I'm telling you because you need to know."

She had no trouble understanding his desperation. She felt it, too. "I'm glad you came back early. Glad that you stood here in the hallway patiently knocking until I heard you and woke up...."

"I love this...." He touched her cheek beside her mouth.

She had no idea what he was talking about. "This... what?"

He made a low disappointed sound. "You frowned. Gone."

And then she knew. She smiled. "Dimples. You love my dimples?"

"There they are.... Yeah." He touched each one, a matched pair of quick, sweet caresses. And then his finger strayed. He tapped the tip of her chin and traced the line of her jaw, raising little shivers of awareness as he went.

"I spent the afternoon and evening with Lucy," she said. Her voice came out sounding husky and a little bit breathless. "I love her already."

"I knew you would."

She shook her head and gently scolded, "You know she's not happy with you right now...."

"She'll get over it."

Alice wasn't so sure. "She seems pretty determined to get going on her own life."

Twin lines formed between his brows. "She's not strong enough yet."

"*She* says that she is."

"Wishful thinking. She's always been a dreamer."

"Noah. I believe her."

"She can be convincing, I'll admit."

"No. Honestly, if I didn't know she'd been sick, I never would have guessed that she spent so much of her childhood in bed."

"That's because she's better, a lot better. And all I want is for her to stay that way, not to push too hard and end up flat on her back again. In time, yes, she'll get out on her own. But at this point, she still needs taking care of. And why are we talking about this right now?"

"Because she matters. Because you love her. Because she has a right to her own life—and I saw her portfolio. She obviously has talent, a great deal of it. How can you ask her to miss her chance?"

"Alice, come on." He'd changed tactics; his voice had turned coaxing and his eyes were soft as a summer sky. He put a finger to her lips. "Enough about Lucy."

Alice longed to say more. But maybe not now. Not in the middle of the night, when he'd flown home on a red-eye just to be with her, when she was so glad to see him she felt like a moonbeam, weightless and silvery, dancing on air.

She reached up and laid her hand on the side of his smooth jaw. He smelled of soap, all fresh and clean. He must have showered before he came to find her. That touched her, the way he cared so much to please her. So much so, evidently, that his housekeeper had gotten fed up with his endless demands and been forced to take him down a peg. "I like Hannah, too."

He turned his head enough to breathe a lovely, warm kiss into the heart of her palm. "She's the best."

She let her touch trail lower and tugged on the collar of his polo shirt. "And did I mention it's *so* good to see you?"

"You did." He leaned closer. His warm breath touched her cheek. "And I have a question…."

"Mmm?"

"If you're that happy to see me, how come you haven't kissed me?"

She wrapped her hand around his neck and pulled him down to her. "You're right. I need to fix that…."

His lips were so close. "Do it." It was a command, one she was only too happy to obey.

Their lips met.

Paradise.

She slid her other arm up to clasp around his neck and he reached out and reeled her in. Her breasts pressed against his hard chest, and oh, my, down against her belly, she felt how much he wanted her.

And it was so good. So right.

She really had missed him. Three weeks since that first day when she had mistaken him for a stable hand. In three weeks he had become…special to her. Important. Almost a necessity. Like air and water and her beautiful horses.

Now that she had him in her arms again, now that she had his mouth on hers, she didn't want to stop kissing him. She didn't want to let him go. She wanted his kiss, his touch, the heat of his body so close to hers.

She wanted everything.

All of him.

Tonight.

He deepened the kiss, wrapping her tighter in his powerful embrace. She pressed her body closer to his heat and his strength.

It wasn't close enough.

With a little moan, she surged up closer still. He took her cue and caught her by the waist, lifting her. She responded instinctively, wrapping her arms and legs around him.

She gasped. He groaned. She was all over him like a fresh coat of paint, and it was marvelous. The hardest, hottest part of him pressed insistently against the soft womanly core of her, with only a few layers of clothing between.

He tore his mouth from hers and his eyes burned down at her, blue fire. "Alice?"

She knew exactly what he was asking. And she knew she wanted to answer yes.

At the same time, she hesitated. The new Alice, the more cautious Alice, nagged at her to put on the brakes.

And the old Alice, the *real* Alice, was having none of that.

How could she call this magic wrong? It *wasn't* wrong.

All right, yes, she did realize that they had a long way to go if they hoped to carve out a slice of forever side by side. She had to know him better, trust him more.

And *he* had to learn to trust *her,* to count on her.

They both had to find a way to reach for each other with open hearts, to be guided by each other, to hold on, to share support, to count on each other when things got rough.

It's too soon. Her wiser self kept after her. *You know*

how you are, always leaping before you look. She needed
to be more careful. She needed to keep from getting
swept away in the heat of the moment.

But no.

Being more careful was the *last* thing she needed right
now. At least, her heart thought so. With every swift,
hungry beat, her heart seemed to insist that it wasn't
too soon at all.

In the weeks apart, when they'd talked and texted constantly, something had been changing. Being so far away
from him had actually brought them closer.

So that now, tonight, when he touched her at last,
when she heard his voice so low and tender, something
special happened. All her doubts melted to nothing. And
she knew a deeper truth.

She knew that it would be wrong to send him back to
his own bed. It would be wrong and it would be false.

And cowardly, too.

What was that lovely thing Rhia had said to her?

That she was a bold person, someone who lived by
her instincts. Rhia had said that she should stop trying
to be otherwise, stop second-guessing and being overly
careful, stop working so hard to be someone she wasn't.

"My God." Noah's eyes blazed down at her. His wonderful mouth was swollen from kissing her, his eyes feral
with need. "Alice?"

And she did it. She took the plunge, gave him the answer they both longed for. "Yes."

"Alice…" It came out on a groan and he claimed her
mouth again, harder and deeper even than before.

She kissed him back. The choice had been made
and she was bound to glory in it. She wrapped her legs
and arms all the tighter around him, pressing her hips

against him, feeling him there, right where she wanted him, tucked so close against the feminine heart of her.

"Alice," he whispered once more, so tenderly now. "Alice..."

And then he carried her over the threshold into the shadowed bedroom, pausing only to kick the door closed before striding straight for the bed.

Chapter Seven

Noah hardly dared to believe.

Now. Tonight. All night.

Alice, in his arms.

They had far too many clothes on. He needed to deal with that. Fast.

And he did. He took her by the waist and lowered her to the rug by the bed, groaning a little at the wonderful friction as her body slid down the front of him until her bare feet took her weight.

She gazed up at him, eyes lazy and hot, soft mouth parted. "Noah…"

He clasped her waist tighter, not wanting to let go, locking her in place. "Do. Not. Move."

She laughed, full-out as always, and husky, too. The sound played over him, making him hungrier, harder. Even more ready than before. She said, "I'm not going anywhere."

"Good." He let go of her and started ripping off his clothes, shirt first. He bent and reached with both fists over his shoulders, gathering the knit material up in a wad, yanking it off and away.

She remained right where he'd put her, looking like an angel in a white robe that seemed spun of silk and cobwebs, her hair wild on her shoulders, her eyes full of promises he fully intended to see that she kept.

He had his zipper down and his trousers dropped when he realized how he'd messed up. A chain of swear words escaped him.

She laughed again. "Oh, come on, Noah. It can't be all *that* bad."

He bent and yanked his pants back up. "I've got to go get condoms," he confessed with a groan.

"Condoms." She looked at him levelly. Calmly. Regally.

He felt like a complete idiot, a dolt of epic proportions. "I'll run all the way to my rooms. I won't be a minute, I swear."

She reached over, pulled open the drawer by the bed and came up with a box of them. "Will these do?"

The woman amazed him. "You brought condoms all the way from Montedoro?"

She tipped up her chin. So proud. So adorable. "I believe it's best to be prepared and responsible. We've had more than one unexpected pregnancy in my family. Those pregnancies ended well, in good marriages and wanted babies. But still, I prefer not to take that chance."

He felt better about everything. "You *were* planning to have sex with me. God. I'm so glad."

Her chin stayed high. "What I *planned* was to be safe *if* I had sex with you."

He wanted to grab her and kiss her senseless, but he had a feeling he'd be better off at that point to fake a little humility. "Yes, ma'am."

She shook the box at him. "Not that I had any intention of using them so soon...."

"Oh, hell, no. Of course you didn't." *And you damn well better not change your mind now.*

Her dimples flashed. He knew then that it would be all right, that she would let him stay with her. That he would have her, hold her, claim her as his own.

Tonight.

She opened the box, took one out and set it on the nightstand. Then she dropped the box back into the drawer and pushed it shut. "Please. Proceed."

And he did. He proceeded the hell out of getting naked fast. When he tossed away his second sock and stood before her in nothing but a little aftershave, she was all softness and sweet, willing woman again.

"Oh, Noah," she whispered, and she stepped in close. She put her hand on his chest, right over his breastbone. "Oh, my…"

He bent and took her mouth. Incredible, the taste of her. No woman ever had tasted so good.

She was a lot more than he'd bargained for when he went looking for his princess. A whole lot more. And he was absolutely fine with that.

He framed her face in his two hands, threading his fingers up into the tangled cloud of her golden-brown hair. And he went on kissing her, feeding off that tender, wet, hot mouth of hers until he was so hard he started worrying he might lose it just standing there naked at the side of the bed, his mouth locked with hers.

No way could he let that happen.

He got to work getting her undressed, first tugging the tail on the bow that held her robe together. The silken tie slithered off and down to the rug. And the robe fell open, revealing a lacy copper-colored cami and a pair of very tiny matching tap pants. He pushed the robe off her shoulders. It fell with a soft airy sound, collapsing around their feet.

Then he pushed down the tap pants, taking longer about that than he'd intended to. But the feel of her skin under his palms, the glorious smooth curves of her hips, the long, strong length of her flawless thighs....

He kind of got lost in the sheer beauty of her. What red-blooded man wouldn't?

But eventually, she stepped out of the tap pants, and he took the lacy hem of that little camisole and pulled it up over her head and away.

And that was it. They were both naked.

And she was so beautiful he almost lost it all over again. Not fragile, not Alice. Uh-uh. All woman, and strong, a true horsewoman, with more muscle than most, with shapely arms and round, high breasts, a tight little waist and lean hips. And those legs of hers...

He couldn't wait to have them wrapped around him good and hard again.

He scooped her up and laid her down. She didn't argue, only sighed and pulled him down with her, offering that tender mouth up to him once again. He took what she offered and kissed her, a hard claiming kiss.

And he went on kissing her, letting his hands go exploring, loving the feel of her skin, the lilies-and-musk scent of her, those hot little cries she made when he cupped her breasts and teased at the nipples, when he spread his fingers across her belly and rubbed.

It got to him, got to him good, to imagine that tight stomach of hers softening, slowly going round and then turning hard all over again—with his baby. He wanted that, to watch her get bigger with their child. He'd done what he had to do in his life to care for his sister, to make a place in the world that no one could take from him or anyone he claimed as his.

Now he had that place. He had the power and the money to earn what mattered—and more important, to hold on to what he earned, to mold the future for his children and his children's children. He had enough to offer a woman like this one, enough to make her his. To give her everything.

To keep her safe and happy and having his babies.

He let his hand stray lower. He parted the closely trimmed curls at the top of those beautiful thighs. And he dipped a finger in.

Wet. Hot. Silky.

She cried out against his lips and caught his face in her two hands. "Noah…"

He dipped another finger in. "Like this?"

"Yes," she whispered. And, "Yes," again.

"So soft. Hot…"

"Noah. Oh, Noah…"

He liked that. More than anything. The way she said his name like he counted, like she couldn't any more get enough of him than he could of her, like he really was the man he'd worked so hard to become—and that other guy, too. The one in the old jeans and the battered boots, sweeping out the stable, dreaming of the day he might have something to call his own. She liked that guy, too, even if she'd been pissed off at him for misleading her.

She reached down between them, wrapped her fingers around him. And then she started stroking.

He was sure he would die. And he knew it would be worth it.

Too bad he couldn't last if she kept that up. He had to reach down between them and capture her wrist.

Her eyes flew open. "Too much?"

His answer was a hard groan and another deep, hungry kiss. She wrapped both arms around him and held him so close.

He wanted to taste her, in the heart of her, where she was so hot and wet. But it had been too long for him. He feared he wouldn't last long enough to feel her sweet body all around him.

So he groped for the night table and found the condom. He had it out of the wrapper and down over himself in a matter of seconds, and then he lifted up on his hands to position himself.

She gazed up at him, eyes dazed, mouth so soft and willing. And she ran her hands over him, across his shoulders, down his chest. Slowly, she smiled, a knowing, wicked smile, those dimples of hers making naughty little creases in her velvety cheeks.

And then she got her feet braced somehow and she was turning him—turning *them*. She must have seen that she'd surprised him, because another of those throaty killer laughs escaped her.

He found himself on his back, staring up at her. "What?" he asked in a growl, though he had a pretty good idea of what—and he didn't mind in the least.

"I want to be on top, that's all." She folded those muscular legs to either side of his waist and sat up on him.

"Be my guest," he managed on a groan. The view was amazing. He couldn't resist. He cupped her breasts, teased the tight dusky nipples with his thumbs.

And then she lifted up again. She reached down between them and she took him in her hand.

They both groaned as she lowered her sleek, strong

body down onto him. She did it slowly, drawing it out, making him suffer and clearly loving every minute of it.

He grasped her waist, trying to take a little control, trying not to lose it when they were so close.

But she just kept right on at her own pace, slowly claiming him, surrounding him with her wet heat, her silky softness, owning him, taking him in. It went on forever, and every second he knew that he couldn't hold on, couldn't last a second longer.

And yet, somehow, he did hold on. For that second. And the one after that, and even the one after that.

Until she had him fully within her.

She stilled. He followed her lead, holding himself steady, though his whole body ached with the need to move. He stared up at her and she gazed down at him through another sweet, endless space of time. He knew he would explode.

Finally, when he was past the point where he couldn't take it anymore and yet, through some dark miracle, kept on taking it without losing it after all, she started to lift up again.

He still clasped her waist and he grabbed on hard—and pulled her back down. She moaned at that and let her head fall back. So beautiful, her long slim neck straining, her hair falling over her shoulders, her mouth open in another cry, a silent one.

After that he lost track of everything but the pure, perfect sensation of being held tight inside her. She rocked those hard little hips on him and he rocked with her.

It was forever and only a moment. Light exploded behind his eyes, and then he was reaching for her shoulders, pulling her down onto him, tight and close. He let his hands glide along the fine shape of her slender back to grasp the twin curves of her bottom and he held her good and tight and rocked up hard against her.

She took him, she pushed right back. A shudder claimed her and he knew she was almost there. Inside, she closed and opened on him in rhythmic contractions. She cried out.

That did it. He was so ready, and now she was going over. He didn't have to hold out any longer.

He lifted his head enough to claim her mouth. She opened for him, her tongue sliding over his, welcoming him with a keening little sigh as her body continued to pulse around him.

So good. Exactly right. Doubly joined to her, he kissed her and he let it happen, let his climax rise to meet hers. No stopping it now. It rolled up through the core of him, a long wave of heat and energy, spreading outward so that everything—his body, her body, the whole of the world—seemed to shimmer, to open.

He surged up harder than ever into her, still holding the endless kiss they shared. She breathed his name into his mouth. He drank it. Drank *her,* as the end shuddered over him in a spinning-hot explosion of burning, perfect light.

Curled on her side facing the bedside table, Alice woke from a deep, peaceful sleep.

The clock by the lamp said it was almost ten in the morning. Daylight glowed around the edges of the drawn curtains.

She rolled onto her back and eased a hand out, feeling her way across the sheet to the other side of the bed. Empty. Frowning a little, she turned her head.

Gloriously naked, feet planted wide apart on the

cream-colored rug, Noah lounged in one of the sitting-area chairs, watching her through hooded eyes.

Alarm jangled through her. Was something the matter?

She bounced to a sitting position, instinctively pulling the sheet against her bare breasts, pushing her hair out of her eyes. "Noah, what...?"

He got up and came toward her. Her heart rate spiked. He really was one magnificent-looking man, wide shouldered and broad in the chest, with lean, hard arms, a sculpted belly and sharply muscled legs nicely dusted with burnished gold hair. She found herself staring at the most manly part of him. It really was every bit as breathtaking as the rest of him, even at half-mast.

Halting at the side of the bed, he stood staring down at her.

She blinked up at him, vivid images from the night before flashing through her mind. It had been wonderful. They'd used three of her condoms and made love till near dawn, finally falling asleep wrapped up in each other's arms. "Um. Good morning."

He held out his hand. "Come here."

She frowned, tipped her head to the side and tried to figure out what exactly was going on with him. "Is everything...all right?"

He nodded. He really was looking so very serious. She kept having the feeling that something terrible must have happened. But what?

He prompted, "Take my hand." He still had it outstretched to her.

And she thought of that night at the palace when she'd first learned he wasn't a poverty-stricken stable worker after all, and she'd been so angry with him. He'd offered his hand to her then. And she couldn't bear not to take it, couldn't leave him standing there, reaching out to nothing. She just had to reach back.

She took his hand. His fingers curled around hers, warm and strong and steady. And her heart gave a little lurch of pleasure. Of hope and happiness. "Last night was so beautiful, Noah."

"It was," he said softly. "Let go of the sheet."

Why not? She'd never been all that overly modest, anyway. And he'd seen every inch of her last night. Plus, he was naked, too. They were naked together. A ragged little sigh escaped her as she let the sheet drop. He tugged on her hand. She swung her bare legs over the side of the bed and stood.

"This way…." He led her across the lustrous mahogany floor to the nearest set of French doors, where he released her hand and drew the curtain back.

Morning light burnished the equestrian fields. Several of his men were out working with the horses. A breeze blew the branches of the trees lining the riding trails. Farther out, the ocean was a perfect shade of blue with a rim of white waves rolling onto the sandy ribbon of shoreline.

She turned to Noah again and saw he was watching her. His gaze seemed approving. And possessive. A delicious little shiver ran up the backs of her bare calves. Butterflies got loose in her belly—and her anxiety eased. He wouldn't be looking at her in that sexy, exciting way if he was about to break some awful bit of news to her.

"I'll tell you what's even more beautiful than last night," he said. "You are, Alice. You knock me out…."

A flush of pleasure warmed her cheeks. She breathed easier still. It was definitely not bad news, then. He wouldn't take time to shower her with compliments if he had something terrible to tell her, would he?

Surely not.

So if not bad news, then what?

"Alice." And he dropped to a bare knee right there in front of her—at which point the situation became all too clear. Oh, she should have guessed. She started to speak, but before she could make a sound, he raised his other hand.

Wouldn't you know? There was a ring in it, a stunning marquise-cut solitaire on a platinum band. The giant diamond glittered at her.

She managed to croak out, "Oh, Noah…"

And then he proposed to her, right there on his knees, naked in the morning light.

"I know what I want, Alice. I've known for certain since that first morning I saw you in the flesh, tacking up that golden mare in the palace stables before dawn. I want *you,* Alice. Only you. Now, tomorrow, for the rest of our lives. Let me give you everything, Alice. Marry me. Be my wife."

Chapter Eight

Alice caught that plump lower lip of hers between her teeth. "Noah, I…" The words trailed off.

Not that he needed to hear anymore. He already knew by the tone of her voice and the way she looked down at him, so sweet and regretful, that she wasn't going for it.

"Crap." He stood. No point in kneeling in front of her stark naked if she wasn't going to give in and say yes.

She stared up at him, those gray-blue eyes soft and maybe a little worried—for him. That ticked him off. He didn't want her concern. He wanted *her.* Beside him. For the rest of their lives.

"You're amazing," she said. "I really am crazy for you."

He took her by her silky shoulders and grumbled, "So why aren't you saying yes?"

"Ahem." She went on tiptoe and kissed him—a quick little peck of a kiss. And then she settled back onto her heels again and suggested gently, "Maybe you forgot? A certain four-letter word seems to have gone missing from your proposal."

He scowled down at her. "Fine. I love you, then. I love you madly. All the way to distraction and beyond. You are my shining hope, my only dream of happiness. Marry me, Alice. Say yes."

She put her hand on his chest, the way she had more than once the night before. "I know you have a heart, Noah. I can feel it beating away strong and steady in there."

"What the hell is that supposed to mean?"

"It means I know what I want now, after years of throwing myself wildly into all kinds of iffy situations."

Just like a woman. She knew what she wanted, but she failed to share it with him.

Patiently, he suggested, "And what, exactly, *is* it that you want, Alice?"

"I want it all. I'll have nothing less. I want everything. All that you have. Not only your strength and protection, your fidelity and your hot body and half of everything you own. Not only your brilliant brain and great sense of humor and your otherworldly way with my horses. I want your heart, too. And I know I don't have that yet. And until I do, I won't say yes to you."

"My heart." He sent a weary glance in the direction of the forged-iron fixture overhead.

"Your heart," she repeated with great enthusiasm. "Exactly."

"I'll play along. What about *your* heart?"

"I get yours, you get mine. That's how it works."

He let his lip curl into something that wasn't a smile. "You're being sentimental. It's all just words, what you're talking about."

"Uh-uh. It's not just words. And until you understand that and give me what I want from you, I'm not going to marry you. It's just not going to happen."

He was tempted to shake her until a little good sense fell out. "Alice. Think about it. I've already offered you everything."

"No, you haven't. But you will." She spoke with confidence. Only the slight tightening around her mouth hinted she might have doubts.

He decided to look on the bright side. She hadn't said no. She'd only said *not yet*. Very few deals were ever finalized on the first offer anyway.

And she did look so beautiful, standing there naked in the morning light. Her skin had a golden cast and the scent of lilies swam around him.

He couldn't resist. He stroked her hair. She didn't object. In fact, she stared at him with shining eyes, even let out a sweet, rough little sigh when he ran the back of his finger along the side of her neck.

"You want me," he reminded her, just in case she might be thinking of telling him that last night had been a mistake. "You want me and I want you."

She answered with no hesitation. "Oh, yes. Absolutely."

He touched the pulse in the undercurve of her throat. It beat fast. Yearning. Eager. "I want to marry you. I'm not giving up."

"Of course you're not." She searched his face. Her voice was gentle, almost tender. He realized he wanted her more than ever right then. "I love that about you, Noah. I don't want you to give up."

He slid his fingers around the back of her neck, up into the warm, living fall of her hair. "If you're not going to say yes to my proposal right now, the least you can do is kiss me."

"Oh, I would be only too happy to kiss you."

Enough said. He lowered his mouth to hers. She swayed toward him, sliding her arms up around his neck.

Her body pressed like a brand all along the front of him. He was fully erect in an instant.

He grasped her waist, the way he had at the door last night, and lifted her from the floor. Those fine legs came around him and she linked her ankles at the small of his back.

They groaned in unison.

He carried her that way to the bed, where he paused long enough to set the ring she'd refused on the night-stand. Then he lowered her down to the tangled sheets.

She made no objections. On the contrary, she went on kissing him eagerly, deeply.

He might not have her promise to marry him yet.

But he *was* in her bed.

An hour later, Alice handed him the fabulous ring, kissed him one last time and then sent him to his room to shower and dress. He was barely out the door when someone tapped on it.

Michelle peeked in. "Good morning." Alice had put on her robe while Noah was getting dressed, but the cami and tap pants lay on the bedside rug where he'd dropped them the night before. Michelle bustled over and picked them up. "Breakfast here in the room or...?"

"I'll go down. We'll grab a quick bite and then I'll get my first look at the stables, followed by a long ride and a tour of the property."

Michelle only stood there, holding the bits of satin and lace, a look of bemusement on her face.

Alice held her hands out to the side, palms up. "What?"

"You look positively...glowing."

Glowing. Hmm. She felt well satisfied, certainly. It

had been a wonderful night. But she didn't feel exactly glowing. That would come later, if things went as she hoped they might.

She smiled at Michelle anyway. "Thanks. I'm working on it." And she turned for the bathroom and a nice hot shower.

"What's going on?" Alice asked Noah when she joined him at the table out in the loggia. Beyond the open French doors to the family room, men and women in white shirts and black trousers bustled back and forth. A big bearded fellow in a chef's hat had taken over the kitchen. Alice had seen the pots bubbling on the giant red-knobbed steel range. It all smelled wonderful.

"We're having a party," Noah said. "Coffee?" He held the carafe above her cup.

"Yes, please—a party *tonight?*"

"A welcome party for you. Just some people I know— neighbors, business associates. Is that all right with you?"

"Of course. It's only that this is the first time anyone's mentioned a party to me."

"I'm sure they assumed I'd told you. And I should have." He attempted to look contrite. "I'm sorry, Alice."

She laughed then—and she leaned close to him to whisper, "You intended to announce our engagement tonight, didn't you?"

He gave her a dark look and dropped the apologetic act. "You're damn straight. You should say yes and not ruin my big plan."

She sat back in her chair and gazed out at the tree-shaded, sun-dappled garden. "I believe you are the most relentless person I have ever known."

"You're right. I don't give up. You should say yes

now. Telling me no is only putting off the inevitable." He said it teasingly. But he wasn't teasing, not really. Alice thought of the night before, of how sweet and eager he'd been to see her. He had so many stellar qualities. But he did have a ruthless side, a side that demanded loyalty rather than graciously accepting it, a side that strove constantly for control.

He might claim her loyalty. But she ran her own life and made her own choices. And with the man she loved, she would be willing to share control. But never surrender it completely.

"Alice!" Lucy hovered in the open doorway to the family room, wearing a gathered red skirt with white polka dots, a red lace bandeau and a jean jacket with big red buttons. She bounced over, grabbed Alice by the shoulders and planted a big kiss on her cheek. "There you are." She took the chair on Alice's other side, grabbed an apple from the bowl in the center of the table and bit into it with gusto.

Hannah came out carrying two plates piled with scrambled eggs, bacon, browned potatoes and golden toast. "I hope scrambled will do." She set a plate in front of Alice.

"Wonderful." Alice beamed at her and picked up her fork as Hannah set the other plate in front of Noah.

"I had my breakfast *hours* ago," Lucy announced, and chomped on her apple. "So what are you going to do today?" she asked Alice, taking great care to ignore her brother. "I mean, besides partying all night with Noah's rich friends."

Alice reached over and put her hand on Noah's. He turned his hand over and laced his fingers with hers. A delicious little thrill skittered through her. He might be ruthless and overbearing at times, but when he touched her, she couldn't help thinking he was worth it. "Noah is showing me the stables and then we'll go riding."

Lucy waved her half-finished apple. "I would go with you, but I don't think I like the company you keep."

"Lucy." Noah sent her a warning frown.

She continued to pretend he wasn't there. "Well, Alice, I'm going to put in a few hours sketching new designs." She jumped up, bent over Alice and placed an apple-scented kiss on her cheek. "Come find me if he gives you a moment to yourself...."

Noah kept a variety of breeds, including Morgans, Thoroughbreds and Arabians. Each horse was a beauty with impeccable bloodlines, well trained and well cared for. And the stables and facilities were top-notch. None of that surprised Alice, but it was lovely to see it all for herself nonetheless. Orion would be happy here.

She met his staff—the two trainers, the grooms and stable hands—and she admired the dressage and jumping areas, the oval-shaped private racetrack and the state-of-the-art hot walker. Once she'd had the tour, they chose their horses. He rode a big black Thoroughbred mare named Astra and she chose Golden Boy, a handsome palomino gelding with a blaze on his forehead and a thick ivory mane. Altus, on a gray gelding, followed them at a discreet distance.

They rode for hours, on the trails around the property and sometimes onto trails that belonged to his neighbors. The horses seemed familiar with the route and comfortable with drinking from the troughs they came upon now and then along the way.

Eventually, he turned onto a trail that went under the

highway and they ended up at the ocean, on the ribbon of golden beach. It was nearly deserted, which surprised her. As they rode side by side on the wet, packed sand at the edge of the tide, he told her that the beach was privately owned by him and a group of his neighbors.

They rode until they reached the place where the rocky cliffs jutted out into the tide, much like the cliffs at her family's private beach in Montedoro. It was all so beautiful and perfect. Too perfect, really.

It had her thinking of the other Noah, the scruffy down-and-out Noah she'd met first. She wondered about his early years, about his life growing up. Really, she needed to know more about the man he'd started out as.

"Alice."

She glanced over at him. The sun made his hair gleam like the brightest gold. He grinned and her pulse kicked up a notch. Really, the man ought to come with a warning label: Too Hot. Contents Combustible.

He lowered his reins, canting slightly forward. She didn't have to hear him cluck his tongue to know what he was up to.

They took off in unison, her palomino as quick and willing as his black. The wind smelled of salt and sea, cool and sweet as it pulled at her tied-back hair. She bent over Golden Boy's fine strong neck and whispered excited encouragements as they raced toward the other end of the beach, where Altus waited, ever watchful.

The race was too short. They ended up neck and neck—and then turned their mounts as one and raced back the other way.

That time, she won by half a length. But of course, he couldn't leave it. A lucky thing she had that figured out ahead of time. Again they turned and made for the other end.

He had the slightest edge on her and won that time. When they pulled to a halt, he sent her a grin of such triumph she *had* to kiss him. She sidled her mount in close. He must have read her look, because he met her in the middle.

She laughed against his mouth as the horses shifted beneath them, pulling them away from each other—and then bringing them together so their lips met again.

"We need to go back," he told her regretfully. "The party starts at eight."

Side by side, they turned for the trail that would take them beneath the highway and back the way they'd come.

At the stables, they let the hands clean the tack but took care of their mounts themselves. They hosed off all the salt and sand. Then Alice gave Golden Boy a nice long rubdown, while Noah did the same for Astra. A groom led both horses away to feed and water them. Noah had a few things to discuss with the trainers, so she left him and went on to the house, with Altus following close behind.

Lucy must have been watching for her. She was waiting at the side door when Alice approached.

"Come on," she said, and grabbed Alice's hand. "Have a cold drink with me. There's plenty of time…."

So they went up to Lucy's room, which faced the mountains and was as bright and eye-catching as Lucy herself, the linens neon yellow and deep fuchsia pink. There were plants in pots everywhere. Lucy's drawings and designs covered the walls, and a fat orange cat lay on the floor between the open doors to the balcony, sprawled on its back, sound asleep.

Lucy scooped up the big cat and introduced him to Alice. "Boris, this is Alice. I like her a lot, so you'd better be nice to her."

The cat looked exceedingly bored, but Alice said hello anyway and scratched the big fellow behind the ears. She got a faint lazy purr for her efforts.

Lucy got them each a canned soft drink from her minifridge and they took comfy chairs in her small sitting area. It didn't take her long to get around to what was bothering her.

"Lately, I have a hard time remembering how much I love my brother and how good he's been to me," Lucy said in a whisper, as though Noah might be standing out in the hallway, his ear pressed to the door. "I swear, most of the time now I never want to speak to him again. But I know I need to try harder to get through to him before I do anything drastic."

Alice didn't like the sound of that. "Drastic. Like what?"

"You don't want to know."

"But, Lucy—"

"Trust me. It's better if you don't know. It just puts you in the middle of this more than you already are."

"All right, now you're scaring me."

"Oh, please. It's nothing that awful." Lucy knocked back a big gulp of ginger ale. "And I'm twenty-three years old. If I want to walk out of here and not look back, he can't stop me. But I don't want to do that."

"You want your brother's blessing," Alice said gently.

"Yes, I do. And that means I'm going to have to talk to him some more. I'm going to have to try again to get him to see that he has to let me go." She waved a hand. "Oh, not tonight. Not with the big party and all, but tomorrow or the next day. And I know, a minute ago I said you shouldn't be in the middle of this. I do totally get that it's not fair to ask you, but will you maybe just think about backing me up?"

Alice had no idea how to answer. She felt a strong sense of loyalty to Noah. But she also sympathized with Lucy. Noah *was* too protective and Lucy deserved her chance at her dream.

Her indecision must have shown on her face because Lucy groaned. "Okay, never mind. It's not your battle, I know that. Like I said, I shouldn't have asked."

And Alice found herself offering limply, "I'll…do what I can."

Lucy jumped from her chair, grabbed Alice's hand and pulled her up into a hug. "Oh, thank you. And whatever happens, I'm so glad you came here—selfishly for me because I like you a lot and you're so easy to talk to. But also for Noah. I'm so glad he found you and I hope you two end up together in, well, you know, that forever kind of way."

Alice eased from Lucy's grip and set her soft drink on the side table next to her chair. Then she took Noah's little sister by the shoulders and gazed into her wide brown eyes. "I can't say for certain yet what will happen between me and your brother. But I *can* say that you are absolutely marvelous."

Lucy giggled. "I try." And then she grew more serious. "I worry about Noah. I do. Before our mom died, he used to be…softer, you know? At least, he always was with me and Mom. I was sick so much and Mom, well, she was so sad all the time. Noah said she missed our dad. I remember him then as so sweet and good to us. He would do anything for us back then."

Alice reminded her, "I think he would do anything for you right now."

Lucy made a scoffing sound. "But you see, the point is, there are things he *can't* do for me, things I need to do for myself."

Alice had to agree. "All right. I see what you mean."

Lucy dropped back into her chair again. She kicked off her shoes, drew up her feet and braced her chin on her knees. "All those years ago? Before Mom died?"

Alice knew she should be getting back to her room to prepare for the evening ahead. Michelle would be waiting, growing impatient. But then again, this right now with Lucy, was a lot more important than primping for a party. She sat down, too. "Tell me."

"Well, Noah also had a wild side then, when I was little."

Alice wasn't surprised. "I believe that."

"Outside the house, he was big trouble. He didn't fit in and he used to get in fights all the time. It got worse as he got older. He didn't make friends easily. He was an outsider. And he never backed down, so every night was fight night. I guess it's kind of a miracle he never got shot. He did get knifed a time or two, though. *That* was really scary. He'd come home all bloody and Mom had to patch him up. He barely graduated high school. And then somehow he got into business college and found this job working for this guy who flipped houses. Mom was pleased he was working and actually getting a little higher education, but every day she worried he'd get kicked out of college for bad grades or lose his job for fighting. She had that sadness inside her, and it got worse because she feared for him, for his drinking, for his being out all night, being out of control. And then we lost her...." Lucy shut her eyes and dropped her forehead down on her knees.

Alice sat in sympathetic silence, hoping that she would go on.

And she did. She lifted her head and straightened her shoulders. She stared toward the open doors to the balcony. "And that was it. After the day Mom died, I don't think he ever got into another fight. He got control of himself scary fast. He started getting straight As at his business school. I never saw him drunk again. I mean, that's good, I know, that he isn't out beating people's heads in, that he's not a drunk. That he's focused and determined and a big success and all that. He's come so far. I get that. I'm proud of him. But he's definitely not as sweet as he used to be back in the day, when it was just us at home. He's not as understanding, not as open-minded." She turned her head, looked at Alice, then. "I've done my best, I promise you, to keep him real, to remind him that he only *thinks* he owns the world. But I really am well now. I'm one of the lucky ones. And I have my own life I have to live, you know?"

"Of course you do...." Alice felt strangely humbled. She'd thought Lucy childlike at first. But today she saw the wisdom in those innocent eyes.

Lucy reached between their chairs and squeezed Alice's arm. "Noah desperately needs a person like you in his life, someone he can't run all over. Someone who isn't the least impressed by his money, someone who really cares about him and who can stand up to him, too."

Alice hardly knew what to say. "You make me sound so much more exemplary than I actually am."

"That's not true. You *are* exemplary. You're the best

thing that's ever happened to my brother, and I only hope he doesn't blow it and not let you into his heart and end up chasing you away."

Chapter Nine

When Alice got back to her room, Michelle was waiting, tapping her foot in irritation. "What am I going to do with you? Is that hay in your hair? The party starts at eight. Have you forgotten?"

Alice didn't even argue. She headed straight for her bath.

She was ready at a quarter of eight, fifteen minutes before the guests were due to start arriving. She followed the sound of music down to the first floor. A quartet was warming up in the wide curve at the bottom of the stairs—a grand piano, bass, drums and a sultry singer in a clinging blue satin dress, her blond hair pinned up on one side with a giant rhinestone clip, her lips cherry red.

Alice had a look around. In the living room, two full bars had been set up, one at either end. The dining room was one fabulous buffet, set out on the long dining table and on each of the giant mahogany sideboards. She moved on to the family room, where the doors were wide-open on the loggia. Outside, there was more food and yet another full bar.

Noah appeared from the foyer. He was looking cool and casual in an open-collared dress shirt and dark trousers.

He swept her with an admiring glance, head to toe and

back again. "You look incredible in that dress and those shoes." She wore a short strapless black cocktail dress, her classic red-soled patent leather Christian Louboutin stilettos and the hammered-gold necklace he'd bought her. He put an arm around her, drew her close and whispered, "So how come all I can think of is getting everything off of you?"

She laughed and leaned against him, the things Lucy had revealed to her earlier foremost in her mind, making her feel tenderly toward him—and sympathetic, too. He'd been through so much and come so very far. She would try to remember to be patient with him. She teased, "I think I'll keep my clothes on, if that's all right with you. At least until the party's over."

He handed her a glass of champagne and offered a toast. "To when the party's over." They touched glasses, sipped and shared a quick champagne-flavored kiss.

The doorbell rang and the party began.

Alice met a whole bunch of handsome, athletic people, most of whose names she promptly forgot. A lot of them were horse lovers. Many knew of her and her family. And she could tell by the gleam in more than one eye that several of them had read of her exploits over the years. Yes, she did feel a bit like Noah's newest acquisition—a famous painting or a champion racehorse brought out and paraded around, yet more proof of Noah Cordell's enormous success.

But she didn't let it get to her. She'd spent too much of her life with people staring at her to become all that upset if they stared at her some more. She didn't let the ogling bother her, only smiled and tried enjoy herself.

Her second cousin, Jonas Bravo, and his wife, Emma, arrived around eight-thirty. It touched Alice that Noah had thought to invite them. She sat out by the infinity pool with them for over an hour, catching up a little. Emma and Jonas enjoyed a great marriage. They loved their four children and they were clearly blissfully happy together. It always made Alice feel good to be around them. They encouraged her to come visit them at their Bel Air estate, Angel's Crest, anytime she could manage it during her stay. She thanked them and promised she would try.

They went back inside together, the three of them. Alice excused herself to mingle with the other guests. She visited with a couple of minor celebrities who lived in the area and chatted with a lovely older lady about the best local beaches and the fine gardens at Mission Santa Barbara. Then she joined Noah, who was talking horses and polo with three of his neighbors. The nearby polo and racquet club was deep into its fall schedule of polo tournaments. After half an hour of that, she excused herself and went upstairs to freshen her lip gloss.

At the top of the stairs stood a tall, attractive fortyish brunette in red silk. "Your Highness. Hello. I'm Jessica Saunders." Jessica had very angry eyes.

Alice was tempted to simply nod and move on past. But she did want to get along with all of Noah's friends. So she paused when she reached the landing and returned Jessica's greeting.

Altus was below her, following her up, staying close as he always did when there were strangers around. She gave him a quick glance and a slight shake of her head to let him know she was fine. He continued the rest of the way up, passing between her and the other woman, stopping farther down the upper hallway, where he could keep her in sight.

Jessica sighed. "Leave it to Noah to bring home royalty." She delicately plucked the cherry from her Manhattan by the stem and popped it into her mouth. Her red lips tipped upward in a smile that managed to be both lazy and aggressive at the same time.

Alice resisted the urge to explain that her family was not strictly considered royal. Montedoro was a principality, not a monarchy. Her mother held a throne, but she didn't wear a crown. It was a distinction most people didn't get, anyway. Plus, in recent generations, with all the media hype, just about anyone with a title could end up mistakenly being called a "royal." So never mind. Let Jessica call her a royal if she wanted to. "Noah didn't 'bring' me here," she said. "I arranged my own transportation, thank you—and the Santa Barbara area is so beautiful. We rode down to the ocean today. It was fabulous."

Jessica was not interested in discussing the scenery. "Slightly, er, tarnished royalty, however. We've all read so *much* about you...."

Alice kept on smiling. "Tarnished? I'm guessing you must have grown up years and years ago, back when women weren't allowed to be as interesting as men."

Jessica took a large sip from her drink. "Humph. Being royalty, *I'm* guessing *you* know about Henry VIII."

"Well, I did see *The Other Boleyn Girl*. I kind of have a thing for Eric Bana, if you must know."

"I only mean, if you think about it, Noah is a little like Henry VIII, isn't he?"

Alice wished she had a drink in her hand. She could toss it into Jessica's handsome, smug face. "Excuse me?"

"Not that he's ever cut off anyone's head. It's only that he becomes bored with his conquests so easily, wouldn't you say?"

Alice gave up trying to play nice. "I'm sorry, Jessica. Could you try being just a little more direct? Are you telling me that you are one of Noah's 'conquests,' and that he dumped you and now you're bitter and out for revenge because he broke your heart?"

Jessica almost choked on her Manhattan. "No, of course not. It's just what I've heard and what I've observed. I'm a *friend,* a neighbor. I have the next estate over to the north."

"You don't behave like a friend."

"I'm only telling you what I've heard."

"Only spreading ugly rumors, you mean—and trying to cause tension between Noah and me."

Jessica huffed. "As I said, *Your Highness,* it was just an observation. There's no need to get hostile."

"Oh, I'm not hostile. I'm merely disgusted. Now, if you'll excuse me, I see no benefit to either of us in continuing this conversation." Alice started walking. She didn't stop until she reached her room. When she glanced back, Jessica was gone and Altus was right where he'd been a moment before, patiently waiting, ever watchful. She gave him a nod and shut the door.

Once alone, she fell back across the bed and stared at the ceiling and slowly smiled. Her mother would have been proud of her. She'd put Jessica Saunders in her place and then some. And she'd done it without causing her usual scene, without so much as raising her voice.

Later, when all the guests had gone home, Noah did what he'd been waiting all day and evening to do. He took off Alice's black dress and her red-soled shoes and made slow love to her. It was even better than the night before.

She cuddled up close to him afterward, and he stroked

her silky, fragrant hair and thought that even if she hadn't agreed to marry him yet, things were going pretty well between them.

Scratch that. Things were going great.

Then she said, "Tell me about Jessica Saunders." Her tone was a little too careful, too neutral.

He wrapped a thick bronze curl around his finger, rubbed it with his thumb and then let it go. "There's nothing to tell. She's always seemed friendly enough. She's a neighbor, a booster of the new Carpinteria hospital— to which I have written more than one large check. She does like her Manhattans, or so I've been told. And she's divorced. I heard she took her ex-husband to the cleaners. He left her for a twenty-year-old dental assistant from Azusa."

"Ouch. I guess that explains the bitterness. At least to a degree. And she was drinking a Manhattan. Maybe she'd had one too many."

"What bitterness?" He took her chin and tipped it up so he could see her eyes. "What happened?"

She wrinkled up her pretty nose as though she smelled something bad. "Jessica caught me on the stairs and told me that you're like Henry VIII. You quickly get bored with your girlfriends and dump them."

"What a bitch. I never realized." He kept his hand under her chin so he could see her eyes as he told her gruffly, "Not bored. Never dumping you—but didn't I tell you that weeks ago, on my last night in Montedoro?"

"You did. And your dumping me or not isn't really what I'm worried about right now."

"Good." He waited. He wasn't sure where this was going, but he already had a feeling it was in the wrong direction.

She asked, "Are you really *friends* with any of the people who came to the party tonight?"

"Not really, no. But I have a good time with several of them. I enjoy their company. Isn't that enough? Do they need to be people I'd take a bullet for?"

She stacked her hands on his chest and braced her chin on them—and didn't answer his question. "It's beautiful here. I love it."

"So, then, why do you sound like you're leading me someplace I'm not going to like?"

She lifted up enough to plant a hard, quick kiss on the edge of his jaw. "I want to know more about you. I want to know *everything* about you."

He scowled up at her. "Why?"

"Noah, come on. You've asked me to marry you."

"Yeah, I have. And in case you've forgotten, you failed to say yes."

"It's not something a person should enter into lightly. We're talking about a lifetime together. *And* about having children."

"Exactly. So when are you going to say yes?"

She puffed out her cheeks with a hard breath. "A woman with any sense at all needs to know everything she can about a man before she says yes."

"You already know me better than anyone else but Lucy—and maybe Hannah."

"I believe that. And still, I don't know you nearly well enough."

He did love her mouth. He loved it even when she was saying things he didn't want to hear. Idly, he rubbed his thumb across those lush, sweetly shaped lips of hers. "Believe me. You know me well enough."

His assurances failed to shut her up. "No, I don't. And

what I'm trying to tell you is that I need to know more. I want you to take me to Los Angeles. I want to see the street you grew up on, the house you used to live in. I want to meet your childhood friends."

That was not going to happen. "Where did you get this idea?"

She bent her head and pressed the sweetest, softest kiss to the center of his chest. "I was talking to Lucy yesterday. She told me a little about how it was for you before your mom died."

He should have known. "Did she tell you that all I did was fight and drink?"

"More or less, yes. But she also said you had a sweeter side then and that you were more open-minded."

He grunted. Of course Lucy would say that he *used* to be sweeter. And maybe it was even true. Being sweet and open-minded had not gotten him what he wanted and needed in life. "I don't *have* any childhood friends, so there's no one there for you to meet."

"That's all right." She laid her head down, her ear against his breastbone. "I still want to see where you grew up."

He eased his fingers under the warm weight of her hair and settled his hand around the back of her neck. He didn't think he could ever get tired of putting his hands on her. It was another of the many things that made her perfect for him. "It's a neighborhood of small older houses, California bungalows and little stucco Spanish-style homes. Nothing special. You'd get nothing out of seeing it."

"Let me be the judge of that." With her index finger, she traced a squiggly pattern along the outside of his arm. It tickled in a very good way. "You can take me to all the places you used to hang out." She sighed, a tender little sound, and snuggled in even closer. "My sister Rhia met her husband in Los Angeles. Rhia was in college at UCLA and Marcus was on some special military fellowship there. They had a favorite hamburger stand." She chuckled to herself. "I want to go to *your* favorite hamburger stand."

He traced a slow path down the bumps of her spine— all the way to those two perfect dimples on either side of her round little bottom. "No, Alice. I'm not taking you there."

She pushed herself up over him and then brought her face down to his, nose to nose. He could smell lilies. Also, sex. Her nipples were like little pink pebbles against his chest. He started getting hard again. She knew it, too. She smiled in that way she had, all woman and all-powerful. "I wasn't asking your permission."

"Listen to me." He cradled the side of her face and gave her his most uncompromising stare. "No."

"You don't intimidate me, Noah. And you don't get to be the only one in control. If you don't go with me, I'll only go without you."

"What in hell did you and Lucy talk about?" he growled against those fine soft lips of hers.

"I'll never tell." She licked him, just stuck out that clever tongue of hers and ran it in a circle around his lips. He got even harder. And then he opened his mouth and sucked her tongue inside.

The kiss was long and wet and wonderful. Before it was over, he'd flipped her onto her back. And once he had her there, well, he had to kiss her everywhere.

She didn't object. She threaded her fingers into his hair and whimpered encouragements, holding him in place against the wet, slick heart of her sex. He kissed her there until she rolled her head on the pillows and whispered his name, the waves of her climax pulsing against his tongue.

He was sure by then that they were done with the subject of the old neighborhood and he was feeling pleased with himself to have so effectively distracted her.

She smiled at him in a dazed and dreamy way and held down her hand. He took the condom from her and smoothly rolled it on. Then he rose up over her. She didn't even try to gain the top position that time. She simply opened to him, soft and giving and welcoming, more woman than any other he'd ever known.

He lost himself in her. It was perfect. Paradise.

And then, sometime later as they drifted toward sleep, with her arms tight around him, her fingers stroking his hair, she whispered, "Tomorrow, then. We can go to East Los Angeles and after that maybe visit Bel Air and see Jonas and Emma and the children."

In the morning, he told her again that they weren't going to East L.A.

She said, "It's all right, Noah. I'll give you a few days to get used to the idea. And eventually, if you keep refusing to go with me, I'll go by myself."

He decided to leave it at that for now. She'd said she would give him a few days. He was hoping that when those days were up, she'd either have seen the light and realized it was a pointless exercise to try to travel backward into his past—or he would have come up with another, better argument to convince her of why there was no need to go.

He left her for his rooms, where he showered and dressed.

When he got downstairs, she was sitting with Lucy out in the loggia. Their heads were together and they were whispering intently.

Then they spotted him.

They straightened away from each other and smiled at him—both of them, Lucy, too.

His sister hadn't granted him a smile in more than three weeks. He knew her so well, knew what that smile meant. She was mounting a new offensive in her campaign to get him to give her the money to go to New York.

Fine. At least she wasn't acting like he didn't exist. Maybe they could work this out. Maybe this time he would be able to get through to her, get her to see that he only wanted what was best for her.

"Noah," Alice said, too sweetly. "Come join us. Hannah is making French toast with raspberries."

He went and sat down and put his napkin in his lap.

Lucy poured him coffee—buttering him up. Definitely.

Hannah came out with the plates full of food.

Lucy waited until he'd had a couple of fortifying bites of his breakfast before she said, "Noah, I want to try one more time to work this out with you, about New York."

He ate another bite of the French toast. Excellent, as always. And then he took a sip of coffee. "Yeah. I think we do need to settle this." He set down his cup and told her sincerely, "You know I want you to be happy." He slid Alice a quick glance. She was concentrating on her breakfast, staying out of it, which he appreciated. He saw the little twitch of a smile at the corner of her mouth, though, the flash of a dimple. She assumed from what he'd just said that he was rethinking his refusal to send Lucy three thousand miles away.

Lucy had known him a lot longer. She regarded him warily. "If you want to settle it, let me have access to my trust fund so I can get an apartment and get ready for the spring semester."

He set down his fork and said gently, "When you're twenty-five, if you're strong enough."

Alice's faint smile had disappeared. She set down her fork, too, and took a slow, thoughtful sip of her coffee.

Lucy said, "I'm strong enough now." She spoke levelly. He could hear the angry undertone in her voice, but she was controlling it.

So far, anyway.

He said, "Listen. Why don't we compromise?"

Lucy cut a bite of French toast and then didn't eat it. "I want to be flexible, Noah. But with you the word *compromise* only means that we'll be doing it *your* way."

"That's not fair."

"It's the truth."

He'd been thinking it over. And he *was* willing to compromise, willing to let her try more than just the online classes he'd been suggesting. He made his new case firmly. "How about this? One year here. At UC Santa Barbara. The School of Art, the College of Creative Studies. Come on. It's UC. It will be challenging and exciting. You'll learn a lot and enjoy yourself. And you can live at home. We'll see how it goes. Then, after two semesters, we can reevaluate, see how you're feeling, see if you're ready to try New York."

From the corner of his eye, he could see the look on Alice's face. It wasn't a happy one. She just didn't understand. Someone had to make sure that his sister was safe. Lucy wouldn't be realistic, so he had to do it for her.

Lucy came right back at him. "I know UCSB is a great school. But it's not FIT New York. I'll only be treading water there, and I have tread water all of my life, Noah. I've always, forever, been waiting—to get better, to be well, to be like everyone else." Tears filmed her big eyes that were just like their mom's.

If only she would face the truth about herself. "But, Lucy, come on. You're not like everyone else. You have to be careful, you have to—"

"No!" Her fisted hand struck the table. Her plate bounced and flatware clattered. "How many times do we have to go over this?"

Damn it, why couldn't she see? He didn't want this fight any more than she did. "Lucy, I—"

"No. Wait. For once, Noah, won't you please just listen to what I keep telling you? Last year I *wanted* to try UC. You said to wait one more year just to be sure I was strong enough. Well, I have waited. I have waited and waited. My doctors have given me their blessing to live a normal life. I keep up with my blood work and exams and stress tests and everything is stable. When I go, it's not like I'm heading off to the ends of the earth. It's New York. Some of the best cardiac doctors in the world are there. I'll get referrals, you know that, the best of the best. I'll keep up with my checkups. I will be fine."

"Lucy. Come on. No."

Her cheeks flushed hot pink. "Just like that, huh? As always. Just *no*."

He felt like some monster. But he knew he was right and he couldn't back down. "If you would only—"

"Stop. Just stop." Tears pooled in her eyes. Furious,

she dashed them away. "I'm a healthy, normal woman now, Noah. Why can't you see that? Okay, Mom died. And Dad. But that doesn't mean something awful will happen to me, too. Why are you so afraid I'm going to keel over dead if I dare to get out on my own?"

Mom and Dad. Why did she always have to bring up Mom and Dad? And Alice was just sitting there, taking it all in. He should have insisted that he and Lucy do this in private.

He said with slow care, "This has nothing to do with Mom and Dad and you know it."

"Oh, please. Get real. You are lying to yourself and I have no idea how to get you to stop. You *have* to let me go, Noah. I'm all grown up, I'm in good health, and you haven't been my guardian since I turned eighteen. I'm getting the money somehow. One way or another, I'm moving to New York before the start of the spring semester." Lucy shoved back her chair and threw her napkin on the table. "You just watch me and see if I don't." She whirled and took off like a shot.

"Lucy, get back here!"

She didn't glance back, didn't even break stride. She stormed through the open doors to the family room and vanished from sight.

Once she was gone, he picked up his fork again. He ate a couple of bites of his fast-cooling breakfast, chewing slowly and carefully, keeping it calm.

Eventually, he sent a sideways glance at Alice. She caught him at it. Because she was just sitting there watching him. She had her hands in her lap.

He supposed he had to say something. "I'm sorry you had to see that."

She picked up her fork without saying a word—and

then set it back on her plate. "This is the thing, Noah. I happen to agree with Lucy."

What? Now she was going to get on his case, too? "Look, Alice, I don't think you—"

She put up a hand. "No. *You* look. Lucy's a grown woman and she has a right to make her own choices now. You should release her trust fund and help her do what she's always dreamed of doing. Think about it. Try to see it from her viewpoint. Finally, it's her turn to have her own rich, full life. And you just keep telling her no."

He wanted to shout at her to stay out of it, to remind her good and loud that she had no idea what she was talking about. Lucy wasn't *her* sister. But he didn't shout. He had more self-control than that. "Three years ago she was in Cardiac ICU at UCLA Medical Center. She weighed seventy pounds and her lungs were full of fluid. They said she wouldn't make it. They'd said that before. I brought in another specialist with a different approach. She survived, barely."

"That was three years ago. And then she had the surgery that made all the difference, you said."

"Nothing in this life is certain."

"Noah. It's been two years since the surgery. Her doctors say she's fine."

"Do you imagine you're telling me something I don't already know? She needs more time at home. I'm not going to bend on that. I *can't* bend. I have her best interests at heart."

Alice pressed her lips together. For a second he dared to hope she would let it go. But no. "I don't think you were really listening to her. I don't think you see how determined and focused she is, how very much like you she is...."

"Of course I was listening. And I know she's determined."

"If you don't help her, she's going to find a way to get the money somewhere else."

"She's twenty-three with no credit and no job history. No way can she afford to relocate to New York by the first of the year without my help." A really bad thought occurred to him. He pinned the woman next to him with his hardest stare, at the same time way too aware of how much he wanted her, how exactly right she was for him in every way. How sometimes when he looked at her, he found himself thinking that she'd somehow wound herself all around his heart, that he couldn't imagine his life without her in it. But if she betrayed him… "My God. You wouldn't."

She drew in a slow breath. "Don't think I haven't been considering it."

"Damn it." The two inadequate words felt scraped from the depths of him. "Don't do that to me."

And then she sighed, softened. "I won't. I wish I could, but…"

"What?" he demanded.

And her eyes went soft as clouds in a summer sky. "I know you would never forgive me. I don't think I could bear that."

It meant a lot. Everything. To hear her say that. He wanted to grab her in his arms and lift her high and carry her back upstairs to bed.

But he knew she wouldn't go for that. Not now. She might be unwilling to betray him, but she was firmly on Lucy's side about the move to New York.

And when he thought about that, when he thought about his sister, it ruined the mood anyway.

Chapter Ten

After breakfast, Alice went up to check on Lucy.

She tapped on Lucy's door and Lucy called out in a tear-strangled voice, "Go away, Noah! I don't want to talk to you."

"It's only me," Alice said.

A sob, then meekly, "Alice?"

"Come on, Lucy. Let me in."

Swift footsteps on the other side of the door. And then Lucy flung it wide and threw herself into Alice's arms. "Oh, Alice, Alice, what am I going to do?"

Alice took her to the bed and eased her down. She sat beside her and handed her the box of tissues from the nightstand.

Lucy blew her nose and cried some more and kept insisting over and over, "I'm going. I will find a way. He's not going to stop me. I'm not missing my chance...."

Alice put an arm around her and reminded her softly, "He does love you and he thinks he's doing the right thing for you. You know that, right? He loves you so very much."

"Of course I know." Lucy's breath hitched on a hard sob. "Somehow that makes it all worse. That he loves me so much and he's being so stupid and stubborn and wrong...." Another flood of tears poured out.

Alice hugged her close and made soothing noises and stayed with her until the storm of weeping had worn itself out.

"I'm okay now," Lucy said at the end with a sad little sniff.

Alice smoothed her thick, short, brown hair. "I'll stay with you for a while."

"No, really. I mean it. I'm fine. I think I'll pull myself together and go to my workroom. Patterns to cut, hems to turn. Working always cheers me up."

"You sure?"

"Yeah. And thanks." She gave Alice's arm a fond squeeze. "For coming up, for being here."

"Anytime."

Noah and Hannah were sitting side by side at the top of the stairs when Alice came out of Lucy's room.

Hannah got up. "How is she?"

"Not happy."

"I'll talk to her." She went into Lucy's room and quietly shut the door.

Noah reached up a hand to grab the banister and stood. He looked tired suddenly. Older than his thirty-five years. The sight made Alice's heart ache. "I know," he said glumly. "She doesn't want to talk to *me*."

Alice went to him. She wrapped her arms around his waist and laid her head on his broad, warm chest. Slowly, he responded, pulling her closer, resting his cheek against her hair.

She whispered, "I need to go riding. I think we both do."

He made a low noise of agreement, but then just continued to hold her. She lifted her head to look up at him and she remembered that dream of hers, way back at the beginning, before she knew who he really was. The dream of the two of them, longtime companions, riding together, stopping in a meadow of wildflowers just to talk.

Sometimes that seemed an impossible kind of dream. And then, times like now, as he held her at the top of the stairs after all that awfulness with Lucy, she couldn't imagine herself ever being able to leave him.

"Alice…" He bent his golden head and kissed her, a chaste kiss, a warm firm pressure, his lips to hers. "I'll meet you at the stables."

"I won't be long."

He let her go, and she went to her room to change.

Alice let a full week go by without reopening the subject of a visit to his hometown.

It was a lovely week, all in all. They rode every day, long rides on the eucalyptus-shaded trails and sometimes along the quiet private beach where he'd taken her that first day. There were picnics on that beach, just the two of them, with Altus standing watch. They attended a polo tournament at the club.

And they had each night together.

The nights were unforgettable. Alice adored being wrapped up tightly in his arms.

But there were shadows on the sunny expanse of their pleasure in each other. Alice spent time with Lucy, but Lucy would have nothing to do with her brother. She remained determined that somehow she was moving to New York.

And Noah wouldn't hear a word about letting her go. Alice stayed out of it. She'd told Noah how she felt about the situation that Sunday morning at the breakfast table. She wasn't willing to go against him head-to-head and give Lucy the money she needed, so really, she had nothing else to say about the matter. She left it alone.

Three times during that week, she called Rhia and cried on her shoulder—about Noah's unwillingness to let his little sister grow up and escape his well-meaning control. About love in general. Because she was falling in love with Noah.

She wanted to tell him so. But she didn't.

Her love made her more vulnerable to him. And she'd begun to fear that she wanted more from him than he was capable of giving her. He had his own ideas about the way things ought to be and he was never all that willing to be guided by anyone else. How could they have a partnership of equals if he insisted on believing—and behaving as though—he ran the world?

She'd said she would give him a few days to get used to the idea that they were going to his old neighborhood. But then he'd had that awful fight with Lucy and Alice had backed off. She ached for him and she wanted to give the man a break, not to push him too hard. Those few days she'd said she'd give him to think it over went by, and she didn't bring up the subject of visiting his childhood home. She knew he assumed she was letting it go.

Wrong. She was just waiting for the right moment to try again.

One really lovely thing did happen that week.

Thursday morning, early, Dami called. The first words out of his mouth were, "I called to make amends."

Both pleased and surprised, Alice laughed. "Do go on."

He confessed, "Mother accused me of being a pig-headed ass."

"That doesn't sound like Mother."

"Well, of course, she didn't use those words exactly. But she said that she believed I had it all wrong, that not only are you serious about Noah, he cares for you, too. She said that I, of all people, have no right to judge a man just because he's, er, enjoyed the company of a large number of women."

"Don't you just love Mother?"

He laughed then. "Sometimes I find her much too perceptive. Not to mention right. Why does she always have to be so bloody right?"

"It's a gift."

His voice changed, grew more somber. "I'm sorry, Allie. Noah *is* a good man, and I was an idiot. I hope the two of you will be blissfully happy together."

I hope so, too, she thought. She said, "Thank you. And you are forgiven."

"Good. Is Noah there?"

"He is, as a matter of fact." Sitting right there in her bed under the covers with her, his pillow propped against the headboard, same as hers. She caught his eye. He arched a brow.

"Put him on," said Dami.

So she handed Noah the phone and sat back and listened to his end of the conversation. He said yes several times and then, "Believe me, I'm on it." And then he laughed. A *real* laugh.

She knew then that it was okay between the two men and she was glad.

Noah reminded Dami that he was always welcome at the estate. "Come anytime. Now, tomorrow… You know you never have to call. The door's always open. You can see firsthand that I'm taking good care of your sister."

Dami must have asked about Lucy, because Noah said in a carefully neutral tone that Lucy was fine. They started talking about some business deal they were apparently in on together.

Alice shut her eyes then and let her thoughts drift away.

She woke when Noah kissed her.

"Your brother forgives me for seducing you," he whispered against her parted lips. "But he's expecting a wedding, and soon."

She lifted her arms and twined them around his neck. "Nice try. But when I marry you, it won't be because Dami expects it."

"*When* you marry me? I like the sound of that…." He deepened the kiss.

She sighed and surrendered to the sorcery in his touch. The man had his flaws.

But when he made love to her, she had no complaints.

On Sunday night, a week after that big argument with Lucy, when Noah joined her in her bedroom as he did every night, she kissed him once—and then she walked him backward to the bed.

She pushed him down, kicked off the purple flats she was wearing and straddled him.

He laughed. And then he commanded, "Take off your clothes. Do it now."

"In a minute." She bent over him, nose to nose, grasped the collar of his shirt in either hand and said, "I need to talk to you."

A little frown formed between his dark gold brows. "About?"

"The place where you grew up. I want you to take me there tomorrow."

He reached up, wrapped a hand around the back of her neck and kissed her. It was an excellent kiss, as usual. It made her want to go loose and easy, to forget everything but the taste of his mouth, the feel of his hand, warm and firm and exciting, stroking her nape, tangling in her hair.

But that was exactly his plan, and she wasn't falling for it.

She lifted away from him, though he tried at first to hold her close. When he gave in and let her go, she said, "If not tomorrow, then Tuesday. And if you won't come with me Tuesday, just tell me now and Altus and I will go alone."

His eyes had gone flat and his jaw was set. "We already settled this."

"Excuse me. We did not."

"I told you—"

"I remember. You told me no. I said I would go anyway. And I will, Noah. Lucy will give me the address of the house you lived in."

He growled, "Lucy's in on this?"

Gee, this was going so well. She rolled off him and flopped to her back on the bed. "No. I didn't want to get Lucy involved if I didn't have to." She turned her head and met his shadowed eyes. "But I will. If I can't get the information I need from you, I'll ask her. It's that simple."

"You would drag my sister into this?"

"That's a bit strong, don't you think? I wouldn't drag Lucy anywhere. But would I ask her for the address of the house you used to live in? In a heartbeat."

"You're being unreasonable."

Was she? And was she pushing this too far? "Why

don't you want to take me there? Why don't you want
me to go there on my own?"

"It's the past. It's got nothing to do with me anymore."

She reached across the space between them to touch
his cheek. "I think you're wrong."

He caught her wrist. "Leave it. Please."

It was the *please* that undid her.

And in the end, what was the point of going if he
didn't want to take her there, if he didn't want her to go?
She would learn nothing about his secret heart by driving
alone past some house where he used to live.

She pulled her hand free of his grip and sat up. And
for the first time since she'd come to stay with him, she
thought of home with real longing. Of her horses, her
villa, the life she'd left on hold. Was this whole thing with
him just an interlude after all? Just two people trying and
slowly failing to be more than a love affair?

"All right," she said wearily. "I give up. If you feel
that strongly about it, I won't go."

Tuesday evening after dinner, when Alice was in her
room catching up on her email and messaging with Gilbert about various minor issues at the palace stables, she
got a call from Emma Bravo.

"Come on out to the house," Emma said in that cute
Texas twang of hers, as though she and Jonas and their
children lived out on the range somewhere surrounded by
tumbleweeds and longhorn cattle instead of at one of the
most spectacular estates in the whole of Bel Air. "You and
Noah and his sister, too. It's still warm enough for a swim
party and a nice barbecue. The weekend is the nicest.
We'll have all afternoon. How 'bout Saturday at two?"

Alice said she'd check with Noah and get back to her tomorrow.

Noah came to join her a few minutes later and she told him about Emma's invitation. "She said to bring Lucy, too."

"Sounds great. I'd love to go. Who knows? Lucy might even agree to come along."

"I hope she will."

"You'd better be the one to ask her," he suggested somewhat grimly. "We'll get an automatic no if the invitation comes from me."

"I will ask her."

"Perfect." He pulled her close and kissed her, a slow, delicious kiss.

He'd been so attentive and sweet since two nights before, when she'd agreed to give up the trip to his old neighborhood. Alice tried to enjoy his kiss and not to think that it would always be that way with him, that he would stonewall her until she did what he wanted and then reward her for being such a good girl by treating her like royalty.

Royalty. That was a good one. She chuckled against his mouth.

He broke the kiss and guided a few stray strands of hair away from her lips, his eyes full of heat and tenderness, his expression openly fond. "Share the joke?"

"It's nothing," she lied. And then she kissed him again.

He scooped her up high in his arms and carried her to the bed. They made love for hours. He knew just the things to do to thoroughly satisfy her body.

Too bad he wasn't quite so willing to satisfy her heart.

* * *

Lucy didn't come to the breakfast table the next morning. Ever since the big argument with Noah a week and a half before, she'd been taking the majority of her meals in her room.

Around nine, after they'd eaten and Noah had gone to his study to make some calls, Alice went upstairs to invite Lucy to Emma's barbecue that weekend. Lucy's empty breakfast tray waited on the floor outside her door, where Hannah or one of the day maids would pick it up.

At least she wasn't starving herself, Alice thought with a smile. The only thing left on that tray was a little corner of toast crust. Her door was open a crack. Apparently she hadn't closed it all the way when she set the tray out.

From inside the room, there was a burst of happy laughter. And then, "Oh, I'm so glad…Yes…Oh, I can't tell you…A lot to ask…Hero…And don't blow me off. You *are* a hero and I…" There was more, but Lucy's voice dipped and Alice didn't catch the rest.

By then she'd reached the door. Curiosity got the better of her. Shamelessly, she eavesdropped.

"No. It will be awful. Please," Lucy wheedled. "Why don't we just go, avoid all that?…But I…Well, all right, if you think it's best…Mmm-hmm…" A hard sigh escaped her. "I know, I do, I understand…"

About then Alice reminded herself that she hated eavesdroppers. And now she was one. She tapped on the door and it swung partway inward.

Lucy sat on the bed, a cell phone to her ear. She caught sight of Alice. Her mouth dropped open and her eyes went saucer wide.

No doubt about it. She had a coconspirator on the other end of the line.

A boyfriend, maybe?

Or someone who'd agreed to loan her money for New York?

Lucy pulled herself together and wiped the guilty look off her face. "Alice!" She waved her forward and spoke nervously into the phone again. "Ahem. Yes...Mmm-hmm. That's right. I really have to go." She disconnected the call and set the phone on the nightstand. "Come on in." She patted the spot beside her on the bed.

Alice shut the door and went to sit beside her. "Sorry I interrupted..."

"Oh? What?" Lucy fluttered her hands about. "The call, you mean? It was nothing. Just a friend. What's going on?"

Alice considered asking Lucy the same question. But she hardly knew where or how to begin. And really, she shouldn't have been listening in on Lucy's conversation. "Have you met my cousin Jonas Bravo and his wife, Emma?"

Lucy blinked. "Jonas Bravo, as in the Bravo Billionaire? The one whose brother was kidnapped by their psycho uncle when he was just a baby?"

"That's the one." Amazing. Even Lucy knew the old story. Jonas's younger brother, Russell, had been nicknamed the Bravo Baby. Russell grew up in Oklahoma under a different name, never knowing his real identity until the truth came out years later.

Lucy picked up her cell phone, stared at it for a moment then set it back down. "I've never met them, but Noah knows Jonas Bravo, I think."

"Yes. They've done business together, Noah and

Jonas. Jonas and Emma were here, at the party Saturday before last."

"I didn't meet them. But I only stayed downstairs for an hour or two...."

"Jonas is a great guy. And Emma is a sweetheart. I love her. They have four children, two girls and two boys. I think the eldest is ten or eleven now. And Jonas has an adopted sister, Amanda, who's in her teens. Emma's invited us out to their Bel Air estate for a barbecue and pool party this Saturday afternoon. You're included."

Lucy wore a distant look. Preoccupied. Not quite present. She frowned. "Um. Saturday, you said?"

"That's right. We would leave in time to be there at two."

"We?"

"You, me and Noah...."

Lucy sighed. "I don't think so."

Alice put an arm around her. "Come on. Consider it, won't you? It will be fun."

Lucy pulled away. "No, really. You two go on. I have... a few projects I'm working on. I need to keep focused."

Alice dressed for riding, and she and Altus went to the stables. She was tacking up Golden Boy when Noah came to find her. She told him that she'd talked to Lucy about Saturday.

"Will she come with us?" He looked so hopeful it made her heart ache.

She shook her head. "She said something about the projects she's working on...."

His big shoulders drooped a little. He stuck his hands into his pockets. "She spends her life hunched over that damn sewing machine."

She turned back to Golden Boy and cinched up the saddle. "Well, I saw her breakfast tray. At least there's nothing wrong with her appetite. I swear she licked her plate clean."

Noah laughed at that and didn't seem quite so sad. He saddled a big gelding named Cavalier and they rode up into the mountains for the day.

She didn't tell him about Lucy's mysterious phone call.

Yes, she felt a bit guilty for keeping that from him. But she shouldn't have been listening in anyway. And Lucy had a right to a secret admirer.

But what if she's found someone to pay her way to New York?

Alice doubted it. It would be a lot of money. Several thousand for an apartment and furnishings, living expenses and tuition, fees, books, supplies and whatever else.

But say, just for the sake of argument, that Lucy did have a generous friend who'd agreed to bankroll her dream....

Alice couldn't help thinking that it wouldn't be a bad thing. True, she couldn't bring herself to write the check that Lucy needed, couldn't bring herself to betray Noah's trust. But Lucy *was* her friend. Loyalty counted with Lucy, too.

So Alice kept her mouth shut about the cryptic conversation she'd overheard that morning.

Saturday, Alice and Noah left for Los Angeles early in the morning. They went in one of Noah's limos, Altus in the front seat with the driver.

The drive only took about an hour and a half.

But Alice wanted to play tourist before the barbecue at Angel's Crest. So they drove down Hollywood Boulevard, past Grauman's Chinese and all the gold stars embedded in the sidewalk. And then they went to Beverly Hills and had coffee at the Beverly Hills Hotel. They drove down Sunset and Alice gawked at all the giant billboards advertising movies and rock groups and lawyers to the stars.

They arrived at Jonas and Emma's right at two. The whole family was there. Alice forgot her worries about Lucy. And Noah seemed more relaxed, too. He laughed often and treated her with open affection. They swam and played Marco Polo and water volleyball with the children. And later they all sat down outdoors to heaping plates of Texas-style barbecue.

At seven Emma started herding her children upstairs for their baths. Alice and Noah changed back into their street clothes. Jonas urged them to stay—overnight, if it suited them. The house was bigger than Noah's, with guest rooms to spare.

But Noah squeezed her hand and she understood that he wanted to get back. That was fine with her. They hadn't planned to stay late anyway. Alice went upstairs to tell Emma goodbye. The kids were running around, the girls and the older boy already in their pajamas. The youngest one, Grady, was still splashing in the tub.

Emma embraced her. "You come back soon...."

The children's voices echoed on the upper landing as Alice went down the stairs. Noah was at the door shaking hands with Jonas.

The car waited right outside, the engine running in the warm twilight.

Altus held the door for her. She ducked in as Noah got in on the other side. He put his arm around her.

She leaned against him. "That was fun...."

His lips touched her hair. "Yeah. A good day...."

Alice felt more hopeful than she had in weeks. Noah *was* a good man. And she wanted to be with him.

Most of the time, it felt so right with him, as though she'd known him all her life—or been waiting to know him. He touched some place deep within her heart that no other man ever had.

Alice sighed, settled her head on his shoulder and thought about how every day she fell more in love with him.

Yes, he had a giant blind spot about Lucy, and serious control issues. And he always seemed to keep something of himself apart from her. Even with all that, she wanted what they shared to last.

She snuggled in even closer, breathed in the wonderfully familiar, deliciously exciting scent that belonged only to him and considered just saying it: *I love you, Noah. I love you very much.*

But then he would only start pushing for a yes on the question of marriage.

And she wasn't quite ready to go that far—not yet, anyway.

The driver pulled up at the foot of the wide steps leading to Noah's front door. Someone had parked a black luxury SUV over by the low wall that surrounded the koi pond.

Noah frowned at her. "Were you expecting anyone?"

"No. Maybe a friend of Lucy's?"

His frown only deepened. They got out. Hannah was

waiting in the open doorway, the light from the foyer behind her silhouetting her tall, slim form. They mounted the wide front steps with Altus close behind.

One good look at the older woman's face and Noah demanded, "What's the matter, Hannah?"

The housekeeper spoke quietly. "Prince Damien is here. He and Lucy are waiting for you in the family room. Lucy has informed me that tomorrow the prince is taking her to New York."

Chapter Eleven

Noah hadn't cracked any heads in fourteen full years. But he burned to crack one now: Damien's, to be specific.

Hannah saw his expression and got out of his way. He headed for the family room.

Behind him, Alice tried to slow him down. "Noah, wait. Please...."

He ignored her and kept going, through the foyer, down the hallway, past the kitchen, to the family room, with the heels of Alice's sandals tapping in his wake.

They were there, the two of them, just as Hannah had said they would be, sitting in the soft white chairs in front of the arched windows. Lucy popped to her feet at the sight of him. Dami rose, too, but more slowly.

A chain of obscenities scrolled through Noah's mind. He demanded, "What kind of crap are you pulling here, Damien?"

Alice came up beside him. "Noah. Can you please just settle down?"

He hit her with an icy look. "Are you involved in this?"

She stared at him. "Involved? What are you talking about?"

Lucy spoke up then. "Stop it, Noah. Alice had no idea that I talked Dami into helping me. You just leave her alone."

He whirled on his sister. "Are you out of your mind? You can't just—"

She cut him off with a cry. "Yes, I can, Noah. And I will. Dami has a place I can stay and he's loaning me the money I need."

Noah felt a fury so hot and so total, it seemed that the top of his head might pop off. He swung his attention to Damien. "Why? I don't get it. Because of Alice? This is some sick revenge because I want to marry your sister?"

Dami stood there and looked at him as if *he* was the one who'd gone over the line. "Of course not, you idiot. Don't be ridiculous."

"I ought to..." He took a step toward Damien.

Alice grabbed his arm. "Noah, don't...."

At the same time, Lucy tried to step in front of Dami as if she was going to protect him, all ninety-eight pounds of her. "Stop it, Noah. I mean it. You stop it right now."

"It's all right, Luce," said Damien, and he took her by the shoulders and moved her out of the way. His bodyguard, who'd been standing by the doors to the loggia, stepped closer. Damien signaled the man back.

Lucy insisted, "I *called* him, all right? I called Dami and I begged him to help me. He's my friend, okay?"

Noah made a low scoffing sound. "Oh. Right. Exactly. Prince Damien is such a hero. The Player Prince only wants to be your *friend*."

"He *is* my friend, Noah! He's my friend, and that's all. Just my friend, and a very good one, thank you. And yes, he's a hero, too. Because he knows how much this means to me and he's willing to help me, willing to go up against *you*. He's not blinded like you are, Noah. By fear and by the things that happened years and years ago. He sees me as I am now, not as I used to be, and he knows how long I've waited, for all of my life so far. He knows it's finally time I came into my own. *He* knows that I'm ready." The tears rose, clogging her voice, making those big brown eyes of hers shine too bright.

About then he started feeling like the monster in the room.

Which was insane. Not true. He was the only one here who understood the risk, the only one determined to keep Lucy safe, to make certain she didn't push herself too far and end up at death's door before he could get there and save her.

"Noah." Alice still had hold of his arm. "Can we just sit down, please? Can we just talk this over like civilized adults?"

"Civilized," he growled at her.

But she had his attention now. She gazed steadily up at him, pleading and determined, both at once.

And from behind them, Hannah said, "Do what Alice says, Noah. Sit down. Lucy will be leaving in the morning, one way or another. Now's the time to make your peace with that."

Noah glanced back at her. She stood next to Alice's bodyguard, and she met his gaze, unflinching. He couldn't bear it. He shut his eyes.

And his father's face rose up, laughing, on the morning of the day that he died. Laughing and grabbing his mother for a hug and a kiss, heading off to work like it was any other day, with no idea that he would never be back again.

He shook his head, blinked away the image—but it only got worse. Next he saw his mother lying on the couch in that cramped run-down bungalow they rented after the bank took their house. His mother, her face sickly pale, clammy with fever sweat, her eyes red and dazed looking, insisting that she was fine, there was no problem. No need for a doctor, it was only a little cold....

Alice still held his arm. And she was nudging him, guiding him to a chair.

He dropped into it, feeling disconnected, as if this was all some weird, awful dream. Alice sat beside him. She took his hand and twined her fingers with his. He let her do that, even held on.

Her hand felt solid, her grip sure and strong. At that moment she seemed the only real thing in the room.

Lucy and Damien sat down again, too. Hannah came over from where she hovered by the kitchen and took the last chair.

He heard himself ask Damien, "When you called to apologize to Alice, were you already planning this?"

Damien shook his head. "Lucy called me a couple of days later."

Alice cleared her throat and asked Lucy, "Was that Dami on the phone Wednesday morning, when I came to your room and asked you to come with us to Angel's Crest?"

"Yes, it was," said Lucy proudly.

"What?" He turned accusing eyes on Alice. "You never said a word." He started to pull his hand from hers.

She wouldn't let go. "I was eavesdropping, and it was none of my business. Lucy left the door open a crack or I never would have heard a thing."

"You should have told me," he insisted. He might have been able to stop this madness before it went so far.

"I shouldn't have been listening," she said slowly and clearly, as if maybe he didn't understand English very well. "It was a private conversation."

Lucy chimed in, "Alice kept it to herself because *she* understands that I'm an adult and I have a right to my privacy."

"You damn well don't have the right to go cooking up harebrained schemes that put your life in danger."

"Oh, don't be so dramatic, Noah. My life is not in danger. I'm perfectly fine." She swung her gaze to Damien. "Listen to him, Dami. And you kept telling me I needed to try again to get through to him. Ha. Like that was ever gonna happen."

Noah winced. Was he really that bad? He only wanted her safety, only cared about her well-being.

Dami said gently, "Easy, Luce. Calm down."

Noah swung his gaze on his so-called friend and longed to leap up and punch his lights out. But he stayed in his seat, held on to Alice and reminded himself that he was thirty-five years old and there were better ways to fight than with his fists.

Lucy turned on him again. "At least I finally got Dami to see that *you* were never going to listen to me. I... Well, I admit I just wanted to sneak away, not to have to go through this." She raised both hands as though to indicate the five of them sitting there, the tension so thick it seemed to poison the air. "But Dami said I had to face you. That you had a right to know exactly what was going on."

He sent another furious glance in Damien's direction. The last thing he needed to hear right now was how wise and enlightened Damien was.

Lucy was still talking. "So here we are. Now you know. Dami's flying me to New York. My things are all packed and outside in the car. Our plane leaves at eight in the morning."

Noah just stared at her. His mind seemed to have locked up. He had to stop her. He just couldn't seem to figure out how.

Damien said, "I own an apartment building in NoHo—near Greenwich Village? There's a vacant one-bedroom. Luce will have that."

Alice squeezed his hand and coaxed, "I've been there. It's a lovely old building. And the apartments are roomy, especially by New York standards."

He blinked and looked at her again. "You're all for this, aren't you?" His voice sounded strange, without inflection, to his own ears.

She answered softly but firmly, too, "I think Lucy is ready, yes. If you'll recall, I've been clear on that. But in the end, Noah, it's not what *I* think that matters. And it's not what *you* think, either. It's Lucy's choice. And now she's found a way to make it happen."

Because of your brother, he thought, but decided not to say. Yeah, he could beat the crap out of Damien for letting Lucy talk him into this, for sticking his nose in where it didn't belong. But Lucy was the key here.

And she wasn't budging. He couldn't get through to her.

She was going. There was no protecting her from herself anymore. One way or another, she would go to New York.

And somehow he would have to learn to live with that.

He met Lucy's wary eyes. "All right. If there's no way to stop you, *I'll* take you. Give me a couple of weeks to put things on hold here. We'll go to New York, get you a place, get you settled in, get your new doctors and services lined up. I'll arrange to get you access to your trust fund. I'll—"

Lucy put up a hand. "No. You're not doing that. You don't get to go with me and take *care* of me, Noah. The whole point is that you have to let me go, let me stand on my own at last, let me make a life that works for me."

He did turn on Damien then. He couldn't seem to stop himself. "So what, then? *You're* going to take care of her?"

"Of course he's not!" Lucy cried. "How many times do I have to say it? *I'm* going to take care of me. Dami's only going to take me to New York, show me my new apartment, loan me an embarrassing sum of money and then go back to his own life—which, if you think about it, is way more than enough."

Damien said quietly, "I'll make sure she's safe, Noah. I won't leave until she's settled in."

Alice leaned close to him. She didn't say anything, just held tight and steady on to his hand. Hannah sat silent, too, her brow furrowed.

None of them agreed with him. Not one of them took his side in this. They didn't know what he knew, hadn't seen what he'd seen.

He couldn't deal. Couldn't take it all in. Couldn't come up with a way to get even one of them to see the situation as he saw it. He turned to his sister again. Her wide mouth was set, her gaze unwavering. He accused, "You'll do what you want to do, then, no matter the cost."

"I *have* to do it, Noah."

"That's a lie."

Alice chided, "Noah, don't…"

He pulled his hand free of hers. There was nothing more to say. "This conversation is through." He stood. "Good night." And he turned on his heel.

Alice called after him. "Noah. Please…"

He kept walking. He didn't stop or look back. Through the kitchen, down the hallway to the foyer, up the stairs to his rooms.

He went inside and slammed the door.

Alice winced at the sound of the door slamming upstairs. She wanted only to go up there, to be with him, to try to ease his suffering at least a little bit.

But it seemed wiser for the moment to leave him alone.

Hannah caught her eye and echoed her thoughts, "Give him a little time...."

Lucy worried her lower lip. "I knew this was going to be awful. I was so right."

Dami suggested rather sheepishly, "You could always slow down a bit, give the poor guy a chance to get used to the idea that you're going."

Lucy shot him a startled glance. "Are you backing out on me now?"

"No. But if you want to think it over a little more—"

"I don't. We're going," she said sharply. And then, more softly, "Please?"

Dami shrugged. "Well, that settles that." He stood. "Allie, a few words, just the two of us?"

Alice got up and followed him out to the loggia.

"You probably don't believe this," he said when they were alone in the cool autumn darkness, "but I'm honestly not the least happy about causing all this trouble."

"So, then, why are you doing it?"

He stared off toward the garden. "I've seen her designs, and she's shown me the clothes that she's made. She's so talented. It's wrong to hold her back."

Alice phrased her next question with care. "I have to ask. Lucy says you're her friend and nothing more.

I'm going to be backing both of you up with Noah after you go. If the two of you are more than friends, I need to know the truth."

Dami groaned. And then he swore. "How can you ask me that? Lucy's very sweet. But she's like a child. I've never been attracted to the wide-eyed innocent type."

"She's *not* a child, Dami. In many ways, she's quite mature."

He stuck his hands into his pockets and cast a glance at the distant moon. "Please. I swear to you on my honor as a prince of the blood. Luce and I are friends. That's all." Alice had known him all her life and she could tell when he was hedging. He wasn't. Not this time. "Peace?" He held out his arms to her.

Alice accepted his embrace. When she pulled back, she said ruefully, "I only wish Lucy could have found someone else to come to her rescue."

Dami made a low ironic sort of sound. "Her options were limited. And for more than a year she's been trying to get Noah to give her a little independence. But he's been locked up tight, absolutely sure something awful will happen to her if he lets her get out on her own. In the end, I couldn't *not* help her. She's got a fine opportunity and she doesn't want to let it slip through her fingers. She has to make the break."

Alice wrapped her arms around herself against the slight chill in the air. "Noah might never forgive you. He might never forgive any of us."

"I think you're wrong. He loves his sister. When push finally comes to shove, he's going to accept that Luce is a grown-up and that she's also fully recovered after that last surgery she had. He'll realize that he doesn't have to take care of her anymore. He'll see that her leaving was the right choice."

Alice blew out a hard breath. "All right, he'll forgive Lucy. But will he forgive *you?*"

"I think so." Dami grinned then, that charming world-famous grin of his. "He'll want to get along with me. After all, I'm going to be his brother-in-law."

She elbowed him in the ribs. "I haven't said I'll marry Noah."

"You didn't have to. It's written all over your face when you look at him. And even tonight, with all hell breaking loose, it was obvious every time he glanced your way that he's found the woman for him."

I hope you're right, she thought. But she decided not to say it. As soon as she did, Dami would ask her why she sounded doubtful. And then what would she say?

That she loved Noah but she hadn't told him so, that for some reason, she couldn't bring herself to say the words? That he kept his heart carefully separate at all times. That he wouldn't take her to the place where he'd grown up and that made her feel that she didn't really have his trust.

She wanted to confide in Dami now, but the timing was all wrong. He'd come to take Noah's sister away. He was in much too deep already. He didn't need her crying on his shoulder, revealing things she ought to be discussing with Noah.

Dami took her hand and wrapped her fingers around his arm. "We'd better go in before Luce gets herself into any more trouble."

They returned to the family room, where Hannah and the two bodyguards waited. Alone.

Hannah sent them a smile that was both wise and

weary. "Lucy went upstairs. She said if *you* two could talk things through, she probably ought to make an effort to work it out with Noah."

Noah expected Alice's soft tap on the door. His pride jabbing at him, he started to bark at her to leave him alone. But his heart wouldn't let him do that.

She infuriated and challenged and thrilled and bewildered him by turns. He was angry at her for not having his back with Lucy, for going so far as to keep crucial information from him. She damn well should have told him about that phone call she'd overheard.

And yet at the same time, in a deeper sense, he knew with absolute certainty that she *did* have his back.

From the first, she'd confused the hell out of him. And she continued to do so.

The soft knock came again.

He left off staring blindly out the sitting-area French doors to go and let her in.

But it wasn't Alice.

It was Lucy.

His gut tightened at the sight of her standing there. "What?" He pretty much growled the word at her and then instantly wished he could call it back.

Lucy surprised him. She refused to let his gruffness send her off in a huff. She stared up at him with her lips pressed together and her eyes full of hope and anxiousness. "Look. You're my brother. I love you so much. And you saved my life. Repeatedly. I know that. I get that. I wouldn't be here without you. I owe you everything. I owe it to you to *do* something with this life I have because of you. I know you're afraid for me and you only want the best for me. I just need you to understand that my going *is* the best thing for me. So please, please, can't you just give me your blessing? Can't you just let yourself be okay with it? Can't you just...let me go?"

Let her go....

As he'd had to let their dad go, and then their mom? No. He couldn't do it. He *wouldn't* do it....

"Please, Noah," she said again. "Please."

And the strangest thing happened. He looked into her upturned face and he saw the naked truth.

He'd lost the damn battle. She *was* going. He could get with the program and help in any way she would let him—or he could let his pride win, turn his back on her, shut the door in her face.

And then never be able to forgive himself if anything actually did happen to her if she felt that she couldn't call him for help because he'd sent her away in anger.

He went with the truth instead of his pride. He gave in. "Lucy..." He let his pain and his love for her show on his face. In his voice. "All right. Yes. I get it. You need to go."

"Oh, Noah..." All at once her big eyes brimmed with tears. "See, I knew it. I did. I knew you would come through for me in the end. Because you always do." She threw herself against him.

He caught her and wrapped his arms around her good and tight. She smelled like cherries and Ivory soap and that made him want to hug her all the harder. "Just...be okay, will you? Just stay safe."

"I'll try. And if I ever get worried I'm not going to make it—"

"You'll call me. I'll be there."

"I promise, Noah. I will."

* * *

Alice hoped against hope that Lucy and Noah would come back downstairs together.

She got her wish.

Brother and sister appeared arm in arm and Lucy announced, "It's okay. We worked it out."

Dami said, "Wonderful." He offered his hand to Noah.

And Noah took it. "She still insists on going with you in the morning, but I'll handle her expenses."

"Fair enough."

Then Noah led Lucy away to his study to write her a check, explain about how he would arrange to give her early access to her trust fund, and no doubt provide endless and detailed instructions on any number of important subjects.

Hannah excused herself. Dami and Alice told their bodyguards to call it a night. They sat and chatted for a while about the family, about the goings-on at home. But Dami kept trying not to yawn. Finally, he had to admit he was jet-lagged. He said good-night. He and Lucy would be leaving before dawn.

Alice lingered in the family room, hoping Noah might finish giving last-minute advice to his sister and come and find her. She was feeling a little unsure.

Was he still angry with her for not taking his side about Lucy's leaving? It made little sense that he would be. He'd ended up accepting the inevitable after all. But then there was the phone call she'd overheard. He'd seemed pretty put out with her for not telling him about that.

Seriously, though. At this point, he should be over that, too. Shouldn't he?

She had no idea if he was or not. And it bothered her. A lot.

Everything had happened so fast at the end. Noah had whisked Lucy off to his study without so much as a glance in Alice's direction. Just a look or a quick squeeze of her hand would have done it, let her know that he'd forgiven her, too.

But then, maybe he hadn't.

The minutes dragged by. Hannah asked her if she'd like some tea or a snack. She almost asked for a vodka tonic—and to make it a double.

But drowning her doubts about Noah in alcohol was no kind of solution. She told Hannah good-night and went upstairs, where she considered calling Rhia and decided not to. It would be seven-thirty Sunday morning in Montedoro.

Alice settled on a bubble bath, heavy on the bubbles. The suite had a nice big tub. She filled it and lit the fat white candles waiting on the rim. Then she undressed, pinned her hair up and sank gratefully into the fragrant, bubbly heat.

It felt so good she closed her eyes and drifted. She tried to forget her worries about Noah, to be happy that what had started out so badly had ended up with Lucy and Noah reconciled and Lucy gaining her freedom at last.

"You look so tempting in that tub I could almost forgive you for not telling me about Lucy's plans...."

Noah.

He might be mad at her, but he *had* come to find her. Her pulse pounded swift and hard under her breastbone. Even in the scented heat of the bathwater, goose bumps prickled across her skin.

She let her eyelids drift open. He lounged against the door to the bedroom, watching her, still fully dressed in the tan trousers and knit shirt he'd worn that afternoon.

"Didn't anyone ever teach you to knock before entering a woman's private space?" she asked him lazily, waving her hands in a treading motion under the water, enjoying the heat and the wet and the feeling of floating.

Not to mention the look in his blue eyes as he watched her. She could stare into those eyes forever and never get bored. A heated thrill of pure anticipation shivered up the backs of her knees.

He undid his belt. It made a soft whipping sound as he pulled it through the loops and off. "I knocked. You must not have heard me."

"But that's the point. If I don't answer, you don't get to come in."

He reached over his shoulders and got hold of the back of his shirt, gathering it in his fists the way he always did, pulling it over his head and tossing it aside. "I wanted to see you." He really did look much too amazing with his shirt off. She admired the depth and breadth of his chest, the power in the muscles of his long arms, the hardness of his belly. And the gold hair in a T-shape, trailing on down to heaven.

Hair dusted his forearms, too. She liked to rub it, just run her hand lightly above the surface of his skin and feel the silky, subtle brush of it against her palm.

What were they talking about?

Right. She was getting on his case for coming in without her knowing. "Still, you shouldn't have."

He undid his trousers and ripped the zipper wide, slanting her a devil's glance as he did it. "Do you want me to leave?"

Her breath came a little shaky. "No. Stay. Join me."

The corners of his mouth curved up and the blue of his eyes grew somehow deeper. Darker. A bolt of heat zipped along her spine, sharp and sweet, pooling in her belly, spreading out slowly like honey in a spoon.

"Happy to oblige." He shucked out of his shoes, lifted one foot and then the other to yank off his socks.

"Lucy all set, then?"

He straightened, barefooted, bare chested, still wearing the tan trousers, though his fly gaped wide, revealing silk boxers beneath. His eyes had changed, gone darker still. There was still heat in them, but there was anger, too. "As set as she's going to be. And I mean it. You should have told me about the phone call."

Alice sat up and shook her head. "I made the right choice on that. You won't convince me otherwise, won't make me feel guilty. Lucy's not only your sister. She happens to be my friend, too. That phone conversation was between her and Damien. I shouldn't have listened in. But then when I did, the only right thing to do was to keep what I'd heard to myself."

His gaze tracked her eyes, her lips. Lower. "You're distracting me, all those wet bubbles on your shoulders, shining on your breasts, sliding down over your nipples...."

She leaned back again, resting her head on the tub rim, letting the bubbles cover her. "Better?"

He made a low sound in his throat and shook his head. And then, swiftly and ruthlessly, he shoved down his trousers and kicked them aside. The boxers followed, down and off. He was fully aroused.

And that turned her on. *He* turned her on.

A lot.

The man was pure temptation—and she'd known it from that first day. From the moment he raised his golden head and met her eyes.

Oh, yes.

Temptation. Coming to get her, to stir everything up—her body, her mind, her heart. To lure her from her home and her horses, to wreak havoc on the careful, well-behaved existence she'd been trying to make for herself after the Glasgow incident.

He came to her then, covering the distance between the door and the tub in five long strides, stepping in at the opposite end and lowering himself slowly until the bubbles covered the proof of how much he wanted her.

His leg brushed hers under the water. She felt his foot sliding along the inside of her calf. And higher. "All right. I forgive you for keeping that phone call to yourself."

She suppressed a low moan of pleasure. "I would prefer if you admitted that I did the right thing."

He regarded her lazily. "Sit up. Let me see your breasts again. You can probably get me to admit just about anything." Something in his voice alerted her.

Something ragged. Raw.

"Oh, Noah…" She did sit up.

"Alice." He said her name low. Rough. And he reached for her.

She went to him, up on her knees between his open thighs, bubbles and bathwater sliding between her breasts and over her belly. Capturing his face between her two hands, she gazed down at him, into his seeking eyes. "What is it?"

He searched her face as though she held truths he needed to find. "Tell me that *I* did the right thing tonight."

She lowered her mouth to him and kissed him. Soft. Slow. Up close, even beneath the floral fragrance of the bubble bath, she caught his scent: sunshine and that aftershave she loved. He tasted of mint. "You did the right thing," she whispered. "Absolutely. The *true* thing." She kissed him again. "And Lucy *is* ready. She's going to be fine. Watch and see."

"God, I hope so. And it wasn't what *I* thought was right. I didn't see a choice, that's all."

She smiled against his lips. "But there *was* a choice. You could have refused to give in. You could have turned your back on her because she wouldn't do things your way. But you didn't. You made the better choice, the *bigger* choice."

"The hell I did," he whispered roughly. And then he caught her lower lip between his teeth, tugging a little before letting go. "She'd better be safe, be all right, or I'll—"

"Shh." She kissed the sound onto his parted lips. "You're not running her life anymore. She gets to be a grown-up now. You're only there for backup *if* she asks you for it."

He laughed low, in equal parts amusement and pain. "You know you're scaring the crap out of me, right?"

"I get that, yes. You had too many losses as a child. You had to make a new life from the ground up, with only your brains and your will to guide you. You had to take control of yourself and your life when your mom died, absolute control. Letting go of it now is not your best thing."

He smoothed the last of the bubbles down her spine, over the curves of her bottom, cupping her, pulling her closer. "I can let go of control."

"Ha," she mocked, trying really hard not to let the teasing sound become a moan.

He brought those wonderful hands between them, sliding them up over her rib cage, cupping both breasts, and he whispered, "You don't know what you do to me. *You* get me out of control."

It pleased her to no end to hear him admit that. She could almost start thinking they were finally getting somewhere. "I do?"

"Oh, yeah…."

"Show me." She kissed him as he caressed her, teasing his lips with her tongue until he let her in, let her taste him slow and deep, let her have control of the kiss. And while she was kissing him, she slipped a hand beneath the water and wrapped her fingers around him nice and tight.

He jerked against her touch and groaned into her mouth. "Alice…"

She stroked him, long, slow strokes. And then faster. Harder. He gave in to her, let her push him back to rest his head on the tub rim, let her guide his hands out to either side, let her slide around and ease her legs under him, bringing his hips above the water and the slowly dissolving bubbles.

He kept those big arms widespread, letting her have him, letting her do whatever she wanted. The sounds he made, low and urgent, drove her on.

She tasted him at her leisure, bending close and surrounding him by slow degrees, letting him free, only to take her sweet time licking all along the length of him.

"Please," he groaned. "Alice…"

And she lowered her mouth on him again, all the way down, then slowly up and down and up again, creating a building rhythm, stroking him with her encircling hand at the same time.

He called out her name. And she felt him, under her palm, at the base, pulsing. She lifted—and then took him in all the way. He touched the back of her throat as he came, tasting of salt and sea foam. She swallowed him down.

A moment later, he reached for her, guiding her around by the shoulders until he could pull her in front of him. He wrapped his arms around her and she lay against him. With her back to his broad chest, the slowly cooling water buoying her, it seemed she felt him all around her, yet she floated above him, too.

He pressed his lips to her temple, murmured rough and sweet in her ear, "We're good together. You know that we are."

She chuckled, a husky, easy sound, tipping her head back enough that they could share a quick kiss. "Spoken like a recently satisfied man."

"I'm serious." Gruff. A little bit angry, but in such a tender, urgent way.

"All right. Seriously, then. Yes, I agree with you. We *are* good together. Mostly."

"You have complaints?" He bent and nipped at the wet skin of her shoulder.

She moaned. "At this exact moment? Not one."

"Good." He cupped her breast with one hand and idly, possessively, teased at the nipple. With the other, he touched her belly, spreading his fingers wide beneath her rib cage, pressing down a little, bringing her into closer contact with his body, making her burn for him within. "I don't want anyone but you." His voice was gruff and soft at once. "I honestly don't. I've been with more women than maybe I should have. But no more. I'm true to you. I *will* be true to you. It's not a hardship. It's what I want."

She reached back, needing her hand on him, and clasped his nape. It felt so good just to touch him. "I'm glad. So glad."

He caught her wrist, brought her hand to his lips, kissed the tips of her fingers one by one. "I started out to find myself a princess."

"Yes. I know."

"I was an ass."

She agreed with him. Gently. "Well, yes. You were. A bit."

"But then guess what happened?" He curved his fingers around hers and brought their joined hands down together under the water. "I went looking for what I thought I wanted—and I found so much more. I found you."

All at once, her throat felt tight and her eyes were brimming. And she couldn't stop herself, didn't *want* to stop herself. She went ahead and said exactly what was in her heart. "I love you, Noah." It came out in a whisper. She made herself say it louder, owning it, proudly. "I'm in love with you. *You're* the one that *I* want, too."

And then he was taking her shoulders again, turning her so that she faced him, so she was meeting his eyes. "Marry me." He said it low. With heat and longing and coaxing intensity. "Say you will. Say yes this time. Be my wife."

Chapter Twelve

Alice longed to give him what he wanted, to tell him yes.

She did want to marry him. She wanted that a lot.

But somehow she couldn't say it. She couldn't quite make herself put that yes out there. She couldn't quite open her mouth and give him the answer he was waiting to hear.

Instead, she only stared at him, mute, her body yearning, her heart aching.

Her silence didn't go over well. The hot, hopeful look left his eyes. They turned cool. Hard.

And then he lifted her off him. Firmly guiding her back to her own end of the tub, he gathered his feet under him and stood.

The water sloshed over the rim and splashed onto the thick bath mat as he got out. He grabbed a towel from the linen cart and wrapped it around his waist. Without stopping to pick up his scattered clothes, dripping water, he headed for the door.

She let out a cry. "Noah, please don't go...."

He kept on walking. Two more steps and he was through the doorway, out of her sight.

She waited to hear the outer door open and shut.

When it didn't, she felt a tiny bit less awful.

He wasn't happy with her, but at least he hadn't stormed out. Well, not *all* the way out. He'd stayed in the suite.

She climbed from the tub, reached for another towel from the stack and dried off, giving him a little time to settle down before trying to talk to him again. At the beveled mirrors over the twin sinks, she took down her hair and shook it out on her shoulders. And then, knowing she'd probably stalled as long as she dared, she snagged her light robe from the back of the door, stuck her arms in the sleeves and belted the sash.

He was standing at the French doors, still wearing the towel, staring out at the moonlit equestrian fields when she found him. She approached with care and drew to a halt a few feet from his broad bare back. About then she realized she had no idea what to say.

Apparently he got tired of waiting for her to find her voice. He demanded, without turning, "What do you want from me, Alice? Heavy use of the L-word? My heart on a pike?"

She fell back a step. "You're being cruel."

He whirled on her then. She startled, certain he would raise his voice to her. But no. He drew in a slow breath and spoke in a tone as even and low as it was dangerous. "I don't know what more to say to you, what else to do to prove to you that I want this, you and me. I want it to last and I intend to do my part to see that it does. I want to be your husband. I want us to have children together. When I get old, I want to be looking over at you in the other rocking chair."

What he said was so beautiful. Her arms ached to reach for him. But she knew he would only pull away from her touch. So she brought her hands up and folded them, prayerfully, under her chin. "I want that, too, Noah. I meant what I said. I love you. I do. You mean the world to me. It's only…" With a hard sigh, she let her arms drop to her sides again. "It's been barely more than a month since we met. I think we need more time."

"Speak for yourself. I *know* what I want."

"All right, then. Speaking for myself, *I* need more time."

"How much time?"

"Some. A little. I don't really know. But when you rush me like this, it only makes me more certain I need to slow things down."

His face looked haggard suddenly. "You say that you love me. But you don't trust me."

Again, she wanted to reach out, smooth his brow, to swear that she *did* trust him, that in the end it would be all right. But she kept her arms at her sides and told him quietly, "It's not you I don't trust. Not really. It's…me."

He threw up both hands. "Oh, excellent. Like there's a damn thing I can do to fix that."

"I don't expect you to fix it. There's nothing *to* fix, not really. There's just…" She struggled for the right words. "Honestly, what you did tonight, making your peace with Lucy, finally letting her go when she's the last of your family and you have this ingrained need to keep her close where you can protect her…. Well, that was amazing. That was really, truly something. It showed me that you *can* compromise, that you're not all about winning, about doing what *you* think is right. That when someone you love finally draws the line on you, you'll do what you have to do to keep the connection. Also, I did hear the things you said to me a little while ago, about being true to me, about wanting me for myself, not because I fit some idea you had of the perfect trophy wife—and then what you said just now, about you and me and the rocking chairs. All of it. It's good. It's right."

He ran a hand back through his hair. "Great. I'm wonderful. Amazing. I say the right things to you. I've proved that I'm flexible, willing to give in. You're in love with me. I'm the guy for you. And still, you keep putting me off."

She wrapped her arms around herself. "I'm an impetuous person. I told you that at the first. My sister Rhia says I do best when I go with that, when I follow my instincts. I think she's right—as a rule. But I do have to be careful about saying yes to sharing the rest of my life. Ten years from now, I don't want either of us to look back and wonder why we said *I do.*"

"That's not going to happen. Not for me."

"I have to be sure, too, Noah."

He was silent, watching her. Then he said, "I think I'll sleep in my room tonight." He started to turn.

"Noah."

"What now?"

"Stay. Please." She held out her hand.

He scowled at it—but then, just when she thought he would turn his back on her, he took it. She pulled his arm around behind her nice and snug, stepping up close and resting her head against his bare chest.

"You don't ask much," he muttered against her hair.

She cuddled closer. "I love you, Noah. Let's go to bed."

Noah let her lead him to the bed. But he'd had enough for the night. Enough of stepping back and letting his sister move to Manhattan where he couldn't protect her.

Enough of having Alice turn him down—even though she claimed to love him.

In bed, she cuddled up close the way she liked to do. He wrapped his arms around her—for a while.

But as soon as her breathing grew even and shallow, he eased his arm out from under her head and slept on his side, turned away from her.

In the morning, they were up before dawn to see Lucy and Damien off. He stood on the front steps with Alice on one side and Hannah on the other, waving goodbye as the black SUV drove away.

Once the car was out of sight, Alice turned to him with a brilliant smile, those gorgeous dimples flashing. He made his lips curve upward in response. But his heart wasn't in it.

They spent the day in the stables and out working with the horses. That night, she asked him if something was wrong.

He shook his head and kissed her. They went upstairs together. He'd been thinking that maybe he'd sleep in his own room. But she kissed him again and he couldn't resist her, so that led where it always led.

Later, as they lay together in the dark, she reminded him that she had to leave on Wednesday. "Next weekend is the Autumn Faire, remember?"

He did remember. "The bazaar and the parade you have to ride in."

"That's it." She settled in closer, pressed her lips to his shoulder. "Come with me. It will be fun."

Was it going to go on like this indefinitely, then, with the two of them constantly together in every way except the one that mattered most to him? "I can't."

"Why not?"

"Didn't I tell you? I have a trip to Amarillo Thursday."

She went very still. And then a small sigh escaped her. "No. You didn't tell me."

He *hadn't* told her, and he knew that he hadn't. In fact, the invitation from Yellow Rose Wind and Solar was open-ended. He'd just that moment decided to go on Thursday. "A West Texas wind farm. I want to have a look before I decide how much to invest."

She rolled away from him, sat up and switched on the lamp. "I'll ask you again." She pulled the sheet up to cover her pretty breasts and settled back against the headboard. "What's wrong?"

He started to insist that there was nothing. But instead, he hauled himself up to sit beside her. "Look. It's hard for a guy. To keep asking and getting told no, all right?"

She kind of sagged to the side and put her head on his shoulder, which felt really good, absolutely right. Damn it. "I'm not saying no. I'm just saying not yet."

He couldn't hold back a grunt of disgust. "Sounds a lot like no to me. And then there's the love thing. You said that you love me."

"Because I do." She clasped his upper arm, squeezing a little. He shifted, easing away from her until she let go, lifted her head from his shoulder and frowned at him. "Is there something wrong with my saying I love you?"

He had no idea why they were talking about this. He never should have let it get started. "It's nothing. It doesn't matter."

"Yes, it does. You know it does."

"It's nothing, Alice."

"That's not true."

"Can you just leave it alone?"

She winced. "You mean it bothers you that I told you I love you and then turned down your proposal?"

It occurred to him that if he said yes to that question, this conversation that made him feel as though poisonous spiders were crawling around under his skin might end more quickly. "Yeah. That's it. It ticks me off. You said you love me—and then you refused to marry me."

She leaned in closer, so their noses almost touched. He wanted to push her away—and he wanted to grab her good and tight and bury his face in her sweet-smelling hair. "How about this? I won't say those dreaded words again until I'm ready to answer yes."

He would prefer that she never said them again. Not ever. But if he admitted that, she'd be all over him, wanting to know what was wrong with him that he had such a big issue with the L-word. The questions would be endless. The spiders under his skin would start biting.

Uh-uh. Not going there.

He said, "It's a deal."

She cradled the side of his face, and then combed the hair at his temples with a fond, gentle touch. "Are you worried about Lucy?"

"Hell, yes."

"She's going to be fine, Noah."

"So everyone keeps telling me."

She kissed him. He breathed in her sweetness. "Reschedule your visit to the wind farm," she whispered. "Come to Montedoro with me."

He shook his head. "You go home. I'll go to Texas. We can't be together all of the time."

"Noah." She held his gaze steadily. "Are you trying to get rid of me?"

"Of course not."

She kissed his chin, his jaw and then nipped at his ear. "Say that again."

"I'm not trying to get rid of you."

"Prove it." Her naughty hand slid down beneath the sheet.

A moment later he flipped her over on her back and showed her just how happy he was to have her around.

Lucy called him the next day. He took the call in his study and couldn't help smiling at the breathless, happy sound of her voice.

"Noah! New York is amazing. The energy here... I could work round the clock and never need to sleep. And my apartment! It's in a beautiful old building. I have tall windows facing the street. There's a claw-foot tub in the bathroom and those old black-and-white subway tiles. The building has seven floors, two apartments per floor, except for the top two floors, which are Dami's for when he's in town. Noah, I'm here just a day and I have so many ideas I can't sketch them fast enough."

He chuckled. "Speaking of fast, have you already moved in?"

"No. Remember? I'm at the Ritz-Carlton for the next few days while I get the place furnished and all that— I mean, at least until I get a bed in and a few basics for the kitchen and bath."

"Good, then." He knew she didn't want to hear it, but he had to caution her, "Don't push too hard. Take care of yourself...."

She laughed. "Oh, I will. I promise you. And I'm feeling great. Fabulous. Never better, I swear."

"How's Damien?"

"He's been wonderful. So helpful and sweet. Plus,

he's easy to talk to and I can ask him anything. He never laughs at me for being so inexperienced and having way too many silly questions."

"Is he...there at the hotel with you?"

"Uh-uh. He's staying at his apartment—the one in my new building?"

Excellent. Noah felt relieved enough to tease her. "Right. *Your* building."

"It *is* my building, because I'm going to live there. Tomorrow he's taking me furniture shopping. But then Wednesday he has to go back to Montedoro." Good. Noah was willing to believe that Dami and Lucy were friends and nothing more, but he would still rest easier when the Player Prince had left New York. Lucy added, "Some festival or something."

"The Autumn Faire."

"That's it. He has to drive a race car in a parade. He's been so sweet, though, Noah. He introduced me to nice Mrs. Nichols across the hall from me. And there's a great building superintendent, Mr. Dobronsky. He takes care of the apartments and fixes anything that gets broken. I met him and his wife, Marie, too. I liked them both a lot."

He couldn't help smiling. "You like *everyone* a lot."

"Mostly, yes. I do." She said it proudly. "And how about you?"

"I'm fine. Perfect."

"Hannah?"

"She misses you already."

"I miss her, too. I'll call her tonight. How's Boris holding up?" Hannah would be taking the cat to her later.

"He'll survive."

"And Alice?"

"Good. Alice is good."

Lucy chided, "You'd better *be* good to her."

A curl of annoyance tightened his gut. "Oh, come on, Lucy. Of course I'm good to her."

"You know what I mean. Treat her right. Take care of her. Let *her* take care of you. Don't close yourself off. Don't boss her around."

"Just what I need." He tried to make a joke of it. "Relationship advice from my baby sister."

But Lucy wasn't kidding. "Someone has to say it. Alice is the one for you. I just don't want you to blow it."

"I'm not blowing anything." *She's the one who keeps turning me down.*

"Oh, I know *that* voice. It's your 'I'm the boss and you're not' voice."

He breathed deep and grumbled, "Lucy. Cut it out."

And she relented. "Okay. Just, you know, try to be open, will you?"

"Open. Absolutely. I will."

"Ha. I love you, Noah."

"Good. Be safe. Don't overdo it."

"I will be fine. I promise. Bye, now."

And she was gone. He set down the phone and thought of all the things he hadn't said: *Watch your back. Hold on to your purse. Stay out of dark alleyways. Set up those first appointments with your new doctors....*

He had so much advice he needed to give her. But she was on her own now. All grown up. And a continent away.

Alice didn't know what to do. Noah was shutting down on her, shutting her out. Whenever she tried to talk to him about it, he denied and evaded.

Maybe he was right. A little time apart wouldn't hurt them. It might do them good.

Or it might just be the simplest way to end it. She would go home; he would fly to Texas on business.

The days would go by, the weeks and the months. Somehow they would never quite get back together again....

She left for Montedoro Wednesday morning.

Noah kissed her goodbye at the front door. "Have a good trip," he said. Nothing else. No urging her to hurry back, not a single word about how much he would miss her or when he might come to her.

His coolness hurt. She longed to tell him she loved him, but she'd promised she wouldn't—not until she was ready to marry him. And how could she be ready when he wouldn't even talk to her about the things that really mattered?

So she kissed him back and whispered, "Take care."

Altus held open the car door and she got in.

And that was that. They drove away.

Noah returned from Texas on Friday. He'd sunk a big chunk of change into Yellow Rose Wind and Solar. And he had complete confidence in his decision to go in and go big.

There were other things he wasn't so confident about. Things like his sister's continued good health and well-being now she'd run off to New York to become a star in the fashion world. And Alice.

Alice most of all.

She'd left him without saying when she'd be back. He was pretty damn furious at her for that.

True, he hadn't *asked* when she would be back. He

hadn't offered to join her in Montedoro. But he felt justified in that. After all, *she* was the one leaving *him*. She should be the one to say when she planned to return.

And she hadn't called or emailed or texted him, either.

Well, all right. One text. To tell him she'd arrived home safely:

@ Nice Airport. Flt smooth. Njoy Texas.

He'd texted back, Thnx, a real conversation stopper. Because he didn't really want to text Alice.

Or talk to her on the phone.

Or correspond via email.

He wanted her with him, where he could touch her and see her smile. He wanted his ring on her finger and her sweet, strong body next to him in bed.

Wanted all that. And wanted it way, way too much.

So much it scared the crap out of him. So much it had him all upside down and turned around inside.

It wasn't supposed to be like this. She was supposed to say yes when he asked her—or at least, if she didn't say yes, he should be able to take it in stride. Patience and persistence were everything. He knew that. You kept your eye on the prize and you never gave up no matter what went down.

He was blowing it. He got that. Blowing it and determined to keep on blowing it.

It made no sense. *He* made no sense.

He was ashamed of himself and pissed off at her. And so lonely for her it made his bones ache.

Saturday, he called Lucy just to see how she was doing. And to give her all the important advice he hadn't managed to impart when she'd called the previous Monday. She chattered away, laughing, sharing way more information about her new life in New York City than he ever needed to know.

And he simply listened. And found himself smiling and nodding and now and then making an encouraging sound. He never did give her all that advice he'd been so anxious to share.

Because he realized she didn't need to hear it.

Somewhere around the time she started detailing how Mrs. Nichols across the landing had invited her over and they'd made cookies together—spice cookies with cinnamon and nutmeg and sugar sprinkled on top—the truth came to him.

Lucy was okay.

Lucy was going to be fine.

If she needed him, she would call him. For now, he'd done all he could for her.

It was her turn to soar, and he really couldn't help her with that.

He was just feeling kind of good for the first time in a week when she asked him about Alice. He didn't know what to say so he answered in single syllables, and she knew immediately that things weren't right. When she found out that Alice had gone to Montedoro and Noah had no idea when she'd be back, Lucy got all over him, calling him his own worst enemy, demanding to know if he'd lost his mind.

Noah let her rant on. What could he say? She was right after all.

When she finally wound down, she pleaded softly, "Go after her, Noah. Do not let her get away."

After that conversation, he felt worse than ever. He

went out to the stables and spent the day with his horses. It helped a little.

But not enough.

Monday, Orion arrived from the farm in Maryland. God, he was beautiful. To see that incredible iridescent coat shining in the California sun, well, that was something. Noah called in the vet to check him over. The vet declared him in excellent health. After the vet visit, Noah tacked him up and rode him. Orion amazed him, so calm and responsive for a stallion, especially a super-sensitive Teke recently cooped up in a trailer for the long ride from Maryland.

He started to whip out his phone and text Alice, just to let her know that Orion had finally arrived safe and well, to give her a hard time for parting with such an amazing animal.

But he didn't call.

What if she didn't answer? He had no idea where he stood with her now.

It had been five days since she'd left him. In some ways, those five days seemed a century. Or maybe two.

That got him feeling down all over again.

Back at the house, he showered and changed and then went down for a drink before dinner. He poured himself a double and drank it, staring out over the equestrian fields. When the glass was empty, he poured another.

Hannah served him his solitary dinner on the loggia.

He sat down and looked at the excellent meal she'd put in front of him and decided he wasn't hungry after all. "Hannah, another drink." He held up his glass to her.

She gave him one of those looks and said, "If you want to get wasted, you can do that on your own." And then she spun on her heel and marched back into the house.

He sat there for a moment after she left, fuming. And then he went after her.

"What the hell, Hannah?" he demanded when he got to the jut of white stone counter that separated the kitchen from the family room. He slammed the heavy crystal glass down. "What is your problem?"

Okay, he shouldn't have asked. He knew that. You didn't ask Hannah Russo what her problem was unless you wanted an earful.

"You," she said low, with a cold curl of her lip. "*You* are my problem, Noah. You, moping around here like someone did you wrong when we all know very well that *you're* the one in the wrong here."

"Now, you wait just a minute here…"

"No. Uh-uh. *You* wait, Noah. When are you going to wake up? You think I can't tell what's happened in this house? You think I don't know that you went out and found yourself the woman of your dreams and then brought her home only to send her away again?"

"I didn't—"

Hannah cut him off with a wave of her hand. "Don't even bother lying to me. I've known you for too long. I know what you're up to. You had some grandiose scheme to get yourself the ultimate trophy wife."

"What the… How did you—"

"*You* told me."

"I didn't—"

"You did. Maybe you didn't know that you did. But you told me all about her, including that she's a Montedoran princess. You said you were going to marry her, and that was before you even met her. I can add two and two and come up with four every time—and where was I? Oh, yeah. You went out to catch yourself a princess and instead you found someone to love you. Someone you love right back. That scares you. Love scares you. Well, you know what? You're not the least special. Everybody's scared. Everybody's afraid that they'll lose what they love the most. Everybody's afraid that they'll end up alone."

"I'm not—"

That time, she slapped her palm flat to the counter for silence. The sound echoed like a shot. "Yes, you *are*. You are afraid. And you are taking yourself way too seriously. You need to get over yourself. And here's a hot flash. Getting snockered on thirty-four-year-old Scotch is not going to give you anything but a headache in the morning. You need to go after her. You need to suck it up and say what's in your heart, Noah. You need to get down on your knees in front of her. You need to tell that sweet girl that you love her. You need to do it right away. Before she does exactly what you're afraid she'll do— which is to decide that you're not worth waiting for."

Chapter Thirteen

Alice was doing her best just making it through one day after another.

In some ways it was good to be back in Montedoro. To share long lunches with Rhia, to spend time with her horses.

The Autumn Faire came and went. She rode Yazzy in the parade wearing traditional Montedoran dress: full pink skirt with black trim, a frothy white blouse, a snug black vest embroidered with twining flowers and a round, flat, wide-brimmed hat with a black ribbon that tied beneath her chin. White tights and flat black shoes completed the ensemble.

Alice waved and smiled at the crowds that lined the narrow streets. A lot of people had cameras pressed against their faces or took pictures with their phones as she rode by. Alice just kept smiling even though she felt vaguely ridiculous. She knew she would end up all over the tabloids looking like a country milkmaid.

Which was fine, she reminded herself. Looking like a milkmaid was a significant improvement over coming off like a refugee from an episode of *Girls Behaving Badly*.

After the parade, she went home to change. Dami showed up and coaxed her out for a coffee with him. They sat in a favorite café and he told her what a delight

Lucy was and then asked her why Noah hadn't come with her for the Faire.

She sipped her espresso and said she didn't want to talk about Noah.

And Dami surprised her by not pressing her to say more. He took her hand and kissed the back of it, and then turned it over and pretended to see her future in her palm. "Great happiness. True love. Horses. Children— lots and lots of children." He faked a look of dismay. "Far too many of them, if you ask me."

She eased her hand away. "You just never know, Dami."

He didn't lose his beautiful smile. "Perhaps *you* don't. But *I* know. You are a ray of boldly shining light in a world that is too often boring and gray. You were born to be happy. And you will be. Just watch."

Alice hoped her charming brother might be right. But as each day went by, she grew more afraid that if there was to be happiness for her, it wouldn't be with Noah.

Michelle clucked over her and whipped up delicious meals to tempt her flagging appetite. Alice ate the wonderful food without much pleasure. Everything seemed gray and sad to her, even Michelle's excellent cooking.

More than once she considered simply hopping a flight and returning to California. But she didn't do it— which was unlike her. She'd always been one to go after what she wanted.

With Noah, though...

It just didn't feel right to go running after him. He'd sent her away alone, though she'd asked him twice to come with her. He wanted her to marry him, but he wouldn't or couldn't say that he loved her. He didn't even seem to want her to say that *she* loved him. It was all too perplexing, and she didn't know what to do about it, didn't know how to get through to him.

So she did nothing.

Rhia gave her a hard time about that. "Waiting. That's what you're doing. You realize that, don't you? Waiting for him to make the first move. It's so...backward of you to wait for a man to make the moves. That's just not you, Allie. You're a woman of action. And you need to go to him, work things out with him, together, the two of you...."

Maybe Rhia was right.

But deep in her heart, Alice didn't think so. Alice thought that Noah needed time to figure a few things out.

She was giving him that time.

At least that was what she told herself.

While she waited.

And did nothing.

Thank God for her horses. Without them, it all would have been too much to bear. She gave her days to them gratefully, rising long before daylight to be the first one at the stables, not going back to her villa until sunset.

On the last Wednesday in October, she woke from her restless dreams even earlier than usual. She went straight to the stables and tacked up the chestnut mare Rosanna to ride. She'd just set the saddle well forward on the mare's fine back when she heard it: the soft rhythmic rustling of a broom brushing the floor.

Her heart roaring in her ears and her gloved hands suddenly trembling, she turned.

He was there at the edge of the shadows, tall, strong, golden. Wearing battered jeans, an old sweatshirt and worn Western boots.

His name filled up her throat. She hesitated to let it

out, struck silent by the absurd certainty that he was only a fantasy brought on by her own desperation and longing, that he would vanish as soon as she dared to acknowledge him with sound.

She made herself say his name anyway. "Noah?"

He dropped the broom. It clapped and clattered against the stone floor. And then he was lifting his head to face her. He tried on a smile that didn't quite make it. In those blue eyes she saw hope and fear and so many sweet, tender questions.

And love.

She did. At last. She saw his love.

He made a noise, a tight, tortured sound. And in a whisper, he said, "Alice." He held out his arms.

It was enough. It was everything.

With a soft cry, she covered the distance between them in swift strides. He scooped her up and she grabbed on tight.

He turned them in a circle there in the darkened stable, so early in the morning it still felt like night. His cheek, rough with morning stubble, pressed to hers—at first.

And then he turned his head just that little bit more. Their lips met in a kiss that told her all the things she needed so desperately to know. A kiss that promised tomorrow.

And the next day.

And all the days after that.

On Friday they flew to Los Angeles.

They took a suite at the Beverly Hills Hotel and made love for hours. When they finally fell asleep, exhausted from jet lag, pleasure and happiness, they slept until the middle of the following day.

At three in the afternoon, they stood on a palm-tree-lined street in the pretty, hilly neighborhood of Silver Lake. He showed her the Spanish-style house that his parents had owned, where he'd lived until the money ran out after his father died.

"It's a comfortable house," he said. "Built in the 1920s and big for that era. Four bedrooms, two baths. A great house to raise a family."

She linked her arm with his and shaded her eyes with her other hand. "You loved it here."

He nodded, his gaze on the house where he used to live. "We were happy. Safe. Until my father died, I honestly thought no trouble could touch me—or maybe I didn't actually think it. It was simply true. A fact of life. But then one morning, he kissed my mother goodbye, walked out the front door and fell off a roof two hours later. Everything changed."

She leaned her head against his shoulder and wished she could think of something both helpful and profound to say. All that came was, "It's so sad. And scary..."

He tipped her chin up and kissed her, just a tender brush of his mouth across hers. "Come on."

They got back in the car and he told the driver where to go next.

Twenty minutes later the car pulled to the curb on another street, where the houses were smaller and more run-down, with barred windows and doors.

They got out and stood on the sidewalk by the car, beneath a beautiful tree with delicate fernlike leaves. "A jacaranda," she said. "We have them in Montedoro, too."

He pointed at the house across the street, a small stucco bungalow painted a truly awful shade of turquoise. The paint was peeling, the doors and windows barred. A battered chain-link fence marked off the tiny bare yard. "One bedroom," he said. "One bath. My mother slept on the sofa. Lucy had the bedroom. There was an extra room, very small, in the back. I had a cot in there. I hated that house. But not because it was so ugly and cramped. It just... It always felt empty to me. Empty and sad. Well, except for Lucy. She was like a bright ray of light, even when she was so sick and I was sure we would lose her like we lost my dad."

"So, then, it wasn't *all* bad."

"Bad enough," he said gruffly, still staring at the turquoise house.

She reached up and guided his face around to look at her. "It means so much to me that you've brought me here."

He turned to her fully then, there beneath the lacy branches of the jacaranda tree, and he gazed down at her steadily, his eyes like windows on the wide-open sky. "I love you, Alice." He said it softly but firmly, too. Without hesitation and with no equivocation. "You are my heart, my life, all the hope for the future I didn't even realize I was looking for. I want you to marry me, but if you're not ready, I swear I can be patient. I can wait as long as you need me to."

She put her hands on his chest, felt his heart beating strong and steady beneath her palm. "Oh, Noah..." Across the street, a woman with long black hair pushed a stroller in front of the house where Noah used to live. Two boys raced past in the middle of the street, laughing and bouncing a ball between them. She thought that it wasn't such a bad street, really, that there were people in the small houses around them who loved and cared for each other, who looked to the future with hope in their hearts. She whispered, "I was so afraid you wouldn't come to find me."

He laughed then, but it was a ragged, torn sort of sound. "Me, too." He took her by the shoulders and met her eyes again. "The love thing. Talking about it, saying it out loud... It's hard for me."

She laid her hand against his cheek. "It will get easier. Love is like that. The more you give, the more you have to give."

"Think so, huh?"

"I know so."

"Hannah got fed up with me," he confessed. "She told me off, said I was scared to love you and I'd better get over myself and deal with my fear before you got tired of waiting for me."

She shook her head and dared a smile. "It would have taken a long time for me to get that tired. But I'm glad you came sooner rather than later."

"I gave some thought to what Hannah said..."

"And?"

His mouth twisted wryly. "It's old news."

"Tell me anyway."

He glanced up into the ferny branches of the tree, then down at the cracked sidewalk and finally into her eyes again. "My parents, that's all."

"They made you afraid to love? But how? From all you've told me, they did love you, very much. And they loved each other...."

He lifted a hand and stroked her hair, his touch so sure and steady—and cherishing, too. "I know. It doesn't make sense. They loved each other absolutely. Even I knew that, and I was only a kid. But my mother was never the same once he was gone. She let everything go.

She was like a ghost of herself. She was…just hanging around, waiting for it to be over."

"Oh, Noah. Are you sure? Did she say actually that?"

"No, of course not. But she didn't have to. It was there in her face all the time. That faraway look, a bottomless sort of sadness. The day we lost her, I think she knew what would happen if she didn't get to the doctor. But she wouldn't go. She wanted to be with my dad. It was where she'd wanted to be all along."

Alice started to speak.

He put his finger against her lips. "I realize I'll never know for certain that she let herself die. I realize she did the best she could and that we survived, Lucy and me."

"But you've been afraid. Afraid to love so much…"

He nodded. And then he bent and he kissed her. It was the sweetest kiss, tender and slow.

When he lifted his head, she said, "Don't be afraid. Or if you are, do it anyway. Love me anyway."

"I will," he replied. "I do."

And then, slowly and clearly, she said, "Yes, Noah. I will marry you."

He looked so startled she almost laughed. And then he demanded, "You mean it? You will?"

"I love you. And yes. I will."

He stuck his hand into his pocket and came out with the ring he'd offered her that first time they made love. When she shook her head in wonderment, he explained, "I've been carrying it around with me all along, just in case. It got to be like a talisman. I kept it on me even after you left California."

"Noah, I do believe you're a complete romantic."

"Shh. Don't tell anyone. Let it be our secret."

She gave him her hand and he slipped it on her finger. It was a perfect fit. "I love it," she whispered. "I love *you*."

They shared another slow and tender kiss.

Then, hand in hand, they turned for the waiting car.

* * * * *

THE PRINCE'S
COWGIRL BRIDE

BRENDA HARLEN

For Connor & Ryan
—the next generation of princes—
the reason for everything I do.
I love you both
with all of my heart.

Prologue

"Does it give you ideas?"

Prince Marcus Santiago of Tesoro del Mar glanced down at his dance partner and found her smiling up at him with big blue eyes filled with promises she was far too young to be making. He'd been holding her at a careful distance, not wanting to give her any encouragement or the press any reason to speculate that he was interested in more than waltzing with a guest at his brother's wedding, but clearly she hadn't taken the hint.

"No." His answer was succinct and unequivocal.

"I'll bet if you met the right woman you'd change your mind."

"Maybe if I met her at the right time," he conceded, though he sincerely doubted it. "But I've got to finish university before I even start thinking about settling down."

She pouted prettily. "Are you really going back to Harvard next week?"

"Only because the university has this annoying expectation that a student attend classes and write exams in order to earn a degree."

She laughed prettily. "But you're not *really* going to be a lawyer."

"Aren't I?"

"Of course not. You're a prince."

"The two titles aren't mutually exclusive," he said dryly.

Her eyelashes fluttered. "I only meant that you don't need to work."

He couldn't prevent the smile that curved his lips. Clearly this girl had no idea what it meant to be a royal. The truth was, he didn't know anyone who worked harder or longer than his brother Rowan. As the youngest, Marcus didn't bear the same burden of responsibilities, but he wasn't exactly given a free ride, either.

She shifted closer to him, lowered her voice. "If you must go away, maybe we could go somewhere to share a private goodbye."

He was relieved to note that the song was winding down to a finish. He touched his lips briefly to the back of her hand and stepped back. "Right now, I must speak with my brother."

Disappointment clouded her eyes as she dropped into a curtsy. "Of course, Your Highness. Maybe later?"

He didn't bother to respond.

That was exactly why Marcus wasn't a big fan of weddings. It wasn't so much that he was opposed to the institution of marriage—not for other people, anyway. No, what he disliked was the effect that they seemed to have on the single females in attendance. It was as if they suddenly couldn't see anything but wedding gowns and bouquets of flowers and any unmarried man who happened in their path as a potential candidate for the altar. No thank you—no way.

There were just too many women out there—fun women, smart women, beautiful women—to want to commit to a single one. If he ever met a woman who was all of those things, he might reconsider his attitude toward matrimony, but he was doubtful.

He snagged a glass of champagne from the tray of a passing waiter and carried it to the terrace where he'd seen his brother Eric disappear. He found him in the shadows, nursing a drink of his own.

"Hiding out?" Marcus asked him.

Eric grinned. "And not ashamed to admit it."

He leaned back against the stone balustrade and crossed his feet at the ankles. "So how many times have you been asked if Rowan's wedding has given you ideas about getting married?"

"I lost count."

Marcus nodded and sipped his champagne, enjoying the stolen moment of quiet camaraderie with his brother.

Then Eric broke the silence by saying, "I wouldn't say I've never thought of it, though."

Marcus nearly choked. "Marriage?"

His brother nodded. "Not with respect to any particular woman, but I've wondered, sometimes, what it would be like to have what Julian had with Catherine, or what Rowan has found with Lara."

"*Mi Dios*—don't let anyone overhear you saying that or you'll have a ring on your finger before you have a chance to recover from this temporary bout of insanity."

Eric's lips curved. "Do you really think it's crazy? Crazier than being alone?"

"Maybe you have been at sea too long."

"And that is exactly why I won't ever have what our brother has. Because I can't imagine ever leaving the navy any more than I could imagine asking someone to share my life when I'm at sea more than I'm home."

"You could ask," Marcus argued. "And not have any trouble finding someone who believes becoming a princess is more than adequate compensation for an absent husband."

Eric shook his head. "You're too cynical."

"Realistic. Isn't that why we all have passports with our mother's maiden name—so we can occasionally escape the attention of being royal?"

"I didn't think you minded the attention."

He couldn't blame his brother for thinking that because there had been a time when it was true, when he'd not only not minded the attention but had courted it. Lately, however, he'd just wanted to get away from it all. To shake free of the media spotlight and everyone else's expectations and figure out what he really wanted. Because the truth was, he still didn't have a clue. For too long, he'd been moving from one thing to the next, from school to school, earning degree upon degree, searching for the one thing that really seemed to fit.

Or maybe Eric was right. Maybe it wasn't some*thing* so much as some*one* that he'd been searching for.

He almost laughed out loud at the ridiculousness of that thought.

Tonight, the only thing he was searching for was a good time. He tossed back the rest of his champagne and went to find it.

Chapter One

Two years later...

Jewel Callahan slid onto a stool at the counter at the Halfway Café and scowled at the slim back of the blond woman who was grinding beans for a fresh pot of coffee. Crystal Vasicek was the proprietor of the popular little café and the creator of the most amazingly decadent desserts in all of West Virginia—and probably the other forty-nine states, too.

Jewel waited for the grinder to shut off before she spoke. "It's your fault, you know."

Crystal dumped the grounds into the waiting basket and slid it into place, then punched the button to start the coffee brewing before she turned. "That's quite an accusation coming from the woman who's always so quick to assume responsibility for everyone else's troubles." Her pretty blue

eyes sparkled with a combination of amusement and curiosity
"What did I do?"

"It's what you didn't do," Jewel told her.

"Okay—" Crystal picked up a pot of coffee that had finished
brewing and poured her sister a cup "—what *didn't* I do?"

"Marry Russ."

Crystal raised a perfectly arched eyebrow. "He never asked."

"He might have." Jewel dumped a heaping spoonful of
sugar into her cup. "If you hadn't run off and married Simon."

"Forgive me for falling in love and not anticipating how
that event might somehow interfere with your plans."

"You always were the type to leap without looking."

"And you always exercised enough caution for both of us,"
Crystal replied evenly.

Because she'd wanted to protect her sister, to shield her
from the expectations—and the disappointments—that were
inherent in being a daughter of Jack Callahan. After all, she'd
had half a dozen years of experience with that before Crystal
came along.

"We were talking about Russ," Jewel reminded her.

"What about Russ?"

"He's leaving."

"Oh."

There was a wealth of understanding in that single syllable.

Jewel's throat was suddenly tight, making it difficult for
her to speak. And what more could she say, anyway?

Crystal went to the bakery display and pulled out a mile
high chocolate cake, then cut a thick wedge and put it on a
plate with a fork. Jewel managed a smile as her sister nudged
it across the counter toward her. Crystal believed that choco
late was a cure-all for every one of life's problems, and

judging by the seven layers of moist cake and creamy icing she'd just set in front of Jewel, she understood the magnitude of this one.

Russ Granger had worked at the Callahan Thoroughbred Center for the last ten years, but he'd been Jewel's friend a lot longer than that, and she couldn't help but be shocked by his defection. He wasn't just leaving his job—he was leaving her. He was the only man she'd ever felt she could truly count on, and now he was moving on.

After pouring herself a cup of coffee, Crystal came around to sit next to her sister at the counter. "Why is he leaving?"

Jewel picked up the fork and dipped the tines into the decadent dark icing. "Because Riley got some big recording contract and he wants to go on tour with her."

"She was wasting her talent singing at The Mustang," Crystal said gently.

Jewel popped a bite of cake into her mouth, but even the rich flavor didn't lift her spirits. "I should have guessed something like this would happen," she admitted. "As soon as he told me he was going to propose to Riley, I should have known. But I was so happy for him that I didn't think about what it might mean for CTC. I certainly didn't think he'd take off in the middle of the season."

"He's leaving soon, then?"

"The end of next week. He's been working closely with Darrell over the past several years and assured me that he's more than ready to take over his duties, but—" she sighed and dug into the cake again "—I can't imagine how I'll get through the season without him."

"You will," Crystal said confidently. "Because there isn't anything you can't do if you put your mind to it."

Jewel had always prided herself on being capable and independent, able to handle anything and everything on her own. And it was a good thing, too, because that was how she always ended up—on her own.

"Jack Callahan might have built CTC, but the only reason it's one of the top training facilities in the state today is because of you," Crystal said, then smiled wryly. "And in spite of me. Lord knows, I never had any interest in staying on the farm or working with the horses."

"You carved your own path." Jewel was proud of her sister's success, and she still got a kick out of the fact that Crystal's spectacular desserts were available not just at the little café where she'd first started baking but in some of the area's trendiest and most exclusive restaurants. "Sometimes I wonder why I couldn't have wanted something else more than I wanted the farm."

"You were a champion barrel racer for three years running," Crystal reminded her.

She smiled, though her memories of that time in her life were more bitter than sweet. "That was a lifetime ago."

"It was what inspired me to do my own thing, regardless of what Jack wanted."

"I would have done anything he wanted," Jewel admitted. Even now, she wasn't sure why she'd always tried so hard to please him, she only knew that she'd never succeeded. Nothing she'd ever done was good enough for Jack Callahan.

"And did," her sister reminded her. "Including giving up your own life to come home when he asked you to."

He hadn't really asked but demanded, as both sisters knew was his way. But the truth was, six years on the rodeo circuit had disillusioned Jewel about a lot of things, and she'd been more than ready to return to Alliston, West Virginia. Her father's heart attack had been both her incentive and her excuse to finally do so and, her difficulties with him aside, she hadn't ever regretted that decision.

She had become his willing assistant, as eager to learn as she was to demonstrate what she already knew, confident that he would learn to trust in her abilities and eventually grant her more authority. But Jack Callahan had continued to hold the reins of the business in his tightly clenched fist until—many years later—they'd finally been pried from his cold, dead fingers.

Jewel and Crystal had stood side by side at his funeral, his daughters from two separate marriages, both sisters painfully aware that they'd been neither wanted nor loved by their father. And more than they'd mourned his death, they'd mourned the distance between them that he'd never tried to breach.

"My life was always here," Jewel finally responded to her sister's comment. "Even when I thought it wasn't."

Crystal touched a hand to her arm. "Maybe the problem isn't that Russ is leaving, but that he found someone and you haven't."

Jewel pushed the half-eaten cake away. "Not this again."

"Honey, you're too young to have resigned yourself to being alone."

"Resigned suggests that I'm settling for less than I want, and I'm not. I'm happy with my life."

"You're happy being alone?"

"I'm hardly alone."

"The horses don't count," her sister said dryly.

"At least they don't hog the bed—or the remote."

"Well, I can't dispute that Simon does both of those things," Crystal said, then a slow smile curved her lips. "But he does other things that more than even the scales—and I'm not talking about taking out the garbage."

Jewel got up and went around the counter to grab the coffeepot for a refill. "You lucked out with Simon," she admitted.

"Then you're not really mad that I didn't wait around for Russ to propose?"

She sighed. "How can I be mad when you're so happy?"

"I am happy," Crystal said. "Happier than I ever could have imagined."

Jewel knew the feeling. She'd experienced that same euphoria of love—and the complete devastation of losing the man she'd thought she would love forever. She only hoped her sister would never have to know that kind of pain, that her life would always be wonderful, that Simon would always love her as much as he did now.

As if following the path of her thoughts, Crystal reached out and squeezed her hand. "Someday your prince will come."

Before Jewel could respond, the jingle of the bell over the door announced the arrival of another customer.

Crystal glanced over, then let out a low whistle.

"Don't look now," she told her sister. "But I think he just walked in the door."

Jewel picked up her cup, sipped.

Crystal frowned at the lack of response.

"You told me not to look," Jewel reminded her.

"Since when do you listen to me?"

She shrugged. "Since the last prince turned into a frog."

Crystal picked up a menu and fanned herself with it. "Six-two, I'd guess. Dark hair, darker eyes. Sinfully sexy.

And—" she glanced pointedly at her sister and smiled "—flying solo."

Her curiosity undeniably piqued by the description, Jewel twisted in her stool—and nearly slid right off of it and onto the floor.

For once, Crystal hadn't exaggerated. The man hovering just inside the door had short, neatly cropped hair, dark slashing brows over espresso-covered eyes, a strong jaw, straight nose, slashing cheekbones and a beautifully sculpted mouth that brought to mind all kinds of wicked fantasies. His olive-toned skin and exotic looks suggested some kind of Mediterranean heritage that made her think of sultry nights and hotter passions, and the punch of lust that hit low in her belly left Jewel almost breathless.

No, her sister definitely hadn't exaggerated. But what she'd neglected to include in her description was "young." Way too young. Probably younger than Crystal even. Definitely too young to make a thirty-four-year-old woman weak in the knees and hot everywhere else.

His gaze moved around the room and collided with hers. Then those beautiful lips slowly curved, and her heart pounded hard against her chest as if it was trying to break free in order to fall at his feet.

"Well, well, well," Crystal said softly.

Jewel felt heat infuse her cheeks as she tore her gaze away from his hypnotic stare. Crystal smirked at her before turning her attention back to the new customer.

"Grab a seat anywhere you like," she called out cheerily. "I'll be with you in just a sec."

"Thank you." His voice was low and deep and as sexy as the rest of him.

"Mmm-mmm," Crystal murmured her appreciation.

Jewel picked up her cup again and sipped before asking, "Weren't we just talking about how happily married you are?"

"I am," Crystal assured her. "But the ring on my finger hasn't affected my eyesight and that is one exceptional specimen of masculinity."

She could hardly deny the fact, nor would she make the mistake of agreeing with her sister aloud, so she only said, "A specimen probably waiting for a cup of coffee."

"Oh. Right." Crystal grinned and grabbed the pot.

Jewel concentrated on finishing her own cup while her sister chatted with her new customer. She couldn't hear what was said, but the low timbre of his voice was enough to create shivers that danced up and down her spine. Crystal's responding laughter bubbled over like a newly opened bottle of champagne, then his deeper chuckle joined in.

Jewel had always envied her sister's ease with other people—her outgoing personality and easy charm, her natural warmth and friendliness. She'd always been more cautious and reserved than Crystal, and though she didn't think anyone would accuse her of being unfriendly, she wasn't often mistaken for warm and welcoming, either. She dealt with a lot of people in her business, not out of choice but necessity, and most of the time, she preferred the horses to their owners. Though lately, she'd been spending a little too much time up close and personal with certain aspects of the thoroughbred training business that she'd prefer to avoid, which reminded her of the other reason she'd come into town to see her sister today.

She waited while Crystal finished serving her "exceptional specimen" and checked on her other customers.

"In addition to Russ leaving, I've got Grady laid up with a broken leg so I'm short a stable hand," she said when her sister returned to the counter. "Do you think Simon's brother would be interested in a summer job again this year?"

Crystal tallied up a bill. "Ted's in Europe with his girlfriend for the next couple of months."

"Oh." Jewel pushed her now empty cup aside. "Know anyone else who might be interested?"

"Most of the local college kids already have their summer jobs lined up."

She sighed. "I guess I'll have to put an ad in the paper then."

"Sorry, I couldn't be more help," Crystal said. "I know how much you hate interviewing people."

"Actually the interviews don't concern me as much as the possibility that it might be too late to find qualified help for the summer."

"What kind of qualifications do you need to muck out stinky stalls?"

"Some experience working around animals would be helpful," she said dryly.

"What kind of animals?" a masculine voice asked from behind her.

She whirled around and found herself face-to-chest with the hunky stranger and couldn't help but notice how the polo shirt he wore stretched across impressive pectoral muscles. Cheeks hot, mouth dry, she lifted her gaze and found his eyes on her again.

Crystal offered profuse apologies as she refilled the cup in his hand.

"Not a problem," he assured her, then shifted his attention back to Jewel and asked again, "What kind of animals?"

She drew in a breath and, along with it, his scent. Clean and sharp and as tempting as the rest of him.

"Horses," she finally managed to respond to his question.

"Thoroughbred racehorses," Crystal elaborated. "My sister runs one of the top training facilities in the state."

Jewel's quelling glance was met with a sweet smile.

"I'm Mac Delgado," the man introduced himself. "I happen to know my way around horses and I'm looking for some short-term employment."

Jewel only said, "And I don't hire anyone without a recommendation," and stepped away from the counter.

"I'll let you know if I find any suitable candidates," her sister called after her.

"Thanks, Crystal." She didn't turn back, but she knew he was watching her. She could feel the heat of his gaze on her as she made her way to the door.

He'd been dismissed—blatantly and unapologetically. It was a new experience for Mac Delgado—aka His Royal Highness Marcus Santiago, Prince of Tesoro del Mar—and not one he'd particularly enjoyed. She hadn't even given him her name, and he was frowning over that fact as he watched her walk out, enjoying the quick strides of long, lean legs and the subtle sway of slim hips until the door of the café swung shut behind her.

A soft sigh drew his attention back to the young waitress with the friendly smile. Crystal, the other woman had called her.

"She really doesn't mean to be rude," Crystal said now.

"And yet, she has such an obvious talent for it."

She smiled again, a little ruefully this time. "She's got a lot on her mind right now."

He shrugged, as if it didn't matter, as if he didn't have a hundred questions about the woman who'd walked out the door without so much as a backward glance in his direction. But he sat down on the stool she'd recently vacated as Crystal waved goodbye to an elderly couple as they headed out the door.

"So what brings you to Alliston?" she asked, turning her attention back to him.

"Road construction on the highway," he admitted.

She smiled at that. "Where are you headed?"

"California eventually."

"Driving?"

He nodded.

"You've got a long way to go."

"I'm not in a hurry," he told her.

"What's in California?" she asked. "Friends? A job? A wife?"

He fought the smile that tugged at his lips in response to her not-so-subtle probing. "None of the above."

"You have to give me more than that if you expect me to answer any questions about my sister."

"What makes you think I have any questions about your sister?"

She lifted a brow. "Then you aren't interested in seeing Jewel again?"

"Jewel?" he echoed, then realized it was her sister's name, and an apt description for the woman with wildly sexy hair and eyes the color of a summer sky before a storm.

And then there were her lips, glossy and full and as perfectly shaped as a cupid's bow. And her hair, miles of honey-gold corkscrew curls tumbled over her shoulders and down her back. And—

He caught a glimpse of Crystal's satisfied smile out of the corner of his eye and forced himself to sever the thought.

Her smile widened. "I believe you were telling me how much you weren't interested in my sister."

"Actually," he said, "you were going to tell me where I could find her."

Jewel was faxing her Help Wanted ad to the classifieds department at the local newspaper when the knock sounded at the door.

"Come in," she said, her eyes never lifting from the machine where she was manually inserting pages because it had a tendency to chew the paper if she used the automatic feeder. She'd been meaning to take the machine in for service, but kept forgetting. With so many other tasks to deal with on a daily basis, those that didn't directly impact the horses tended to get shifted to the bottom of the list and frequently forgotten.

The door creaked as it was pushed open, reminding her that oiling the hinges was another one of those tasks that she never seemed to get around to doing. On the other hand, she didn't have to worry about anyone sneaking up on her.

She fed the last page into the machine before turning around, and found herself looking at a pair of very broad shoulders—not covered in flannel or denim, as was usual around the stables, but a royal-blue polo shirt, complete with the embroidered logo of pony and rider on the left side. The shirt stretched over those shoulders, across a broad chest and tucked into a pair of belted jeans that fit nicely over narrow hips and long, muscular legs.

Her eyes shifted and discovered that the face was just as spectacular as the body, and not entirely unfamiliar.

It was the man from the café, and along with the sense of recognition came a quiver inside—a humming vibration that rippled from her center all the way to her fingertips and churned up everything in between. The sensation was both unexpected and unwelcome, and she fought against it as her gaze locked with his.

Amusement lurked in the depths of his dark eyes, as if he'd been aware of her perusal and wasn't bothered or surprised by it.

He was probably used to women ogling him—a man who looked that good would have to be—but that didn't excuse her own behavior. It had just been so long since Jewel had looked at a man and recognized him as such.

Around the stables, the men were her employees or customers, and over the past few years, she hadn't had much of a life beyond the stables. Her instinctive reaction to this man's arrival at the café had been proof of that. Her response now only reinforced that truth.

"Can I help you?" she asked, the politely neutral tone giving no hint of the hormones zinging around inside of her.

"Actually, I'm here to help you." His warm, rich voice was as sensual as a caress and caused another quiver of sensation deep in her belly.

She mentally cursed her sister, certain that Crystal was somehow responsible for this man's appearance here now.

"How do you think you can help me?" she asked cautiously.

"By taking the job you were talking about at the café."

She looked him over again—had, in truth, not been able to take her eyes off of him—and shook her head. While she didn't doubt that long, lean body was more than capable of the physical work she needed done, she did doubt that he'd ever done such physical labor. "I'm looking for someone to muck out stalls as well as groom and exercise my horses."

"That's what Crystal said," he agreed.

Yep—her sweet but interfering little sister's sticky fingerprints were all over this ambush.

"And you are?" she asked, vaguely recalling that he'd offered his name at the café but unable to remember what it was.

"Mac Delgado."

Her father had taught her that she could learn a lot about a man from his handshake, so she moved forward to take his proffered hand, undeniably curious about this one. His grip was firm, strong and the contact of his palm against hers sent an unexpected jolt of heat through her.

She saw a flicker of something in his eyes, as if he'd felt the jolt, too. Or maybe she was just imagining it. She disengaged her hand and lowered herself into the chair behind her desk. "I have to be honest, Mr. Delgado, you don't look much like a stable hand."

He shrugged. "I have a lot of experience with horses and I'm between jobs at the moment."

She eyed him skeptically but gestured to the chair across from her desk. "Tell me about your experience."

He sat, somehow owning the space rather than merely occupying it. There was an aura about him, a sense of command, as if he was accustomed to giving orders rather than taking them. It made her wonder again why he was really here, because she didn't believe it was to muck out her stalls.

"I assume you're asking about my experience with horses?" There was just the hint of a smile on his lips, and the gleam in those sinfully dark eyes suggested he was flirting with her.

She'd known guys like Mac Delgado before—guys who

usted their good looks and easy charm to get them what they wanted in life, whatever that might be. Jewel wasn't going to fall for it, not this time, no matter how hard her heart pounded when he smiled at her.

Still, there was a part of her—a shallow, sex-deprived part—that was tempted to hire him just so she could have the pleasure of looking at him every day. Because she had no doubt that those muscles would ripple very nicely as he mucked out stalls—if he knew which end of a pitchfork to grab hold of. But hiring a man who obviously expected to get the job by offering little more than his name and a smile would be a mistake, and Jewel Callahan didn't make mistakes. Not anymore and especially not when it came to the business that carried her name.

"Yes, Mr. Delgado. I was asking about your relevant job experience."

He propped one foot onto the opposite knee, a casual pose that allowed her to picture him in Levi's and flannel, rather than the designer threads he was wearing. "I grew up around horses," he told her. "Even before I could walk, I was sitting on a pony."

"That doesn't prove you know the difference between a curry comb and a hoof pick," she noted.

He shrugged again, and she couldn't help but notice how his shirt moulded to the broad shoulders. "I've groomed more than a few horses, even helped train some of them."

"Do you have references?"

"Give me a trial period," he said. "A week to prove that I can do the job."

"No references," she concluded.

"I'm a hard worker."

"This is a busy stable—"

"Three days," he interrupted.

She shook her head with more than a little regret as she pushed her chair back from her desk. "I don't have the time or the patience to train anyone."

"Give me a chance—I promise you won't be disappointed."

"I might have been willing to give you that chance, if not for your hands."

His brows lifted. "What's wrong with my hands?"

"They lack the calluses of a man accustomed to physical labor."

"I've spent the last few years at school," he admitted. "But I wouldn't risk my life around animals who weigh more than six times as much as I do if I didn't know I wasn't capable."

She leaned back in her chair. "At school where?"

"If I give the right answer, do I get the job?"

"You're assuming there is a right answer."

His smile was filled with confidence and charm, and she felt a distinctly feminine flutter in her belly. "Isn't there?"

"No," she said. "And no about the job."

She might end up regretting her hasty decision if no one else responded to her ad, but she instinctively knew that hiring Mac Delgado would present a bigger risk than turning him away. Not just because his experience was unproven, but because of the way her heart raced whenever he was near.

Chapter Two

Four hours later, Marcus had checked out of his hotel and was retracing the route to Callahan Thoroughbred Center after Jewel had—reluctantly—reversed her decision about hiring him.

He wasn't sure he believed in fate, but he couldn't deny feeling that he'd been in the right place at the right time—first, when he'd walked into the café and noticed Jewel sitting at the counter, and again when a young stable hand rushed into her office to warn that an expectant mare was having trouble with her labor.

Not just any mare, as it turned out, but one Jewel had raised since it was a newborn filly, and she'd been frantic at the thought of losing both mother and baby.

With the vet more than an hour's drive away and most of her own personnel at the track in preparation for the next day's race, she'd had almost no choice but to trust Marcus's assurance that he could turn the breech foal. Of course, she'd given it her own best effort first, demonstrating more strength and stamina than he would have expected of a woman who was about five-feet-three-inches tall and hardly more than a hundred pounds. And only when her own efforts proved futile had she stepped aside for him.

He'd been sweating when he was done, not just because it was a messy and physically demanding task, but because he knew this was *his* only chance to convince *her* to give him a chance. He hadn't considered why it mattered or why the opinion of a woman he'd only just met meant anything to him, he only knew that it did.

Having been born royal, even if he had been the last of four sons, meant that he was accustomed to a certain amount of deference from the cradle. The wealth he'd inherited aside from his title ensured that he could live his life as he chose, while dictates of custom and tradition established the parameters within which he was expected to make those choices.

Now he was twenty-five years old and still didn't have a clue about what he really wanted to do with his life—except that at this point he wanted to know Jewel Callahan better. The woman in question, however, had made it clear that she only wanted a hired hand.

Of course, she didn't know who he was. He'd enrolled in school as Mac Delgado, trusting that the use of his mother's maiden name as his own would help him avoid media scrutiny and allow him to concentrate on his studies. And it had worked—more successfully even than he'd anticipated. In fact, soon after coming to America he'd realized few of his classmates could find Tesoro del Mar on a map. They certainly never suspected that Mac was a member of the royal family.

His anonymity hadn't made him any less sought after by the female coeds, confirming that his looks, charm and intelligence were almost as big a draw to members of the opposite sex in America as his royal status had been in Europe. And he found it interesting that the characteristics that had attracted so many women in the past were the same traits that made Jewel wary.

She was grateful to him—he was sure of that. Whether she felt anything beyond appreciation for his actions in delivering the foal he was less certain. But now that he'd been hired on, albeit on a trial basis, he would have some time to find out.

What he found, when he detoured to check on the new foal, was that the woman in question had the same idea.

She was standing at the gate, her arms folded on top of it, her attention riveted on the mare nursing her baby.

"Hard to believe she caused such a fuss only a few hours ago," Marcus noted.

"And scary to think how differently things might have turned out." She turned to face him. "I didn't expect you'd be back so soon."

"I didn't have a lot to pack," he told her.

But before he'd checked out of the hotel, he'd taken the time to shower and change, as he saw she had done, too.

Her jeans had been discarded in favor of a pair of khaki pants, the navy T-shirt replaced by a soft yellow one, and the band that tied her hair back had been removed so that the riotous golden curls tumbled over her shoulders.

She dug something out of her pocket, held it out to him. "The apartments aren't big or fancy, but they're conveniently located, a fact which you'll appreciate at 4:00 a.m. tomorrow morning."

He nodded and took the key she offered. "Thanks."

"There's a cafeteria on site, but also a refrigerator and microwave and some dishes and cutlery in your room."

He nodded again.

She tilted her head, and studied him as if he was a mystery she was trying to figure out. "When I told you I didn't think you were right for the job, I thought that would be the end of it."

"So did I," he admitted.

"Why did you follow me to the birthing shed?"

"Curiosity. Impulse." He lifted a shoulder. "I'm not entirely sure."

"Well, I'm grateful you did," she told him. "I could have lost both of them if you hadn't been here."

He touched a hand to her arm, to reassure her. When he felt the muscles go taut and heard her breath catch, he knew she was feeling more than just gratitude. Whether or not Jewel Callahan liked him, she wasn't immune to him.

He let his hand drop away and kept his voice light. "She's a beautiful filly."

"'The prettier they are, the more trouble they are.'"

His brows rose in silent inquiry.

"Jack Callahan's words of wisdom," she explained.

"I'm guessing you gave him a lot of trouble."

Her cheeks flushed in response to the compliment, but there was sadness lurking in the depths of those stormy blue-gray eyes as she shook her head. "Not really."

"Well, if I'd had to put money on it, I would have guessed the foal was a colt," he said.

"Why's that?"

"Because you said that she wasn't due for another couple

f weeks, and it's been my experience that females are rarely
n time for anything, never mind early."

Her lips quirked at the corners, just a little. "I could
retend to take offense at that comment, except that I set
ny watch ten minutes ahead to help me get where I'm
oing on time."

It was the first insight she'd given him of her character, and
hile it wasn't a significant revelation, it was enough to give
im hope that she might be warming up to him.

"Does it work?" he asked.

The smile nudged a little wider. "Usually."

The foal, her hunger now sated, curled up in the straw to
eep, and Scarlett moved to the feed bucket for her own dinner.

"Of course, the process of birth doesn't fit into any kind
f schedule," he acknowledged.

"You obviously have some experience with that," she noted.

"I was eight years old the first time I saw a foal born."

And a few years after that, he'd witnessed a breech birth,
nd the complicated and time-consuming process of turning
ie foal. Even now, so many years later, he remembered the
rofound sadness that had washed through him when the roan
lly was finally pulled free of her mother's womb. Even
overed in what he'd referred to at the time as the slime of
irth, he'd thought she was perfect and beautiful—and he'd
nown that her complete stillness was unnatural.

"You grew up on a farm?" she asked.

Her question drew him back to the present and made him
ant to smile. He'd never heard the royal palace described as
ich, but he supposed, in a way, it might be considered that.
The horses were more of a hobby than anything else."

"How many?"

"It varied. Sometimes half a dozen, sometimes more than twice that number."

"We have between eighty and a hundred here at any given time," she told him.

"I guess that means I'm going to be busy."

She nodded, her gaze drifting back to the mare and her foal. Another minute passed before she said, "This is a prestigious establishment. The races around here draw crowds from around the world and focus a lot of attention on Callahan. Two years ago, a former British prime minister was at the derby. Last year, it was the Princess Royal from some small country in the Mediterranean."

"You have a point, I'm guessing, other than name-dropping."

She nodded. "I can't afford to make mistakes where the business is concerned."

"You didn't make one in hiring me," he assured her.

"We agreed to a one-week trial period," she said. "If we're both satisfied with the way things are working out by the end of the week, we can discuss further terms."

"Then I'll look forward to our discussion at the end of the week."

"Cocky, aren't you?"

"Confident," he corrected, and smiled.

"In any event, I'm only looking for someone to fill in for a couple of months while Grady has a cast on his leg."

"Riding accident?"

"No. He tumbled off a ladder while taking down his Christmas lights."

"In May?"

Now she *really* smiled. "He didn't want to do it in January when it was icy and snowy because he might slip and fall."

She was even more beautiful when she smiled, when her eyes sparkled with humor and her lips tilted up at the corners. His gaze lingered on her mouth for a moment, wondering if it would taste as soft and moist as it looked, and certain that putting the moves on his new boss would be a good way to lose his job before he'd started.

He took a mental step back, because as attracted as he was to Jewel, he really did want this job.

He had three university degrees and countless royal duties waiting for him at home, but what appealed to him right now was the opportunity to work in these stables.

It was nothing less than the truth when he told Jewel he'd been riding since before he could walk. His father had taught all of his sons to ride, and with the duties of his office monopolizing so much of his time, the brothers had grown to appreciate those all-too-rare occasions when they'd raced across the hills together.

After his father's death, Marcus had started spending even more time in the stables, because it was there that he could recall his fondest and most vivid memories. It was when he was with the horses that he felt his father's presence most keenly. He hadn't realized how much he'd missed working with animals until this opportunity had come up and he wasn't going to blow it because of a woman—no matter how much she tempted him.

Still, he couldn't prevent his gaze from skimming over her again, couldn't help wondering if he'd ever seen eyes such an intriguing shade of gray-blue, if her hair was as silky as it looked, if the pulse fluttering at the base of her jaw would race if he brushed his fingertips over it.

He curled his fingers into his palms to resist the temptation to do just that.

* * *

Something had changed.

Jewel wasn't sure how or when, she only knew that it had.

One minute they were joking about Grady's clumsiness, then he was looking at her as if nothing existed but the both of them, as if there was no time except in that moment.

The very air around them seemed to be charged with an electricity that heightened her senses, amplified her awareness of him, magnified the needs that had been too long ignored.

She wasn't the type of woman whose knees went weak at the sight of an attractive man—at least, she never had been before. But that was precisely what had happened when she'd caught her first glimpse of Mac Delgado in the café.

He was a man who would make any woman look twice, so she didn't fault herself for doing so. Even her sister, who was unquestionably devoted to her husband, had sighed in appreciation when he'd walked in the door.

But he was also young—probably a decade younger than her—and she was old enough to recognize the dangers of getting involved with a man just because he was nice to look at.

Okay, he was a lot more than nice to look at, and he'd already proven that he was more than a pretty face. But she'd made the mistake of following her heart once before. She'd ignored her sister's concerns and her father's demands, and she'd let herself get swept away by her dreams. And she'd come home with those dreams and her heart shattered.

It was a mistake she wouldn't ever make again.

She pushed away from the gate. "I've got other animals to see to, and you need to get settled."

But as Jewel walked briskly from the barn, she felt anything but settled.

She'd meant what she said when she told him she couldn't afford to make mistakes with respect to the business. She was even less willing to take risks where her heart was concerned.

Though the idea of a casual affair held a certain and undeniable appeal, Jewel didn't dare let herself think about it. Because she'd never been able to share her body without first opening up her heart, and she had no intention of opening up her heart again.

You're too young to have resigned yourself to being alone.

Jewel tried to ignore the echo of her sister's words in her head, along with the admonition of her conscience that she'd lied to Crystal when she'd claimed she wasn't settling for less than what she wanted. Because the truth was, she wanted a husband, a family, a life outside of the farm where she'd grown up.

But while it wasn't entirely accurate to say that she was happy being alone, she was content. She'd become accustomed to quiet nights and an empty bed, accepting that was the price to be paid to protect her heart.

And if she sometimes desperately yearned for a baby of her own to hold in her arms, well, she'd just have to accept that wasn't going to happen for her—not without a ring on her finger first. And since she had no intention of falling in love again, she would just have to be satisfied with her role as doting aunt to any children her sister might have.

As for Mac Delgado, she was probably misinterpreting her feelings for him because she was grateful for his help in delivering Scarlett's foal, exaggerating the attraction because it had been so long since she'd been with a man.

She frowned, trying to figure out exactly how long it had been, then realized if she had to think about it that hard, she probably didn't want to know.

* * *

When Jewel left the stables, she saw that Russ had returned from his errands in town, and her lips curved with genuine pleasure as she made her way toward him. Her smile slipped a little when she noted the scowl that darkened his usually handsome face.

"Did you see Scarlett's foal?" she asked.

His only response was an abrupt nod. Then he jerked his head in the direction of the barn. "Was that him?"

"Who?"

"The guy who drove up in the fancy wheels. Is he the new groom Cody said you hired?"

She nodded. "Mac Delgado."

His scowl deepened. "What do you know about him, JC?"

"I know that he doesn't panic under pressure."

"You hired him because he helped deliver a foal?"

"It's not my usual interview technique, but I'd say he more than proved himself. If he hadn't been here, I might have lost both Scarlett and the baby."

"Cody would have come through for you."

"Cody was shaking so badly I'm surprised he managed to dial the phone when I asked him to call the vet."

"You're mad that I wasn't here."

She shook her head. "There's no point in being angry about anything. There weren't any of the usual indicators that she was going to foal so soon and, truthfully, if she'd waited another couple of weeks, you'd be gone anyway."

"Is that why you hired the first guy who showed up here?"

She shifted her gaze away, not willing to admit that she still had her own reservations about Mac—though they were more personal than professional. And considering the way he'd come through for her, she figured she owed him a chance. "I don't answer to you, Russ."

"No," he acknowledged. "But it used to be we talked about things, made decisions together."

"That was before you decided to leave."

"Are you going to throw that up at me in every single conversation we have over the next nine days?"

"Maybe."

His jaw tightened.

She sighed. "I'm sorry, Russ. I know that wasn't fair."

"I'm not abandoning you, Jewel." The quiet words were filled with understanding.

She nodded, grateful that he didn't say what they were both thinking. Like her mother. Like Thomas and Allan and everyone else who had ever claimed to love her. And she knew he honestly didn't see his leaving as yet another abandonment—but it sure felt that way to Jewel.

Marcus worked closely with Russ over the next seven days, learning the routines of the farm and getting acquainted with the animals and the people who worked with them. He barely crossed paths with Jewel during that time and she certainly never stopped to engage him in conversation. In fact, the most response he ever got from her was a nod acknowledging his presence—certainly no more than any other employee.

At first, he enjoyed the novelty of being treated just like the other men. But after a few days, her indifference started to frustrate rather than amuse him. Until he realized it was *studied* indifference—and that she would only have to make such a deliberate effort to ignore him if she was as aware of his presence as he was of hers.

He heard her name come up in conversations and blatantly eavesdropped, trying to piece together a picture of who the woman referred to by most of her employees as "JC" really was. He was surprised to learn that she'd spent some time on the rodeo circuit before her father's first heart attack several years earlier, after which she had come home to help with the running of the facility. He also learned that she was both liked and respected by the men in her employ, most of whom had been with the Callahan Thoroughbred Center for years.

The owners who came to the onsite track to monitor the progress of their horses weren't as unanimous in their praise. While they thoroughly approved of the facility, they weren't sure that "Jack's daughter"—as Jewel was frequently labeled—had her daddy's head for business. And then they'd look across the fields and shake their heads. Mac had yet to figure out what that was all about.

By the end of the week, he was exhausted. But it was a good exhaustion—the kind that came from hard physical work. His hands weren't as soft as they'd been the first day he came to the farm, but the sting of blisters was a small price to pay for the enjoyment of working with the horses and the satisfaction of knowing he'd done a good job.

"Hey, Mac." Crystal tossed him an easy smile and a quick wave as she passed by the track, where he was watching some of the yearlings work out.

"Hi, Crystal. Where are you racing off to?" he asked, falling into step beside her.

"Haven. And I'm late."

"Where's Haven?"

She stopped in her tracks and stared at him. "How long have you been working here?"

"My seven-day trial period ended today. Since your sister hasn't fired me yet, I assume she's willing to keep me on."

"I can't believe she hasn't told you about Haven," Crystal said, picking up her pace again. "She never misses an opportunity to rope someone into helping out, if she can."

"Helping out with?" he prompted

She stopped outside of a barn that was on the far side of CTC's property. He'd noticed the building before, but because it was so distant from the hub of CTC, he'd assumed it was owned by someone else. There was a brass oval on the door with the silhouette of a horse's head inside it and the word "Haven" spelled out in brass letters above it.

"This is Haven," she told him.

He followed her inside, immediately noting that it was as clean and organized as any of the buildings at CTC if somewhat more utilitarian in design. The floor was concrete rather than cobblestone and the names of the stalls' residents noted on white boards rather than engraved on brass plates, but the stalls were still twelve-by-twelve and filled with straw bedding.

"Jewel started Haven for old or injured racehorses. The big money winners are well taken care by their owners, but those with less successful careers are sometimes neglected and often resented because of the high cost of their maintenance. Those unwanted animals come here until she can find them new homes."

A huge draft horse tossed his head over the stall door and whinnied.

"That isn't a thoroughbred," he said.

"No," Crystal agreed. "Some of them are, some aren't. But they're all horses that have been rescued or are in need of rehabilitation."

"So this is what she does in her spare time," he murmured.

"Jack Callahan established the Center," Crystal told him. "Jewel took over running it after he died because she could, and because she loves horses. But CTC is a business. This is her passion.

"And this—" she indicated a powerfully built chestnut in the end stall "—is Cayenne. Also known as The Demon Stallion."

"Temperamental?" he guessed.

"You might say," Crystal agreed. "His trainer thought a heavy hand with the crop would teach him to obey. Instead it taught him to be mean. And then there was an incident in the stables and—" She shook her head. "Let's just say his owners wrote him off."

Marcus had heard about trainers like that and thought the crop should be used on them. How anyone could abuse such a beautiful animal—or any creature—was beyond him. And while he didn't doubt Cayenne was capable of acting like a demon, right now the horse just looked wary, and scared.

He moved closer, keeping one eye on the stallion and his voice low. "How did he end up here?"

"Jewel heard about him from a friend of a friend, or something like that. It's hard to keep all of their stories straight sometimes."

He was starting to realize there was a lot more to the story of Jewel Callahan than she wanted him to know.

"Anyway," Crystal continued, "the owner was looking to unload him rather than invest in further training, so Jewel made him an offer. Now she's faced with the challenge of undoing the damage that has been done so that she can find a good home for him."

"Who decides what a good home is?" Mac asked.

"Jewel, of course. But never before a personal interview with the potential buyer and a thorough inspection of the premises."

"Is there anything she doesn't do?" he wondered aloud.

Crystal grinned. "She doesn't make a cheesecake that compares to mine."

"I have a weakness for cheesecake," Mac admitted.

And he had a growing fascination with Jewel Callahan. The more he knew about the beautiful, stubborn woman who had reluctantly given him a job, the more he wanted to know. And he had a pretty good idea about how to get what he wanted.

Cayenne was in the paddock when Jewel returned to the farm after her trip into town, so she knew her sister was cleaning his stall. Knowing how much Crystal hated that job, she felt a twinge of guilt that she'd been gone as long as she had, but only a slight twinge. Crystal had been helping out at Haven since they took in their first horse, but with her own business turning into such a success, she'd had to severely cut back her volunteer time. Since she was only able to put in a few hours on Tuesdays and Fridays now, Jewel figured mucking out a couple of stalls was actually necessary to keep her in practice.

But as she carried the bags of vitamin supplements through to the storeroom, she couldn't resist teasing. "You must be losing your touch, Crys, if you didn't manage to sweet-talk some cute stable hand into doing that for you."

But the head that popped up in response to her comment was neither blond nor female, and "cute" was far too bland a description to do it justice.

"Hey," Mac said.

"Obviously she hasn't lost her touch," Jewel muttered beneath her breath.

But not so quietly that Mac didn't hear, because he flashed her an easy grin that, even from a distance of twenty-five feet, made her tummy quiver.

"Does that mean you think I'm cute?" he asked.

She ignored the question. "You haven't mucked out enough stalls already this week?"

"More than enough," he assured her, leaning on the handle of the pitchfork.

"Where is my sister?" Jewel asked. "And how did she con you into doing her job?"

"She didn't con me—she bribed me."

"With?"

"Promises of homemade cherry cheesecake."

Jewel began stacking bottles and jars on the appropriate shelves. "I'd say she got the better end of the deal, but she does make a spectacular cheesecake."

"Pot roast was also mentioned," he told her.

"Crystal invited you up to the house for dinner?" Not that she objected, exactly. And since Simon had a late meeting and Crystal would be dining with them, she had no reason to object. But she was still a little wary of her sister's reasons for issuing the invitation.

"She thought it would give you and I an opportunity to talk about my duties for the next several weeks."

"If you want to stay on, I'd be happy to have you continue doing what you've been doing."

"I want to stay on," he told her. "And I want to help out here."

She closed and latched the door. "Why?"

"Because it's obvious to me that you could use a couple extra hands."

"I could use a dozen extra hands," she admitted. "But

Haven doesn't have the funds to hire any help. Mostly we take on coop students from the local high school."

"And you come in every day after they're finished to redo what wasn't done properly," he guessed, tossing fresh bedding into the stall.

She shrugged. "They're kids. They do the best they can."

"And they're scared to death of Cayenne."

"There's no shame in being afraid of a twelve-hundred-pound animal. Randy Porter trained horses for more than thirty-five years and even he watches his step around Cayenne."

Mac finished spreading the straw before he turned to her. "I could work with him."

She'd have to be crazy to let him. He'd proven he was a competent groom, but what he was suggesting was way beyond the scope of anything he'd been doing in the past week, and Cayenne wasn't like any of the horses he'd encountered at CTC. The Demon Stallion had earned his nickname by being both difficult and unpredictable, and though Jewel had been working with him personally over the past couple of months, she'd made little progress.

But while she might worry about Cayenne's inconsistent behavior, her own had been no better. When she'd started training him, she'd planned to spend a couple of hours with him every day. The reality was that she didn't always have a couple of hours to spare, there were simply too many demands on her to be able to dedicate the time and attention he needed.

And there were too many reasons why she should refuse Mac's offer, not the least of which was that if he started hanging out around the Haven stable, their paths would cross more often.

On the other hand, if she spent enough time around Mac

she might become inured to his presence so that warm tingles didn't dance through her veins every time he looked at her and her heart didn't skip a beat every time he smiled.

"Dinner's at six," she finally said. "We can talk about it then."

Chapter Three

Jewel decided to grab a quick shower after she finished up at Haven and was just tugging on a clean pair of jeans when she heard a knock on the back door. A quick glance at the clock confirmed that it was almost six. Confident that the housekeeper would let him in, she didn't hurry. She was combing her fingers through the unruly mass of hair she'd released from its ponytail when the knock came again.

Ignoring the socks she'd tossed on the bed, she made her way to the kitchen. Where she expected to find Bonnie hovering at the stove, she instead found a note.

Crystal is driving me into town to pick up a package at FedEx. Dinner is in the oven. Enjoy.

She noted the two place settings along with the candles and wine on the table and seriously doubted that there was any package. She'd invited Mac to dinner because she'd believed

Crystal and Bonnie would also be there. But somehow her conniving sister had managed to take what was supposed to be a business discussion over a meal and made it look like a date. And while she understood her sister's motivations, she had no intention of being manipulated.

She tucked the candles and wine into the pantry, returned the stemware to the cupboard and moved the place settings to opposite ends of the table before she went to answer the door.

The first thing Mac noticed when Jewel opened the door was that she'd showered and changed since she'd left the stable. Her hair tumbled freely down her back, her freshly scrubbed skin glowed and her feet were bare. She wasn't wearing any makeup that he could tell, but she looked beautiful, natural.

She noticed the flowers in his hand and frowned. "You shouldn't have brought me flowers."

"They're only for you if you cooked the pot roast." He was pleased to note that his response had surprised her, because he suspected that the only way he was going to make progress with Jewel was to give her the unexpected and keep her off her stride.

"I didn't." She smiled wryly. "For which we should both be truly grateful."

He smiled back. "Then the daisies are for Bonnie."

"You've met Bonnie?"

"Not yet, but your sister did such a good job extolling her culinary virtues I almost feel as if I have."

"Well, you won't meet her tonight, either. She had an errand to run in town." Jewel took the flowers from him. "But I'll put these in water for her and tell you that she'd appreciate the thought."

As he followed her into the house, he thought *she* smelled good enough to eat, though he didn't think the citrusy scent was perfume. She didn't seem the type to bother with such frills. More likely the scent was from some kind of lotion or cream that she'd rubbed onto her skin after her shower.

He firmly shoved *that* tempting image from his mind and glanced around the kitchen.

The table and chairs appeared to be solidly built and obviously well used. The dishes were stoneware rather than china, the cutlery was stainless instead of silver, the napkins made of paper not linen. It was a family table, and the rich aromas that filled the air were those of a good, home-cooked meal, and he found the simplicity of everything appealed to him.

As Jewel appealed to him.

Noting that the table was set for two, he said, "I thought your sister would be here for dinner."

"So did I."

Something in her tone suggested that she wasn't only surprised—but annoyed—by Crystal's change of plans. And he wondered if it was the thought of dining alone with him that bothered her.

"Does her absence mean there's no cheesecake?" he asked.

"No." She smiled as she carried a tray laden with thick slices of beef and chunky roasted vegetables to the table. "The cheesecake's in the fridge."

"Well, that's a relief," he said.

She gestured for him to sit, but he scooped the basket of warm rolls and the pitcher of steaming gravy from the counter to set on the table before she could do so.

She slanted him a look, as if his willingness to assist with domestic chores was something else she hadn't expected, but silently took her own seat on the other side of the table.

He loaded his plate with a generous helping of beef and vegetables and noted that she did the same. When he passed her the pitcher of gravy, she smothered her plate with it.

They chatted casually while they ate, about the horses and the routines in her stables and then about thoroughbred training and racing in general. He enjoyed her company as much as dinner because of her sharp intelligence and wry humor and found he was reluctant for the meal to end.

When she got up to get dessert, she frowned at the clock. "Is it seven-thirty already?"

"Looks like," he agreed. "Is there somewhere else you need to be?"

"No." She slid a generous slice of cake onto a plate. "I was just wondering what kind of errand could have kept Bonnie out so long."

As if on cue, the phone rang. Jewel passed him the plate then excused herself to answer the call.

"That was Bonnie checking in," she said, when she returned to the table. "Apparently she and Crystal decided to stop for coffee and got caught up chatting with some mutual acquaintance."

He stabbed his fork into the cake, noting that while she'd started to relax over dinner, she wasn't so relaxed now. Was she anxious for him to leave? Or nervous because the phone call had reminded her that they were alone together?

She sat back down with obvious reluctance and cut herself a much smaller piece of cake.

"Tell me about Haven," he said. "The more I know about it, the more useful I can be."

"Why are you so eager to help out?"

"I figured that was obvious," he said. "I'm trying to ingratiate myself to you so you'll keep me around, maybe even consider having a hot and torrid affair with me."

Jewel glanced at Mac across the table. "Was that comment intended to fluster or flatter me?"

He shrugged. "I'm guessing it failed on both counts."

Actually it had succeeded on both counts, but she wasn't willing to let him know it. Or know that she'd given some thought to the same thing.

"Are you always so suspicious when someone offers you help?" he asked her.

"Let's just say that I've learned to look for the strings that are usually attached."

"I like horses," he said. "And, for some reason, I like you, too. Maybe it did occur to me that spending time at Haven might result in spending time with you, but my motives are no more nefarious than that."

"Well, you were right about extra hands being needed at Haven," she said. "And if you really want to spend your spare time there, I have no objection."

"That's incredibly gracious of you," he said.

She smiled at his dry tone. "Yeah, Crystal's always telling me I need to work on my social skills. But the horses don't usually complain."

"I'm not complaining," he said.

She took the tray of leftovers to the counter to wrap up. She heard the scrape of chair legs on the floor as Mac pushed away from the table, too, then brought their plates to the counter.

"Are you going to question my motives for clearing the table, too?"

She bit down on her lip, because she'd been tempted to do exactly like that. Instead she said, "I appreciate your help, but I can handle it."

He ignored her and began loading the dishwasher.

"You've got to be up early in the morning," she pointed out.

"And you'll be up just as early," he noted. "Whatever time I walk into the stable, you've already been there."

"It's my stable," she pointed out.

"No one's disputing that." He nudged her aside with his hip so he could move around to the other side of the dishwasher.

The brief contact shot arrows of awareness zinging through her system.

She stepped back quickly and braced her hands on the counter behind her. As she did so, her elbow bumped a water goblet on the counter and sent it crashing to the floor. The glass shattered, jagged shards flying.

Silently cursing her clumsiness, she started toward the closet for the broom.

"Watch," Mac said.

"I am," she snapped irritably, then swore when she stepped down on a piece of glass.

She lifted her foot, saw the blood was already dripping.

Before she could say anything, he scooped her up off her feet and lifted her onto the counter. Her breath whooshed out of her, though she wasn't sure if that was because of the un-expected jolt when he plunked her down or the surprising thrill of being held by a strong man.

He took a step back and picked up her foot. His hand was warm, his touch firm but gentle, and somehow incredibly sensual.

"Mac—"

He snagged a paper towel from the roll. "Just let me take a look."

She didn't see as she had much choice in the matter. And when his thumb slid over her instep, she didn't protest because she was incapable of speaking.

He dabbed gently at the blood. "You up-to-date on your tetanus shots?"

"I had one a couple of years ago," she said.

"It doesn't look like it needs a stitch, but it definitely needs some antiseptic cream and a bandage."

"There's a first-aid kit in the bathroom. If you let me get down, I'll—"

"You stay put," he said. "I'll get it."

"You give orders better than you take them, Mac," she noted when he returned with the box of medical supplies.

He shrugged. "I didn't figure you wanted to get blood all over the floor by hobbling around before that cut was tended to."

She didn't, of course, but that wasn't the point. "I would have managed just fine if you weren't here."

In fact, she probably wouldn't have knocked the glass off the counter if he hadn't been there to distract her—not that she was going to admit as much to him.

She sucked in a breath when he wiped an antiseptic pad over the bottom of her foot.

"You're being ungrateful again," he told her.

She frowned at that. "I'm used to doing things on my own."

"Then it's not just me," he noted, dabbing some cream onto the pad of a Band-Aid before affixing it to her wound.

"No."

His fingers smoothed down the edges of the dressing,

and caused those tingles to dance and swirl through her system again.

"Maybe," she muttered under her breath.

Not quietly enough, obviously, because he looked up at her and grinned.

"That should take care of it," he said, finally releasing her foot.

But he didn't move away, and she was suddenly aware of the intimacy of their positions—of the cupboards behind her back, and the man standing between her thighs.

"I need to, uh, get that glass swept up."

He stayed where he was, his hands on the counter, bracketing her knees. "Are you always this skittish when anyone gets too close?"

She laid her hands on his chest and tried not to think about the solid muscles beneath her palms, the strong beat of his heart, or the heat of his skin as she pushed him back a few inches.

The intensity in his gaze made everything inside her quiver, but she managed to keep her eyes level with his and her voice steady when she responded. "I have this thing about personal space—as in, I don't like people in mine."

Before he could say anything else, a flash of headlights warned of a vehicle coming up the driveway.

"That will be Crystal dropping Bonnie off," she told him, torn between relief and disappointment that their time alone together was about to be interrupted. Because as much as she did tend to veer away from intimacy, she occasionally experienced pangs of loneliness, moments when she was sometimes even tempted to open up her heart again. Usually those moments were quick to pass and her life would go back to normal.

But Mac Delgado had shaken up the status quo the minute

he walked into the Halfway Café, and Jewel didn't know what—if anything—she was going to do about him.

Mac's knowing expression suggested that he'd picked up on her mixed emotions, that he knew how confused she was and how tempted she didn't want to be. She found it strange that a man she'd met only a week earlier should be able to see through all the layers she'd worked so hard to build up over the years and recognize the longing that was buried deep in her heart.

And she knew that if she wasn't careful, he might find a way to tunnel through those layers.

As Mac found the broom and quickly swept up and disposed of the broken glass, Jewel promised herself that she would be careful. Very careful.

Jewel was making some adjustments to the yearling training schedule on her computer when Caleb Bryant came into her office. He'd started as an exercise boy for her father when Jewel was still riding ponies and they'd grown up and into the business together. Now he wasn't just an Eclipse-winning trainer but a good friend.

The ready smile faded when she saw the concern etched between his dark brows.

"Gabe Anderson was here," he told her.

It was all he said, and yet those few words said so much. Gabe Anderson had been a client of Callahan for a long time, and he'd never made any secret of the fact that he had doubts about JC's ability to run the facility as her father had done. Jewel would have liked to be able to tell him to take his horses elsewhere, but the fact was, he had a fair amount of clout in the racing world and a lot of horseflesh in her stables. So she gritted her teeth and tried to accommodate his needs and wishes whenever possible, but something in Caleb's eyes warned it wouldn't be so easy this time.

"Is there a problem?"

"After Midnight came ninth in a field of fourteen at Belmont on the weekend."

She rubbed at the throb in her temple. The headache had been hovering there for a couple of hours, but she'd managed to stave it off with a handful of aspirin and focused determination. Until now.

"Should he have done better?"

Caleb only shrugged. "He's a young colt with a lot of potential, but right now, he has more enthusiasm than focus."

And that was the reason, she suspected, that Caleb had recommended not racing the colt so early in the season. The two-year-old had been a late season foal and would have benefited from a few more months training before being loaded into a starting gate. But he was also a foal with impressive bloodlines and a price tag to match, and she knew that Anderson was focused so intently on seeing a return for his investment that he couldn't see anything else.

"I just wanted to let you know that he's blustering," Caleb said. "About the possibility of taking his horses elsewhere— as he threatens to do at least once a year, or—and this is a new one to me—maybe building his own stables."

She nodded, and wished she hadn't when her pounding head protested the motion. "I appreciate the heads-up."

He turned to leave, pausing in the doorway to say, "We both know he won't find another facility in the state that compares to this one."

She managed a smile. "Or a trainer like the one here."

Caleb smiled back. "Well, that goes without saying."

After he'd gone, Jewel thought about the training schedule she had yet to finish, and decided it could wait. She wasn't going to sort anything out while her head was pounding.

"Dinner will be ready in a few minutes," Bonnie said when she tugged off her boots inside the back door.

"I'm not really hungry," Jewel said.

"You didn't come in for lunch, so unless you have a kitchen in your office that I don't know about, you haven't eaten since breakfast."

"I had a chocolate bar and a Diet Coke."

"Which would explain the headache."

"Which is why I just want a bath and bed."

Bonnie's lips thinned. "You've forgotten."

Jewel winced, because obviously she had, though even now, she couldn't remember what it was that she'd forgotten.

"The boys are giving Russ his big send-off at The Mustang tonight," the housekeeper reminded her.

Jewel wasn't sure if she'd forgotten or deliberately put it out of her mind, because to think about the party was to think about Russ leaving, and that was still too painful. "I'm not up to going out tonight."

"You most certainly are going." Bonnie folded her arms across her chest in a posture that clearly communicated the matter wasn't open for debate.

She had been Jack Callahan's housekeeper since long before he married Jewel's mother, and when Lorraine Callahan ran out on her husband and daughter, Bonnie had taken over the day-to-day care of the child Jack had shown even less interest in than had the woman who'd left her behind. She was so much more than an employee to Jewel—

she was a mother figure, a role model and a trusted friend, and she never hesitated to speak what was on her mind.

"Now take something for your headache and go have that bath before dinner," she continued. "You'll feel better then and you won't have to spend the next six months wallowing in guilt and regret that you didn't take the time to say goodbye to your best friend."

Jewel wanted to resent the housekeeper's high-handedness, but the truth was, she was right. And after she'd popped a couple of Tylenol, soaked in the tub for half an hour and had a quick bite, she was feeling better. Maybe not quite looking forward to a night on the town but accepting of the fact that she needed to make an appearance.

And then she walked out to her truck and found Mac waiting for her.

She'd caught glimpses of him now and again around both the CTC stables and at Haven, though she'd taken care to ensure that their paths didn't cross any more than was absolutely necessary. She'd needed the distance to figure out the feelings he'd stirred inside of her, and had almost managed to convince herself that the warm, tingly feeling she got when he looked at her was just gratitude tangled up with the joy and relief that Scarlett's foal had been delivered safely.

But a week and a half had passed since then and nothing had changed. He was looking at her now, and that warm, tingly feeling was back, and she feared the explanation wasn't that simple. It wasn't gratitude she was feeling but attraction.

And the dark glint in his eyes told her that he was feeling the same thing.

When she'd dressed, she hadn't known that Mac would be there. The possibility had crossed her mind, of course, as thoughts of him had crossed her mind all too frequently over the past several days, but she hadn't been certain. She'd pretended that she didn't care one way or the other, but she found herself taking extra care with her appearance anyway. Nothing too obvious, just a touch of mascara to darken her lashes, a swipe of gloss over her lips, a spritz of perfume that had rarely been taken out of the box.

But as his eyes moved over her, his lips curving in a slow smile of obvious appreciation, she was glad she'd made the effort—and still more than a little wary about the tingly feeling inside.

"What are you doing here, Mac?"

"I was hoping to ride into town with you."

"What's wrong with your Navigator?"

"Nothing. I just thought it made sense to carpool, since we're both going the same way."

"Did my sister put you up to this?"

He ignored her question, asking instead, "So what do you say—can I hitch a ride?"

The last thing she wanted was to be trapped in the cab of her truck with a man whose mere proximity put every one of her nerve endings on high alert. Unfortunately, she had no valid reason to refuse his request, not when they were both heading in the same direction. After a moment, she finally shook her head.

"No—" she tossed him the keys "—you can drive."

Chapter Four

Jewel didn't worry about any speculation that might result from her showing up at the Mustang with Mac. The men she worked with knew her well enough to know that she wouldn't get personally involved with an employee, though in the close confines of the truck's cab on the way to the bar, she'd had to consciously remind herself of the same thing.

Limiting their interactions over the past week and a half had done nothing to lessen her response to him, but she knew that maintaining a physical distance was necessary if she was going to keep a clear head and continue to resist the attraction that seemed to be drawing them inevitably closer together.

She excused herself and slipped away from him as soon as they entered the bar, and he let her go without protest, making her question that conclusion. As she wandered through the crowd, exchanging greetings with familiar faces, she had to wonder if the attraction she felt wasn't reciprocated. Maybe the only hormones running riot were her own.

"If you don't stop frowning, the guest of honor might think you're not having a good time."

She turned to smile at Russ. "My mind was wandering."

"Apparently." He was carrying two glasses of beer, handed me to her. "You missed your sister. She and Simon stopped in for a quick goodbye."

"I'm glad she was able to make it." She followed him to a table in the corner.

"Then you're not still mad at her for not marrying me?"

Jewel rolled her eyes. "Is there any part of our conversation she didn't share with you?"

"Probably not," he said.

They chatted a little more, about the farm and Riley's tour, ordered another round of drinks.

"You haven't asked about Mac," he noted.

"Was I supposed to?"

"I figured you'd want to know how he was working out."

"And I figured if there was a problem, I would have heard about it before now."

He nodded at that. "He catches on fast, isn't afraid to get his hands dirty and gets along well with the other guys."

"Why do I hear a 'but' in your voice?"

"Because there's just something about him that I still can't figure out."

She glanced over her shoulder, saw that Mac was looking at her, and felt the tingles of awareness skate all the way down her spine.

She'd had lovers. True, she could count the number on one hand, but she wasn't completely inexperienced. But she had never experienced the instant tug of attraction she felt when her eyes had locked with his the very first time. A tug that had only become more insistent with each passing day.

"Everyone has secrets." She turned back to Russ, unwilling to admit she'd spent too much time trying—and failing—to figure out Mac Delgado. "All that matters is that he's capable of doing the job he was hired to do."

"Then your interest in him isn't at all personal?"

"You *have* been talking to my sister."

"I already told you I was," he said. "But I also have eyes in my head."

"Those must come in handy when you need to get back from way out in left field."

He grinned. "You're forgetting that I've known you for a long time."

"Then you should know me well enough to know that I would never jeopardize a professional association by getting involved in a personal relationship."

"Never say never," Russ warned.

Marcus wasn't worried about the fact that Jewel was cozied up in the corner with Russ Granger. He might have wondered about their relationship when she first hired him on, about the easy camaraderie they shared and their obvious rapport, but over the past week and a half, he'd realized their closeness was friendly rather than romantic. A definite relief to him since he'd decided that he wanted Jewel in his bed and her potential involvement with someone else would be a major obstacle to those plans. His playboy reputation aside, he'd never let himself get tangled up with a woman who was otherwise engaged. Not knowingly, anyway.

Still, the fact that Jewel didn't share an intimate relationship with Granger didn't mean she *wasn't* involved with someone else. And when the other man finally said goodbye and walked away, he decided it was time to stop wondering.

He ordered another draft for Jewel and a Coke for himself, then slid into the now vacant seat across from her.

"It just occurred to me," he said, "that this is my first Alliston nightlife experience."

"Has it been memorable?" she asked.

"It has potential."

"If you want nightlife, you won't find much of it here," she told him. "There are a couple of restaurants in town, this bar, a movie theater and a bowling alley."

He sipped his Coke. "If I wanted to take a woman on a date, where would you suggest I take her?"

"Charleston," Jewel responded without hesitation.

"You want to go to Charleston with me sometime?"

She shook her head without a hint of reluctance or any hesitation.

"It's okay if you need to think about it or want to check your calendar," he told her.

"I don't need to think about it or check my calendar, because I'm not going on a date with you, Mac."

"You might have at least made an effort to let me down easy."

"Have I dented your pride?"

"Inflicted a mortal wound," he said solemnly.

"Somehow I doubt that."

"Are you involved with someone?"

"No." She picked up her glass, sipped her draft. "Nor am I looking to complicate my life with any personal involvements right now."

"My father once told me that it's only when we stop looking that we find our heart's desire."

Her lips curved, offering him just a hint of a smile that made him want to see more.

"Sounds like he's either a philosopher or a romantic," she said.

"He was a lot of things," Mac said. "Mostly a good man and a great father who was taken away from his family far too soon."

"How long ago was that?" she asked gently.

"Almost eight years."

"It must have been difficult, losing him when you were so young."

He smiled at that, as he realized she was trying to gauge exactly how old he was. Because she was interested? Or just curious?

"How young do you figure I was?" he countered.

"Fourteen?"

"Actually I was seventeen."

"And you said you just finished school," she said, considering. "So you must have taken some time off before college, goofed off in college, or you have more than one degree."

"Something like that."

"You never did tell me where you went to school."

Damn—he should have seen that question coming. But he only shrugged and answered, "Harvard."

Her brows arched. "Definitely not a goof-off."

The last pounding notes of an AC/DC song that had been playing on the jukebox faded out and an Aerosmith ballad took its place.

"Dance with me," he said, pushing away from the table and offering his hand.

She shook her head. "I can't."

"Can't dance?"

"I can't dance with you," she said.

"Because—" he prompted.

"Because this bar is filled with people both of us work with and—"

"Actually almost everyone else is gone."

She glanced around in surprise, then at her watch. "Oh, my goodness. I had no idea it had gotten to be so late." Then she looked up at him. "Why didn't you catch a ride back with someone else?"

"Going home to a cold, empty bed or enjoying the company of a warm, beautiful woman—" he grinned "—it seemed an obvious choice to me."

Jewel was flattered—how could she not be? But she also knew that it was important to set some boundaries between them. No doubt he was aware of her attraction to him, but she needed to let him know that she had no intention of acting on that attraction, no matter how tempted she might be.

"Look, Mac—"

"It's just a dance, Jewel."

She wasn't sure that was true, but when he took her hand, she forgot all of her protests and let him lead her to the tiny dance floor. There were only two other couples dancing, another with their heads close together in the corner and a handful of men lingering at the bar. It was a Thursday night, after all, and morning came early in a town that had been built around the thoroughbred racing industry.

It's just a dance, she reminded herself as Mac turned her in his arms.

And yet, dancing with him was like something out of a fantasy. He had an innate grace for someone so big and strong, and though he pulled her close, he didn't hold her so tight that their bodies were pressed together like those of the other couples on the dance floor. Just close enough so that their thighs brushed as they moved, close enough that she could smell the heady masculine scent of him, close enough that her own body was starting to melt from the heat of his.

In the short time he'd been employed at the farm, he'd been working hard, as evidenced by the calluses that had already started to build up. The hardness of the skin on his palms made her think about the delicious sensation of those work-roughened hands moving over her naked body, and she had to keep her face averted so he wouldn't see her flushed cheeks.

She was so caught up in the erotic fantasy that she stumbled on the next step. He shifted easily, so that the miscue was hardly noticeable. Except that he was holding her closer now, so that the tips of her breasts rubbed against the solid wall of his chest, and her nipples hardened in instinctive response to the delicious friction.

Did he know? Could he tell how aroused she was becoming? She was mortified to think that he could—until she realized that certain parts of his body had responded to the contact, too. Apparently she wasn't the only one who was aroused.

Though the realization set every nerve ending in her body on fire and made her want to press herself tight against him, she managed to resist, all too aware that giving into such impulses would result in her getting burned.

Jewel breathed an almost audible sigh of relief when the song finally ended. She moved out of his arms, determined to keep her own desires under control—and Mac at a safe distance.

* * *

It took more willpower than Marcus would have thought to leave Jewel at her door and walk away without giving in to the temptation to kiss her. She'd looked so damn beautiful in the moonlight, and when her head had tipped back and his gaze had dropped to her lips—

Mi Dios, the woman had a mouth that was made to be kissed.

Her lips were full and soft, and when the tip of her tongue had swept over her lips, leaving them glistening with moisture, it had been all he could do not to haul her into his arms and cover that delectable mouth with his own.

She would have kissed him back—he had no doubts about that. When he'd held her in his arms on the dance floor, he'd felt the beat of her heart against his own. When he'd looked at her, he'd seen the awareness and desire that stirred in his own blood. Yes, she would have kissed him back. And then she would have kicked him out on his butt.

He smiled wryly at that thought as he walked to his rooms over the stables. It would have been just the excuse she needed to get rid of him, to push him away and pretend she didn't want him as much as he wanted her. And though he suspected that one kiss from Jewel Callahan would be worth it, he knew it would be a mistake to push for too much too soon. For now, he would simply have to be content himself with contemplating the possibilities.

Had he ever been so preoccupied with thoughts of a woman?

He didn't think so. On the other hand, having been born rich and royal, he'd never had to make more than a minimal effort to get a woman into his bed.

Of course, Jewel didn't know he was rich and royal, and he was happy to keep it that way for now. If she knew his true identity, she'd likely use it as an excuse to fire him and he'd probably never see her again.

And he wasn't nearly ready to say goodbye to Jewel Callahan. She was the most intriguing and frustrating woman he'd ever met, and every step she took in retreat only made him more determined to advance.

Her comments about his youth suggested that she was bothered by the age difference between them. Though he didn't know exactly what that difference was, he wasn't worried about it. He'd had other lovers who were older—one or two who were definitely older than Jewel—and age had never been an issue for him.

Nor was the fact that she was his boss. Not that he'd ever had an affair with an employer, and in fact, royal duties aside, he'd never really had a job before. But he sensed that the employer-employee relationship would present another problem for Jewel, another explanation for her resistance.

Disregarding both the age and employment issues, he'd forced himself to consider the possibility that she simply might not be interested. And he'd discarded that thought the minute he took her in his arms on the dance floor.

There had been a definite spark between them, and a wary awareness in the depths of those stormy eyes.

She might pretend she was uninterested, but he knew differently.

Just as he knew that if he pushed her for too much too soon, she'd push him away.

He'd never been a patient man—he'd never had to be. But he knew that seducing Jewel was going to require both patience and perseverance—and that the end result would be worth the effort.

With that thought in mind, he stripped off his clothes and climbed into bed. The sheets were crisp and cool against his heated skin, but he knew nothing and no one but Jewel would douse the fire in his blood.

Chapter Five

It was the end of a long day at the end of a long week, and it seemed to Jewel that she hadn't had much time to spend at Haven recently. Probably because she'd been so busy trying to court new clients for CTC in case Gabe Anderson followed through on his threat to withdraw his horses from the stables. Which was why, at the end of yet another eighteen-hour day, she found herself heading to the stables instead of her bed. Tired and cranky as she felt, she didn't want to short-change Haven's residents.

She moved through the barn, checking water buckets and hay nets along the way, noting the cleanliness of the stalls, the gleaming coats of the horses. When she reached Wizard's stall, she noticed the horse was swaying from side to side, a sure sign that he was bored and needed exercise. Despite her fatigue, she decided to take him out onto the track.

But she paused at Cayenne's stall first, spoke briefly to the skittish stallion and coaxed him to take an apple. The stallion snorted his protest when she moved on, and pawed impatiently at the ground.

She felt herself waver. Cayenne was a big animal—almost seventeen hands—and spirited, and all of her student helpers were terrified of him. He was also one of her favorites.

His pedigree wasn't anything spectacular, but that didn't matter to anyone who had seen him run. He was purchased for a paltry sum at the Keeneland September Yearling Sale and won a substantial amount of money for his owner in the next ten months.

Then there was an accident at the stables—the horse got spooked and kicked out at the owner's six-year-old daughter. The child suffered broken ribs and bruised kidneys; her father beat the colt within an inch of his life then abandoned him in a distant pasture. He stayed there, injured, isolated, neglected, for more than six months before anyone contacted Haven.

He'd been with Jewel for almost a year now and both she and Crystal had gradually managed to earn the stallion's trust. He was still wary of everyone else, however, and men in particular.

There had been some interest in him when he first came to Haven, potential buyers who remembered his early performances as a two-year-old, who understood that the horse shouldn't be held responsible for an accident that occurred because a child was left unsupervised in the barn. But the interest waned when they realized the skittish animal wouldn't let visitors come near enough to examine him never mind put a saddle on his back.

He'd made significant progress in the past twelve months,

but Jewel worried that she might have already missed out on any opportunities to find him a good home.

"Tomorrow," she promised, and gave him a last pat before gathering her tack and grooming kit, then heading back to Wizard's stall.

She opened the door and the old gelding came to her, butting his head gently against her shoulder in greeting. Smiling, she took another apple from her pocket and offered it to him. He took it happily—and more mannerly than Cayenne had done.

She led him out of the stall and gave him a quick grooming, pleased to see that the high school kids who had been helping out had done a good job of that already. She positioned the blanket then slid the saddle onto his back. Recognizing the feel and weight of it, the gelding trembled with barely suppressed excitement.

"You remember, don't you?" she said softly. "The crowds, the excitement of the race, the thrill of victory."

The horse snorted again and tossed his head in agreement.

"And some people say that animals can't talk," a familiar male voice noted from over Jewel's shoulder.

She finished buckling the girth before she turned, but her heart was already pounding with recognition—and anticipation. "I'm not so sure about talking, but he definitely knows how to communicate."

Mac stepped closer, so that he was no longer hidden in the shadows, and her heart pounded even harder.

She eased the bridle over the horse's head, grateful to focus her attention on the task rather than the man who had dominated her thoughts far too often lately. Wizard took the bit eagerly.

"What's his story?" Mac asked, watching as she buckled the nose and chin straps.

"He has good bloodlines, but even as a yearling, he was out-of-control—too spirited to train never mind race. So his owners decided to geld him, thinking that would settle him down. It did, and he spent several years on the circuit. He finished in the money more often than not in his career, but never big money. When he started to slow down, his owners didn't know what to do with him. They couldn't retire him to stud, obviously, so they were going to put him down."

She saw the muscle in his jaw tighten, and knew he was as infuriated as she had been at the thought of a horse being euthanized simply because it was no longer winning races.

But when he spoke, it was only to ask, "How did you find him?"

"A friend of a friend."

"And what are your plans for him?"

"The same as all of the other horses that come here—to try to find him a new home. But right now—" she rubbed her hand over Wizard's cheek "—we're going to ride."

"Does he prefer to ride alone?"

She shrugged. "He just likes to ride, and he doesn't get nearly enough opportunities these days."

"Why don't you let me saddle up one of the other horses and go out with you?"

"You don't have anything better to do?"

"Not right now."

"Okay, then." She considered for a moment. "Peaches is overdue for a run."

Mac nodded, apparently unfazed at being asked to ride a horse named after a fruit. "Give me ten minutes to saddle her up."

* * *

Jewel mounted the gray and trotted him around while they waited for Mac.

She wasn't surprised when he took less than the ten minutes he'd asked for. She still had questions about him, but she no longer doubted his aptitude or abilities where the horses were concerned. And if she wished she knew a little bit more about the man, she reminded herself that nothing was as important as his doing the job he was hired to do.

She let Wizard begin to canter, and Peaches pulled up alongside, keeping the easy pace. Mac didn't seem to have any trouble handling the spirited mare. It was as if he instinctively knew when to exercise control and when to let the horse take the lead so that it didn't turn into a battle of wills—a battle that no man could win against a thousand-pound horse, though there were many who were foolish enough to try.

Mac didn't strike her as the foolish sort.

Though she wondered about the wisdom of her own actions in agreeing to a moonlight ride with a man who stirred feelings inside of her that hadn't been stirred in a very long time.

"This is quite the place you've got here," he said, as they guided their respective mounts toward the dirt oval.

She looked around, at the grounds and buildings that were the landscape of not just her business but her life, and felt a sense of contentment and satisfaction. She still marveled sometimes at the fact that everything she saw—as far as her eyes could see—was hers.

"There are times I still can't believe it was a twist of fate that made it mine," she said softly.

"Fate?"

"Long story."

"And one you don't particularly want to talk about," he guessed.

"It's not really a big secret, and if you hang around long enough, someone is bound to comment on the fact that I'm only running CTC because my father was killed on the way to his lawyer's office to change his will."

"He was going to write you out of it?"

She shook her head. "Nothing that drastic. I might not have been the son he wanted, but I was still his oldest child and he wanted the business to stay in the family. But he also wanted all the decisions to be made by his hand-picked management team, including his lawyer, Russ, and Brian Murray."

"That would be the same Brian Murray who owns the place down the street—the one your father wanted you to marry?"

She turned to glance at him over her shoulder. "Is there anything my sister hasn't told you?"

"She didn't give me any details," he told her. "So why don't you tell me about this marriage your father tried to arrange?"

"He wanted me to marry Brian in order to merge the two businesses. When I told him it wasn't going to happen, he decided that I was incapable of making decisions for myself. If I wouldn't accept Brian as my husband, I'd have to take him as my boss."

"And what were Brian's thoughts on all of this?"

"He wanted the merger. He made enough money betting on horses that he decided to try his hand at owning a few, then breeding one or two. After a dozen years in the business, he realized it was going to take a lot longer than that to build the kind of reputation Callahan has."

"Unless he married a Callahan," Mac guessed.

She nodded.

"And yet you managed to resist such a temptingly romantic offer," he said dryly.

She smiled at that. "Hard to believe, but somehow I did."

"Still, it must have been hard to lose your father when you had those kind of issues unresolved between you."

"The only thing that would be different if he hadn't died that day is CTC wouldn't be mine."

"What about your sister? Where does she fit into this?"

"I bought out her share of this business, then Crystal helped me found Haven."

"And this—" he gestured expansively "—is this what you've always wanted?"

"No." She grinned. "I used to want to be a champion barrel racer."

"What changed your mind?"

"Six years on the rodeo circuit. It seemed there was always one more town, one more season, and I realized I didn't want to spend my life on the road, moving from one hotel room to the next. I wanted a home—and a family."

"And so you gave up barrel racing and came home to train thoroughbreds."

"I came home," she agreed. "Though CTC requires that I spend more time with paperwork than the horses."

"I can't imagine that," he said, "considering how much time you spend in the stables and at the track."

She smiled. "It's my job to know what's happening with every one of the horses."

"You mentioned that you came back here because you were tired of life on the road—that you wanted a home and a family."

She nodded.

"So why aren't you married?" he asked.

Her eyes clouded. "Because life doesn't always work out the way we hope it will."

"Sometimes that's not a bad thing."

"What are *your* plans?" she asked.

He shrugged. "Nothing's carved in stone right now."

"You said you had a business degree," she recalled. "Why aren't you looking for a job in business?"

He felt a twinge of guilt. It wasn't so much that he'd lied to her as that he hadn't been entirely honest. He'd done more than study business—he'd earned a master's in business administration before continuing his education at law school. But he knew that if he'd admitted all of that, Jewel would have a lot more questions about why he was working as a stable hand at CTC, questions that he wasn't sure he was ready to answer.

"I'm just taking some time to do what I want to do first," he said, speaking the truth if not all of it. "I missed the horses, the physical labor of working in the stables, while I was at school. I'm looking at this as an opportunity to recharge before I spend the rest of my life at a real job."

"You don't think of what you're doing here as a real job?" she challenged.

He grinned and shook his head. "This has always been my passion—so much that I almost feel guilty earning money for doing it."

She laughed. "I'm not sure that's something you should admit to the woman signing your paychecks."

"That makes things a little bit awkward, doesn't it?"

"How so?"

He held her captive with nothing more than his gaze. "Because I really want to kiss you."

She knew what it meant when a man looked at a woman

the way he was looking at her, and she knew that they were treading on dangerous ground. "That would make things more than awkward."

"I know." He smiled. "Doesn't make me stop wanting you, though."

"I can't get involved with you, Mac."

"Why not?"

"For starters, you work for me."

"Okay, I quit."

She laughed, though the intensity with which he was staring at her made her suspect that he wasn't entirely joking. As they came upon the track, she could feel Wizard quivering with excitement and was grateful for the opportunity to end their conversation. "Are we going to talk or ride?"

"If those are my only two options—"

Jewel didn't wait to hear his response. She loosened the reins and Wizard, sensing his freedom, took off like a shot.

She heard Mac shout—a combination of surprise and protest—and then he gave chase.

Wizard got off to a good start and had an impressive lead over the mare coming up to the first marker. His eagerness and experience allowed him to hold on to the lead over the younger horse for a while longer, but they were neck-in-neck coming into the backstretch. Then, not surprisingly, Mac and Peaches edged ahead. But Wizard didn't let up. He fought back valiantly, racing with his heart as much as his legs, and approached the final post neck-in-neck with the other horse. When they crossed the imaginary wire, he'd actually stretched his nose out to take the mock race by a nod.

Jewel slid off of Wizard's back and wrapped her arms around his damp neck. "You were incredible," she told him.

"And you," Mac said from behind her, "are a speed junkie."

She turned around, grinning. "I have to admit, I love the feel of the wind in my face."

"You must have been a force on the rodeo circuit."

"Three time national champion," she told him.

He took a step closer. "But not everything in life should be a race to the finish line."

"You're just saying that because you lost."

"It was a tie."

"You lost."

"You cheated."

She lifted a brow. "How do you figure?"

"You started first."

"Just because you were slow out of the gate—"

The rest of the words lodged in her throat when his arm snaked around her waist. "No one's ever accused me of being slow out of the gate."

"Well—" she gave herself a moment to acknowledge the delicious little sparks that zinged through her system "—you were this time."

"Maybe I was," he acknowledged, drawing her closer. "Or maybe I chose finesse over speed."

"You still lost."

He smiled. "I don't think so."

Then he kissed her.

And he definitely chose finesse over speed this time.

His lips brushed over hers—once, twice, testing, teasing—then settled.

And Jewel realized he was right. In this, at least, she didn't want to hurry at all.

He kissed her softly, slowly and very thoroughly.

His tongue glided over her lips and she felt the sizzle right down to her toes, a jolt of electricity that melted the last of her resistance along with everything else inside of her.

Her hands were on his shoulders now, her fingers digging into the taut muscles, trying to hold herself steady in a world that was suddenly spinning out of control.

His hands slid up her back and down again, and she trembled against him. It had been a long time since she'd had a man's hands on her—so long, in fact, she'd almost forgotten how it felt to be touched, wanted, cherished. And she almost didn't want him to stop.

His hands skimmed upward again, over her ribs, the sides of her breasts, and she sighed.

She definitely didn't want him to stop.

But somewhere in the back of her mind, she knew that there were too many obstacles to a personal relationship between them.

He'd graduated from Harvard—she'd chosen the rodeo circuit over college. She'd eventually got her trainer's certificate and later picked up some night courses at the local college to help with the running of her business, but nothing that compared to his Ivy League education.

How he happened to be working for her right now was nothing more than some kind of cosmic fluke, an inexplicable mystery that could change in a heartbeat.

Then there was the obvious age gap. It still boggled her mind that she should be so intensely attracted to a man who was closer to twenty than thirty when she could see forty in the distance. So as good-looking and smart and sexy as he was—and every one of her hormones was in full agreement with that assessment—she couldn't forget that he was young enough to be…a much younger brother.

And it was just a cruel twist of fate that he could kiss with such masterful skill that an ordinarily sane and rational woman would be tempted to forget all of the reasons that she shouldn't jump into bed with him.

She pulled away, and drew in a long, deep breath.

Mac didn't protest her withdrawal. In fact, he didn't say anything at all, but only stroked a hand down her back in a gesture that was somehow both soothing and arousing.

"I can't do this, Mac." Her lips were still tingling from the pressure of his, and her body was still quivering with longing. It would be so easy to lean into him again, to let him take her where they both wanted to go. Instead she took a step back. "I need you here, at CTC, and I can't afford to lose you if I let things get personal."

"I'm not going to push for more than you're ready to give," he promised her. "But you should know two things—I'm not going anywhere, and things are already personal."

Chapter Six

The man was driving her mad.

Five days after Mac had kissed her, Jewel had barely caught sight of the man around the stables. Oh, she knew he was there, knew he'd been doing his job as well as putting in extra hours at Haven. But he hadn't sought her out, and though thoughts of him had hovered at the back of her mind, she sure as heck wasn't going to go looking for him.

The cocky self-confidence that fit him as nicely as his faded Levi's suggested that he was well aware of the effect he had on women, and she refused to swoon like the masses. She refused to admit that her heart did beat a little bit faster and her blood pulsed a little bit hotter whenever he was near.

It had been so long since she'd been attracted to any man that she couldn't help but wonder what it was about this one that kicked her hormones into overdrive. She frowned over hat thought for a minute before considering that maybe it wasn't this man at all. Maybe it was simply…proximity.

After almost three years of self-imposed celibacy it was a logical explanation. And even before that, her affair with Allan hadn't been much more than a fling, and a somewhat disappointing one.

She'd hooked up with him a few months after Crystal had gotten married, after waking up one morning and realizing she was thirty-one years old and tired of going to bed alone every night. In retrospect, she realized she hadn't been attracted to him so much as she'd been attracted to the idea of being with someone. The relationship had lasted all of three months and she'd been more relieved than disappointed when they'd both finally agreed it wasn't working.

There had been no one since then. She'd wanted no one since then—until Mac Delgado had walked into the Halfway Café.

The knock on the door jolted her from her reverie.

The sight of the man himself standing in her doorway jolted all of her hormones to attention.

"Are you busy?" Mac asked.

"I'm always busy," she said, as much to remind herself as him that she didn't have time for anything other than business, and certainly no time to be distracted by the feelings he stirred in her.

"Too busy to take a drive into town to grab some dinner?"

She glanced at her watch, surprised to see that it was dinnertime already. And as Bonnie had gone to Michigan to visit her sister for a couple of weeks, there would be no dinner waiting for her when she finally headed up to the house.

But driving into town with Mac? Sitting at a table and sharing a meal with him? She wasn't sure that was a good idea. And, after five days of silence, she wasn't going to jump just because he'd asked her to.

"I'm not really hungry," she said, then felt her cheeks heat when her stomach chose that exact moment to growl in contradiction of her statement.

Mac grinned, and the flutters in her tummy were suddenly stronger than her appetite. "You sure?"

She sighed, because it was just dinner. And the fact that she hadn't seen or heard from him in the past few days was a pretty good indication that she'd misinterpreted his feelings for her, overreacted to a casual look, an innocent touch, and a single mind-numbing kiss.

"Okay," she admitted, "I am hungry, but I've got some things I have to finish up here and—"

"I'll wait."

"As much as I appreciate the invitation," she continued, "I'm going to be a while so you should just go ahead."

He shrugged. "Your call."

She forced a smile, refusing to acknowledge the twinge of disappointment she felt that he'd relented so easily. "Enjoy your dinner."

Nearly an hour passed before Jewel shut down her computer and returned to the house. She was comparing the merits of leftover week-old lasagna and microwave popcorn when there was a knock at the door.

"You said you wouldn't go out for dinner with me," Mac said. "You didn't say you wouldn't share a pizza with me if I brought it to you."

She opened the door wider, too tempted by the flat cardboard box in his hand to turn him away.

He grinned as he stepped into the house, while she worried that she'd made the wrong choice in refusing to go out with him earlier. Sharing a meal in a public restaurant seemed much less risky than inviting him into her house, where they would be alone together. And that thought was niggling at her mind even before he passed her the bottle of wine he carried in his other hand.

She frowned at the familiar label as she asked, "What's on the pizza?"

"Pepperoni, sausage, hot peppers and olives."

"Did you happen to run into my sister in town?"

"As a matter of fact, she and her husband were in line at the movie theater."

Which was, coincidentally, right next door to the pizza parlor.

"Nice guy—Simon," he said. "Though he certainly isn't the type of guy I would have expected your sister to marry."

It was the reaction most people had when they met Crystal—who still looked like the perky cheerleader she'd been in high school, and Simon—a stereotypical nerd with thick glasses and thinning air. The technologically challenged dessert chef and the diabetic computer geek, as Crystal referred to them. And yet, there was no denying that they were madly in love and truly committed to one another.

While Jewel got the plates and napkins, Mac opened and closed drawers until he found the corkscrew.

"By the way," he continued, "they're having a dinner party in a couple of weeks. Simon said you already know some of the other guests, so he's putting you on the invite list, and Crystal suggested that you should bring me as your date."

"My sister has a habit of sticking her nose into things that are none of her business," Jewel told him.

"She thought the merlot might persuade you to at least

consider it." He deftly uncorked the bottle and poured it into the two glasses she'd set on the counter.

She smiled at that. "It would take more than a bottle of wine—even if it is my favorite—to make me abandon all common sense and go out with a man I barely know, who is at least ten years younger than me, and an employee."

"I'm hardly a stranger, I'm only eight years younger than you, and as much as I'm enjoying this job, I'd give it up in a heartbeat if that's all it would take to get you to change your mind about going out with me."

As flattered as she was by the latter part of his statement, it was the middle that caused her to frown. "How do you know how old I am?" Then she shook her head. "Obviously from the same source that told you what toppings I like on my pizza."

"I was surprised," he admitted. "I wouldn't have guessed that you were a day over thirty."

"And I wouldn't have guessed that you were a day over twenty-two."

He shrugged. "So we were both wrong."

"And eight years is pretty close to ten."

He just smiled and handed her a plate with two slices of pizza on it. "Hungry?"

"Starving." She took the plate and pulled back a chair.

He took a seat on the other side of the table and loaded up his own plate.

"What movie were they going to see?" Jewel asked.

"The new Sandra Bullock film. Simon said it was a chick-flick, but he said it with such a dorky smile on his face, it was obvious he didn't mind."

"Or he was hoping to get lucky after the movie," she said dryly.

"And people say that I'm cynical," he noted, picking up his wineglass.

She slid into the chair across from him. "What else do they say about you?"

"That I'm attentive, considerate, charming—"

"Modest?"

He grinned and shook his head. "No one's ever accused me of that."

"Hard to believe."

They polished off the whole pizza, and while they ate, they talked about everything but nothing of importance. And as they talked, Marcus noticed that Jewel finally started to relax, her smile started to come more easily and her words were less censored.

"When I first saw you at the café with Crystal, I wouldn't have guessed that you were sisters."

"We're half sisters," she admitted.

"Same mother or father?"

"Father." She picked up her glass, took a long sip of wine before continuing. "My mom walked out before my third birthday. Jack hooked up with Alice—Crystal's mom—a few years later. Then she walked out, too, a few years after that, but she had the sense to take Crystal with her."

"And left you," he guessed.

She shrugged. "She was willing to take me, too, and told Jack she wanted us to stay together. Jack wouldn't hear of it—not that he wanted me around, but he didn't want anyone else to take what was his. And since she wasn't my mother, she had no legal claim to custody.

"She kept in touch for a few years—bringing Crystal back

for regular visits—more for me than Jack. Then she remarried and moved to Washington.

"When Crystal was twelve, Alice and her husband were killed in a car accident. She was sent back here to live with Jack, but I was already gone."

And she felt guilty about that, he could tell. She'd spent her whole life being neglected by the man who'd fathered her and wanted only to save her little sister from the same fate.

"That's when you ran off to be a rodeo star?" he asked lightly.

"Something like that."

They ate in companionable silence for a few minutes, then Marcus heard himself say, "My mom died when I was seven."

She looked up, surprise and compassion evident in her beautiful blue-gray eyes. "That must have been hard."

He wasn't sure why he told her that—it certainly wasn't a usual topic of conversation. In fact, he couldn't remember sharing such personal details with a woman. But when she reached across the table to touch her hand to his arm, he realized the explanation might be as simple as that he'd never met another woman who would understand as he'd known Jewel would.

"How did she die?" she asked gently.

"A brain aneurysm." And he'd taken so much for granted before she'd died. Being a prince had ensured there was almost nothing he couldn't have or do. Until all he'd wanted was his mother to wake up—and no one could make that happen for him.

"One minute she was there, and the next she was gone," Jewel murmured.

He knew the loss she'd experienced had been similar, that her scars probably ran as deep.

"Did your dad ever remarry?" she asked gently.

He shook his head. "My mom was the love of his life. After she died, he focused on his duties."

"Duties?"

He mentally cursed himself for the slip and quickly amended, "His job."

"And he raised you on his own?"

He managed to smile now, thinking of his father with genuine love and affection. "My father didn't have a clue about raising kids," he admitted. "But he did have a nanny."

"A nanny," she echoed and leaned back in her chair, removing her hand from his arm so that it felt almost cold after the warmth of her touch. "Which again makes me wonder—what the heck are you doing mucking out my barn?"

"Have you been dissatisfied with my work?"

"You know that's not what I mean."

"I like my job here, and I think I've proven that I'm good at it. Why does anything else matter?"

"Because you're a Harvard graduate working as a stable hand."

He refilled her glass. "You're making this more complicated than it needs to be."

"I doubt that." She traced the base of her glass with her fingertip, her brow furrowed. "You don't fit in here, Mac.

"I'm not talking about your work," she continued. "You obviously know horses, and I'm grateful that you signed on. But you're not the drifter you're pretending to be."

"That's exactly what I am," he told her.

She shook her head. "Drifting from place to place, from job to job, doesn't make a man like you a drifter."

He quirked a brow. "What does it make me?"

"I haven't quite figured it out," she admitted.

"Maybe I'm just a man who's trying to figure out his place in the world."

"Maybe." But she didn't sound convinced. "If I had to guess, though, I'd say you were running from something."

He smiled, as if he was amused by her assessment when, in fact, he was a little unnerved by the accuracy of it. "A fugitive from the law?"

She sipped her wine. "Nothing so dramatic. More likely family expectations and responsibilities." She looked at him over the rim of her glass, considering. "I'd bet you have family connections to the Vanderbilts or Rockefellers or Kennedys. And you probably have some blueblood fiancée back in Boston who you convinced you needed to take some time for yourself before you settled down."

"There's no fiancée. Not in Boston or anywhere else." He laid his hand over hers, and this touch had nothing to do with offering comfort or compassion, and they both knew it. Her breath caught before her eyes lifted slowly to meet his. His thumb brushed over her wrist, felt her pulse race. "I wouldn't be here with you if there was."

"And this is why having dinner together was a bad idea," she said softly.

"I think it was a good idea," he said. "We finally had a chance to talk about something more personal than horses and manure, and now you can't say I'm a stranger anymore."

She pulled her hand away. "You're still ten years younger than me."

"Eight," he corrected again.

"And somehow, despite the age factor weighing on my side, I get the impression I'd be totally out of my league with you."

"Personal relationships aren't team sports."

"No," she agreed. "But they often do involve a lot of game-playing, and I don't have the interest or inclination."

He felt his lips curve. "Are you going to tell me that you haven't thought about it?"

"I've occasionally considered a foolish course of action, but recognizing it as such usually prevents the mistake from being made."

"Usually?"

She swallowed. "I can't afford to make any mistakes at this point in my life."

Everything she was feeling was in her eyes—attraction, confusion, desire and uncertainty. It was the uncertainty that held him back. As much as he wanted her, he needed to know that she wanted the same thing.

Until then, he would force himself to be patient.

Tearing his gaze from hers, he glanced at the clock on the stove. "I didn't realize it was getting to be so late."

"Neither did I," she admitted.

He pushed away from the table. "I should go."

She nodded and got up to walk him to the door.

"Mac?" She touched a hand to his arm, forcing him to turn back, to look into those gorgeous blue-gray eyes that were shining a little brighter than usual because of the wine, cheeks that were flushed, lips that were slightly parted.

He had to remind himself of his vow to be patient. "Yes?"

The tip of her tongue swept along the curve of her bottom lip. "Thanks for the pizza. And the company."

He curled his fingers into his palms to resist the urge to reach for her. "You're welcome."

Chapter Seven

Jewel wasn't surprised when Crystal popped by her office late the next morning. An impromptu visit from her sister was a rare occurrence, but Jewel didn't need two guesses to ascertain the reason for this one.

"Aren't you supposed to be at work?" she asked.

"The morning rush is over," Crystal said. "And the blueberry muffins just came out of the oven, so I thought I'd take a break to see how you were doing."

Jewel opened the paper sack her sister set on her desk and hummed her approval at the mouthwatering scent that wafted out.

"Apparently I'm hungry," she said, reaching into the bag.

"Probably because you haven't eaten anything since the pizza you had for dinner last night."

"Thanks for that, by the way."

Crystal looked wary. "You're not going to chastise me for matchmaking?"

"I didn't realize you were," she fibbed as she broke the top off of a muffin. "I thought you were just ensuring that I had something to eat."

Her sister huffed out a breath. "Are you honestly telling me that you shared pizza and a bottle of wine with Mac last night and *nothing* happened?"

"We talked."

"He didn't even kiss you?"

She considered her answer while she chewed, and decided evasion was the safest response. "Why all the interest in my personal life all of a sudden?"

"Because you seem to have a personal life all of a sudden."

Jewel took another bite of muffin. "Does that mean you'll be wanting all the details of how we did it on the kitchen table after we finished the pizza?"

"You didn't do it on the kitchen table or anywhere else," Crystal stated confidently.

"How do you know?"

"Because if you had, you'd be looking a lot more relaxed than you do right now."

"Maybe he just isn't very good."

Crystal smirked. "Do you really expect me to believe that?"

"I expect you to know me better than to think I would fall into bed with a man I've barely known three weeks."

"I fell in love with Simon after only three days," Crystal told her.

"Thanks for the muffins," Jewel said, trying to nudge her sister along. "But I have a dozen things—"

"I didn't only come here to bring you muffins," Crystal interjected. "Or to dig for information about Mac."

Jewel looked at her sister, only now noticing the extra sparkle in her eyes, the natural flush of color in her cheeks. And that suddenly, she knew what Crystal had come to tell her.

Her baby sister was going to have a baby.

Jewel was stunned, thrilled—and a tiny bit envious. But it was only after she'd finally said goodbye and Crystal had gone that the tears came.

There were tears of joy for her sister, who had been trying for so long to start a family with her husband. And tears for herself, because while Crystal's dreams were finally starting to come true, her own were still so far out of reach.

It was the click of the latch as the door closed that warned Jewel she was no longer alone even before Mac knelt down beside her. "What's wrong?"

She brushed the moisture from her cheeks, as embarrassed to have been caught indulging in such an emotional display as she was ashamed of the selfish nature of her tears. "Nothing."

"It doesn't look like nothing."

"I just found out my sister is going to have a baby," she told him.

"Crystal?"

She managed a smile. "She's the only sister I have—the only family I have."

He pulled a tissue from the box on her desk and gently wiped her eyes. "When's she due?"

"January."

Mac smiled. "My brother's wife is expecting their first child in a couple of months."

"I didn't know you had a brother."

"Two of them, in fact." His eyes clouded for a moment before he said, "There used to be four of us, before my eldest brother and his wife died in a boating accident."

"I'm sorry."

He shook his head. "I'm sorry," he said. "We were talking about your happy news. I didn't mean to put a damper on the conversation."

She reached out and touched a hand to his arm. "How long ago did your brother and his wife die?"

His gaze dropped to her hand, as if he was surprised by her touch. And though she was suddenly conscious of the taut muscle in his forearm and the heat of his skin, she didn't pull away.

"Two and a half years," he said.

He was still grieving, she could hear it in his voice. She knew as well as anyone that time didn't really heal all wounds, it just made the pain a little more bearable.

"Did they have any kids?" she asked.

He nodded. "Three."

He heart ached for those children, and she found herself thinking about the loss of her own mother—a woman whose presence was taken from her daughter's life not by the fickle hand of fate but through her own conscious choice, and wondered why it somehow seemed even harder to accept that the woman who'd given birth to her hadn't loved her enough to stay.

She pushed the thought aside, refused to let the bitter memories cast a pall over the moment.

"So you have nieces? Nephews?"

"One niece, two nephews, so far."

"Do you see them often?"

"Not as much as I'd like in the past few years," he said.

"They live far away?"

His lips quirked just a little. "Yeah."

That was all he said, and though it was an answer to her question, she was somehow more aware of what he didn't say, the information he held back, evidence of yet another secret between them.

She wanted to press him for more, to learn the answers to all the questions she had about him. He'd given her little pieces of himself, yet she sensed there was still so much that she didn't know.

"They're in Europe," he finally said. "My family lives on an island in the Mediterranean."

"Oh." She was surprised by the revelation and glad that he'd finally volunteered some information. "You don't sound European," she said inanely. "Except—" she broke off, her cheeks flushing.

"Except?" he prompted.

Her cheeks burned hotter. "When you're flirting with me," she admitted. "Then your voice deepens and picks up just the slightest hint of an accent."

He touched a hand to her cheek, the lazy stroke of his thumb over her skin causing shivers to dance down her spine. "Does it?"

And just those two words, and the light touch, had everything inside her quivering.

She forced herself to take a mental step back, to remind herself—to remind both of them—how ill-suited they were.

"I want a baby."

She hadn't intended to blurt out that thought, but when his face went pale, she couldn't help but laugh.

"I didn't mean right now, and I certainly didn't mean with you."

He frowned at that. "Why 'certainly' not with me?"

She shook her head. "You've made it clear that you have no interest in a serious relationship, never mind marriage or children, yet you're somehow offended by the statement that I don't want to have a child with you."

"Well, it's not flattering for a man to be told he's not good father material."

"You'd probably make a great father," she said. "When you stopped being such a child."

"Ouch."

She laughed again. "I couldn't resist—your instinctive panicked reaction was just so typical."

"Typical?" He sounded more offended by that than being referred to as a child.

Jewel waved the question aside. "I assume there was a reason you're here—other than to wipe my tears?"

"Yeah." He stroked a finger over the curve of her bottom lip. "That was just a bonus."

"The reason?" she prompted.

"Cayenne."

She jumped to her feet.

"Nothing's wrong," he hastened to assure her. "I just wanted to let you know that Harold Emerson was looking at him today—and hinting that he might be interested in adding him to his stable."

"He wants to buy Cayenne?"

"Maybe."

She understood his caution—but any interest in the wayward stallion at this point was far more than she'd expected.

Impulsively she threw her arms around his neck and gave him a smacking kiss on the lips. "This is almost as good as Crystal's news."

"And that was even better," he said, tightening his arm around her when she started to draw back and kissing her again.

What it was, she immediately realized, was a mistake. Because the minute his mouth took possession of hers, she wanted more.

In the time that had passed since their first kiss, she'd managed to reassure herself that she'd been smart to put on the brakes, that she couldn't have an affair with him. She'd even managed to convince herself that the kiss wasn't as spectacular as she'd remembered. It was just that it had been so very long since she'd been kissed that she'd exaggerated both his skill and her response.

This kiss blasted that theory to smithereens.

And when his tongue touched hers, her mind went completely blank. There was no thought or reason. There was nothing but Mac and an acceptance of the passion that had been simmering between them since the first—a passion that was everything she hadn't even known she'd wanted.

But now, there was no denying how very much she wanted. She wrapped her arms around him, pressed her body closer to his to absorb his warmth, his touch, his taste.

His hands slid up her back, her breasts brushed his chest and sparks of electric heat zinged through her system.

Oh, yeah, he knew how to kiss.

His mouth moved over hers with a skillful mastery that made everything inside her tremble and yearn. His hands tangled in her hair, tipping her head back. His tongue dove deeper between her parted lips, tasting, tempting.

It seemed as if he would kiss her forever, and she knew that even if he did, forever wouldn't be long enough. So she let herself savor the moment, steeped herself in his flavor and gloried in the press of his hot, hard body against hers.

"Usted me está conduciendo insano." He murmured the words against her lips.

"I have no idea what you just said," she told him.

"I said you are driving me crazy," he admitted. "When are you going to stop torturing me?"

"Believe it or not," she said, "I'm not trying to torture you."

He nibbled on her lip as his hand found her breast, his thumb circled the nipple, testing, teasing. "Just a coincidence then?"

Her only response was a moan, deep in her throat, when his thumb brushed over the turgid peak.

He said something else, speaking softly again in Spanish. She didn't understand the words—she didn't need to. The tone was pure seduction, and she was helplessly entranced.

She didn't realize he'd unfastened her shirt until his lips moved down her throat, then lower to nuzzle between her breasts. His cheek was rough against her sensitive skin, his breath was warm, and the little flicks of his tongue were deliciously erotic.

He freed one breast from the lacy constraint of her bra, then his mouth was on her, hot and hungry. She gasped as fiery spears of pleasure arrowed to her core. Her fingers dug into his shoulders, holding on while the earth seemed to tilt on its axis.

She was tempted—oh, so tempted—to follow where he was leading, to let her world spin out of control. But she was afraid—of the desire she tasted in his kiss, of the needs churning inside herself, of the enormity of feelings she hadn't known before. And her fear was stronger than her desire.

She pulled out of his arms and drew in a long, shuddering breath as she refastened the buttons of her shirt.

Mac lifted a hand, as if to touch her, and she took another quick step back, out of reach. Her blood was still pulsing, her body aching, and she wasn't entirely sure she could be trusted not to jump his bones if he touched her again right now.

His hand dropped to his side.

"I'm not playing hard to get," she told him. "I'm just not looking for a relationship right now, or a quick fling, or anything else you might be thinking of."

"I was thinking it wouldn't be quick," he said, in a tone that had her blood pulsing again.

She swallowed, hard. "Mac."

"You know what I want, Jewel. The next step is yours."

And then he was gone, and she was left alone and wanting.

Marcus was up earlier than usual on race day, and though there was a lot of work that needed to be done, he stole a private moment to make his weekly telephone call home. It was Lara who answered the prince regent's private line, and the pleasure and warmth in her voice made him feel just a little bit homesick.

"We weren't expecting you to call until tomorrow," she said. "Rowan's tied up in meetings all day today."

"I'm going to be out most of the day tomorrow," he told her. "And I'd rather talk to you anyway, so I'm glad I caught you."

"It's easy to catch me these days," she admitted. "It's hard to move fast when you waddle."

He chuckled. "Rowan e-mailed me some photos—you're not that huge yet."

"Now that I'm in my seventh month, I seem to be getting

bigger every day." Then, in an obvious change of subject, "Tell me what you've been up to."

"Working."

"And loving every minute of it, I can tell."

"It's been a good experience," he agreed.

"You've been there several weeks already," she noted. "And you're not getting bored yet?"

"No. In fact, I can't remember when I've had more fun."

"Mucking out stalls?" she asked dubiously.

"I've met someone," he admitted. He wouldn't have confided the fact in his brother, but he'd always found it easy to talk to Lara.

"A female someone, I'm guessing."

Marcus grinned. "Yeah."

"Details," Lara demanded.

"She's beautiful and smart and sexy."

"Does she have a name?"

"Her name is Jewel."

"You sound smitten, Marcus." And she sounded genuinely pleased by that fact.

"I think I am," he admitted.

"When am I going to get to meet her?"

"Well, that might be a bit of a problem."

Lara groaned. "She doesn't know who you are, does she?"

"I'm going to tell her."

"When?"

"When I'm sure that it won't make a difference."

His sister-in-law sighed.

"How are things there?" he asked, in a deliberate attempt to deflect the inevitable lecture.

"We're gearing up for the Independence Celebrations."

"I hope you're not overdoing it."

He could picture Lara rolling her eyes as she responded to his comment. "Rowan is hardly letting me do anything, and when he's not here to keep an eye on me, he's got someone else hovering."

Marcus smiled. "How are the kids?"

"They're doing great," she assured him. "But they miss you and keep asking when Uncle Marcus is coming home."

"I miss all of you, too," he said. "And you can tell them I'll be home for the celebrations, if not sooner."

"Will you be coming alone?"

Marcus smiled at his sister-in-law's subtle prodding. "I'll let you know."

Jewel had been at the track since before dawn, when the grandstands had stood silent and empty and the infield was covered with mist. Now it was nearing post time, and the stands were quickly filling up. There was an energy in the air—a buzz of excitement and anticipation.

She had a *Daily Racing Form* in her pocket and had placed her minimum bets. She'd never been much of a gambler and didn't pay any attention to odds or handicaps, but she believed in making a customary wager to demonstrate confidence and faith in her horses.

After Midnight was entered in the fourth race on the ticket, and though the horses for the third were just now being escorted onto the track, it was After Midnight that was on her mind. She needed him to race well today. Gabe Anderson had demanded it, and she'd known him long enough to know he was serious about his threat to take all of his horses elsewhere if he didn't get the results he wanted with After Midnight.

Over the past several years, there had been more than enough times when she'd wished she didn't have to deal with Anderson and his overinflated ego, but she'd put up with him simply because his defection could be a serious blow to CTC.

Caleb had assured her the colt was both ready and eager to race. Jewel knew she couldn't ask for more than that—though she wouldn't turn down a little luck.

"Nervous?"

She turned to find Mac beside her. "Do I look nervous?"

He studied her for a moment, and if she hadn't already been aware of the nerves in her belly, the intensity of his gaze would have started them stirring. "Maybe focused rather than nervous."

He took her hand, turned it over and pressed something against her palm.

She glanced at the pale blue stone, still warm from the heat of his hand, then at him. "What is it?"

"Aventurine," he told her. "For luck."

"You don't strike me as the type to carry lucky stones in his pocket."

He shrugged. "It was given to me by a friend—now I'm giving it to you."

She closed her fingers around the smooth, polished quartz. "Thanks."

The nerves in her belly jolted when the bell rang and the starting gates sprang open. Mac took up position beside her as the horses thundered onto the track, and though every nerve ending in her body was acutely aware of his nearness, she somehow found his presence comforting. Or maybe it was just the distraction from her other concerns that she appreciated.

She didn't even take notice of who won that race—it was the next one that held her attention.

She watched the post parade, noted the familiar royal and white colors that After Midnight and his jockey were wearing as they were escorted onto the track. Even from this distance, she could see the nervous excitement of the horse, the focused intensity of his rider, and she felt her own muscles knot in anticipation as After Midnight was loaded into the starting gate.

"Arianna's running later today, isn't she?" Mac asked.

"In the seventh."

"She looked good this morning," he said. "She knows why she's here, and she's ready for it."

Jewel nodded. "I'm not worried about Arianna."

"Then it's Gabe Anderson's entry that has you gripping the fence until your knuckles are white."

She pulled her hands back and tucked them into her pockets. "Don't you have work to do?"

There was no censure in her question, so he only lifted a shoulder in response. "There's always work to do, and so few opportunities to spend time with a beautiful woman."

Her brows lifted. "Flirting with your boss could be dangerous, Delgado."

"I keep hoping," he assured her.

"Mac—"

"I do have to get back to the shedrow," he interrupted. "But there was one more thing I need to do first."

And before she could even ask what it was, he touched his mouth to hers in a brief but potent kiss that had the knots in her stomach twisting for reasons that had nothing to do with the race about to take place.

"Was that for luck, too?" she asked when he drew away.

"No—" he grinned "—that was for me." Then he turned and walked off, whistling.

Chapter Eight

After Midnight came second in a field of nine. It was a more than respectable finish and the colt had run well, but Jewel knew Anderson would be ticked that his horse had given up the lead in the backstretch, coming under the wire almost two full lengths behind the winner.

She tucked her hands into her pockets as she went to rustle up a cup of coffee and found the stone Mac had given to her earlier. Russ had once said that she'd learned more than the business from her father—she'd learned to keep her emotions bottled up inside. Her cool demeanor and level-headedness had served her well in business, and she was a little unnerved that a man she'd known for such a short time had seen through the facade and recognized the feelings she'd managed to hide from everyone else. But she was also touched by the effort Mac had made to take her mind off of her worries, pleased by the thoughtfulness of his gesture.

She shook her head, wondering what was wrong with her that she was getting sentimental over a silly rock even as she reached into her pocket for it. It was just a stone—but it was a pretty stone. And while she didn't really believe it had helped After Midnight's performance, she didn't see any harm in holding on to it until after Arianna's race.

Mac didn't have any trouble picking Jewel out of the crowd, and while she watched the horses, he watched her.

When Arianna was led onto the track, her hands dipped into her pockets. He wondered if she was looking for the aventurine he'd given to her earlier for luck, or if she just wanted to make sure she couldn't twist her fingers together, as she sometimes did when she was anxious.

He saw her gaze zero in on the purple and gray silks her jockey wore and knew she probably didn't see anyone or anything else as the horses were loaded into the starting gate. Some of them entered more willingly than others, and it took a while before it was Arianna's turn. She'd drawn the tenth post position in a field of twelve, and though it was a little more outside than Jewel probably would have liked, he knew Arianna liked space to run. If she shot out to an early lead, as she liked to do, she could then move to the inside.

Caleb joined Jewel to watch the race, just as the horses sprang from the gate. Their hooves pounded like thunder in the dirt, and though it looked like a tight race, he was pleased to see that Arianna had already started to edge out in front. Steadily she moved forward, her legs stretching out, pulling her ahead of the pack, and seeming to increase her lead with every long stride. By the time she flew under the wire, she was more than five lengths ahead of her nearest competitor.

The next time he caught sight of Jewel, she was leaving the winner's circle with Arianna. She was waylaid several times on her way back to the shedrow by people she knew or other spectators just wanting to offer congratulations.

She smiled warmly at an older man who approached, nodding in response to something he said. Mac's attention shifted, along with Jewel's, to another man who was being introduced to her by the first, and his gaze narrowed.

No. It couldn't be…

The second man turned slightly, giving Mac a more direct view, and he felt his jaw clench instinctively as his suspicion was confirmed.

He was looking at none other than Prince Cameron Leandres.

Which led him to wonder—what the hell was his cousin doing in West Virginia? And, more importantly, did Cameron have any idea that Marcus was there? Because if he did, he could ruin everything.

Jewel let her groom lead Arianna back to the shedrow for a much-deserved rubdown and celebratory dinner while she turned her attention to Hugo DaCosta.

The older man was a former acquaintance of her father who had introduced himself to her earlier and expressed an interest in renewing a business relationship with CTC. Jewel had accepted his invitation to dinner in order to discuss the possibilities.

"I want you to meet a friend of mine," Hugo said to her now. "This is Prince Cameron Leandres of Tesoro del Mar."

"Nice to meet you." She offered her hand.

He caught her hand, but instead of shaking it, he brought it to his lips. "The pleasure is mine."

Though his charm seemed a little too practiced, he was good-looking. Not quite as tall as Mac, not quite as dark, and with eyes more hazel than brown—she broke off, appalled to realize she'd been comparing the two men, and forced her attention back to the one in front of her.

"Do you have an entry on the card?" she asked politely.

"No, I'm...observing today."

"And have you been impressed with what you've seen so far?"

He smiled as his eyes skimmed over her. "Very."

"Ms. Callahan owns and operates one of the finest training facilities in the state," DaCosta interjected.

"Some would say *the* finest," Jewel felt compelled to add.

DaCosta grinned. "And Cameron's family has one of the finest thoroughbred stables in his country."

"And I would argue that it is *the* finest," the prince told her. "Although Hugo has me thinking that I should invest in some quality racehorses in this country. Perhaps you could give me some advice."

There was something about the man, prince or not, that made her a little uneasy. But she was too savvy a business person to pass up such an opportunity. "And I'm guessing you would also need a local facility to board and train those horses."

"Of course," the prince agreed.

"Then you should come out to CTC and talk to Caleb Bryce," she suggested.

"I'd rather talk to you," he said.

"Excellent," DaCosta proclaimed. "You can discuss it over dinner."

* * *

Unfortunately there wasn't much of an opportunity to discuss business over dinner. The group that DaCosta had assembled numbered more than twenty, most of whom wanted only to talk about themselves and their personal successes. Even more unfortunately, Jewel found herself seated beside Prince Cameron, who demonstrated a fondness for personal contact. She managed to grit her teeth and tolerate it while it was just her shoulder or her arm that he was touching, but when his hand slipped beneath the tablecloth to her knee, her irritation threatened to overcome reason. Then his palm started to travel upward on her thigh.

Reaching beneath the table, she removed his hand from her thigh and held it up. "I believe this belongs to you," she told him.

He dropped his hand onto the back of her chair and leaned in to whisper in her ear. "I believe we're wasting our time here. Why don't we go back to my hotel room and continue our discussion in private?"

She pushed back her chair. "I really need to get back to the stables. If your interest in CTC is genuine, please feel free to stop by to visit the facilities."

The prince's gaze raked over her. "I'll do that."

Then he turned his attention, and his wandering hands, to the woman seated on his other side.

Jewel said a quick thank-you and goodbye to Hugo DaCosta before making her escape.

When she finally got home, she was tired but too wired to sleep. After a quick shower to scrub away the last remnants of the prince's groping touch, she went down to Haven and saddled up Daizy Mae. She hadn't realized how much she was looking forward to the possibility of seeing Mac until she felt her heart expand in her chest when she caught sight of him at the top of the hill.

She noted, with both surprise and amusement, that he'd chosen Medicine Man from the stable. The twenty-three-year-old stallion had little spark left in him and wasn't any kind of a challenge for an experienced rider like Mac. But like an elderly man trying to prove he was still useful, the old horse would trot or canter or gallop when prompted to do so.

"Interesting choice of mount," she noted.

He shrugged. "I figured they all needed a turn at some exercise."

"They do," she agreed, pleased that he'd recognized the fact. She was also pleased that he'd taken such an interest in Haven, even if she felt a slight twinge of guilt for the same reason. "I have to wonder—between your job at CTC and the extra hours you've been putting in at Haven—when do you find time to sleep?"

"Why don't you come up to my apartment after the horses are put to bed and find out?"

Coming so close on the heels of Cameron's crude invitation, she'd expected to be offended by his offer. But his words were without guile and his smile was easy, and she found herself smiling back.

"A tempting invitation," she assured him. "But I think I'll pass."

"An open invitation," he assured her, with another smile.

And though she realized she was probably missing out on what would undoubtedly be an incredible experience with Mac, she figured it was a fair trade for keeping her heart intact. She'd gotten to know him pretty well over the past few weeks and already started to care for him. If she let herself get any more personally involved, it could only lead to heartache when he left the farm. As he was planning to do when Grady returned.

Maybe she could convince him to stay a little longer—but for what purpose? He might be satisfied with his menial chores in the short-term, but they both knew he was destined for greater things. And she was destined to remain exactly where she was.

They rode together in silence for several minutes before Mac said, "I heard you had another confrontation with Anderson today."

"Good news travels fast."

"For what it's worth, he's an idiot."

She smiled. "He knew my dad for a lot of years and doesn't seem to accept that I do things differently than the infamous Jack Callahan did."

"Such as not run the business into the ground?"

Her head swiveled.

He shrugged. "People talk."

"I didn't think anyone knew," she said softly.

"The ones who do also know that you turned CTC around, and they respect and admire you for it."

"I'm…surprised," she admitted. "Spending so much time at the track lately, I've been hearing stories about my father. Listening to other people share their memories of him, contrasting their images with that of the man I knew."

"What do you remember differently?"

"Everything." She guided Daizy around a stand of trees toward the stream. "He did spend most of his weekends at the track, and not just checking on the horses we trained. He liked to gamble, and he liked to drink, and he liked women. And because he was good-looking and charismatic and didn't mind throwing his money around, the women liked him right back.

"Of course, none of them stuck around for very long. Not once they realized what a selfish sonofabitch he was, and more devoted to the gambling and drinking than he could ever be to any one woman."

"Even you?"

"Especially me. When he died—" She shook her head. "You wouldn't have believed the mess he left behind. It took more than two years after he was gone to straighten everything out, to put CTC firmly back in the black."

"And you tried to do it so that no one else knew," he mused. "Without asking anyone for help."

"In this business, reputation is more important than a lot of other things—I didn't want people speculating, clients worrying.

"I didn't build this place from the ground up, as Gabe Anderson likes to remind me my father did. But I built it back up, and only then, only when I knew the business was back on solid ground, did I start building the facilities for Haven."

"Did you ever consider doing something completely different?"

She shook her head as she dismounted to lead Daizy to the water to drink. Marcus followed her lead. "The horses have been my life for as long as I can remember. I never knew or wanted anything else. Except…"

"Except?" he prompted.

"There was a time when I thought about going to school to get a degree in animal husbandry and expand our breeding program."

"Why didn't you?"

She looked away. "It was made very clear to me that

breeding horses wasn't woman's work and that I was to choose a more appropriate occupation."

They were walking side by side in the moonlight, and he couldn't remember a staged scene that had ever felt more romantic. "But it's obvious that you love your horses."

"My father always said that a man who makes decisions based on emotion is a man who makes mistakes," she quoted.

"And he wouldn't consider an exception to that—even for his daughter?"

"Especially not for his daughter. It was bad enough that I had to be born female without compounding the mistake by acting like one."

The more he heard about Jack Callahan, the more Marcus was certain the man had been a sonofabitch. "I don't think I would have liked your father."

"I'm not sure many people did," she admitted. "But they admired and respected him."

"I admire you," he told her.

She managed a smile at that, and they walked a few more minutes in silence before she turned her head to study him in the moonlight.

"What about you?" she asked. "Are you doing what you want?"

He thought about his family, and about the responsibilities that were waiting for him back home. Responsibilities that he'd shirked for too long. Then he looked at Jewel, at the serious intensity in her stormy eyes, and there was no doubt about what he wanted.

"Right now—" he dipped his head toward her "—I'm doing exactly what I want."

And he settled his mouth over hers.

His hand moved up her back to cup her neck, his fingers sifting through her silky curls and tipping her head back to deepen the kiss. Her lips parted willingly for him, her tongue teased his. She was soft and warm and passionate, and he wanted her desperately.

"*Usted es tan hermoso, tan perfecto.*" He whispered the words against her lips.

"I have no idea what you just said, but it sure sounded beautiful."

"Not as beautiful as you," he told her.

She drew away slightly. "You're trying to seduce me, aren't you?"

"No," he denied. "I told you the next move would have to be yours."

"And are you a man of your word?"

"Always." But he brushed his lips over hers once more before he drew away. "And because I am a man of my word, I should see you back to the stables before I forget that's true."

They rode back and tended to the horses in silence. It was only when they were walking out of the barn together that she spoke again.

"That dinner party at Crystal and Simon's is next weekend."

Despite her deliberately casual tone, he sensed the nerves beneath her words, and it was those nerves that let him hope that she might be getting ready to make the next move.

"Are you asking me for a date?"

"I'm asking you to go with me to a dinner party at my sister's house. Crystal doesn't like to set thirteen places at a table so she asked me to bring a date." She sent him a mischievous grin. "I thought I'd invite you instead."

"Ouch." He pretended in wince in pain.

"Are you interested in a free meal?"

"Always," he assured her. "Can I kiss you good-night at the end of the evening?"

She considered his question before finally responding, "Maybe."

Marcus raised his brows. "Maybe?"

"We'll have to see how the evening goes."

"When?"

"Saturday night. Seven o'clock."

He was already looking forward to it.

Marcus enjoyed spending time with Jewel's sister. She was outgoing and fun—and a valuable ally in his battle to overcome Jewel's reservations about getting involved with him.

"Has she invited you to be her date for my dinner party yet?" Crystal asked, when she caught up with him at the stable Tuesday afternoon.

"Yes, although that's not quite how the invitation was issued."

"What do you mean?"

"She asked me to go," he admitted. "Because if she showed up alone, there would be thirteen at the table and that would be bad luck."

Crystal rolled her eyes. "If that's the explanation she gave for inviting you, I'm surprised you didn't turn her down."

He shrugged. "I figure dinner at your place means you're making dessert."

"Black Forest Cake," she promised.

"Mmm." He hummed his approval before asking, "Who else is going to be at this dinner party?"

"Mostly business associates of Simon's," she told him. "Several of whom have some connection to the thoroughbred industry—as most people living in Alliston do. And Hugo DaCosta, one of Simon's oldest and biggest clients, is bringing a friend—a prince, he claims."

Mac stilled. "A prince?"

Crystal nodded. "Yeah. From some obscure little country in the Mediterranean."

He nearly groaned. Knowing that Cameron was in West Virginia, there was no hope that Crystal's royal dinner guest was anyone other than his cousin. Which meant that he had to find a way to back out of his date with Jewel, because there was no way Cameron wouldn't blow his cover, and he wasn't nearly ready for Jewel to learn the truth of his identity. Not until he knew that the feelings she was starting to have for him were real and wouldn't be influenced by his title.

"Have you met this guy—this prince?" he asked casually.

"No, but Jewel did. He was at the race in Arlington with DaCosta last weekend." She grinned at him. "Why? Are you worried that my sister will fall head over heels for him just because of his title?"

"I'm sure it happens." He spread fresh bedding in the stall.

"I'm sure it does," she said. "But not with Jewel. In fact, she specifically asked not to be seated next to him at the table." She winked at him. "Which is when I told her that she would have to bring a date to ensure that didn't happen."

Marcus lifted another forkful of straw and wondered how he was now going to extricate himself from a situation he'd deliberately maneuvered himself into.

He'd told Jewel the next move would need to be hers, and she'd finally made it. Now he had to change those plans—and he had a feeling she wasn't going to appreciate that at all.

* * *

Jewel told herself it was ridiculous to feel nervous. This was a business dinner at her sister's house, not unlike other events she'd attended there in the past. Except that this was the first time she had a date, and she couldn't forget the warmth in Mac's eyes when he'd agreed to come with her tonight.

Still, there was a part of her that wondered if inviting him had been a mistake. They were moving toward something she wasn't sure she was ready for yet didn't seem to know how—or even want—to avoid.

Which was one of the reasons she'd opted to run some errands in town and meet him at the house, rather than arriving with him. She figured there would be fewer expectations if they didn't show up and leave together. Or maybe she was just a coward—afraid to face her feelings for Mac, afraid to go after what she really wanted. Because she really wanted Mac.

She looked around for his car, but didn't see it anywhere on the street or in the driveway. She hoped he wasn't running behind schedule. As nervous as she was about this date, she was even more uneasy about facing Prince Cameron again without Mac by her side.

She was almost at the door when her cell phone rang. She flipped it open, her eyes scanning the street for any sign of Mac arriving.

"Callahan," she answered.

"Jewel—I'm glad I caught you."

She frowned as she recognized Mac's voice. "Where are you?"

"That's why I'm calling," he said. "I'm sorry to do this at the last minute, but as it turns out, I'm not going to make it."

"What is it? Is there a problem at the stables? Do you need me to come back?"

"No, there's not a problem." There was a slight hesitation, as if he wasn't sure what to say to her. "I'm sorry."

"You call me as I'm walking into my sister's house to tell me you're sorry?"

"I'm having trouble hearing you, Jewel. I think the call's about to drop."

And she knew then, even before the line went dead, that he was going to hang up on her.

Chapter Nine

Jewel was still fuming when she drove home at the end of the evening.

Not only had Mac stood her up, but he'd lied to her.

The only good thing to transpire from the evening was that Prince Cameron had kept his hands to himself—although the fact that he was seated on the opposite side of the table might have had something to do with that—and agreed to come out to the farm to discuss with her *and* Caleb the training of a two-year-old he was in negotiations to buy. Her anger at Mac was pushed aside for a moment as she considered the possibility that the royal might choose CTC to train the promising colt he'd recently purchased. It would be a coup for the business—and a relief to her personally. If she had the sought-after chestnut colt in her stable, it wouldn't matter what Gabe Anderson chose to do with his horses.

But her focus—and her fury—swung right back to Mac Delgado when she pulled into the long, winding driveway toward home. She didn't care that he'd changed his mind about going to Crystal's dinner party, she just wished he'd had the decency to let her know five minutes *before* she was on the verge of walking into the door of her sister's house. And she absolutely wouldn't tolerate being lied to.

As angry as she was, she knew it would be smart to wait until morning to confront him, but her emotions were too churned to be rational. So she parked her truck beside the house and stormed across the yard to the apartments above the stables.

There was no response to her knock on his door, a fact which only fuelled her anger. Maybe he'd gotten a better offer—a chance for a "real" date and everything that might entail. Her stomach twisted at the thought. Of course, he had every right to go out, to date whoever he wanted. She had no claim on him, nor did she want one.

She was just furious—more at herself than Mac. She'd actually started to think she could trust him, which only proved that she was a fool. How many times did she have to be let down before she finally learned that there was no one she could count on?

She stormed back to the house and up to her room, where she kicked off her shoes and yanked her dress over her head. She tossed it toward the chair, not caring when it landed in a puddle of crimson silk on the floor. Then she tugged on a pair of jeans and T-shirt and headed back outside. If she couldn't kick Mac Delgado's ass, she could at least work off some of her bad mood down at the stables.

She went directly to Cayenne's stall. Jewel had been so busy with other responsibilities that the spirited stallion had been sorely neglected over the past few days, and with a prospective buyer in the wings, she couldn't allow that to happen.

It was Mac, she remembered now, who had directed Harold Emerson's attention to Cayenne. Mac who had made the man look beyond the horse's reputation to see his beauty and potential. She could acknowledge that fact and be grateful to him for it—but it didn't make her any less mad at him.

She came to an abrupt halt outside of Cayenne's stall. Cayenne's *empty* stall. She turned around, checking the stall across from his. Mystic stared back at her, head bobbing in acknowledgment of her presence. Jewel gave the aging mare an absent pat before she retraced her steps, checking every stall, as if someone might have simply misplaced a twelve-hundred-pound animal.

She then went outside to check the paddocks, hoping he'd just been forgotten outside. She would certainly reprimand the student who had been in charge of ensuring the animals were bedded down for the night, but so long as Cayenne was safe, there was no real harm done.

Except he wasn't in the paddock.

But from her vantage point behind the stable, she could see the lights on in the arena. She should have spotted them when she'd made her way to the Haven stable, but she'd been so preoccupied with her anger at Mac that she hadn't been paying attention to anything else.

She headed toward the arena, relief surging through her when she found that Cayenne was, in fact, inside. And so was Mac.

His back was to her, allowing her to approach without

being noticed, though he was so intently focused on the horse she wasn't sure he'd have seen her even if she was in his line of sight. The fury and frustration that had bubbled up inside her when she'd spotted him there were tempered now by curiosity and confusion. She didn't say anything, not just because she didn't want to break his concentration, but because she wanted to observe without Mac knowing she was there. So she folded her arms on the top of the boards and settled in to watch.

Judging by the sheen of the horse's coat and the perspiration that dampened the back of Mac's shirt, he'd had the stallion on the longe line for a while. But Cayenne appeared to be resisting all cues, and yet Mac persisted. He wasn't harsh but he was relentless, not mean but demanding. And through it all, he spoke to the stallion, using a firm but level tone to indicate he was the one in charge. Whether Cayenne finally accepted that fact or Mac simply wore him out, the horse stopped fighting and let Mac run him through some basic exercises.

As Jewel watched, the last of her anger and frustration drained away leaving other more complicated feelings in their wake. She shook her head, wondering how he managed to do this to her, how one man could pull so many conflicting emotions out of her.

She didn't like knowing that she had so little control over her own feelings where he was concerned. And she especially didn't like that she felt things for Mac she hadn't felt in a very long time, if ever before.

She watched the muscles in his arms bunch and flex, noted the way the thin, damp fabric of his T-shirt moulded to his lean, hard torso. As she watched, her throat got dry, her knees got weak and her heart pounded. And she realized it was desire that stirred inside her now—hot and insistent and undeniable.

He drew the horse close, rubbed a strong hand over its long neck as he spoke quietly to the animal. She couldn't hear his words, just the low timbre of his voice, a sound that apparently soothed the strong stallion even while it stirred her.

He turned to exit the arena, and halted abruptly when his gaze landed on Jewel.

"How long have you been here?" he asked her.

"A while," she said. "You've made some progress with him."

He shrugged. "I'm not sure it's enough."

She wasn't, either, but the only thing that mattered to her right now was that he'd made the effort—and that the horse was responding to him as he hadn't responded to anyone else.

She fell into step beside him as he walked Cayenne back to the stable. He kept his focus on the stallion, checking him for signs of heat when they got back to the stable, sponging him down to wash away the sweat and refresh him and examining his feet for stones. Only when the animal had been properly cared for and returned to his stall did Mac turn to her.

"I'm sorry for canceling at the last minute," he finally said.

"Is that why you're here? Is this supposed to be some kind of penance for standing me up?"

He shook his head as he washed up. "I'm here because I knew you couldn't be, because we only have five more weeks before Emerson's deadline and with every day that passes, I'm more certain it isn't enough time."

She wondered at his use of the term "we." They *had* been working together a lot at Haven and she knew he genuinely cared about the animals. But she'd thought he cared about her, too, as she was starting to care about him. She'd thought inviting him to the dinner party at her sister's house would show him that she was finally ready to acknowledge her growing attraction to him.

Either he hadn't understood the magnitude of that step for her, or it just hadn't mattered to him. Regardless, the mistake had been her own.

When would she learn? When would she realize the folly of opening up her heart to men who wanted no part of it?

She pushed aside her hurt and disappointment and said, "I appreciate your efforts."

"But you're still mad," he guessed.

"I was mad," she admitted. "Now I'm not entirely sure what I'm feeling."

He took a step closer and brushed his knuckles down her cheek. "Let me make it up to you."

The sincerity in his tone, the tenderness of the gesture, had her resolve weakening again. "There's no need."

"It's not about needing—" his hand dropped to her shoulder, then stroked down her arm from shoulder to wrist, and his fingers linked with hers "—but wanting."

He was holding her hand, but it was the desire in his eyes that held her spellbound. "Are we still talking about our date that didn't happen tonight?"

"The night's not over."

She swallowed. "But it's late."

"Not too late, I hope."

"Mac—"

"Why did you invite me to dinner tonight?"

She'd already told him why, though her explanation about the number of guests at the table hadn't been the real reason.

She could recite that same excuse now, or she could take a chance and tell him the truth. Except that she'd just finished berating herself for putting her heart on the line too many times in the past, and if she told him the truth now, wouldn't that just give him the power to hurt her again? Or would it give her the opportunity to experience something new and exciting, the possibility of which tempted her every time he was near?

"Because I've been thinking about you a lot lately. And not just in reference to the work you've been doing with the horses."

She saw the flicker of surprise in his eyes and knew he hadn't expected such a candid admission. They'd been dancing around the attraction for weeks now, and every time he'd taken a step forward, she'd taken two in retreat.

"I think about you all the time." His lips curved upward, just a little. "And rarely do my thoughts have anything to do with horses."

Her heart pounded harder, faster, urging her to forget about logic and reason and go after what she really wanted. "I've been thinking about sleeping with you."

It wasn't surprise that flickered in his eyes now, but desire that flared, searing her with intense heat that made her wonder how she had resisted him for so long—*why* she had resisted him for so long.

"How much longer till you get past the 'thinking' part?" he asked.

She took another step. She splayed her hands on his chest, and felt the thunderous beating of his heart beneath her palms. "About thirty seconds."

"Thirty seconds?"

Her hands slid upward to link behind his head.

"Give or take," she said, and pulled his mouth down to hers.

* * *

Mi Dios—the woman knew how to kiss. And like everything else Jewel did, she poured her heart and soul into it. He tasted her passion—and the promise of more. And the flavor—*her* flavor—was so tempting and intoxicating, it made him dizzy with wanting.

More. He murmured the word against her lips and drew her closer. She gave him more. More than he'd thought was possible from a kiss. And more than he had a right to take.

When he'd canceled their plans earlier, he'd known she would be annoyed, angry even, and he'd told himself it was for the best. He was only going to be in town a few more weeks, and though he'd never promised any woman more than that, he'd wished he could give her more. And it was the wishing that warned him he was already in too deep.

He couldn't risk falling in love. It wasn't something he'd ever worried about before, because he'd never met another woman who made him feel and want so much. In fact, he'd started to wonder if he was simply incapable of that emotion, if he might never fall in love. Then he'd met Jewel, and he'd been off balance ever since.

Which was exactly why he'd believed he'd done the right thing in canceling their date. There was no point in starting a relationship with Jewel when there could be no future for them together. Though he had no doubt that both of them would be extremely satisfied if he took her to his bed, doing so with so many secrets still between them would only end up hurting her in the end.

He didn't want to hurt her, though he knew he'd done so tonight. He couldn't tell her why he'd stood her up. He couldn't explain why he'd stayed away when he'd wanted nothing more than to be by her side. And even if he tried, he wasn't sure she'd believe him.

But as her lips parted and her body pressed closer, he realized she'd forgiven him. Or maybe it was just that, at the moment, she didn't care. As, at the moment, he was having trouble caring about anything but the willingness of the woman in his arms.

He'd wanted her from the first minute he set eyes on her, and with each day that he'd been at the farm, the wanting had grown. But what he'd accepted as a basic and primal desire— no different than what he'd felt for other women before—had somehow changed over the past few weeks. Into something deeper, dangerous.

She eased her lips from his, and when her eyes opened, they were dark and clouded with desire. "Come up to the house with me, Mac."

He was torn between taking what he wanted and doing what was right, between what he needed and what was wise. His body urged him to accept what she was offering before she had a change of heart, his mind warned him that it would be a mistake to let himself get involved any deeper, and his heart worried that she deserved more than he could ever give her.

"I've been working all day," he warned her.

"I know."

She was nearly a foot shorter than he, yet somehow she fit perfectly in his arms. She was warm and soft and fragrant—and he was hot and smelled like horses, if not worse. "I'm sweaty."

She nipped at his bottom lip, tugging playfully on it with her teeth. Blood pounded through his veins, in his head, blocking out all thought and reason.

"I'm hoping we'll both be even sweatier before we're done," she told him.

It would take a stronger man than he to resist a woman he'd wanted so much and for so long, and he gave up the pretense of even trying. "I'll race you to the house."

She pulled out of his arms and took off running. He chased after her, letting her keep the lead until they were almost at the back porch, then he caught her around the waist and pulled her back against him.

"Not a bad effort—for a girl," he teased.

She tilted her head back, her eyes narrowed. "I would think, at least right now, you would appreciate the fact that I'm female."

"Believe me—" he brushed his lips over hers "—I'm appreciative."

She pushed open the door and led him inside.

"Bedroom?" he asked.

"Upstairs." She reached for his hand, but he reached for her, scooping her into his arms.

Jewel let out a breathless laugh as he took the stairs two at a time. "I really love a strong man."

"And I love a willing woman," he said, tumbling onto the bed with her.

She gloried in the weight of his hard body against hers, the thrill of those talented hands moving over her, the pleasure of his avid mouth sampling hers.

Her mind blurred, her body yearned. She was more than ready to stop thinking and start doing.

But while she was eager to move things along, Mac seemed determined to draw out the experience, savor the moment.

He spoke softly to her. There was more than the hint of a

Spanish accent now—he was speaking fluently in the language, a fact that might have puzzled her if she wasn't so aroused. She could barely hear the words, never mind understand them, yet the sensual tone sent shivers of anticipation dancing over her skin. She hadn't expected romance, didn't need seduction. But with every pass of his hands, every brush of his lips, he patiently and thoroughly seduced not just her body but her heart and her soul.

"Mac." His name was a whisper, a plea, though she wasn't entirely sure what she was asking of him.

But he was, and while he still didn't rush, he did—finally—strip away their clothes. First hers, then his own. Then they were naked together, and the heat of his skin against hers, all those wonderfully taut muscles at her fingertips, was almost more than she could stand.

She moaned in sensual pleasure as his tongue slipped into her mouth, and she instinctively arched against him, silently pleading for a more intimate penetration.

But he only continued to kiss her, deeply, thoroughly, endlessly. She responded to his kiss, learning the shape of his lips, exploring the texture of his mouth, savoring the flavor that was uniquely Mac. Though her experience was admittedly limited—and no doubt a lot more limited than his—she'd long accepted that kissing was a means to an end as far as the male gender was concerned. A starting point on the road to seduction, the enjoyment of which was forgotten in the push toward the finish as soon as clothes were shed.

But here they were, their naked bodies tangled together, and still Mac only kissed her.

And then he touched her.

Light, gentle strokes of his hands.

Lazy, tantalizing caresses.

As if he wasn't just discovering, but memorizing every dip and curve of her body. The palms of his hands weren't smooth anymore, and the scrape of the rough skin against her sensitive flesh was deliciously erotic. With each pass of his hands, the pleasure and anticipation built inside of her until she was quivering with need.

After what seemed like an eternity, his mouth moved away from hers, his lips trailing across her cheek to nibble on her earlobe, then nuzzle the tender skin beneath. She shivered and moaned, and his mouth skimmed down her throat, over the curve of one breast. His tongue swirled around the crest in a sensual journey that slowly meandered closer to the tight bud. He touched his tongue to her nipple, a gentle lick, a leisurely nibble. Then his lips closed over the aching peak, and she closed her eyes and bit down on her bottom lip to keep from crying out as he suckled and tugged. Sparks of fiery pleasure shot through her, accelerating the flames of a heated passion that was already burning out of control.

She wasn't sure she'd ever known such an intensity of need or experienced such a raging storm of desire. It was as if nothing existed outside of the moment, as if nothing else mattered.

"Mac," she said again.

He responded by shifting his focus to her other breast, giving it the same delicious attention and driving her closer and closer to the edge.

She wanted him—desperately. But she didn't want this seductive exploration to end. She wanted to discover every inch of him, with her hands, her lips, her body.

His mouth was moving lower now, simultaneously enticing

and tormenting. Her hands slipped from his shoulders, her fingers curling into the bedspread beneath her back as he continued to tease and tantalize every part of her body. His lips caressed her belly, his tongue dipped into her navel, his teeth grazed her hip. She trembled—with anticipation, desire, need.

He lifted her hips off the mattress and zeroed in on the ultrasensitive spot at the apex of her thighs, and she cried out in shocked pleasure as he drove her to the edge of oblivion and beyond.

Her body was still trembling with the aftershocks when he finally rose over her. His body pressed down on her, into her. He groaned; she gasped. He more than filled her—he fulfilled her.

She moved with him slowly at first, then fast, faster. Her hands cupped his taut buttocks, her hips arched to take him deeper and her legs wrapped around him. His mouth covered hers, swallowing her sighs and moans as their bodies mated and merged, moving toward the ultimate pinnacle of pleasure, and finally leaping over the edge together.

Marcus had thought about making love with Jewel, but whatever fantasies his mind had conjured up didn't even begin to compare to the reality. Had he ever known a woman who gave so much? Who was so openly passionate? Or who made him want so much that even now, when their bodies were still joined together after lovemaking, he wanted her again?

He disentangled himself from her warm embrace and went to the bathroom to dispense with the condom. When he returned, she hadn't moved a single muscle. Her body was naked, her eyes were closed, her lips were curved.

She looked sated and sensual and just looking at her had his body stirring to life again.

He grabbed another condom before he slid into bed beside her again. Propping himself up on an elbow, he gently brushed her hair from her cheek.

Her eyelids fluttered, opened.

"I've wanted this," he told her, "wanted you just like this, from the very first time I saw you."

She smiled. "And I worried, from the beginning, that getting involved with you would be a bad idea."

"Are you sorry?"

"No." She pulled his head down to kiss him again. "I'm not sorry."

"Good." He lifted himself over her again, slid into her slick heat, and swallowed her gasp of shocked pleasure.

The first coupling had taken the sharpest edge off of his need for her, this time, he was determined to show her a little more patience, a little more finesse, a lot more pleasure.

Chapter Ten

Jewel woke up alone.

She was more relieved than surprised by the realization because she wasn't sure what she would have said or done if she'd found Mac beside her this morning. While she wouldn't go so far as to say it had been a mistake to take him to her bed—how could she possibly regret something that had been so incredible?—it had definitely been an impulse, and Jewel wasn't usually the type of woman to act on impulse.

Of course, now she couldn't help but wonder why he'd gone. Because he didn't want anyone to see him sneaking out of her house in the early light of morning? Or because he'd got what he'd wanted and he was finished with her?

No, she didn't believe that. She wouldn't believe it. Not after the incredible night they'd spent together.

And yet, despite the intimacies they'd shared, she was

aware that there was still so much she didn't know about him. Too much she didn't know.

This thought plagued her as she showered and dressed and went through the motions of her day. She didn't see Mac at all, though she found him at the center of her thoughts far more than he should be.

It was late and she was doing a final check on all of the horses at Haven when he came into the barn. Her heart did that now-familiar skip and jump, and the heat in his eyes when he looked at her was enough to have her flushing from the roots of her hair to the tip of her toes.

"Is everyone else gone?" he asked her.

She nodded.

"Good," he said, and pulled her into his arms for a long kiss. "I've been thinking about doing that all day."

"Kissing me?"

He smiled as his hands slid up her back, drawing her closer. "For starters."

They went up to the house together and made love again, slowly and very thoroughly. And when their bodies were finally sated, he kissed her again. There was more than passion in his kiss this time. More than she'd expected—more than she was ready for. She'd decided that she would have an affair with him—there really didn't seem to be any way to avoid it at this point. But she hadn't wanted any more than that.

"I'm thirty-four years old," she said.

His lips curved and he brushed them over hers. "You really have to get over this age thing."

"I am. Mostly."

She couldn't speak to him of the feelings that were in her heart. It would serve no purpose to admit that she was on the verge of falling in love with him. He would be gone in a few weeks and she would go on without him. But she would always be grateful to him for the memories he'd given her, and she wanted him to know that.

"I wasn't pointing out the fact that I'm older than you," she continued, "but that in my entire life, no one has ever made me feel the way you do."

"Nadie ha significado tanto a mí como usted."

"You know it drives me crazy when you speak Spanish."

"Usted me hace loco con el deseo."

She looped her arms around his neck and drew his head back down to nibble on his lips. "I warned you."

He grinned. "Are you going to punish me now?"

She pushed him onto his back and rose over him. "You have no idea."

Visitors to CTC weren't uncommon. Jack Callahan was proud of the facility he'd built and had implemented an open-door policy to show it off. Jewel had never seen any reason to change that, although her staff sometimes grumbled about the inconvenience of having to give impromptu tours. But while visitors in general weren't rare, female visitors wandering around on their own were. The woman she spotted by the paddock with Mac early Tuesday afternoon was clearly solo, undeniably gorgeous and definitely flirting with him.

Jewel paused in the shade of the barn and watched as the woman leaned closer to Mac, putting her hand on his forearm as she spoke to him. Mac smiled in response to whatever was said, then whistled for the chestnut filly, who trotted over to the fence.

The woman's glossy, painted lips curved wide and she took her hand off of Mac's arm to touch Ruby's nose.

Jewel felt a twist in her stomach. She couldn't deny the surge of annoyance that rose up in her, but she refused to dwell on it. She might have let Mac Delgado into her bed, but regardless of her ever-growing feelings for him, she had no illusions that they were involved in anything but a temporary and strictly physical relationship. She had no claim on him, and she wasn't going to start acting proprietary and jealous just because they were sleeping together.

But she noted with satisfaction that he stepped away from the other woman, deliberately putting the horse between them. Or maybe it only seemed deliberate to Jewel, because she wanted to believe he wasn't interested in anyone but her.

As she walked past the paddock, his head turned toward her. When he smiled, she felt the now-familiar but still-frustrating slow and liquid yearning spread through her veins. She'd thought the intensity of the attraction would start to fade—had, in fact, counted on it. But after almost two weeks of making love with him every night, it still only took a glance or a smile and shivers of anticipation danced over her skin.

It was undeniably exciting—and a little scary. Over the past few years, she'd been so focused on CTC and Haven that she'd had neither the time nor the interest in anything else. She hadn't wanted or needed any personal involvements.

Then, suddenly, Mac was there, and she found that she enjoyed his companionship too much. She liked talking to him, riding with him, just being with him. But what worried her was that she was starting to count on him being there, because she knew that he wasn't going to hang around indefinitely.

Despite the way his smile melted everything inside of her,

she was tempted to keep going, to prove that she could. But he waved her over, and she found herself moving toward him, wondering if it was already too late for her to walk away.

"...you should talk to Ms. Callahan," Mac was saying. Then to Jewel he said, "Ms. Spring has some horses in Texas that she's interested in moving up this way."

Jewel would bet that wasn't all the woman was interested in, but she forced a smile and offered her hand, noting the glint of rings and painted nails on the other woman's slender fingers.

"J.C. Callahan," she said. "And I promise, you won't find a better facility than ours anywhere in the state."

"J.C.?" The woman's exotic violet-colored eyes widened. "Oh, my goodness. It *is* you."

Now Jewel felt at even more of a disadvantage because, aside from Mac's reference to her as "Ms. Spring," she had no memory of having met her before.

"It's Natasha," she continued. "Formerly Natasha Kenesky. I grew up down the street—you used to babysit me."

The name clicked, and Jewel worked to keep her smile in place as she nodded. She remembered now, though the memory she had of nine-year-old "Nat" with pigtails and scraped knees bore little resemblance to the stunning beauty before her now. She was dressed casually for a visit to the farm, but her slim-fitting jeans and scoop-necked T-shirt bore designer labels.

"It's been a long time," Jewel said inanely.

Natasha laughed. "Almost twenty years. We moved away when Daddy got transferred to Houston for business. I always wanted to come back to Alliston, but I married a Texan who hated to travel. So after the divorce, I decided to make the move on my own.

"Now it's just me and the horses." Her voice dropped a notch, though not so much that Mac wouldn't clearly be able to hear every word she spoke. "I never guessed how lonely a big house would feel with no one to share it."

"You should get a puppy," Jewel suggested. "The local shelter has lots of dogs who need a good home."

Natasha laughed again. "Maybe I will, once I'm more settled. At the moment, I'm looking to make arrangements for my thoroughbreds."

"Who's training your horses?"

"They were working with Duane Watters in Texas. He gave me a couple of names, Caleb Bryce and Evan Horton. I want to meet with both of them before I decide."

"I imagine Evan's at the track today, prepping for the race tomorrow, as Caleb is," Jewel told her. "But you're welcome to check out the facilities while you're here."

"That would be good," Natasha said.

"Why don't you give her a tour, Mac?" Jewel said.

Natasha turned her attention and her megawatt smile on the man next to her again. "That would be even better."

The look he shot Jewel was both puzzled and wary, but he didn't protest the offer she'd made on his behalf.

"It was nice seeing you again, Nat," Jewel said, then continued on her way to the Haven barn.

Marcus knew women, and he knew without a doubt that Jewel was ticked about something. Actually he had a strong suspicion that it was some*one* rather than something—a suspicion that was strengthened when Natasha Spring sidled closer.

He dragged his attention away from the subtle sway of Jewel's hips to focus on the woman she had left in his charge.

"Have you worked here a long time?" she asked him.

"A couple of months," he said. "But I can honestly tell you that I've never worked anywhere else like this."

"I heard Gabe Anderson has his horses trained here."

"He does." Marcus turned to her. "Is he a friend of yours?"

She wrinkled her nose. "He's a self-important windbag, but he knows horses."

It would be completely inappropriate for Mac to agree with her derogatory comment about one of the farm's biggest clients, but he was impressed with her perception. Her obvious flirtation aside, she seemed to be an intelligent and savvy woman.

This opinion was further enforced by her comments and questions as he guided her around the facilities. She wasn't a discarded trophy wife who got the horses as part of her divorce settlement, but a woman who truly admired and cared for her animals and was determined to ensure they had the best housing and training.

While he went through the motions with Natasha, his mind kept drifting. He'd never objected to the company of a beautiful woman, nor had he ever had difficulty focusing on the woman in his company. But as he walked and talked with Natasha, it was Jewel who was on his mind. Jewel who was always on his mind these days.

He'd been attracted to other women, even infatuated with some of them. But never had any other woman captivated him so completely. Never had any other woman been the first thought in his mind in the morning and the last before he fell asleep at night. Never had he known another woman who made him want her all over again even while their bodies were still linked together after lovemaking. Never had another woman made him think of the physical act in terms of making love.

"She's a lucky lady," Natasha said softly.

Marcus started.

She smiled.

"Do you think I haven't noticed how your gaze keeps drifting toward the barn?"

"I'm sorry if I've seemed distracted—"

"*Distracted* isn't the word I would have used." The teasing light in her eyes dimmed just a little. "My husband used to look at me like that—as if I lit up the room just by walking into it."

"I'm sure you do," he told her.

She smiled again. "It's a little late to try charming me—I've seen where your interest lies."

"Have you seen the tack room?" he asked, steering her in that direction.

"I believe that was at the beginning of the tour, which means I've kept you from—" she paused significantly "—other things…long enough."

"I hope we'll see you back here again."

"You can count on it." She offered her hand. "Thank you for your time."

"It was a pleasure," he assured her.

She started to turn, then glanced back at him. "Can I give you some unsolicited advice?"

"Sure, but I won't promise to take it."

"Make sure she knows how you feel about her, Mac. Don't keep her guessing." Then, with a last smile and a wave, she was gone.

Mac watched her go, thinking about what she'd said, and wondering how he was supposed to share his feelings with Jewel when he wasn't even certain what they were anymore.

There was no doubt that his emotions were a lot deeper

than he'd anticipated, stronger than he'd wanted, more intense than anything else he'd ever known. But even if this was love, there was nothing to be gained by telling Jewel what was in his heart. Nothing that could be changed. She had hired him on for three months, and he had to be back home shortly after that. The celebrations for the four-hundredth anniversary of Tesorian independence were already underway and the whole royal family was expected to be in attendance. Even if he forgot about his other plans and opted to stay in West Virginia for a couple more weeks, it would only delay the inevitability of their parting, making it that much harder to leave her behind when he went back to his life in Tesoro del Mar.

No, there was no reason to change anything—and plenty of reasons to take advantage of every minute they had together now.

Nearly two hours passed between the time Jewel left Mac with Natasha until he came down to the Haven stable.

Jewel had just finished a workout with Cayenne and she was concerned about the animal's inconsistent behavior. It seemed he would take instruction when he was in the mood, but his moods were fickle, and Jewel knew that she had to find a way to change that if she was going to convince Harold Emerson to take him home.

She was toweling off the stallion when Mac came into the barn. He didn't say anything at first and she hadn't heard his steps, but the air was suddenly charged with an electricity that alerted her to his presence. The awareness between them had been almost tangible from the beginning, and was heightened rather than diminished by their intimacy.

"What did Ms. Spring think of the facilities?" She kept her tone casual and light, her focus on Cayenne.

"She was impressed." He picked up a brush and began making circular strokes over the stallion's flank. "She wants to meet with Caleb, of course, but I think she'll want to bring them here."

"I've no doubt she will," Jewel said, not quite able to mask her irritation this time. Frustrated with him, angrier with herself, she moved to the feed room to ready the evening meals for the animals.

"Why are you mad at me?" he asked.

She took her time measuring out grain. "I'm not mad."

"You don't sound not mad," he noted.

"I'm...annoyed."

"Why?"

"Only a man would need to ask such a question," she muttered.

"I am a man," he reminded her unnecessarily.

Yeah, she was well aware of that. As, she thought irritably, was any living, breathing female within a ten-mile radius. "She was flirting with you."

His brows drew together, though, to his credit, he didn't deny it. "That's right—*she* was flirting with *me*."

Jewel said nothing else as she worked her way from one stall to the next, automatically adding the required supplements to each animal's feed. Mac put Cayenne back in his stall and worked along with her, filling the water buckets. They'd established an easy rhythm of working together over the past several weeks, and only now did she realize how much help he'd been, how much she'd come to rely on him. And that worried her.

It was already the end of June—Grady's cast would be off in a few weeks and he'd be ready to return to work shortly after that. Mac had agreed to stay on until Grady came back, but she had no idea what his plans were beyond that. He had a life somewhere, she was sure of it. A future that involved some kind of corporate job with a big desk in a corner office, a secretary to manage his schedule and a girlfriend whose attention would be focused solely on him.

So why was he here? Why was he with her when he could be with someone unburdened by so many obligations and responsibilities? Someone younger and beautiful. Someone like Natasha.

She scowled at the thought as she shoved the scoop back into the bag. "I used to babysit her."

Mac put away the hose and wiped his hands. "She mentioned that. So what?"

"Let's just say it was a wake-up call."

"I'm sure there's a logical thought progression somewhere in your brain, but I'm not following it."

"She's older than you are."

"I'm still not following."

She shook her head at his stubborn refusal to see what was so glaringly obvious to her. "I used to babysit a woman who is now older than the man I'm currently sleeping with, which made me realize that if you had lived in the area as a kid, I might have been your babysitter, too."

He frowned at that. "It's back to the age thing again, isn't it?"

"Now you get it."

"What I get is that you're making a big deal out of something that shouldn't be."

"I graduated high school before you'd even started."

"How is that in any way relevant to what's happening between us now?"

She couldn't believe he couldn't see it. Or maybe he really didn't care because he was getting exactly what he wanted out of their relationship. "It highlights—at least for me—the fact that we're at different stages in our lives, that we want different things."

He slid his arms around her waist and drew her back against him, then dipped his head to kiss her neck, touching his lips to the ultrasensitive spot he'd discovered the first time they'd made love, and she couldn't help but shiver in response.

"I think our wants have meshed pretty well," he said, his breath warm on her ear.

She wouldn't let herself melt. She couldn't. But her voice wasn't quite steady when she responded. "Sex just clouds the issue."

His hands slid over her hips and down her thighs, caressing her through the denim. "Let's cloud the issue."

Those wickedly talented hands moved upward again, tracing her curves, skimming the sides of her breasts, stoking the fire that burned within her until she was aware of nothing but him, wanted nothing but him.

"How do you do this to me?" she wondered aloud.

His tongue traced the outline of her ear, his teeth tugged at the lobe. "Do what?" he whispered the question, the warmth of his breath making her shiver.

"Make me want so much," she whispered her response.

"What do you want, Jewel?"

She turned and lifted her arms to link them around his neck. "You."

"Well, that's handy," he said against her mouth. "Because I want you, too."

Her lips responded eagerly to his kiss. Her body yielded to

his. And her heart trembled, teetering for just a moment on the edge of something that was both tempting and terrifying before she yanked it back. She would gladly give herself over to the passion he evoked, willingly share the joys of making love with him, but she wouldn't let herself fall in love. Not again.

His lips moved across her jaw, down her throat. He nuzzled between her breasts, the coarse stubble of his unshaven jaw scraped against her tender skin and shot delicious arrows of excitement and anticipation zinging through her system.

"We can't do this." It was a weak protest at best, and they both knew it.

His gaze caught and held hers as his thumbs traced circles around the nipples straining against her bra. Her breath caught in her throat, his lips curved.

"I'm pretty sure we can," he told her.

His thumbs brushed over the turgid peaks and she had to bite down on her lip to hold back the moan as her brain completely short-circuited.

"Okay," she breathlessly relented. "But we can't do this here."

His lips cruised over hers again, savoring, seducing. "Let's go up to the house."

"Too far away," she said.

He lifted a brow. "You have a better idea?"

She just smiled and took his hand.

Chapter Eleven

Marcus stroked a hand over Jewel's hair, his fingers threading through those glorious silky curls that spilled down her back. And what a nice back it was, too—long and pale, soft skin over taut muscle. And then there was the delicious curve of her butt, and the endlessly long shapely legs.

He felt his body stirring and gave himself a mental shake. He'd only just had her and he wanted her again. But his desire for her more than just physical, and if he let himself think about that too deeply, it might worry him. For now, he wasn't thinking—he was just enjoying the moment, savoring the sensation of her warm, naked body draped over his, the synchronicity of her heart beating in rhythm with his.

He'd never felt this kind of connection, this sense of rightness, with another woman. When he was with Jewel, there wasn't anywhere else in the world that he wanted to be.

Make sure she knows how you feel about her...don't keep her guessing.

Natasha's words nudged at the back of his mind. It was good advice, except that he wasn't entirely sure how to label what he was feeling.

Was this feeling of contentment and completion love?

How could he know when he'd never been in love before. Or maybe it was more accurate to say that he'd never let himself be in love. He'd always kept his relationships brief, ending his affairs long before either he or the woman concerned could start to think that it would turn into anything more.

He'd already been with Jewel longer than he'd been with any other woman, and still, he wasn't nearly ready to let her go. He wasn't sure he ever would be.

Of course, what he wanted wasn't really the issue. He was due back in Tesoro del Mar by the end of July to take part in the Independence Celebrations, and his participation in the scheduled events was a privilege as much as an obligation. But that meant he only had five weeks left to figure out what was happening with Jewel—and maybe convince her to visit his home with him.

As confused as he was about his own feelings, he was completely clueless about hers.

He knew the age difference bothered her, though he didn't understand why it should. Why did it matter that she was eight years older than he when there was such powerful chemistry between them?

But whether it was because of the age gap or for some other reason, it was obvious to Marcus that she was holding something back, and he didn't know how to break through the barriers she'd erected around her heart.

Even now, he had no idea what was going through her mind, though he was sure he could hear the gears turning.

"You're thinking again, aren't you?"

"Just about the fact that we actually did it in the hayloft." She shook her head, though the hint of a smile tugged at the corners of her mouth. "I haven't done this since I was seventeen—and even then, it wasn't anything like this."

He brushed a strand of hair from her cheek, then let his finger trace over her skin, following the curve of her jaw, the line of her throat. He loved touching her—the softness of her skin, the way her breath hitched and her eyes darkened.

"I haven't ever done anything like this before," he confided.

"Really?"

"Why does that surprise you?"

She shrugged. "I just figured you were a man who had been everywhere and done everything."

He frowned at the deliberately casual tone. "You don't think very much of me, do you?"

"Sometimes, I find myself thinking about you far more than I should," she said lightly.

"That's not what I meant, and you know it."

"Mac—"

"What I know is that you don't seem to mind sleeping with me so long as no one knows we're sleeping together."

She pushed herself up and reached for her shirt. "I just don't like the details of my personal life being subject to public scrutiny."

"Is that the real reason?" he demanded. "Or is it that you're ashamed of our relationship?"

"I'm not ashamed of our relationship—I'm just not entirely sure what our relationship is."

"Why can't we figure that out together?"

"You want me to be honest, Mac? The truth is—I don't trust that you'll stick around long enough to figure anything out."

"That's blunt enough," he said.

"Are you surprised?" She fumbled with the buttons on her shirt. "How can I trust you when you deliberately hold back from me? Anytime I try to talk to you about your family or your life outside of this farm, you sidetrack the conversation. Oh, you're good at it," she said. "So good that it took me a while to even realize you do it, but there's no doubt that you do.

"You want my heart and soul—and what have you given me, Mac? I don't know how you happened to show up at the café the day I was there, why you were even in town. I was so grateful you were there to help Scarlett birth her foal that I ignored my own questions and concerns. But you've been here almost two months now, and I still don't know anything about you. You haven't let me know anything about you."

"You're right," he said quietly, and noted that the confession had surprised her. "There are parts of my life that I didn't want put on display, but I wasn't intentionally hiding them from *you*."

"If not me, then from who?"

"Everyone else."

She sighed. "That's another one of those responses that seems to answer the question but doesn't really give anything away."

He tugged his shirt over his head. "My name isn't Mac."

She was reaching for her jeans when he spoke, and her hand dropped away. She looked up at him with questions and hurt and confusion swirling in the depths of her stormy eyes. "I thought that part, at least, was true."

"My real name is Marcus Andrew Charles," he said. "Hence Mac."

"Hence?" She shook her head. "I don't think I've ever known anyone else to actually use that word in a sentence. On the other hand, Marcus sounds a lot more Harvard than Mac." Her gaze narrowed. "You did go to Harvard, didn't you?"

He nodded, then, when it was apparent she was waiting for him to expand on that response, he added, "Law School."

"Oh." She blew out a breath. "Where did you get the business degree?"

"Management Studies at Cambridge."

"An internationally educated lawyer and a barrel-racer-turned-horse-trainer—talk about odd couples."

He wanted to tell her more—to tell her everything—but he wasn't sure she was ready to hear it, and he wasn't ready to lose her if she decided a relationship with a prince was more than she was ready to handle. So he only asked, "Why is that so odd?"

She shook her head. "I actually thought I was falling in love with you, Mac. But how can I love a man I don't even know?"

Four days after her argument with Mac—*Marcus*—Jewel was still feeling hurt and confused, still trying to figure out why a Harvard law graduate was mucking out her stalls and sleeping in her bed.

And yes, he was still sleeping in her bed, because everything else aside, she couldn't deny the connection between them was real. And if he was only going to be at CTC for a few more weeks, as they'd agreed from the beginning, she wasn't going to waste a single moment of that time. She also wasn't going to delude herself into thinking their relationship was anything more than purely physical and strictly temporary.

A knock at the door helped her push these thoughts from her mind, though the automatic smile she'd put on her face froze in place when she recognized the woman standing in the doorway. The last person Jewel wanted or expected to see in her office Friday morning was Natasha Spring.

"I just met with Caleb," Natasha said to Jewel. "And I have to say, I was really impressed with his ideas and philosophies. Of course, he wants to see my horses before he'll discuss the possibility of working them into his training schedule."

"That sounds like Caleb," Jewel agreed.

"So if it's all right with you, I'd like to make arrangements to have them sent up here, to be boarded and trained at CTC."

"How many horses are we talking?"

"Half a dozen."

Jewel nodded. "That would be fine."

In fact, it would be more than fine. It would help fill some of the stalls that would be left vacant when Gabe Anderson pulled his animals out, as she knew he was on the verge of doing.

"Great." Natasha's smile was wide and friendly. "There was something else I wanted to talk to you about, if you've got another minute."

"Sure. What is it?"

"Haven," the other woman said. "I have a lot of free time these days, and I was hoping I could spend some of it helping out at Haven."

"I can always use more help." And with the date of the annual charity auction coming up fast, she could use a lot of extra hands, but as she glanced at Natasha's perfectly manicured nails, she wasn't sure they were the right kind.

"But?" Nat prompted, sensing Jewel's hesitation.

"But I can't help wondering if you really want to help with the horses or you just want to hang around here to get to know Mac better."

"I really want to help out with the horses," Natasha said. "Considering my track record with men, I've decided to concentrate my attention on the horses for a while. Besides, as easy as Mac is on the eyes, I got the distinct impression that he only has eyes for you, and I would never poach on a friend."

"I have trouble reconciling the gap-toothed child I knew with the woman you are now," Jewel admitted.

"Does that mean we can't be friends?"

"No." Jewel stood up and offered her hand. "Welcome to Haven."

Over the next couple of weeks, Mac spent every free moment he had with Jewel, conscious of how little time they had left. Grady had stopped by the farm the day before, to show Jewel that he was mobile again and remind her of his imminent return to work. And when Grady came back, there would be no reason for Mac to stay.

No reason except Jewel, and as much as he wanted to stay with her, to be with her, he had his own responsibilities and obligations. Marcus was expected to be back in Tesoro del Mar along with the rest of the royal family for the independence festivities. And he wanted to be there—he just wished he could take Jewel with him.

There had been so many times over the past couple of weeks that he'd thought about telling her the truth about who he was, and each time, something had held him back. So many women had wanted to date him because of who he was—as if it was some kind of coup to be seen on the arm of a prince. He didn't think Jewel was the type of woman to care that he was royalty, but he was certain she wouldn't be pleased y his deception. And it was this certainty that made the truth tick in his throat whenever he tried to tell her.

Tonight, he resolved that he would find a way—until he saw the look of abject misery on her face.

He coaxed her to take a walk, and they ended up down by the stream. It was a beautiful summer night, warm and clear, and they sat on the bank of the creek. Jewel was cradled between his knees, her back against his front, his arms around her.

"Gabe Anderson gave me his notice today," she told him.

"I'm sorry."

"I thought I would be, too," she said. "In a lot of ways, though, I think it's probably for the best."

"It probably is," he agreed. "But I bet you still feel as if there was something you could or should have done to convince him to stay."

"He was angry that I backed Caleb's decision to scratch After Midnight from a race. I couldn't have done any differently. But you're right, I do wonder if I might have handled it better.

"It's a little overwhelming at times," she admitted. "Knowing that there are so many people—owners and employees—who are depending on me."

"Not to mention the horses," Mac added.

She smiled. "Though they're usually not as vocal in their displeasure."

"You're doing great work here—both with CTC and Haven."

"Cayenne is still balking at being handled by strangers."

He tightened his arms around her. "We still have a week."

She sighed as she leaned into his embrace. "Why does it seem there are never enough hours in a day?"

"Because you try to do too much for everyone," he told her.

"I just do my job," she insisted.

"Still, I wish I could take you away from here—for a day, a week, a month."

She smiled at the thought. "Where would we go?"

He pretended to consider the question for a minute before he said, "An island somewhere, where the sand is soft and white, the sky is clear and blue, and the waves lap gently against the shore." He felt a pang when he thought of it—both a longing for home and regret that his time here was marching inevitably toward its end.

She tipped her head back against his shoulder, oblivious to his thoughts, unaware of the realities of his life. "That sounds heavenly."

But of course she thought he was only spinning an elaborate fantasy for her. She had no idea that he could really give her everything he was offering—and more. And he was surprised by how very much he wanted to give her everything.

Was this love?

The question had been nagging at the back of his mind for weeks now, though he was still uncertain of the answer. And if he did love her, could he be lucky enough to find that she loved him, too? Maybe even enough to forgive him his deceptions.

"Let's do it," he said.

"Do what?"

He chuckled. "Go away together. There's an island in the Mediterranean—Tesoro del Mar. The name means treasure of the sea and I can honestly say I've never been to anyplace more beautiful."

"Tesoro del Mar," she echoed. "It does sound beautiful. And vaguely familiar." She frowned, as if trying to remember where she'd heard the name before.

"I'd love to take you there," Marcus continued.

"You're serious?"

"Absolutely," he assured her.

She sighed wistfully. "Oh, Mac. It sounds incredible, but have responsibilities here that I can't just walk away from n a whim."

"You also have excellent staff who are more than capable f taking care of all the details if you wanted a break."

"I know they're capable," she agreed. "But I'm still the one vho's ultimately responsible. I can't just run off into the unset because it's what you want."

"What do you think I'm asking of you—a vacation on the each with lots of sun and sand and sex?"

"Isn't that exactly what you were asking?"

"Imbécil," he muttered.

She turned to glare at him. "I don't need to speak Spanish o understand *that.*"

He took her in his arms and pressed a brief, hard kiss to her ips. *"¿Cómo puede usted ser tan inteligente sobre tan muchas osas y tan estúpido sobre mis sensaciones para usted?"*

Her brow furrowed. "Okay, that one I don't have the first lue about."

"You don't have the first clue about a lot of things."

"Meaning?"

He raked a hand through his hair, frustrated that she was naking this so difficult and he was bungling it so badly. Tesoro del Mar is my home," he finally said to her. "I'm sking you to come home with me."

Her eyes widened. "Oh."

He managed a smile. "I've never asked another woman to ee where I come from, to meet my family."

"Oh," she said again.

"I have to go back at the end of the month, I'd like you to go with me."

"There's so much going on around here right now with planning for the auction and—"

He silenced her with a kiss. "Just take some time to think about it."

Jewel was able to think of little else over the next few days, and she was more tempted by Mac's offer than she would have expected. She'd traveled extensively throughout the U.S. but had rarely ventured outside of its borders. She'd been to Canada a couple of times—to Woodbine and Fort Erie, and to Mexico once. But she'd never been to the Mediterranean and the promise of sun and sand and some time alone with Mac was almost irresistible.

But the timing he'd suggested was less than ideal. Though Natasha and Crystal had happily taken the reins of the Fourth Annual Haven Charity Auction, Jewel wouldn't feel right dumping the whole project in their laps. Not that she didn't trust them to handle all of the details, she just wasn't used to relinquishing responsibility. After the auction would be better timing, and she thought she might suggest that possibility to Mac if he brought up the subject again.

Cody poked his head into Jewel's office. "There's a Prince Cameron Leandres here to see you."

Jewel managed not to groan out loud.

"He said you invited him to come by and tour the facilities," the young stable hand prompted.

"I did," she admitted, and reluctantly abandoned the papers on her desk to greet the prince.

Cameron scrutinized the lush green paddocks, the immacu

ate buildings and neat landscaping before turning to her. "I was just thinking the view couldn't get better, and then the sun suddenly shone brighter."

She forced a smile as she offered her hand. "I'm glad you were able to make it."

He took her hand and, as he had the first time, brought it to his lips. "Turning down an invitation from a beautiful woman is something I would never do."

"And I'm sure you'll find this visit worth your while." She pulled her hand from his and led the way to the main barn.

She looked up to see Mac coming toward her, and her heart did that funny little skip and jump that it always did when he was near. She smiled, not just relieved but genuinely pleased to see him, but noted that the light in his eyes dimmed when they landed on the man at her side.

She turned to Cameron, noted the sudden glint of what might have been satisfaction in his eyes, though she didn't have time to wonder about it. "Your Highness, I'd like to introduce you to—"

"No introductions are necessary." Though the prince was speaking to her, his gaze was on Mac.

She could feel the tension in the air and was suddenly filled with a deep sense of foreboding. "You've already met?"

"We have," Mac said shortly.

Cameron smirked. "Though I have to admit," he said, "that I didn't quite recognize you at first, Marcus. You look like a stable hand."

Mac's gaze slid to Jewel's, then away again. "Could I speak to you outside for a moment, Cameron?"

The prince shrugged. "Excuse me, Ms. Callahan, while I have a word with my cousin."

Chapter Twelve

*C*ousin?

Jewel stared. Surely Cameron had misspoken, but the flash
of guilt in Mac's eyes assured her that he had not.

And suddenly she knew why the name of the island Mac
had mentioned sounded familiar. Tesoro del Mar was Prince
Cameron's home, and the prince and Mac were cousins, which
meant that Mac could very well be some kind of royalty.

But he wouldn't have kept something like that from her.
At least, she didn't want to believe he would, but she was no
longer certain of anything.

The men had gone outside for some privacy, but Jewel
found herself inching toward the door. Though she knew she
might regret eavesdropping on their conversation, she had to
know the truth.

"Why are you really here, Cameron?" Mac asked.

"I've bought a horse and I'm looking for somewhere to have it trained."

"How did you know I was here?"

"I saw you at Arlington, though again, I wasn't entirely sure it was you. This whole stable hand persona was quite a surprise. On the other hand, it really does suit you."

"You came here to stir up trouble because you're still pissed that Rowan's wearing the crown instead of you."

"I've dedicated my life to the people of Tesoro del Mar."

"You've dedicated your life to no one but *you*," Mac said derisively.

"It should be me on the throne," Cameron persisted. "Not your brother."

Jewel sagged against the door.

Mac's brother was the ruler of the country?

If that was true—and it seemed to be—then Mac wasn't some distant relative of the royal family but in direct line to the throne. And the only reason she could think of for him to have kept this information from her was that she hadn't mattered enough to him that he wanted her to know.

I'm asking you to come home with me...to meet my family.

His words echoed in her mind, taunting her.

What if she'd taken him up on his offer? Would he have told her then? Or had he never actually intended to take her to Tesoro del Mar or acknowledge the truth? Had everything they'd shared together—everything they'd meant to one another—been a lie?

She didn't want to believe it, but the sense of betrayal slashed like a knife through her heart.

She didn't hear any more of Mac's conversation with Cameron. She couldn't hear anything except the pounding in her head. Until the distant ring of a cell phone penetrated.

She managed to pull herself together and step out of the barn.

Prince Cameron, apparently having decided that he'd accomplished what he wanted to with respect to his cousin, had stalked off. Jewel could see him in the distance, talking to Natasha.

Mac looked at her—his eyes filled with regret and apology. He opened his mouth, as if to say something, then closed it when the ring sounded again. He yanked his cell out of his pocket, frowning at the display before answering with a terse, "Hello."

And then his face drained of all color.

Marcus heard the tension in his brother's voice and immediately knew something was wrong.

"There's been an accident," Rowan said.

And he was immediately transported to a different time and place, to another phone call that had started in exactly the same way.

He swallowed, but before he could even ask, Rowan continued, "It was a naval training exercise—or supposed to have been an exercise—and somehow Eric was shot."

Marcus closed his eyes.

"He's alive." Rowan's voice was hoarse. "But they couldn't give me any more details than that."

Alive.

Marcus clung to the word, trying to find both hope and solace in it. He couldn't face the possibility of losing another brother. It had been hard enough to accept Julian's and Catherine's tragic deaths, but his oldest brother had at least lived a little. He'd fallen in love, married and fathered three beautiful children.

Eric had never done any of those things. What he'd done was serve his country, not just willingly but happily. And now he was fighting for his life because of that service.

"Where is he?" Marcus managed to ask.

"He's being airlifted to Memorial Hospital in Port Augustine right now."

"I'll be there as soon as I can get a flight," Marcus said.

"Henri's on the other line right now making arrangements for a charter out of Alliston," Rowan told him. "I'll send you the details as soon as I have them."

"Thanks."

He disconnected the call, his thoughts filled with Eric. Memories of the times they'd spent together, the hopes and dreams they'd shared. Hopes and dreams that Eric, barely thirty-one years old, had never had a chance to realize.

"Mac?"

He blinked in response to her question, but it took a moment for his gaze to focus on her, another for recognition to set in.

"What happened?" Jewel asked gently.

"My brother." He swallowed. "Eric. I don't know all the details. Rowan said there had been an accident. He's being airlifted to the hospital."

He was in shock, and the realization had compassion pushing aside her own hurt and resentment. She touched his arm. "Do you want me to take you to the airport?"

He nodded slowly and glanced at the screen on his phone as a text message came through. "Rowan's secretary has arranged a private charter out of Alliston."

"It's only a fifteen-minute drive from here," she assured him. "Did you want some help to pack up your things?"

"There's nothing here that I need," he said.

And those words told Jewel everything she needed to know.

Turning away to hide the tears that burned her eyes, she said, "I'll go get my keys."

For the next twenty-four hours, Jewel was glued to the television. She watched the news, anxious for any information about Marcus's brother. Few details were revealed about the incident beyond the fact that His Royal Highness Prince Eric Santiago, an officer in the Tesorian royal navy, was seriously injured in a training exercise off the coast of Crete. A later update indicated that the prince was in recovery after a seven-hour surgery and his condition was noted as critical.

She hadn't heard anything from Mac, though she didn't expect to. Not only because she knew his thoughts would be focused on his brother, but because she'd sensed a finality in his goodbye before he'd stepped onto the plane that would take him back to Tesoro del Mar and out of her life forever.

When Crystal stopped by the next day, she found her sister inside the house, her eyes riveted to the television. "What are you—"

"Shh!" Jewel waved her hands impatiently to silence her, as the now-familiar photo of Prince Eric in his naval uniform appeared in the corner of the screen.

Crystal stepped closer, frowning at the television.

"—no change in the prince's condition this morning," the perky reported announced, "but doctors remain optimistic. No statement has been released by the palace.

"In other news—"

Jewel muted the sound as Crystal sank onto the edge of the sofa beside her. "Was that…Mac?"

Jewel shook her head. "His brother, Eric."

"But it said…he's a…prince?"

Her sister's shock mirrored what Jewel had felt in response to Prince Cameron's big revelation the day before.

"Fourth in line to the throne of Tesoro del Mar," Jewel informed her matter-of-factly. "Mac—whose real name is Marcus, by the way—is younger, so he's fifth."

"Ohmygod. When did you find this out?"

"Yesterday. Just before he got the call about his brother's accident. I obviously forgot to ask about any royal connections when I interviewed him."

"I can't believe you've been dating a prince." Her sister's voice was filled with awe.

Jewel shook her head. "I was sleeping with a man who never told me he was a prince."

Marcus had paced the waiting room floor so constantly over the past four days, he was surprised he hadn't worn through the linoleum. But he couldn't tolerate sitting still and feeling helpless. So long as he was moving, he was at least doing something, even if it was only counting the steps—thirteen—that it took to get from one side of the room to the other.

"You've been restless since you got off the plane," Rowan noted dryly.

"I've had a lot on my mind," Marcus said.

"As we all have," his brother agreed. "But Eric's condition has been downgraded from critical to serious and the doctors have promised that he's on his way to recovery."

Marcus finally sank down into a chair across from him. "He'll live," he agreed, and they were all grateful for that fact. The bullet had caused some serious internal damage before lodging near Eric's spine. Surgery had been necessary to control the internal bleeding but it was also extremely risky. The tiniest error could have resulted in paralysis, and though the procedure was deemed a success, the doctors still didn't know if there was any permanent damage.

"The doctors aren't making any promises," Rowan acknowledged.

"They won't even guarantee that he'll walk again."

"Because they don't know him like we do. They don't realize there's nothing Eric can't do if he sets his mind to it."

Marcus nodded. "So he'll walk again." He made the statement as if it was already fact. "But his career will still be over."

"He has a lot of other options."

"Except returning to the navy."

And Marcus knew that was all Eric ever dreamed of, all he ever wanted.

He shook off the thought, because he knew he should be grateful that his brother was alive—and he was. But the whole incident made Marcus realize how quickly everything could change and had him looking more closely at his own life.

And somehow, thinking about what he wanted made him think of Jewel—and how completely he'd blown things with her.

Now that Eric's condition was no longer critical, his mind had started to wander. Mostly in Jewel's direction.

And he knew he'd never forget the look on her face—the shock, the disbelief, the disappointment—when Cameron revealed Marcus was his cousin. He could almost see the pieces click into place in her mind, and he could imagine the conclusions she'd drawn.

Of course, he hadn't had a chance to explain. And while he was certain Jewel would understand why he had to leave the way he did, he wasn't sure she would understand anything else.

He should have told her. He'd known that all along, but he'd been sure that he would have time to find the right words and the right moment. Then Cameron had shown up and everything had gone downhill from there.

He didn't remember much of what happened after Rowan's phone call. He knew Jewel had driven him to the airport, and before he'd boarded the plane, she'd squeezed his hand and whispered something like, "I hope your brother's okay."

He wasn't even sure if he'd said goodbye. And he didn't know if the tears he thought he'd seen were in her eyes or his own.

"Have you called her?"

Rowan's question jolted him back to the waiting room. "Who?"

His brother's brows lifted. "Do you really think I'm that clueless?"

"I don't think you're clueless at all."

"And yet, you still haven't answered my question."

"No, I haven't called her."

"Don't you think she'd appreciate hearing from you?"

"Right now, no. In fact, I'm guessing she'd prefer to never hear from me again."

"You blew it," Rowan said mildly. "That doesn't mean you don't deserve a chance to make things right."

Marcus wasn't sure Jewel would agree.

It had been a crazy few weeks, Lara thought, as she settled her eight-day-old baby at her breast.

Only a few years ago, she'd been alone. Oh, she'd worked for the royal family and lived in the palace, but she'd had no real home or family of her own. Now she was a wife and a mother, and she felt like she was the luckiest woman in the world. Not just because she was married to a prince and part of his family, but because she knew she was loved.

But it was Rowan's brothers who were on her mind now. Eric had been released from the hospital the same day she and the newest member of the royal family had come home. Though his injuries were going to require extensive physiotherapy and he would probably never again see active duty, he was alive. Less than three years after the deaths of Julian and Catherine, the possibility that the family might have suffered another tragedy—well, she couldn't even let herself think about it or she'd start blubbering again.

Rowan had played the part of stoic prince so well in public. It was only when they came home from the hospital at the end of the day that he would hold her close and she would feel him tremble, know how terrified he was of losing another brother. Only when they knew for certain that Eric would survive that he let himself cry.

She didn't know how Marcus was dealing with this latest crisis. He'd rushed home as soon as he'd learned of Eric's accident and had spent almost every minute with his injured brother. As prince regent, Rowan had duties to attend to that couldn't be put off even while Eric was fighting for his life. She had Christian, Lexi and Damon to care for as well as being in the last weeks of her pregnancy, so it was Marcus who had stayed at the hospital every minute that no one else was there.

Because he'd spent so much of his time at the hospital, she hadn't spent much time with him. But Lara could tell that he'd changed in the few months that he'd been away.

He'd always been the most easygoing of the brothers, the playboy prince whose natural charm and easy smile meant he was always surrounded by friends—and somehow still alone. But there was a new maturity about him, an intensity that she didn't think was solely the result of his brother's accident. Maybe it was because he'd graduated law school, maybe it was a natural maturation process, but she suspected it was something else—or some*one* else.

And while she knew it was really none of her business, she couldn't help wanting to help, wanting him to be as happy as she was.

Whether he would appreciate her interference or not, Lara resolved to find Marcus after she'd finished nursing Matthew and settled him down for his nap.

As it turned out, Marcus found her first. She was just buttoning up her top when he came into the nursery.

She shifted Matthew onto her shoulder, only to have her youngest brother-in-law scoop him right out of her arms. She felt a pang of loss and longing, her body's instinctive response to the baby's absence, but then she looked at Marcus cuddling his tiny nephew and her heart sighed and settled.

"Well," she said, "this saves me having to track you down."

"Why were you going to track me down?"

"To thank you for agreeing to make the trip to Ardena in Rowan's place." It wasn't her only reason, of course, but it was a valid one.

"It's just a goodwill visit—nothing I can screw up too badly."

Lara shook her head as she rose from the chair. "You always underestimate yourself—and the importance of what you do for your family and your country."

"I don't do much," he insisted. "Not compared to Rowan or Eric."

"You're younger than both of your brothers," she pointed out.

"The Aimless Heir," he said, quoting one of the less favorable monikers he'd been given. He gently rubbed his nephew's back and touched his lips lightly to the top of the baby's bald head.

The gesture was both easy and natural, and she wished some of those nasty reporters could see the so-called Playboy Prince now—looking like nothing more than the doting uncle he'd always been to his niece and nephews. Of course, what woman wouldn't melt at the sight of a strong, handsome man cuddling a tiny baby?

"You're not aimless," she denied. "You just haven't found your focus."

He settled in the rocking chair with the baby and smiled. "You always did know how to put a positive spin on things."

"And you always managed to get exactly what you wanted," she said. "So why have you given up this time?"

He rubbed a hand over the baby's back as he rocked. "Are you talking about Jewel?"

"She is the reason you've been moping around here for the past couple of weeks, isn't she?"

"I'm going to regret ever mentioning her name to you, aren't I?"

"It was obvious, at least to me, that you were doing more in West Virginia than taking care of her horses."

"I thought we had something really great going," he said. "But she hasn't returned any of my calls since I got back.

"I've called every day for more than two weeks. I've spoken with her sister, her housekeeper and her head trainer, but I haven't managed to talk to Jewel."

"I don't imagine it occurred to you that she might not want to talk to you?" Lara asked dryly.

"Of course it occurred to me," he admitted irritably, "but I didn't think she would hold out this long. It's been almost three weeks."

And with each passing day, he'd grown more frustrated, a reaction that had amused her at first. She'd thought that Marcus was annoyed at being stonewalled simply because it was a new experience for him, but she'd soon realized that he genuinely cared for this woman he'd left in America.

"You lied to her," she felt compelled to point out.

"I had to—she never would have hired me if she'd known the truth about who I was."

Lara nodded in acknowledgment of the fact. "But there was probably an opportunity later on—maybe before you slept with her?—that you might have let her know."

He sighed. "Yeah, I should have told her."

"Instead you let Cameron blow everything out of the water, not only blindsiding her but giving your cousin the satisfaction of screwing up your life."

"He certainly seemed to take pleasure in revealing my title to Jewel."

"Which he wouldn't have been able to do if you'd been honest with her."

He was silent, unable to dispute the fact.

She'd known Marcus for years and had never known him to be so captivated by a woman as he was by Jewel Callahan. Usually his interest peaked and waned in a predictable fashion, but there was nothing predictable about his involvement with this woman. It certainly piqued her curiosity about the American horse trainer who had her brother-in-law so unexpectedly tied in knots.

"Do you love her, Marcus?"

He considered the question as he carried the now-sleeping baby to his cradle and settled him into it. "I don't know," he finally responded.

And even if he did know, even if he did love Jewel, Lara wasn't sure he was ready to admit it—even to himself.

"Maybe that's something you should figure out before you pursue this," she said gently.

"I know I don't like the way things ended."

"But they did end," she pointed out. "As you knew they would. As she knew they would. Because you never made her any promises, did you?"

He shook his head.

Of course he didn't. Marcus didn't make promises. He didn't do long-term relationships and probably broke out in hives if a woman so much as uttered the word "commitment."

Lara didn't have a psychology degree, but she understood—even if he didn't—it was the pain of losing both of his parents that had taught him to guard his heart. The tragic deaths of Julian and Catherine would have reminded him of the dangers of getting too close to anyone, of the pain of losing someone he loved, and reinforced the barriers he'd already put into place.

But she suspected that somehow Jewel Callahan had managed to breach those barriers, even if neither she nor Marcus realized it.

"Can I ask another question?"

"Can I stop you?"

She ignored his sarcasm. "If Cameron hadn't blown your cover, if Eric hadn't been injured—where would you be right now?"

This time, he answered without hesitation. "With Jewel."

"Why?"

"Because I can't imagine moving on with my life without her in it."

It wasn't until the words spilled out of his mouth that he realized they were true. For so many years, he'd been searching for some direction or purpose without ever guessing that what he really wanted was some*one* to share his life with.

He was a prince, with all of the inherent rights and privileges of that title. And he'd never realized how empty his life was until Jewel filled it, had never known how lonely his heart was until it had belonged to her.

Lara smiled at him. "I think maybe you've already figured it out."

Chapter Thirteen

Natasha fairly danced into Jewel's office Saturday afternoon. "Guess who I just talked to on the phone?"

Jewel finished punching the last number in the calculator, then winced at the total she entered into the ledger. Since Harold Emerson had backed out of his agreement to purchase Cayenne—understandably, considering the way the horse had been acting since Mac left—and she'd had to repay his deposit, the Haven books had been in dire straits. Something was going to have to change—and soon—if they were going to continue to operate the facility as they were doing.

Tearing her attention from the book, she looked up at Natasha. The other woman's cheeks were pink and her eyes glowing with obvious excitement. "I'm not in the mood for guessing games," she told Natasha. "I have a lot on my mind."

"A lot?" Nat's brows lifted. "Or one man?"

Jewel dropped her gaze back to the keyboard. "Was there a reason you came in here?"

"Of course." The Haven volunteer lowered herself into the chair facing Jewel's desk. "We've got a buyer for Cayenne."

Her head jerked up in response to this unexpected news. "Harold Emerson changed his mind?"

Nat shook her head but her smile never wavered. "A new buyer—and an honest-to-goodness prince."

Jewel's excitement quickly turned to apprehension.

"Can you believe it?" Natasha continued. "One of the horses you rescued is going to find a permanent home in a royal stable. Just think of the publicity this will bring to Haven."

"Who—" Jewel had to clear her throat before she could continue. "Who is it?"

Nat glanced at the message pad in her hand. "His name is Rowan Santiago, prince regent of Tesoro del Mar." She looked up and shrugged. "I've never even heard of the country, and I don't know what a prince regent is, but royalty's royalty, right?"

Jewel knew, because she'd searched for information on Marcus's family on the Internet after she'd learned the truth about who he was. And she knew that Rowan was his oldest living brother who had become prince regent—ruler of the country only until his eldest nephew was of age to assume the throne—when the reigning prince and princess had died a few years back.

"Royalty or not," she pointed out to Natasha, ignoring both the knot in her belly and the ache in her heart, "the stables have to be investigated and approved before we can allow the sale to take place."

"Of course," Natasha said. "I told His Royal Highness as

much, and he said he would make the arrangements for your travel and accommodation at your convenience."

"*My* travel?"

Nat's lips twitched, as if she was fighting a smile. "Unless there's some reason you don't want to go to Tesoro del Mar."

It was a challenge more than a question, and though Jewel had never told Natasha that Mac Delgado was really Prince Marcus Santiago, it was obvious her new friend had somehow learned the truth.

"Is there?" Nat prompted.

"No," Jewel lied. "No reason at all."

As Jewel waited for her call to the prince regent to be connected, the knots in her stomach twisted and tightened. She tried to picture the prince's office in the palace, where he would be sitting when he responded to her call. Of course, her mind was a blank canvas because she knew nothing of palaces except for pictures of castles that she'd seen in fairy tales. She knew nothing of Marcus's life away from CTC. In fact, if there was one thing she'd learned over the past several weeks since he'd been gone, it was that she didn't know Marcus Santiago at all.

"Ms. Callahan?"

Jewel started at the sound of a lightly accented male voice on the line. "Yes."

"I'm putting your call through to the prince regent," the briskly efficient secretary told her.

Then there was another click, and another voice came on the line. "Ms. Callahan?"

"Yes," she said again.

"Thank you for getting back to me so promptly." The voice

was similar to Marcus's. Similar enough to make her heart ache, but not the same.

She swallowed around the tightness in her throat and forced herself to focus on the business at hand. "I understand you've expressed an interest in adopting a horse from Haven."

"I'm interested in a stallion known as Cayenne," the prince said. "I've heard good things about him."

"He's a beautiful animal, but he hasn't had an easy life and—"

"I know he's had some difficulties with training, but I'm confident we can work with him here."

"With all due respect, Your Highness, that's a bold statement coming from someone who's never even seen the animal."

"My brother has worked with him," he said. "And there isn't anyone whose opinion I trust more when it comes to horses."

Jewel was silent for a moment.

"Will ten thousand American dollars prove my interest in the stallion is genuine?" he asked.

It was an insultingly low offer for a horse of Cayenne's potential. On the other hand, it was ten thousand more than anyone else had been willing to pay and would go a long way toward putting her books back in the black—at least for a while. "You're offering to pay ten thousand dollars for the stallion?"

"No, Ms. Callahan, I'm offering ten thousand dollars to compensate you for your time and trouble if you will come here so that we can conclude our negotiations."

She sank into her chair, stunned—and even more wary. "You're going to pay me to come to Tesoro del Mar?"

"Consider it a contribution to your facility," he said.

"That's very generous," she murmured.

"And yet, you're still uncertain," he guessed.

"It's really not a good time for me to leave."

"I would come over myself," Rowan said, "but my wife just had a baby and I really don't want to be so far away from them right now."

She'd read about the birth, of course. Since Mac—Marcus, she mentally amended—had gone, she'd scoured the Internet on an almost daily basis for information about the royal family of Tesoro del Mar. So she knew that Marcus's sister-in-law had given birth to a seven-and-a-half-pound baby boy whom they'd named Matthew, and though no photos had yet been released of the baby, Jewel imagined he had what she now knew was the trademark Santiago dark hair and eyes, and the image stirred a fierce yearning inside of her for a child of her own.

"Fifteen thousand," he said, when she remained silent.

As his offer increased, so did her wariness. "Why are you so anxious for me to come to Tesoro del Mar?"

"I'm not sure if you're aware of it or not, but Marcus's birthday is coming up and, as he's spoken at length about this stallion, I thought he would be an appropriate gift for the occasion."

She wondered if the prince regent knew that she and Marcus had been involved. Maybe he didn't. Because she'd bet that if he did, he wouldn't be so anxious for her to come to the island. She could just imagine the scandal if it became public knowledge that the young prince had been sleeping with an older woman who wasn't just a commoner but a lowly horse trainer.

"When is his birthday?" she heard herself ask.

"The end of the month. Obviously that's one of the reasons I would like you to come over and check out the stables as soon as possible. The other reason is that Marcus is out of the country right now, so you wouldn't need to worry about crossing paths with him—if that was a concern."

Okay, maybe he did know about her relationship with Marcus. But Jewel found she wasn't bothered by the fact so much as she was relieved to find the last of her concerns eradicated. "If we agree on terms for the purchase of Cayenne, the fifteen thousand will be credited toward the purchase price."

"That sounds more than fair," Rowan agreed. "When can you come?"

She flipped through her calendar, knowing there would be some major juggling required regardless of the date she chose. But she figured the sooner the better, especially if it allowed her to make the trip there and back before Marcus ever knew she'd been in Tesoro del Mar.

"I could come Tuesday," she said.

"I'll make the arrangements."

Jewel spent the next forty-eight hours making sure everything would be taken care of at both CTC and Haven while she was away. The last person she told, and the person she most dreaded informing about her trip, was her sister. Though when she made the announcement, Crystal didn't even blink.

"Why aren't you surprised?" Jewel demanded.

Her sister's smile was indulgent. "Because you love the man. I can recognize the fact even if you refuse to admit it."

"I don't know what I feel for Marcus," she lied. "And my decision has nothing to do with him, anyway. In fact, he's not even going to be in the country."

Crystal frowned at that. "Where is he?"

"On a diplomatic tour of some neighboring islands."

"For how long?"

Jewel shrugged. "A couple of weeks."

"Oh." Crystal pouted for a moment, then asked, "Well, you'll go to the ball, anyway, won't you?"

"What ball?"

The question was met with a dramatic eye roll. "The Midsummer's Night Ball is Saturday night and it's the biggest annual fund-raising event for PACH—The Port Augustine Children's Hospital in Tesoro del Mar. Prince Marcus is a patron."

Obviously her sister had been spending some of her spare time on the Internet, too.

"I'll be home on Friday," Jewel told her.

"You should pack something appropriate—just in case," her sister advised.

"There won't be any 'just in case,'" Jewel assured her. "My return flight is booked, I have no intention of staying any longer than is absolutely necessary, and even if my departure was somehow delayed, there is no way I own anything appropriate to wear to a royal ball."

Crystal's brow furrowed. "You're probably right. Maybe you should borrow my midnight-blue Valentino gown. The one Simon bought for me when we were in Italy last year." She glanced down at her slightly expanded waistline. "I certainly won't be wearing it anytime soon."

"That's a generous offer, but I don't think I need a designer dress to check out the royal stables."

"I'm starting to think that ornery horse has more sense than you do," her sister grumbled.

Jewel took her sister's hand and squeezed it gently. "I appreciate what you're trying to do, but the only reason I'm going to Tesoro del Mar is to make sure that the environment is suitable for Cayenne."

"You doubt that it is?"

"No," she admitted. "But if I approve it without an inspection, it looks like I'm either ignoring the rules because the buyer is a prince or because I can't handle seeing Mac—Marcus—again."

"And even if that was true, you wouldn't admit it," Crystal noted.

"He's just a man who happens to be a prince, and even before I knew he had blue blood, I had no illusions about a future with him."

"I did."

Jewel raised her eyebrows; Crystal smiled.

"Not for me," she clarified. "But for you. The way he looked at you, I really thought—"

"He never promised me anything more than what we had," she told her sister. Then, she stood and picked up her suitcase. "I have to go."

"I hardly think the plane is going to leave without you."

"Maybe not, but I don't want to keep the pilot waiting." She kissed her sister's cheek.

"There's no harm in taking a week or two of vacation while you're away," Crystal called after her.

"I'll be back on Friday," she said again.

Jewel didn't know what to expect when she boarded the plane for Tesoro del Mar, and throughout the eight-hour flight, her apprehension continued to build.

She was still angry with Marcus and couldn't help but feel betrayed by his continued lies and deceptions. And yet, there was a part of her that desperately wanted to see him again, to be held in his arms just one more time.

She let out a sigh. It was a good thing he wasn't going to be in the country, because she wasn't sure she had the will-power to stay away from him. As upset as she'd been with him for deceiving her, her anger and hurt didn't compare to the emptiness she felt inside when she'd watched him get on that plane and fly out of her life.

She picked up the glass of wine she'd been served with lunch and marveled at the luxury of being the solo passenger on a private plane. She did a lot of flying, from one race track to the next, but she'd never even sprung for a first-class ticket before, so this was beyond anything in her wildest fantasies.

Except that in her wildest fantasies, she wouldn't be a solo passenger—Marcus would be there. And she knew now that dream couldn't ever come true.

She took another sip of her wine and tried to banish him from her mind, with as little success as she'd had over the past few weeks. She had no business fantasizing about a man who could never be hers, who probably hadn't given her a second thought since he'd walked out of her life.

Okay, she knew that was both untrue and unfair. Though she hadn't heard from him at all during the first week after he'd gone, she knew his brother's condition had been critical and she didn't blame him for focusing on that above all else. The day after Eric's condition was downgraded to serious, he'd called and left a message on her machine.

She hadn't called him back. She'd still been too hurt and angry then to want to talk to him.

He'd called again the following day, and every day after that for the next two weeks. She hadn't taken or returned any of his calls. As much as she'd longed to hear his voice, she'd managed to convince herself that it was best to make a clean

break. It was one thing to let herself fantasize about the possibility of a future with him when he was just a young Harvard
grad and quite another to do so after learning he was royalty.

She felt like such a fool.

She'd made a mistake when she'd run off to the rodeo with
Thomas—believing she could be everything he wanted, as he
was everything she wanted. But it turned out that she wasn't
quite good enough. Just like she'd never been good enough
for her father.

If she wasn't good enough for either of them, how could
she possibly expect she'd be good enough for a prince?

The simple answer—the obvious answer—was that she
couldn't. And it would be for the best if she just forgot she'd
ever met Mac Delgado, never mind been foolish enough to
fall in love with him.

Jewel met both of Marcus's brothers at the palace.

Eric, though currently wheelchair-bound, was in good
spirits, and as charming and good-looking as his younger
brother. Rowan shared both of his brothers' dark good looks
but with an added air of maturity and a sense of contentment.
It was readily obvious to Jewel that he was in love with his
wife and infatuated with his infant son. As for Marcus's niece
and nephews, she fell in love, hard and fast, with all of them.

But she was here to check out the stables, and after a casual
luncheon with the prince regent and his family, Jewel was
anxious to get down to business.

The stables were, not surprisingly, both impressive and
immaculate, and Frank—who called himself a groom but
seemed to manage the facilities—was gruff but charming.
Within an hour of meeting him, Jewel was wishing she could

take him back to West Virginia to work at CTC with her. Frank responded by offering her a job at the royal stables. In the end, they both agreed they would be most content staying where they were, though Jewel couldn't help remembering how much happier she'd been when Mac had been at CTC with her.

Marcus knew his visit to Ardena had been a success. He'd performed all of the necessary duties and attended all scheduled functions with a practiced smile, all the while wishing he was in West Virginia instead of western Europe. On more than one occasion, he found himself wondering how his brother managed the endless and often tedious responsibilities of his office without going out of his mind. But Rowan did so—and happily. And Marcus knew that his sister-in-law was primarily responsible for his brother's newfound happiness and contentment.

He used to believe that he was incapable of falling in love. He certainly never wanted to commit to a relationship with any one woman. And then he fell in love with Jewel.

He'd been fighting the truth for weeks now, certain that returning to Tesoro del Mar and leaving Jewel was inevitable from the beginning, that Eric's injury had only hastened his departure.

But so much had changed while he was in West Virginia with her, and he was no longer willing to accept that their relationship had to end. Rowan had fought for Lara, and Marcus was determined to do the same for the woman he loved.

But first he had to finish this tour for Rowan.

There was a morning newspaper delivered to Jewel along with a breakfast tray laden with everything from pastries and fresh fruit to oatmeal and eggs, a silver carafe of fresh coffee and an elegant cut-crystal vase holding a trio of cream-colored roses that she suspected had been snipped from the beautiful garden in the courtyard.

She was on her second cup of coffee when she opened the paper.

MIA Prince Back in Action.

The headline article was accompanied by a full-color photo of Marcus with a woman.

Prince Marcus of Tesoro del Mar enjoys a waltz with Princess Francesca at a gala reception held in his honor at the Ardena Royal Palace last evening, the caption read.

Jewel stared at the picture for a long time, as if to commit Marcus's face to memory when she already knew she would never forget a single detail. And as she absorbed every bit of the image, she could no longer deny that she'd fallen in love with him.

But just as there was no longer any denying that fact, nor was there any hope that their relationship could have ever been more than it was. He was a prince—and she was not a princess.

The girl in the photo was a princess. Not only royal but young and stunningly beautiful, and clearly besotted with the prince.

Marcus looked a little less enchanted by his dance partner, as if his mind might be somewhere else—or maybe that was only wishful thinking on her part.

She chided herself for the fanciful thought, knowing there was no way he could have been thinking of anyone other than the beautiful, blue-blooded female in his arms. And the sooner she accepted that and got back to the reality of her own life in West Virginia, the better.

She'd almost finished stuffing her clothes into her suitcase when Princess Lara stopped by her suite of rooms.

"I was hoping I could talk you into lounging around the pool with me for a while this afternoon," Lara said.

"Actually, I was just—"

"Packing?" The princess's eyes grew wide. "You're not planning on leaving already, are you?"

"There's no reason for me to stay," Jewel said. "And I can't imagine that Prince Rowan wants me hanging around here when the sooner I get home, the sooner I can make arrangements for Cayenne to be transported."

"There's every reason for you to stay," Lara argued. "Most notably that I've been overwhelmed by all the testosterone around here lately and am desperate for some female company."

Jewel hesitated for just a second, and the princess pounced.

"You'd planned to stay for three days—I really wish you would."

So Jewel spent the morning with Lara and the children at the pool. After lunch, the three older children had other activities, leaving the two women and the baby alone, and finally giving Jewel a chance to catch her breath.

"I don't know how you do it," she said.

"Do what?" Lara asked.

"Manage four kids without a nanny."

Lara laughed. "It was a matter of some contention between Rowan and I when I was expecting Matthew," she confided. "But what you may not know is that *I* was the nanny before I married Rowan, and I didn't want Christian, Lexi and Damon to feel that they were any less important to me because of the new baby coming along."

"*You* were the nanny?"

The princess nodded. "Going back to when Damon was still in diapers."

"I don't mean to be nosey," Jewel said, "but I thought a prince had to marry someone with royal blood."

"Every country seems to have its own rules regarding royal unions. Here it was that the bride of a prince has to be— among other things—if not of royal birth, then a citizen of Tesoro del Mar or France or Spain." She grinned. "But Marcus found a loophole of sorts—a legislative provision that allowed Rowan to marry me, anyway."

She stiffened automatically at the mention of Marcus's name, but the princess was gracious enough to pretend she hadn't noticed.

"And then, after we were married, he helped draft an amendment to the law so that a royal can now marry anyone who is, if not already a citizen of Tesoro del Mar, at least willing to become one."

Jewel didn't know why Lara was telling her any of this. She couldn't—didn't dare let herself—imagine how it might possibly be relevant to her.

"He talked to me about you," Lara said softly. "I've known him a long time, and yours is the first name he's ever introduced into a conversation."

"I think you're making it into something more than it was." As she'd done when she'd deluded herself into thinking that they'd shared something special, that she really mattered to Marcus. Then she'd found out he was a prince, and realized what a complete fool she'd been.

"Then you're not in love with my brother-in-law?" the other woman challenged.

Jewel shook her head. "My feelings aren't important."

Lara's gaze softened. "You know, I've been exactly where you are—in love with a man I didn't think could possibly love me back."

"I think this situation is a little different," Jewel said.

"Why?"

"For starters, we don't even live in the same country."

"That might require some creative juggling," Lara admitted. "But it's not an insurmountable obstacle."

"I'm eight years older than he is."

"Did that seem to be an issue for him?" the princess asked mildly.

"Not as much as it was for me," Jewel admitted. "And that was before I knew he was a prince.

"The thing is," she continued, "after I found out the truth, and when I had a chance to think about it, I was actually relieved he'd been called away."

"Why?"

"Because it gave us both an out—an opportunity to move on with our separate lives without accusations or recriminations."

"Or an excuse to avoid acknowledging your true feelings for one another."

"Whatever feelings I had were for Mac Delgado, not Prince Marcus Santiago."

Lara shook her head. "You're obviously well-suited for one another because you're just as obstinate as he is."

"We're not suited at all," Jewel insisted. "But I have some wonderful memories of the time we spent together, anyway, and that's why I have to leave before he gets back. If I see him again, if I let myself hope and believe that we could somehow work things out and that isn't what he wants, then I lose everything."

"What if he does want to work things out?"

Jewel's heart skipped a beat, then began to hammer furiously against her ribs. Because it wasn't the princess who had spoken. No, Lara was just sitting there, smiling, as the question came from somewhere behind Jewel, spoken by a deep male voice that was achingly familiar.

Chapter Fourteen

Jewel turned around slowly, and her breath caught.

Marcus stood behind her.

And seeing him there, so close she could almost reach out and touch him, made everything inside her weak.

She hadn't seen him in weeks, and she'd never seen him looking like this. He was wearing a dark suit with a snowy-white shirt, paisley tie and shoes so polished she could probably see her reflection in them. He looked so incredibly handsome, and so very much a prince, her heart ached.

Lara rose from her chair, the baby in her arms. "I think it's time I put Matthew down for a nap." She stopped beside Marcus, kissed his cheek. "Welcome home."

He touched a hand gently to the baby's head and smiled at his sister-in-law. "Thanks."

"You can thank me by not screwing this up," Lara said, then disappeared inside the palace.

Alone now with the prince, Jewel didn't know what to say. The brief exchange between the princess and her brother-in-law confirmed that Lara was responsible for bringing Marcus home ahead of schedule. The fact that he hadn't questioned Jewel's presence proved that he wasn't surprised to find her there and probably already knew why she'd been summoned to Tesoro del Mar.

Marcus, too, remained silent, though his gaze moved over her avidly, hungrily.

"I heard you were in Ardena," she finally said. And because she'd known he was away, she'd made the mistake of letting herself relax, thinking she might actually be back in America before his royal duties allowed him to return to his home.

"Rowan doesn't like to be away from Lara and the baby for too long and Eric's obviously in no condition to go anywhere, so that left the onus on me to represent the family. Every now and again, I'm entrusted with the responsibility and sent off with fervent prayers that I won't embarrass the country."

"I hardly think that's a concern."

"Maybe not so much anymore," he acknowledged. "Apparently I've matured since I first went away to college."

"That happens sometimes," she agreed lightly.

"I don't think it was college that made the difference—I think it was you."

"Well, hanging out with an older woman might have an influence, too."

"Don't downplay what was between us," he said.

"What *was* between us—except a lot of lies and deceptions?"

"I should have told you the truth—"

"That would have been nice," she agreed.

"And the truth is, I've never felt about another woman the way I feel about you," he told her.

"Maybe because you've never before spent more than a couple of weeks with any one woman."

"You've been reading the tabloids."

She shrugged. "Well, you certainly didn't volunteer any personal information, and when you left, I realized I didn't know anything about you. I didn't know you at all."

"You do know me," he insisted. "My title doesn't change anything."

She shook her head sadly. "Your title changes *everything*."

"Only if you let it," he insisted.

She managed a laugh. "You're a prince, Marcus. That's a fact that exists apart from all else."

"And that's exactly why I didn't tell you," he said. "For the first time in my life, I was with a woman who wanted to be with me because of me, not because of my title."

"And you thought that would change if you told me who you really were?"

"I didn't know."

"Then I guess we're even, because you don't know me at all, either."

"I made a mistake," he said softly.

She tore her gaze from his, afraid he'd see the yearning in her heart. "You don't fight fair," she protested.

"I don't want to fight at all."

"Why are you here, Marcus?"

"I wanted to show you my home and introduce you to my family," he reminded her.

"I've had the grand tour and I've met everyone already."

"And?" he prompted.

"It's beautiful," she admitted. "The palace, the island, everything. And your family is wonderful."

He settled his hands on her shoulders, and that simple contact had everything inside her melting.

"I'm glad you're here." His hands stroked down her arms to link with hers. "I've missed you, Jewel."

"I can't do this, Marcus." She couldn't let herself hope and dream, not again. Because she knew it would only be that much more painful when it finally ended.

"Do what?" he asked gently.

"Whatever it is you're asking of me."

"Right now, I'm only asking you to stay. Just for a while."

"I've left Crystal and Natasha with a ton of things to do for the auction and—"

He kissed her.

It was just a brush of his lips against hers, but it was enough to wipe every coherent thought from her mind.

It had been weeks since he'd touched her, kissed her, and though she was still hurt and angry about his lies and deceptions, all of that was forgotten in an instant—burned away by the heat of that contact, replaced by a soul-deep yearning.

"I know I don't have any right to ask," he told her. "But I'm asking anyway. Please."

He would beg. Marcus realized he was close to doing so already, but he didn't care. What was pride when she'd already stolen his heart?

But she didn't make him beg.

Instead she lifted her arms to link behind his head and rose up on her toes to kiss *him*.

Her mouth was soft and moist, and even sweeter than he remembered. He wrapped his arms around her and drew her against his body. She sighed and yielded.

The tip of her tongue touched his, a tentative stroke. He coaxed her to give more, to take more, and they both lost themselves in the passion of their kiss.

From the beginning, there had been something between them. A spark, a sizzle—he wasn't quite sure how to describe it. But over time, it had grown and deepened, and he was relieved to know that not even his betrayal had extinguished it.

When at last she drew away, they were both breathless.

"I want you, Jewel."

Her tongue swept over her bottom lip, erotically swollen from their kiss. "The wanting is the easy part," she told him.

He shook his head. "Wanting you these past few weeks, knowing you were beyond my reach—not just in physical distance—was killing me."

"Marcus—"

He laid his fingers against her lips. "Come inside with me. Please."

He saw the hesitation in her eyes, the caution, but she nodded.

He took her hand, linking their fingers together. He led the way quickly through the maze of corridors, partly because he was afraid she'd change her mind if he gave her the opportunity, and partly because he was just in that much of a hurry to be with her again.

Jewel barely had a moment to take in her surroundings— the antique carpet beneath her feet, the art on the walls or the huge four-poster bed that was neatly covered by a thick duvet and fluffy pillows before Marcus tore back the covers and tossed them aside.

But as soon as he laid her down on the bed, all sense of urgency seemed to vanish. His hands slowed and his lips lingered as he slowly stripped away her cover-up and then the scraps of material that comprised her bikini.

"Mi Dios," he breathed. "We would never have made it to my room if I'd known what you were wearing."

"I didn't bring a bathing suit," she told him. "So Lara had this one sent over from a local boutique."

He dispensed with his own clothes and knelt astride her on the mattress. "I'll be sure to thank her. Later."

Then he kissed her again, deeply, thoroughly. With his lips and his hands and his body, he brought her slowly but inexorably to the brink, and only then did he ease into her.

Her hands moved over his shoulders, following the contours of hard taut muscle and relishing the feel of warm tight skin as he pressed into her, giving and taking. She arched toward him, wanting and welcoming. They moved together, a perfectly choreographed rhythm that built toward a spectacular crescendo. His mouth covered hers again, swallowing her cries as she sobbed out his name.

He plunged one more time, giving himself to her, and everything inside her shattered.

It was a long time later before either of them spoke, and it was Marcus who did so first.

"You were wrong," he said to her.

Jewel was snuggled against his chest, warm in the embrace of his arms, and too contented to take offense at his words. "What was I wrong about?" she asked sleepily.

"The wanting being easy."

She tipped her head back. "It's not?"

"Not as easy as the loving." He brushed his lips over hers. "I do love you, Jewel."

Her heart—recently and not yet thoroughly recovered—tripped again. This was exactly why she hadn't wanted this—and exactly why she hadn't been able to walk away. Because she loved him, too. But rather than simplify things, it seemed to Jewel only to complicate matters.

"I don't want you to love me." Her voice was an anguished whisper. "And I don't want to love you."

He kissed the tears that slipped onto her cheeks, first one side, then the other. "But you do?" he asked hopefully.

Her arms tightened around him. "Yes, I do."

"I've had a lot of relationships," he told her.

"I know."

His smile was wry. "Not nearly as many as the tabloids would lead you to believe, but still a fair number."

"Why are we talking about this now?"

"Because more than one of my ex-girlfriends accused me of being emotionally stunted. Not that I believed it, but over the years, as one relationship after another ended, I started to wonder. Because I did date a lot of women, but I never fell in love with any of them." His lips brushed hers again. "Until you."

She sighed and melted into his kiss. "My life is in West Virginia. You understand that, don't you?"

"We'll work something out," he promised her.

She stayed for the ball, though with each day that passed, her trepidation grew. By all accounts, this charity ball was a big deal—there would be celebrities and dignitaries in attendance and a lot of media coverage of the event. But what made it an even bigger deal for Jewel was that it would be her first official public appearance with His Royal Highness Prince Marcus Santiago, and she couldn't have imagined being more nervous.

In the two days that preceded the ball, he'd taken her to the beach, to some of the shops in Port Augustine, the art gallery and the theater. While they were alone together, it was easy to forget his title. But everywhere they went in public, the press was close on their heels.

Jewel tried not to let the media attention bother her, but she wasn't used to being the subject of such scrutiny. And though headlines such as The Playboy Prince's New Playmate? were a little unnerving, the press really started having fun once her identity had been revealed and they could dig up all kinds of other information about her. Then the captions read The Prince's Rodeo Prize, Prince Marcus's American Mistress and, her least favorite of all, The Youngest Prince's Older Woman, which firmly negated his claim that no one cared about the age difference between them but her.

Still, Marcus didn't seem to pay much attention to the newspapers. He certainly didn't give any indication that he was bothered by what they said, but it wasn't so easy for Jewel to take in stride.

So when the day of the ball dawned and she learned that Lara had arranged for a hairdresser and stylist and a bevy of other assistants to help Jewel get ready for the event, she put herself in their hands. Willingly and gratefully.

The makeover was both time-consuming and thorough, so much so that she barely recognized herself when she was finally allowed to look in the mirror. Her hair had been piled high on her head, with a few curls artfully arranged to frame her face. Her makeup was flawless, highlighting her features without overpowering them. And her gown was Dior—a shimmering bronze creation that looked like something out of a fairy tale and made her feel like a princess.

Looking at the unfamiliar image in the mirror, Jewel could almost believe she was worthy of a prince—a thought that both excited and terrified her, because she knew the woman staring back at her wasn't real.

When Marcus took her hand and led her onto the dance floor, she couldn't help remembering the first time they'd danced, the first time he'd held her in his arms. On a scarred wooden floor in a country-western bar to tinny music playing from a jukebox. It seemed like a lifetime ago, in a different world, and in many ways, it was. Tonight, the floor was gleaming, the chandeliers sparkled and the music entranced.

But at the center of everything, at least for Jewel, was Marcus. He was dressed in military uniform, reminding everyone that he'd done his service in the army, if only the required two years, before he'd moved on to other things. Still, he was breathtakingly handsome in his formal attire. And he was, at least for tonight, hers.

As they waltzed slowly around the room, she was conscious of the many pairs of eyes that followed. She could almost hear the whispers and see the speculation in narrowed eyes.

"I feel as if everyone is looking at us," she confessed softly.

"Everyone's looking at me," he said. "And envying me because I have the most beautiful woman in the room in my arms."

She smiled at that, because she knew it was expected.

But his comment wasn't very reassuring. Sure, it was fun

to play dress-up and dance at a royal ball—or it might be fun if she could forget about all of the eyes focused on them— but she was so far removed from her life she hardly recognized herself.

"You look incredible in that gown," he said. "But you're just as beautiful to me in a pair of jeans and a T-shirt." His thumbs caressed her ribs through the fabric of her dress, the gentle touch causing sparks to skitter through her veins. "And even more beautiful in nothing at all."

"Marcus," she whispered his name, part warning, part longing.

His lips curved in a slow, sexy smile that was intended only for her.

The flurry of flashbulbs that went off proved otherwise.

She blinked and misstepped.

He smoothly executed a turn, moving her away from the cameras and allowing her to regain her composure.

"Sorry," she apologized.

"No need to be," he assured her. "You'll get used to the crowds and the cameras. Not to the point where you forget they're there, but enough to accept and pretend you don't mind."

"You've dealt with this your whole life," she realized.

"Not nearly as much as Rowan, especially since he became prince regent. I figure it's a small price to pay for the perks of being a prince."

And yet, she didn't believe it was. And she finally understood why he'd so carefully guarded his true identity when he'd been in West Virginia.

Jewel thought she would get a reprieve from the press when she returned to Alliston. She certainly never expected that the paparazzi would follow her back home. But that's exactly what happened, and it seemed she couldn't go to the store to buy a quart of milk without someone snapping pictures of her.

Still, it was more of an annoyance than anything. At least until one of the young colts at CTC started exhibiting symptoms of serious colic and Dr. Anderson, the local vet, couldn't get past the media vans that were parked at the end of her laneway. The vet ended up parking on the road and jogging down the mile-long driveway to the barn, by which time the colt's condition was so severe he required immediate abdominal surgery.

The colt was resting now, and Dr. Anderson was optimistic, but the owner was furious and Jewel couldn't blame him.

She was furious, too. At the parasitic press who were camped out in her driveway, and—irrational though she knew it was—at Marcus, too.

It was one thing to put up with the media spotlight when they were together—she could put up with almost anything when she was with him. But she didn't know how to handle any of this on her own, she didn't want to handle it on her own. She didn't *want* to live her life long-distance from the man she loved. And as much as she did love him, she couldn't do this. Not anymore.

The Independence Celebrations had finally concluded, and while Marcus had enjoyed participating in all of the festivities and especially the time he'd spent with his family, he was glad that everything was done so he could go back to West Virginia and be with Jewel again. He'd missed her terribly over the past few weeks and it was only the knowledge that he would be seeing her again soon that got him through the long days and longer nights without her.

He was packing for his trip when the phone rang. A quick glance at the display revealed Jewel's number, and he was smiling when he connected the call. But his smile quickly faded when she told him about the colicky colt and how close she'd come to losing him.

He could hear the tears in her voice, knew she was fighting against them. But what worried him more was the niggling suspicion that she was upset about more than just a close call with one of her animals.

"I'll be there tomorrow," he promised her. "We'll get an injunction to keep the media—"

"No," she interrupted.

"Why not?"

"Because I don't want you here, Marcus."

It was her tone even more than the words that had everything inside him go cold. "You don't mean that."

"I do mean it. I can't live my life under a microscope, and being a prince, you don't have any choice except to live your life that way."

"I know the media attention has been a little intense—"

"Don't try and downplay what happened here. I'm not complaining about a zealous photographer taking my picture on a bad hair day," she interrupted. "I'm talking about the fact that an animal almost died because the damn media vans were blocking the driveway so the vet couldn't get through."

"Let me make some calls," he said. "We'll get a restraining order—"

"No," she interrupted. "A restraining order might keep them off my property, but it will also fuel interest and speculation."

"I'm sorry, Jewel. I know this had been difficult."

"Sorry doesn't change anything," she said softly. "But at

least the press will lose interest in me when they know we're not together anymore."

And before he could say anything else, she'd broken the connection.

Eric figured if anyone had a right to be cranky and miserable, it was him. After all, he was the one with a cast on his leg and question marks in his future. But it was his little brother who was cleaning the floor with his chin, and who had been doing so for days. Though right now they were in the media room, sharing a bowl of pretzels and a couple of cold beers while a rugby game played out on the television.

"So you got dumped," he said unsympathetically. "It can't be the first time."

Marcus raised his eyebrows.

"Or maybe it is," Eric allowed. "In which case, it was long overdue."

"You're not seriously going to try to give me dating advice, are you?"

"I wouldn't dream of it," he said dryly.

"Good."

"I was actually just wondering if you were really over her," Eric said. "Because if you are, I thought I might take a trip to West Virginia when I get this cast off my leg."

"Only if you want both of them broken," Marcus muttered.

Eric lifted his bottle to his lips to hide his grin. "Okay, maybe that's a little tacky. I just figured she seemed to like you well enough, and people often said we could pass for twins."

"Except that you're dutiful and I'm charming," his brother reminded him.

"No one's seen much evidence of that infamous charm

lately," Eric pointed out. "In fact, you've been more temperamental than that stallion Rowan brought over from America."

Marcus ignored him, though his scowl darkened.

"On the other hand, she wasn't really any different than any of the other women you've dated over the years," he commented idly. "I mean, it's not like you planned to marry her or anything, right?"

Instead of going pale at the thought, as the Marcus of old would have done at the mere mention of marriage, his brother just continued to stare straight ahead. And that was when Eric realized how serious Marcus really was about Jewel, and that he wasn't just moping, he was nursing a broken heart.

The realization stirred his sympathies, but Eric knew that it was a brother's job to rub salt in the wounds—and though he knew it might be painful for Marcus now, it was also necessary to prod him to action.

"For what it's worth—not that I'm giving you advice, I'm just offering my two cents—I think you're doing the right thing. Chasing after a woman can never lead to anything but trouble."

"Thanks, Dear Abby." Marcus pushed to his feet. "On that note, I'm going down to the stables."

"Don't let that horse kick you when you're down," Eric called after him.

He was still grinning when Rowan came into the room.

"What did you say to set Marcus off?" he asked.

Eric shrugged. "I simply agreed that he'd done the right thing in ending his relationship with Jewel."

His older brother frowned. "You can't believe that—he's obviously miserable without her."

"Of course, I don't believe it," he agreed. "But I know the surest way to get Marcus to do something is—"

"—to tell him not to," Rowan finished with him.

Eric nodded.

Rowan eyed him with new respect. "And I always thought Marcus was the smart one."

"Marcus is the good-looking one. *I'm* the smart one."

Rowan chuckled at that, but then he asked, "Which one am I?"

"You were always the responsible one."

His brother winced. "I guess I asked for that."

"You were the one we looked up to," Eric explained to him. "The one who instinctively did the right thing—as you did when you left London to come home and raise Julian and Catherine's kids. Of course, we changed your moniker when you married Lara."

"To what?" Rowan asked warily.

"The lucky one."

Rowan smiled. "You're right on that one," he said. "Because not a day has gone by since Lara and I exchanged vows that I haven't thought about how fortunate I am."

"Because you fell in love?"

"Because she loves me back."

And that, Eric knew, was truly lucky. Just as he knew that Marcus was on the verge of finding the same happiness—if only he was smart enough to grab hold of it with both hands.

As for himself, well, Eric was going to take that one step at a time. As soon as he was able to get back up on his feet again.

Chapter Fifteen

Jewel had asked Marcus not to come to West Virginia. She'd told him in no uncertain terms that their relationship was over, so there was no reason for her to feel so dejected and miserable just because he'd complied with her wishes. No reason at all except that she missed him. And with every day that passed, she missed him more.

She tried to fill her days with work, but not even that succeeded in keeping him from her thoughts. Every morning when she woke, she wondered where he was and what he was doing. And every night when she went to bed, she wished only that he was beside her.

Bonnie was unsympathetic to her moods; Crystal and Natasha were even worse. So Jewel kept her unhappiness and her heartache to herself. Mostly, anyway.

It was Wednesday, ten days before the Fourth Annual

Haven Charity Auction, when Crystal dropped a copy of the local newspaper on her desk. It was folded open to an ad for the event, and as her eyes skimmed the details, her heart pounded harder in her chest.

"Why does this say that Prince Marcus Santiago will be in attendance?"

Her sister frowned. "Didn't Natasha go over the draft press release with you?"

She'd wanted to, Jewel remembered now. Shortly after she'd returned from Tesoro del Mar, but Jewel had been more than a little distracted at the time, wallowing in her misery, and assured Natasha that she had free rein with respect to the ad campaign.

"We'll have to get the paper to print a correction," she said now.

"Why?" Crystal demanded.

"Because he's not coming."

"Actually, I am."

Jewel's heart skipped a beat, then raced, as she drew in a deep breath before she swiveled in her chair to face the man himself, standing in the doorway. "You have a bad habit of dropping into the middle of conversations, Your Highness."

He shrugged. "And you have a habit of assuming things that aren't true."

She felt her fingers curl around the arms of her chair as she tried to find her balance in a world that had suddenly been turned upside down just by his presence. And while he was here, she was suddenly conscious of the distance between them, a distance she knew she was responsible for and still wished she could breach.

"I'll, um, give you some privacy," Crystal said. Then, with

a quick smile for Marcus and a narrow-eyed look for her sister, she slipped out of the room.

"Why are you here, Marcus?"

He saw the wary hope in her eyes and wondered why he'd ever doubted his decision to come—and why he'd waited so long to do so. But she'd trampled all over his heart once already, and he wasn't going to make it so easy for her a second time. "Other than the auction, you mean?"

She shrugged. "If there is another reason."

"I came to see if you've grown up in the past couple of weeks," he said mildly.

Her eyes flashed. "I think you're forgetting which one of us is older than the other."

"And I think you're mistaking age with maturity."

"Is there a purpose to this conversation?"

"I just want you to know that I'm not going anywhere and I'm not giving up on us. We can make this work." He pinned her with his gaze. "If you're not afraid to go after what you really want."

He wouldn't have thought she'd balk at a challenge, but her eyes shifted away. Obviously he'd underestimated her obstinacy.

"I have everything I want right here," she told him.

"Do you?"

"Yes."

It was the defiant tilt of her chin that gave her away, and he couldn't help but smile. "It's always all or nothing with you, isn't it?"

"What's that supposed to mean?"

"You don't know how to compromise."

"I do so."

His brows rose; she frowned.

"You believe that giving a little means giving in. So rather than trying to work things out, you ran away."

"I tried," she said. "I just can't live my life the way you do."

"You shut me out."

"You let me!"

And the hurt and frustration in her voice took the edge off of his own anger. "And that's what it comes down to, doesn't it?"

She swallowed and looked away.

"Your father was a sonofabitch, Jewel. There's no denying that. He made you jump through hoops like no child should ever have to do, and still he withheld his love and affection."

"That's old news," she said.

"And then there was Thomas."

Her gaze swung back to his. "What do you know about Thomas?"

"I know he was the guy you ran off to the rodeo with, the one you thought you would marry, the one who wasn't willing to give up his nomadic lifestyle to settle down."

"Which proves that he never really loved me."

"Maybe he didn't," he said softly. "Or maybe he just wasn't willing to play your games.

"Maybe I did let you shut me out," he continued. "Maybe I was a little ticked off at being dumped and needed some time to figure things out, to decide if I was going to let you pull my strings."

"I wasn't—"

"Turns out I was," he interrupted. "At least this one time. Because I do love you, and because I realized you have a lot of insecurities about relationships and trust, so I'm willing to cut you some slack."

She stared at him. "Am I supposed to thank you for that?"

He ignored her sarcasm. "But from this point on—no more games, Jewel. No more excuses. I want a future with you, a life together. A baby." He saw her eyes grow wide, read the heartfelt yearning he knew she wished she could hide, and he smiled a little. "Maybe even two or three."

Her eyes filled with tears, though she valiantly held them in check.

"I've spent the past several years trying to figure out what I wanted," he told her. "I didn't have a clue until I met you. Now I'm just waiting for you to catch up.

"My brother Rowan proposed to his wife three times before she said 'yes.' I've decided that when I finally ask a woman to marry me, I'm only going to do it once. So I'm giving you some time, Jewel, to figure out if you want the same things I do, to decide if you're willing to compromise so that we can build our life together."

Marcus touched her face. "It won't be easy," he admitted. "I have duties and responsibilities to my country, but I respect that you have obligations here, and I know we can find a way to balance everything—if that's what you want."

It was the longest speech of his life—aside from any that had been prepared by one of the palace's press secretaries— and the most heartfelt. But when it was over, he knew he'd said everything he wanted to say. The rest was up to Jewel.

Jewel didn't see Marcus at all in the nine days leading up to the auction, though she knew he'd been busy promoting the event and giving interviews about Haven, no doubt trying to show her that the media attention she'd shunned could be used to advantage at times. And she could hardly object when the auction turned out to be a huge success.

She kept a mental tally of the bidding from the background, and she was more than a little stunned at the revenue that was being generated, and thrilled that Haven would be able to operate for at least another year. As for her own future, well, she wasn't so certain.

She'd thought long and hard about the things Marcus had said the last time they were together, and she'd realized he was right. She wouldn't go so far as to say that she'd been pulling his strings, as he claimed, but maybe she had been testing him, needing to know that she really mattered to him.

But for all of his talk of marriage and babies—and yeah, he had to know mentioning babies would make everything inside her turn to mush—he'd been nowhere to be found in the past week-and-a-half. And after agonizing over this fact for a while, she realized he was testing her, testing her trust in him and his love for her. And she finally accepted that he did love her—maybe even as much as she loved him. But was love enough to overcome the obstacles they would face? Because she knew that building a life with Marcus wouldn't be easy. Any marriage required adjustments and compromise; a union between a prince and a commoner would necessitate changes she probably couldn't even begin to imagine. There were so many things she didn't know, so many things they hadn't ever talked about.

She knew so little about his life as a royal, his responsibilities as a prince, his hopes and dreams.

I want a future with you, a life together. A baby.

On the other hand, maybe she knew everything she needed to.

She didn't delude herself into thinking it would be easy. She didn't want easy—she wanted Marcus.

There were a lot of details to figure out, but she wasn't going to figure them out backstage at an auction, and she certainly wasn't going to figure them out on her own. Whatever answers needed to be found, she and Marcus would find them together.

Now, she just needed to find him so she could tell him.

It was only when Crystal elbowed her in the ribs that the applause registered and Jewel realized the bidding on the last item had concluded. She smoothed a hand over her skirt and stepped onto the stage, figuring that she'd waited ten days to tell Marcus the truth of what was in her heart, she could surely wait another ten minutes.

She stepped up to the podium and spoke into the microphone. "I want to thank everyone for their generous and continued support of the Fourth Annual Haven Charity Auction. Tonight's event was an unprecedented success and your private contributions and successful bids will go a long way toward allowing Haven to continue its work as a rescue and rehabilitation facility. I'd also like to thank—"

"Please excuse the interruption," Natasha said, speaking into a microphone from the other side of the stage. "It appears we may have been a little premature in concluding this event."

Jewel was careful not to let her irritation show, though she wondered what kind of stunt the other woman had planned.

"There is one final item up for sale tonight that was added to our inventory at the last minute."

Nerves began to gnaw at the pit of Jewel's stomach, but she stayed where she was, her smile firmly in place.

A pedestal was carried out to center stage and set beneath the spotlight. An enlarged image was projected onto the wide screen against the back wall, and prompted several audible gasps and numerous "oohs" and "aahs."

The crowd pressed closer to the stage, as curious potential buyers sought a closer look at the stunning ring on display.

"I would like to call His Royal Highness Prince Marcus Santiago up here to tell us a little about this ring and the conditions attached to its sale here today."

Marcus stepped out from the wings, answering Jewel's question about where he had been, and making so many others swirl in her mind.

He took the spare microphone Natasha offered. "First I want to say that not only am I offering this ring today, but with it a check to Haven in the amount of one million dollars."

"A royal heirloom and a cool one mil for the charity," Natasha said. "Tell me, Your Highness, what is the catch?"

"I don't know that I would call it a catch so much as conditions that I've attached to the sale of this ring," he explained.

"You've got everyone's attention now," Natasha assured him, clearly in her element and playing to the crowd.

Marcus looked out at the assembled group and smiled. Then his gaze shifted across the stage to where Jewel was standing, and it was as if everyone else in the room faded away.

"It was my grandmother's ring," he said. "And when it was passed on to me, it was with the express wish that it remain in the family. So that is the first condition—the woman who buys this ring must marry me."

"I'll start the bidding," a female voice called out from the back of the crowd.

There were a few chuckles mixed in with various comments shouted back at the speaker.

"The second condition," Marcus said, interrupting the good-natured banter, "is that I will only sell the ring—and my proposal—to one particular woman."

There were good-natured groans and protests from the crowd, but no one walked away as the prince turned toward Jewel. No one wanted to miss the ending of this unexpected event.

Crystal stepped closer to nudge her sister forward, but Jewel felt as if her feet were glued to the floor.

"That woman," Marcus continued, "is Jewel Callahan."

She still couldn't move, so he started toward her. As he drew nearer, she could see, very clearly, the love shining in his eyes. And it was that which gave her courage, and helped her to meet him halfway.

Still, her stomach was a jumble of nerves and her voice wasn't quite steady when she said, "Did it never occur to you to propose like an ordinary person? Maybe over dinner by candlelight?"

He grinned. "I'm not ordinary—I'm a prince."

"I'm not likely to forget that," she assured him.

"So what do you think—" he took her hand and drew her over to the pedestal, to take a closer look at the ring "—do you want to bid on it?"

She had to clear her throat before she could speak. "How much?"

"The minimum bid is one dollar," he told her.

"I give you one dollar and you give me a check for a million?" She wondered if this was really a proposal or some kind of publicity stunt.

He shook his head. "I wouldn't want anyone to think I had to buy myself a bride. The check has already been made out to Haven. So the only question now is—do you want the ring?"

She didn't even look at the ring. She didn't care if it was a huge diamond in a platinum setting or a carved piece of tin, all that mattered was that she was going to spend the rest of her life with the man she loved.

"I want you," she told him softly.

He smiled. "Then you need to ante up."

She reached into her jacket for a dollar and flushed when she found her pockets were empty, save for the lucky stone she'd taken to carrying with her since the day Marcus had given it to her at the racetrack. She closed her fingers around it now. "I don't have any money."

Crystal pressed something into her other hand. "It's a five," she whispered. "It's all I've got."

Jewel took a deep breath and stared straight into Marcus's eyes—his beautiful, espresso-colored eyes that she wanted only to stare into every day for the rest of their lives together.

"I bid five dollars," she said. "And my whole heart, forever."

His hand closed over hers holding the money and he pulled her toward him and into his arms. Then he kissed her, as if he'd been waiting for weeks to do so. And she kissed him back, because she'd been waiting just as long.

And as the kiss deepened, they both forgot they were standing on the middle of the raised stage in front of a crowd of curious onlookers and eager media personnel.

"And that," Natasha announced, "concludes the Fourth Annual Haven Charity Auction."

As the crowd slowly filtered out, Jewel drew away.

"I never actually heard a proposal," she said to Marcus.

"Because I promised myself that I would only ask once, and I wanted to be sure of the answer before I did so."

"Are you sure now?"

He gazed into her eyes for a long moment before he finally nodded. Then he took the ring from the box and held it out to her. "Will you marry me, Jewel?"

And finally she had the chance to tell him everything that

was in her heart, but when she looked into his eyes, she realized that he already knew, that there was only one word he was waiting to hear from her.

"Yes."

He smiled as he slipped the ring on her finger, though she noted that his hand wasn't much steadier than hers, and Jewel's heart felt as if it would simply overflow with love and joy.

Then he kissed her again, and she knew that he felt exactly the same way.

When he finally drew away, she had to ask, "Did you really mean what you said about wanting babies?"

"I meant everything I said," he promised her.

"You do understand, with me being so much older than you, I'll want to get started on those babies as soon as possible."

He smiled again. "As soon as I get you home."

Epilogue

Prince's Bride Trades Stetson for Tiara
by Alex Girard

Last summer, Prince Marcus Santiago put his heart on public display along with an heirloom fourteen-carat diamond ring when he proposed to Jewel Callahan, former champion barrel racer turned owner of Callahan Thoroughbred Center in Alliston, West Virginia.

Yesterday, the prince regent's youngest brother and his cowgirl bride exchanged their vows.

As if a royal wedding wasn't enough cause for celebration, Prince Eric stood beside his brother at the altar, a remarkable feat considering it was less than a year ago that doctors weren't sure he would ever stand up again.

But all eyes were fixed on the bride as she made her

way up the center aisle of the cathedral in her stunning Vera Wang gown, a bundle of ivory tulips in hand. And none were focused so intently as those of her groom.

When the newlyweds rode off into the sunset together, there was no doubt that the beautiful horse-trainer had firmly lassoed her husband's heart—or that the prince had finally found his own crown Jewel.

* * * * *

MILLS & BOON
MEDICAL
Pulse-Racing Passion

Set your pulse racing with dedicated,
delectable doctors in the high-pressure
world of medicine, where emotions run
high and passion, comfort and love are the
best medicine.

JOIN US ON SOCIAL MEDIA!

Stay up to date with our latest releases, author news and gossip, special offers and discounts, and all the behind-the-scenes action from Mills & Boon...

 millsandboon

 millsandboonuk

 millsandboon

It might just be true love...